VOWS OF EMPIRE

VOWS OF EMPIRE

BOOK THREE OF THE BLOODRIGHT TRILOGY

EMILY SKRUTSKIE

NEW YORK

Copyright © 2022 by Emily Skrutskie

All rights reserved.

Published in the United States by Del Rey,
an imprint of Random House, a division of
Penguin Random House LLC, New York.

DEL REY and colophon are registered trademarks of
Penguin Random House LLC.

Library of Congress Cataloging-in-Publication Data
Names: Skrutskie, Emily, 1993– author.
Title: Vows of empire / Emily Skrutskie.
Description: First edition. | New York: Del Rey, 2022. |
Series: The bloodright trilogy; 3
Identifiers: LCCN 2021050658 (print) | LCCN 2021050659 (ebook) |
ISBN 9780593128954 (hardcover; acid-free paper) |
ISBN 9780593128961 (ebook)
Subjects: CYAC: Kings, queens, rulers, etc.—Fiction. |
Government, Resistance to—Fiction. | Gays—Fiction. |
Science fiction. | LCGFT: Science fiction.
Classification: LCC PZ7.1.S584 Vo 2022 (print) |
LCC PZ7.1.S584 (ebook) | DDC [Fic]—dc23
LC record available at https://lccn.loc.gov/2021050658
LC ebook record available at https://lccn.loc.gov/2021050659

Printed in the United States of America on acid-free paper

randomhousebooks.com

1st Printing

First Edition

Book design and title-page illustration by Edwin Vazquez
Title-page art: © istock.com/dottedhippo (asteroid)

To "Temple Battle" from the *Kingsman 2* score
and the airport fight from Civil War, for fueling the three-year
process of choreographing that midpoint brawl

VOWS OF EMPIRE

CHAPTER 1

ETTIAN

MY STOMACH DROPS with the shuttle.

"Ruttin' hell," I mutter, one hand flying to catch the overhead straps, the other snapping to my forehead to keep my circlet from tipping off. It's a gusty day over Ichano, and the pilot isn't doing us any favors. My eyes catch Wen's across the hold.

She gives me the subtlest shake of her head, a wry smile twisting her lips. I know she wants to storm the cockpit as badly as me. The pilot couldn't stop either of us if we demanded he hand over the controls.

But both of us have higher duties than shouldering through turbulence.

So I grit my teeth through the *utterly avoidable* rattling and try to bend my focus back to my responsibilities for today. Beneath my feet sprawls Ichano, a newly liberated Archon city and the capital of Osar, a newly liberated Archon system. We've strung the second jewel in our belt after a month of fighting like hell—and all that my thoughts keep circling back to is that it's been a month since Gal slipped past our fleet and disappeared into the black.

Because you let him, an ugly voice in my head reminds me. *Because you gave him the* Ruttin' Hell *and told the fleet to let it go.* And then Gal refused, kissed me breathless against its hull, and told me he wasn't doing a damn thing I said. I took him at his word. I wanted so badly for it to be real. For him to be choosing me, siding with me, throwing off the shackles of his bloodright to fight this war at my side.

It was the happiest I'd been in months. I practically floated out of that hangar.

As far as I can tell from the tattered scraps of the security logs, the moment I left was the moment Gal got to work. He hadn't meant a word of it. All along, he'd been biding his time, waiting for his opening. From the holes in the camera footage and the drugged guards we discovered left in their wake, it seems his team sprang Hanji from her cell, rendezvoused with Gal, stole the powersuit, and flew the *Ruttin' Hell* free from the *Torrent*'s core without a single person lifting a finger to stop them.

If it hadn't torn my heart out, I'd almost be impressed.

Another gust of wind shakes the shuttle, and I let out a soft groan. No weather's ever been enough to put a fear of flying in me—and I've flown through a hell of a lot worse—but the grating on my nerves is the last thing I need ahead of today's event. "Five minutes to the drop," the horrible pilot announces over the intercom.

Wen rises from her bench, resplendent in platinum-trimmed tac armor that almost makes up for the fact that she *should* be wearing that powersuit. Her feet are encased in a pair of boot prototypes welded to a carbon fiber exoskeleton that frames her hips—a poor substitute, but enough to get her airborne. Her vibrosword hilt is latched to the magnetic sling on her waist, a reminder that power-suited or not, she's still the Flame Knight. To top off the look, her shoulders are mantled by a fine emerald cape that's been cut with vents.

It takes the breath out of me a little to see her like this—though certainly some of that comes from the wound Hanji bored through my gut two months ago. Wen Iffan's come a long way from the chaotic little troublemaker I found on the streets of Isla. I had no way of knowing the girl dressed in rags trying to sell me a skipship with no engines would one day singlehandedly win the battle for my birth system by taking out a dreadnought with nothing more than a powersuit and her sheer force of will, but there was a little voice in my head that day telling me to bet on her—a little voice that's never steered me wrong.

"You're staring," she says, checking over the straps of her armor. "Again."

"Can you blame me?"

When her eyes catch mine, my smile falters. No happiness of mine can stand up under scrutiny—especially not hers. I've tried to keep the effect Gal's abandonment has had on me concealed, throwing myself headlong into the war effort. I've been burning myself out on strategy meetings and resourcing meetings and gods-of-all-systems-know-whatever-else I can involve myself in, praying that somewhere in the middle of all of it, I'll shovel enough into the hole Gal left inside me to patch it over.

Wen hasn't been faring much better. I've seen a darkness eating at her ever since the battle that claimed the Tosa System and cost us her mentor, Commodore Adela Esperza, in the process. After Esperza's capture, Wen threw herself into repairing the damage her powersuit sustained at the Battle of Dasun. When Gal and his operatives stole it, she dug up the boot prototypes and all but stormed the battlefield. I feared for her, but she held her promise—the Flame Knight has burned enough for one lifetime. Even without the protection of the powersuit, even with Umber armies throwing everything they have at her, Wen Iffan is untouchable.

Within a month, we'd liberated a new Archon system, so . . . at least there's that.

"C'mon," Wen says, crossing the hold and laying her hands on my shoulders. "For the people, right?"

"For the people," I echo numbly. The past month has ground me down to dust for the people. I'm their emperor. I was born to serve them, and it's eating me alive. I pitch forward, letting my forehead rest against the cool shell of the armor plating her stomach. It grinds the circlet into my skin, but at least that wakes me up a little.

Above me, Wen huffs a sigh, barely audible over the rumble of the shuttle's engines. "Look, I think there's something I need to tell you." Her grip on my shoulders tightens. "I can't take watching you mope around like this anymore and if this . . . Okay, I'm just going to say it."

Then she doesn't.

"Wen?" I ask after the silence stretches on for an uncomfortable minute.

"I arranged Gal's escape."

The pilot's flying steady, but I feel like the shuttle's just been shot out of the sky. "You . . . No," I choke as my body locks rigid, braced for a spinout that's only happening in my head. *"No,"* I repeat louder. I try to wrench back from her, but she locks one hand around the back of my head, keeping me from looking her in the eyes.

"I had to. I'm sorry—I *had to.* I struck a bargain, and when you filed the clearance for the *Ruttin' Hell* to leave, I knew it was an opportunity I couldn't miss."

"You struck a bargain with Gal?" I seethe against her plating. The circlet digging into my forehead is the only pain that makes sense anymore, so I lean into it. "What could he possibly have offered—"

"I struck a bargain with Hanji Iwam."

My stomach convulses involuntarily at the mention of her name, the scar burned across it twinging. Modern medicine has worked its miracles for my gut wound, but it can't take away the memory that bullet seared into me. "I don't understand," I grind out, and Wen's grip on me softens enough that I'm finally able to pull back and tip my head up to search her face for answers.

I regret it instantly. I can't handle the way she's looking at me— the way this is tearing her apart just as much. She's trusted me so absolutely, and I thought I could trust her the same. *"You* told me you were going to set him free," she says, her eyes glimmering in the hold's low light. Another burble of turbulence hits the shuttle, forcing her to tighten her grip on me to keep upright. "*You* told me that we couldn't protect him anymore."

"And he *chose to stay.*"

If I thought she was torn before, it's nothing compared to the way her expression breaks now. "He did," she says, her voice choking on a sob she's desperately trying to suppress. The confirmation tears through me like she's just speared me on the end of her vibro-sword. "He fought. He didn't want to go, but . . . It never would have worked. I know you wanted to believe—"

"I am *emperor.* I don't need to believe. I can make it happen. I could have—"

"Ettian," she murmurs, and even in the wake of a betrayal that should render us blasted apart, I still can't stand to see the tears spilling haphazardly out of her eyes. I reach up and catch her scarred cheek, my heart seizing as she leans into the touch like she always does. "Tell me we would still be here, right now, above a liberated city on a liberated planet in a liberated system, if Gal was working freely at your side. Tell me you could have negotiated your way through the infighting on your advisory. Tell me you could have held up your legitimacy against Iral's shadow."

Her words saw their way to bone. Letting Gal stay was what I wanted, but it wasn't in the empire's best interests, and the blood-right in my veins is nothing if I lose sight of the fact that I was born to serve the people. I shouldn't need her to remind me. *No empire . . .* a little voice in the back of my head starts, but I grab it by the throat. "I wouldn't have just had him by my side," I reply. "I'd have the Flame Knight too."

The flattery earns me a soft, sad smile that forces another spill of tears down her cheeks. They sear along my thumb as I brush them away. "Don't make me throw myself into another dreadnought engine trying to be enough for you."

She may as well have kicked me in the gut for the way it knocks the air out of me. "Wen . . ." I breathe, not knowing what I could possibly follow it with. Has she felt like this all along? Have I been letting her give herself to my rebellion, not realizing that she saw it as taking? I've already lost Gal—now I realize that I may have lost her as well.

The intercom crackles overhead like a slap to the face. "One minute to the drop," the pilot announces.

"I did what I had to," Wen murmurs, stepping back out of my reach. "What I always do. I did what it's going to take to win this rusting war."

Without her locking me in place, a sensation of weightless nausea envelops me. I haven't felt this fragile in the air since my earliest days at the academy. "What was the bargain?" I ask numbly. What price could possibly be worth all of this? What did she pay to bring me a month of suffering, thinking that Gal had deliberately abandoned me?

"I proposed a trade. I gave them their prince, and they have three months to pay me back with Commodore Esperza's freedom."

My gut reaction is fury. Gal wasn't just a prisoner—he was a guarantee. The most effective shield we had against the wrath of Iva emp-Umber was the knowledge that she couldn't risk eliminating her own heir in her effort to reduce us to dust and ash. Commodore Esperza was Wen's mentor and a critical part of my advisory, but there's no way her value matches Gal's.

But as the shuttle ramp comes down and the hold floods with furious daylight, I feel my own perspective burn away until all I'm left with is what Wen so clearly sees. Esperza was a cornerstone, one that's been knocked out from under my administration's foundations. Ever since her capture, I've had to fight twice as hard to balance out General Iral's attempts to wrest power from me—a tall order when I was still recovering from a hole in my gut. I need her moderation, and after all she's done for me, I owe her whatever chance we have at saving her life.

My anger shifts its target. How could I have abandoned the commodore to Iva emp-Umber's clutches? Over the past month, I've barely thought of her capture as I found myself pulled aside by the Osar campaign and the thousand other responsibilities hooked into my shoulders. It never even crossed my mind that we might have a chance to rescue her, to spare her the fate of my parents. What does that say about my ability to serve my people?

Wen swings her way to the shuttle ramp by the handholds overhead, reaching down and pulling a set of darkened goggles from her neck up over her eyes. Her cape flaps frantically against the wind as she squares her shoulders. Her hand drops to the sword hilt magnetized to her hip.

My heart aches at the sight of her against the city skyline—proud, unflinching even before a terrifying drop, and so willing to do what's necessary that she'll rip me in two to make sure we win. There's a solidity to Wen that defies the rocking of the shuttle, a confidence that the universe will stabilize around her will. I've tried to learn that confidence from her, but I've never been able to pin it down. The rug's been pulled out from beneath me one time too many.

And speaking of my traitorous, doubting heart—

"If you just gave them Gal, what's to guarantee they'll return Esperza?" I holler over the scream of the shuttle's engines as it wheels into position over the arena. "What's holding them to that promise?"

Wen turns around, pulling her vibrosword from her belt as her lips twist in a smile that's a thousand times more menacing with her eyes blacked out behind the goggles.

"Me," she says, then extends the sword with an electric snarl and topples backward out of the hold as below the crowd begins to roar.

CHAPTER 2

GAL

THERE'S A MONOTONY to most court sessions. It's an endless cycle of system governors and their emissaries wasting time with issues that are almost entirely self-engineered to ensure that their dominion stays relevant in the minds of the imperials.

I can't speak for my mother or father, but for me it's done the opposite. Even with each representative dressed in peacockish finery designed to distinguish them from the crowd, their issues are so pointless and so similar that they all blur together in an irrelevant, noisy miasma. I often end up staring at the ceiling, trying to divine patterns in the abstract, angular brass panels that arc overhead in asymmetric sweeps.

Not so today.

Today, the governors and their retinues have been pressed back to the corners of the grand cathedral by a ring of guards armed with wicked-looking pistols and even meaner shock batons. They form a circle around the focal point of the court, where spears of daylight reflect off the brass paneling to illuminate the room's core. The effect is meant to heighten the grandeur of imperial attention. You can only bear to stand in our sight for so long.

Like most of the Umber Empire, it's brutality masquerading behind civility. Torture dressed up with artistry. If you make your instrument beautiful and clever, people will praise its design over any cruelty it commits.

In the center of the chamber's focal glow, her arms cuffed behind her back, is Commodore Adela Esperza.

She doesn't give us the satisfaction of shifting uncomfortably in the heat. She doesn't even look up. Ever since the guards marched her in here, she's kept her eyes firmly fixed on the soft canvas shoes that she was given to replace the fine boots she was dressed in when they dragged her off her ship. Her hair's been bound back out of her eyes, but from the lack of care put into it, I'm almost certain the lopsided work was done by someone else—and if so, it was done at my mother's instruction.

The empress sits side by side with my father before me on thrones of rough-cut obsidian. Both of them are dressed in simple, understated blacks that make the garishness of the court fashion all the more ridiculous and draw the eye to their angular brass crowns, the only marks of authority they'll ever need. I've been placed above and behind them, both elevated and distanced from the scrum of the court's proceedings. I'm here to learn and observe. They're here for a sentencing.

But they're making the rest of the room hold their breaths for it. There are no murmurs from the eaves—not even whispers. If the rest of the court is talking, they're doing it through surreptitious messages back and forth on their datapads. They know the consequences of breaking the empress's silence.

A sheen of sweat is starting to build on Esperza's forehead.

I'm trying my best not to mirror it. In the weeks since my return, I've gotten plenty of practice composing my features in the public eye. The governors and staffers will scrutinize me from all angles, waiting for me to show a weakness worth exploiting. Thus far, I've kept them hungry.

Truth be told, the only person who has any chance of realizing I'm up to something is the one who taught me how to carry my secrets in the first place.

Fortunately she has her back to me, but I wish *I* could see my mother's expression. Iva emp-Umber sits with poise, her head tilted in a way I think reads as condescending but can't quite pin down without her face to complete the picture. We've been frozen like this ever since the last guard stepped into place, all of us waiting for someone to make the first move. The empress seems determined to roast it out of the commodore.

Esperza won't give in. I can see it in the rigidity of her posture, in the way she betrays no interest in anything beyond her own toes. Before she was a commodore, she was a pirate scraping a living on the fringes of the Umber Empire, and if the stories I grew up with are anywhere near true, she'll burn before she bends to my mother's wishes.

In fact, there's only one person in this room with the latitude to break the silence and have it cost nothing. I'm meant to be learning, after all. I'm excused for not being perfect.

"Ruttin' hell," I groan. "Could we *please* get on with it?"

Thrillingly enough, Esperza actually lifts her eyes at that. She fixes me with a withering look, taking in the brass circlet tipped insouciantly across my brow and the way I've slumped against one arm of the Heir's Throne, my foot propped up on its edge. She's smart enough to realize that what I've just done is a favor—and smarter still, to know it makes no difference for her predicament.

My mother's chin tips downward, and now I'm a little less eager to see the look on her face. Better to face the consequences later. It'll be a lecture at worst, probably with some colorful examples from her long history of wrangling bloodthirsty system governors to heel. It's nothing compared to what the commodore is in for.

"Yes, might as well," Iva emp-Umber starts, her voice so smooth and even that you couldn't possibly tell we're two hours into this court session. "I'd hoped that our guest would treat us to some of that fiery, fighting rhetoric her silly little uprising is so intent on spewing, but it seems she's understood the inevitability of her circumstances."

Esperza's gaze glides back to her oh-so-fascinating feet.

"As some of you are aware, a spate of unrest has overtaken a few of the systems on the outer fringes of the empire," my mother continues. I feel like I've heard her repeat a hundred variants of that line in the month since I returned to the Umber Core. From here, light-years away from the war Ettian's been waging to reclaim his empire, it's easy to minimize the scale of the conflict as a bit of unrest at the border. "The woman who stands before us today is one of the figureheads of that movement, captured from an engagement a month ago."

Again—minimizing the Battle of Imre and the Battle of Dasun as "engagements." Never mind that both were Umber losses.

"Her name is Adela Esperza. She styled herself 'commodore' to her followers, but it is neither a rank she earned nor one any proper command would ever bestow upon her. In fact, there's quite the legal paper trail connecting the name Adela Esperza to a full decade of crime in our borderworlds ranging from piracy to mass murder. Her ideological rot is a threat to the empire on its own, but factoring in her record, it's clear that she's earned the starkest justice the throne can offer."

None of what the empress says is surprising, but a murmur rises from the back of the court anyway, a chorus of low voices muttering their approval. *Sycophants,* I grumble internally, but my mother has warned me about showing open contempt for these people. The system governors are an equation that must be carefully balanced. They need constant reminders of how far above them we imperials sit, but likewise we can never allow them to think that we're not on their side or that we don't value their contributions. If they attempt to buck our rule, we slap them down, but we can't sneer at them for being vicious, conniving little—

"An important anniversary in our history is a month away," the empress says, throwing a little extra power into her voice so that the obsidian of her throne projects it deep into the court's recesses. It's enough to get Esperza to shift her gaze to the throne once more—or maybe it's just that she's determined to look her fate in the eyes. "When Lucia enters its next lunar cycle, it will have been eight years since the end of the War of Expansion. Eight years since we ended the Archon imperial line. I believe it would be most fitting for Adela Esperza to meet justice on that day, as a reminder to all in the Archon territories who might have been infected by this woman's foul commitment to upending our grand peace."

Again, I'm forced to balance my expression into the careful neutrality that's expected of an imperial in a court setting. My parents have their backs to me, and everyone else is too far away to clock it save for Esperza herself. Her eyes slip up to me, her lip curling.

Which I guess means I'm nailing it. Esperza thinks I flew the coop and abandoned Archon to their doom. She must be convinced I've told my parents everything from my time as an Archon prisoner, that I'm thrilled to be home among my people once more.

I can't *wait* to see the look on her face when my Wraiths and I spring her and send her packing back to Ettian.

Unbeknownst to anyone in the room, my mother has just given me our hard deadline. I've flipped entirely from feigning eagerness to leave to genuinely trying to conceal how badly I need to get out of here. A month is barely any time at all, especially considering the audacity of the plan we've been cooking up.

"As for the punishment," Iva emp-Umber continues, "I believe that death is the only method fitting for such a menace. A public execution would be an appropriate marker for the solemnity of the war's end. Adela Esperza, while part of this sentencing is for the information of the court, as a show of mercy, I would be most pleased if you selected the manner of your end."

I'm about to jump out of my skin with the need to bolt from this room, and for a moment I dread that Esperza's going to make the silence stretch long again. But the commodore draws herself up tall, sweat rolling freely down her forehead as the full power of the afternoon sun bores into her, and declares, "If it's all the same to you, Your Majesty, you can honor me with the ax."

I can't keep the smirk off my face. If anyone dares ask me about it, I'll chalk it up to another slipup in my court manners, but I just can't help the delight that sparks through me, listening to Esperza take my mother's free rein and slap her across the face with it. Nearly eight years ago, the empress marched Marc and Henrietta emp-Archon down the Triumph Way and beheaded them for the entire empire to see. If my mother is so intent on connecting Esperza's death to that event, the commodore will use the manner to legitimize the reason for her execution.

Adela Esperza will not die for a spate of unrest in the borderworlds. She'll die for the Archon Empire.

If she dies. If we fail.

Fortunately her metaphorical spit in my mother's face is more than enough reason for Iva emp-Umber to wrap up court quickly. "With that settled, I believe we've taken care of all the business of the day," she says, rising from her throne.

My father, as ever, moves in concert with her, his movement so matched to his wife's that it's clear he anticipates her every thought. They've always been like this, to the point that when I was younger I was taken with the fantasy that some advanced neural tech had intertwined their minds. It instilled an even greater fantasy—one I soon realized was even more out of reach than linking brains.

I've always wanted a partnership like theirs. One built on an understanding of one another so complete that you could coordinate entire battles without ever once speaking. One built on a love so unbreakable that it could withstand nearly two decades of the violence necessary to hold the throne. Love matches have always been rare among imperials. It isn't always the case that the person who holds your heart is the one with whom you can most effectively rule a galaxy.

My thoughts bend back to Ettian, and I feel the last dregs of that childhood dream filter cleanly out of my system. Obviously my younger self had no way of knowing I'd be brainless enough to fall for the Archon heir—heavens and hells, I didn't even know he was the Archon heir when I was falling for him. But now that he's declared himself to the galaxy, the idea that we could ever rule together is laughable at best.

As is the idea that we could ever *be* together, but at least I'm brainless enough to keep the embers of that dream alive.

I wait to stand until the guards have closed around Esperza, spinning her roughly around and marching her back toward the fore of the court. Through their bodies, I catch a flash of the gesture she's locked her silicone prosthetic right hand into.

This is the smirk that my mother catches. "Something amusing?" she asks, setting her hands primly behind her back as she allows my father to steer her around the thrones toward the court's back exit, where another set of guards is waiting for us.

"The futility of it all," I reply with a dismissive shrug. "She thought she could land a barb with her choice of the ax, but if you ask me, it'll only remind the people of Archon's inevitable failure."

My father, Yltrast emp-Umber, smiles softly, clapping a gentle hand on my shoulder. This is his way—he rarely speaks, keeps his tone and manner pleasant, and takes the rug out from under his enemies when they fail to anticipate the vicious plots he's been brewing. But that's for his enemies. For me he only has kind encouragement and guidance that's been honed to an atomic edge.

My mother is less forthcoming. "I respect that woman for the attempt," she says tautly, "but she'll pay for it. A month gives us plenty of time to extract that payment."

Bile creeps up my throat. I've kept eyes on the prison block since my return. I know what goes on in there. The notion that it's about to escalate makes me wonder if Esperza will walk the Triumph Way on her own two feet by the end of it.

I shrug off my father's hand as we pass through the court's narrow rear entrance and into the corridor that connects with the network of the Imperial Seat's sprawl. Sweeping around in grand halls is for public appearances—for posturing in front of system governors and playing to the hordes of people who flock to see their imperials' brutal theater. For the rest of imperial life, there's these cramped throughways where with one guard ahead and one behind, you can never be taken by surprise.

Returning to them after months on an Archon dreadnought was like returning to the safety and security of the womb. I felt myself *loosen* within a week, dropping tension that I'd become so used to carrying that I never truly realized its burden. Of course, a different kind of tension has slipped in to fill the void. As long as I keep up the lounging, devil-may-care prince act, I'm safe.

But there are so, so many people around me who aren't. People I risk every time I find myself teetering toward a slipup.

Speaking of. "Your interruption today was unbecoming," my mother says, slowing to a stop at an intersection that lets us space out for some breathing room. "You knew exactly what I was doing, and despite that, you acted in your own self-interest."

An anxious impulse rises in me with the force of a whale surging from an ocean surface, and it takes a similar effort to keep my expression locked in vague boredom. This is the reality of every direct confrontation I have with my mother, and by this point I've become so well practiced in it that I hardly miss a beat, answering, "I just said what everyone else in that room was thinking."

The empress's eyes narrow a fraction. "You are not a child anymore—you've been crowned as an equal in this administration. Your behavior should not hinge on whether or not you're *entertained*."

I'm walking a perilous tightrope over the urge to reply with outright petulance. I could probably get away with it, but it does me no favors, only encouraging my mother's scrutiny. "I'm sorry," I say instead, stiffening to make it seem as if that admission was peeled from my pride like a slice of skin. "I suppose I'm still not used to the pace of court life after . . ."

I don't expect softness from my mother, and I'm right not to. She takes my confession like a scientist with new data, folding it into her predictive modeling with a single nod. It turns my stomach a little to make implications about my time in Archon captivity that are light-years from my experience, but from the look in my mother's eyes, I've said exactly what I needed to get her to drop the subject.

"If you'll allow me to take my entertainment in a more appropriate setting, I'm due for a drink with the Wraiths," I add with a perfunctory filial tilt at the waist.

The empress's gaze sharpens, and for a moment I'm not fooling anyone. In her cold, richly brown eyes, I'm transparent as the void. My breath lodges in my chest. At last, she says, "There's more for us to discuss, but it can wait until tomorrow. Go. Have fun."

I wait to exhale until I'm twenty feet around the next corner.

CHAPTER 3

ETTIAN

EVERY LAST DROP of exhaustion has left my body by the time I've finished my speech. I know I'll pay the toll later, most likely in the hold of the shuttle that whisks me out of this city and back to the safety of the *Torrent* hung in orbit overhead. But before a crowd of thousands—and with both the electric hum of deflector armor packed under my shirtsleeves and sheets of bulletproof plex set up between me and any possible angle of attack—I feel myself come alive.

I wonder if this is bloodright, when you get down to it. I've never had someone to ask about what it really means to have the blood that rules the stars within my veins. My parents were executed before I could start asking the right questions, and back when he was within reach, Gal had never known this feeling—the electric awe of standing before an entire city screaming your name. The way it feels right, and good, and even though part of you is still an academy cadet astonished they'll let you fly the Viper on your own, the rest is ready to stand tall before it.

This is the first and last gift my parents gave me. I'm trying so goddamn hard not to waste it.

I ease back from the podium, and a familiar scream kicks up from the stage behind me. Wen arcs up overhead to another swell of cheering, throwing her vibrosword out ahead of her in a classic suited knight pose as she wheels into a lap around the arena. Her showboating is meant to cover the logistics of ferrying me offstage and preparing for General Iral's entrance and address, but I can't help watching her for a second as around me the imperial skin drums kick into a frantic, triumphant rhythm.

We were never supposed to have suited knights again. Not after Iva emp-Umber purged them all at once, opening the War of Expansion with a devastating move that stole our heroes in a single cataclysmic moment. It was a miracle that a powersuit survived Knightfall, and an even greater miracle that after a decade, General Iral chose to hand it over to Wen Iffan.

And then, of course, came the greatest miracle, but that makes it sound like a thing of chance. Wen carving through the field at the Battle of Dasun to sink the *Fulcrum* and claim the system for Archon was that flashpoint combination of raw skill and the intimate knowledge of dreadnought systems she'd spent months building. Whispers around my court have jokingly started calling her Wen sys-Tosa in honor of the victory.

The people love her. I feared they wouldn't—that they might reject the notion of a Corinthian suited knight, especially after the suit went missing in the wake of Gal's sudden exit. But Archon has embraced its newest hero with joyous shouts and open arms.

Doesn't hurt that she embraces it in turn. Wen eats up the crowd's affection like it's the first meal she's had in days, throwing her boot thrusters into complicated spins, flipping her cape and hair around with flair, and even beckoning the noise louder just when it seems it's starting to drop off. I duck backstage to a roar that tells me she must have done that terrifying little trick where she pitches the vibrosword up, lets it spin a bit, and then snatches it out of the air.

A unit of guards closes tight around me as I make my way through the fabric paneling and looming sound equipment, then down a set of creaky metal stairs to the hard-packed dirt outside the stage. Everything around me moves in perfect clockwork—a machine that's been engineered to preserve my place in the center of the empire. I scan the ground until I find the twin burn scars that mark where Wen lifted off. As the noise of the crowd swells with a sudden fervor that marks Iral's entrance, I cross over to the marks and start halfheartedly scuffing them away with the toe of my shoe.

The guards lurch back in my periphery, so the sudden *thunk* of Wen landing behind my back doesn't startle me in the slightest. I keep kicking at the dirt, but my attempts to cover it up only reveal how deep the burn goes.

"That went well, I think," Wen says, and the forced nonchalance in her voice is almost too much to take. I haven't had time to process her confession, and the anger is still a raw nerve begging for hurt. She must see the way my shoulders square up, ready to fight, because she hesitates on the next breath, then tells the guards, "Leave us."

They pause the obligatory half second, giving me a chance to counter the order, then obey.

I wait until the last of their footsteps have faded before I dare turn around. In the wake of Gal's departure, I devoted myself wholeheartedly to maintaining a perfect imperial image. I had to show them all that I'd hardened my heart against the foreign prince and the way he played us. The furious tears welling in my eyes are poised to take all of that down—but now it's just me and her.

"For the past month," I start, utterly failing to keep my voice even, barely managing to keep it low, "I believed that Gal conspired against me. That he worked with Hanji to arrange his extraction, that everything he said to me when I tried to let him go was a lie. It made no ruttin' sense. He ran your comms in the Battle of Dasun. He did that . . . that stupid thing with my crown . . ." I break off, breathing deep before the hysteria overtakes me completely. "I had to live with that not making sense for a month, and it tore me apart. I'm past the point of wondering why you did it. In fact, I think I understand it. I'm halfway to accepting that it was what needed to be done. All I need from you is to explain how, exactly, you managed to pull this off."

Wen's wearing that wild-eyed look she gets when she's fresh off a battlefield. The tumult of her flights has blown her braid into a messy array of flyaways, and her unscarred cheek is still pink from the wind. The overall effect should make her seem sloppy, but instead she's suffused with an energetic glow that only makes her more magnetic.

The kind of magnetic you need to slap your hand away from before you get yourself electrocuted.

As she strips off her goggles, her eyes make a careful study of anything but mine. I can't tell if she's aiming for contrition, but I'm almost certain she wouldn't bother. "I . . . need to sit," she says, and only then do I realize how she's leaning her hips hard into the exoskeleton's supports. "Sit first. Then talk."

Our shuttle isn't meant to depart until Iral's remarks are finished, so I steer her into the stadium's hypocaust, which has been swept and swept and swept again by our security teams. An empty electric cart is waiting for us in the wide, brightly lit tunnel we find down there, which will eventually ferry us to the staging zone. I let down the gate of its bed, and Wen turns and collapses back into its rear, wrestling with the straps that bind the exoskeleton to her hips.

"That's better," she breathes as I set myself down next to her. "Rust and *rocks,* I miss that powersuit."

I snort. I know I shouldn't. There is absolutely *nothing* funny about the hell she put me through, but I guess part of me can't help in delighting in the way it's cost her too.

As she kneads her aching thighs, Wen lets out a long breath. "It all started on the day Hanji shot you," she says after a pause. "Obviously."

I don't remember much of that day. It started with the procession celebrating the liberation of Ellit, followed by the thunderous speech I delivered to the crowd—and then the bullet cleaved into my stomach, the pain a perfect crystal of memory, rendering the rest of the afternoon a hazy blur. I came to in a hospital room a day later, my guts a mess of tubing and my mind plastered with so much pain medication that I asked for Gal at my bedside before anything else.

"I never let you see how badly it undid me," she continues. "I didn't want to stress you even more, so I tried to handle it all myself. I conducted Iwam's interrogations. I used Gal to bait information out of her. And what I discovered was this: she and her little Wraith Squadron—"

My spine stiffens abruptly. Wraith Squadron was what Tatsun Seely called the twenty Archon defectors who revealed Gal's true identity with a coordinated assassination attempt.

"—yes, Wraith Squadron. They told me what it means and no, I don't think it's as funny as they think it is either."

I grit my teeth. *Typical Hanji.*

"Anyway, they were on a mission meant to kill them by pitting them against two impossible goals. Iwam explained it plainly. The first part was killing you. The second was getting Gal back."

And I thought I had understood before, but now her thought process is heartbreakingly clear. Hanji and her team had gotten close enough to strike once. Wen needed to shift their focus to their second objective. To put Gal's rescue firmly within reach, if only so they didn't make another run on the first task.

From the look she's giving me now, Wen knows I've understood. "I put Gal in a room with her and had him wheedle the next steps of their extraction plan out of her. I let him think I'd use it to hunt the rest of them down. He only wanted to protect you—though he'd tied it up in this big complicated justification about keeping Iral from killing *him* that I think anyone could tell was bullshit."

I can't tell if it hurts or helps—whether I need to tell her to stop or keep going. My hands clench so hard my knuckles ache, and I stare down the maw of the service tunnel as if its seemingly infinite stretch will center me in what I really want. But as ever, there's no right choice. To try to reduce it to one or the other is to strip it of its complexity.

Wen chooses mercy. "I only wanted to protect you too," she says. "It was a vulnerable moment for your bloodright. Iral started pushing hard for command of the war, and I've seen what happens when a boss lets an upstart lieutenant get a little too much control." As if to underscore her point, there's a distant roar above. Something the general said must have rallied the crowd.

Iral is . . . complicated. He's been many things to me over the span of my life, from the Archon general I idolized as a child to the bane who dragged the War of Expansion on for two years after my parents' surrender and execution to the enemy I had to manipulate to keep Gal safe. And now, though we stand on the same side, fighting the same war, a new war has grown between us—one Iral is completely justified in waging.

He *should* doubt me. He *should* challenge an emperor who spent most of his life crawling out of the rubble of his empire instead of learning to rule it. I deserve every ounce of his doubt, but for me, the line is my bloodright, and the general is coming dangerously close to stepping on my claim to the throne itself.

And it's about to get so much worse. Before I was ever a part of this movement, Maxo Iral cultivated a strong diplomatic relationship with the Corinthian Empire. He had guarantees from the emprex themself that if Archon proved it could reclaim a single system from Umber, Corinth would step into the arena as an ally. They have a vested interest in not becoming the next jewel on the belt of Iva emp-Umber's conquests, and they support the restoration of a buffer empire between them and Umber's greed.

Now we sit in a truck bed under the noise of a packed stadium celebrating Archon's second reclaimed system. We rolled so quickly into the next offensive that the Corinthian delegation didn't have time to catch up to us before we'd brought Osar into the fold. Any day now, the Corinthians will arrive, and we'll start negotiating the next stage of the war as a united front.

The Corinthians, who have an established relationship with General Iral. The Corinthians, who I'm told doubt me for my many Umber indiscretions, from having the nerve to be educated in one of their military academies to my entanglement with their prince. The

Corinthians, who stand to shape our next victory and all the victories to come.

Framed like that, well . . .

"So Gal managed to get a direct line to the rest of the Wraiths out of Hanji, and he handed it right to me," Wen says. "I made contact with them immediately."

"It's the other three, isn't it?" I ask. Even back at the academy, Hanji made all of her trouble as part of a tight quartet.

"Ollins Cordello, Rin Atsana, and Rhodes Tsampa," Wen confirms. "They had a stealth ship, a nasty little tool bag, and at least two decent brains in the batch, and I had access to the *Torrent*'s systems. We got them aboard the dreadnought before the Battle of Dasun and hid 'em in the walls."

I can barely reconcile the mental image of a weeks-long stakeout with my last memories of them. That group was never a patient sort, and I never knew the three of them to go that long without stirring up chaos in our entire tenure at the academy. But I got the logs from Hanji's first interrogation. It wasn't even the stories she told—about being punished by the academy head for their role in helping me escape the base and claim my crown, about being thrown to the front for downright suicidal missions. It was the tired, hard look in her eyes.

Those weren't the eyes of my friend. They were the eyes of a young woman willing to do whatever it took to survive this war.

"After the battle, I knew we had to move. When you told me you were letting Gal go in the *Ruttin' Hell*, it all fell into place around that. They were supposed to extract Hanji, then sneak aboard the Beamer and hide themselves under the floorboards. That part went according to plan. What didn't was Gal *refusing*."

Gods of all systems, there's the weight of it again, pressing on my chest like a dreadnought's just parked on top of me. I try to slow my breathing, try to keep myself from seeing red. *Yes, you complete asshat,* I tell myself. *Gal really did choose to stay. We know this now. Can we stop acting like this every time we think about it?*

"The plan was scrambled. We knew there wasn't a clear path from Gal's quarters back to the *Ruttin' Hell*. Someone had to go get him and meet the Beamer *outside* the *Torrent*. We had to think on the fly, and the only thing I could come up with on short notice was the powersuit. I'd just gotten it operational again, and it killed me to lose it so soon after that, but we had an unmissable window. So Iwam and I ran for it. I strapped her in, sent her off, and cleared a path to the nearest airlock. And that's . . . how."

"And he fought?" I ask, my voice raw. Part of it's from oration, but not all of it.

"I met them halfway down the service tunnel. She had him slung over her shoulder, and he was trying his damnedest to squirm free. He thought I'd come to rescue him for a hot second." Wen shakes her head. "Are you going to strangle me if I tell you it was a little bit hilarious, the moment he realized I was working with Iwam?"

"No, but only because of that thing," I reply tersely, jerking my chin at the vibrosword on her belt. I tip my head back, staring at the concrete overhead as if I can divine the shape of the truth in the patterns of water stains. Finally, the question I've been dying to ask burns its way out of my throat. "If he fought, and if he chose, why did he take that *ruttin' crown*?"

It's the question I know she doesn't have an answer to, which is why I nearly choke on my next breath when she answers, "For the exact same reason you took yours, dipshit."

Wen's the only person in the galaxy who knows what was going through my head right before I stormed the newly liberated Archon court and started waving my signet ring around. I wasn't thinking of empires or bloodright or what I owed to my people when we sat in the hollow shell of an underground parking garage and pooled our resources. All I wanted to do was save Gal's ass.

"You're telling me that Gal's trying to play inside man from the Heir's Throne?" I ask, but I know the answer by the time the last word's left my mouth. It's hard to accept that Gal truly never meant to leave my side—that he was committed to fighting for Archon if only because it meant that he'd be keeping me safe. But once you take that as fact, you realize he's absolutely foolish enough to think he could pull that kind of thing off under his mother's nose.

"I have . . . limited information," Wen says. "A communication channel I built with Iwam. I don't speak to Gal directly, only the Wraiths. So I can't speculate on motivations he hasn't expressed to me—I can only relay what they report back."

"You're sharing this channel with me immediately," I tell her, and hold up an imperious finger when she opens her mouth to argue. "It's not one of those 'the less you know, the better' type things, and don't you dare try to convince me that it is."

"This is a delicate time for the administration," Wen mutters urgently. "The Corinthian delegation is arriving any day. We need to be focusing on establishing trust with them, and if they find out the emperor is colluding directly with Umber agents—"

"*Fine,*" I hiss. Heavens and hells, it's maddening to have a means to communicate with Gal so close at hand and not be able to use it. I have a million questions I need him to answer and a thousand things I want to say to him, but I'd be fed for the rest of my life by the sound of his breath on the other end of a comm line, a quiet promise that he's still with me.

And I wish I could want these things without feeling like my existence is the tragedy of my parents' legacy. Marc and Henrietta emp-Archon fought to preserve the ideals of our empire even in the face of Umber's rapacious push to tear them down. We're servants of the people. We put their needs above our own. Their partnership wasn't a love match—it was a political ideal, forged between the two people best suited to guide the empire. I was supposed to be the logical extension of their deep, faithful bond, all but engineered to be the Archon people's next beacon.

If the war hadn't torn my throne out from under me, I'd have been raised to revere that goal. I would have been encouraged to look for my co-ruler in the remote corners of the empire, selecting from the most promising young heirs to borderworld governorships.

My father found my mother all but single-handedly shaping the Utar system into a paradise of political function. It took him a full year to negotiate the proposal—she had prior commitments, of course, and it took all of Marc emp-Archon's considerable charm to prove to her that she could be of greater service to even more people at his side.

I think about the fact that they were scarcely a few years older than I am right now while they were doing all of this and want to crawl out of my skin. There's a world of difference between being peacetime imperials and a wartime one, but I feel like my parents had an essential spark that they failed to pass on to me—some inner motivator that got snapped over Iva emp-Umber's knee.

I lean forward, pulling the circlet off my skull with one hand so I can bury my face in the other. I knead at the skin on my forehead, massaging out the divots the weight of the platinum left in it. "You'll keep me informed, then," I groan. "With the understanding that if anyone gets wind of this, you'll have to take complete responsibility."

"Now you're getting it," Wen says, a little grin tugging the corner of her mouth.

Anger sparks through my veins again, but I quell it. This isn't *fun*. There's nothing to be smiling about here. And my trust in Wen should be in pieces. An Umber ruler would cut her loose and make an example of her on the spot—in fact, I can imagine Iva emp-Umber pulling her out of the sky to face justice before the crowd gathered in the arena above. An Archon ruler . . .

Well, whatever an Archon ruler would have done was lost to the shambles of my education and the ruins of the palace that collapsed on me when I was ten. All that's left is what I'm going to do now.

"You had some choice words for me before the drop," I murmur.

Wen's grin slips away.

"You asked me not to make you throw yourself in another dreadnought engine." I fix her with a look that she dodges with her most classic trick, turning to give me more of the scarred, less readable side of her face. I hop out of the truck bed and round on her, forcing her to look me in the eye. "Wen," I breathe. "You've been doing too much."

"I've been trying to keep up with you," she replies evenly.

"I sit in meetings and give a few speeches. I saw you at the Battle of Hana. You tore through those mining tunnels like water. You rallied the infantry when Umber pinned them in a tunnel and fought clear of a choke point that would have turned the tide in the enemy's favor. And then less than a cycle after, you came to the Osar strategy meeting. You hadn't even showered."

"That was a strategy."

"*Wen.*"

She falls stubbornly silent again.

"If I lose you, I've lost this war. And that's far too much for one person to be carrying on their back."

"If your war hinges on one person, I've got some doubts about your strategy."

"Gods of all systems, can you let me call you important without making me look like an ass for thinking it?"

"Well, if the crown fits . . ."

I let out an exasperated wheeze, and for a moment we're back where this hellish endeavor began—the two of us underground, spinning harebrained plots that betray everyone but each other.

Wen must see the way I soften, because she lifts her eyebrow and says, "So can I assume you're not mad at me?"

"I'm ruttin' *furious* with you, Wen," I scoff. "I'm just madder at myself for getting this bent out of shape over you making a play that was absolutely correct." And there's a part I don't say—partly because I'm not sure I can admit it, partly because I think she already knows. I'm just so sick of losing people. I lost Gal. I lost Esperza. Gods, I lost my parents—I can't afford to lose her too.

"Good enough for me," she says, flopping back in the bed of the truck and folding her hands behind her head.

I set myself down next to her. "Just promise me," I start, turning my circlet over and over in my hands. "Promise me you won't keep me in the dark anymore." Before she can open her mouth to argue that sometimes for a plan to work, I need to stay in the dark, I clarify. "Promise me you'll ask for help before it comes to another dreadnought engine."

Mollified, Wen sticks out a hand. I take it, and we shake. A rightness floods me with the firmness of her grip. Nothing makes me feel more unstoppable than the two of us against the galaxy.

Footsteps sound from the stairwell, and Wen's hand wrenches from mine to drop to her vibrosword hilt as she jerks upright. One of my aides crashes down into view, looking out of breath. "Jenks," I say, throwing up a hand to hold back Wen's sudden suspicion. "What is it?"

"A communication's come through from Umber, Your Majesty."

I shoot Wen a backward glare, but she gives me a slight shake of her head. This isn't one of hers—of course it isn't, her methods have to be far more subtle than this. Which means this is *Umber* Umber. "Umber as in . . ."

"The crown," Jenks confirms. "An encrypted broadcast to one of our high command channels." He shifts uncomfortably on his toes. "It was decrypted and disseminated to the core council before they realized the nature of its contents. It should have been delivered to you first—I take full responsibility for—"

Before he can trip over himself to eat dirt, I hold up a hand, and Jenks's fountain of information sputters to a merciful halt. "What, exactly, is the nature of the communication?"

Bafflingly, Jenks goes even redder. I half expect steam to start pouring out of his ears. He shoots a nervous glance at Wen, and I remember that most of my support staff still haven't quite gotten a grasp on where a street-rat-turned-lieutenant-turned-knight fits in the Archon hierarchy.

"Out with it," I command. "The Flame Knight is well past authorized to hear."

"Well, Your Majesty," Jenks says. "It appears to be some sort of . . . marriage proposal."

CHAPTER 4

GAL

WHEN I FIND OUT, I'm lucky I'm alone.

There have been a few times in my life when a hot, violent rage has overtaken me so completely that I lose control of myself. The first time it happened, it was because a man was trying to kill me. I beat him half to death with a stone coaster before I got my brain back. The second time was when Hanji shot Ettian. Again, I tried to beat her face concave—only stopped because my escort finally caught up to me and pulled me off her.

It's a bit of a shock when I come back to myself and realize that this time, I haven't moved an inch. The datapad is still clenched in my hands, the communication from my mother still open. I'm weirdly proud of myself for not snapping it in half over my knee.

Maybe I've grown as a person.

Granted, even if I had flipped shit, there isn't that much to break in my rooms. When I last lived in the citadel, I was kept in a secure suite far beneath it, built for a child and meant to conceal my existence. Now that I've returned as an adult, I've been granted my own set of chambers in the imperial residences, but I have no idea what

I'm supposed to put in them. Back at the academy, my lack of personal effects wasn't out of the ordinary, especially not with a roommate like Ettian, who—at least on the surface—had nothing to his name.

Now I'm a crowned imperial, and all I have to show for it is a few bland pieces of furniture that look even more drab against the light panels that serve as "windows," concealing the fact that within the citadel residences, we've got at least twenty feet of concrete between us and the outside world. My only bit of décor is a cutting of a weird little plant Rin pressed on me one day in a way that made me think she was worried about my mental health.

I rolled my eyes at the time, but watering it does help.

"I'm going to see the empress," I announce as I blow through the doors of my quarters, shrugging on my jacket haphazardly. Two guards sweep in to flank me, one moving ahead, the other behind as we forge a path through the narrow corridors from my residence to the grand imperial one that will be mine in seven years. Another pair of guards meet us at the door—not a quartet, which sends a shiver of relief down my spine. I always feel smaller when I have to confront both parents at once. The weight of twenty years of experience is a little easier to stand up to than forty years combined.

I'm the only person in the galaxy who could get away with the way I enter the room. Not even my father has the bloodright necessary to slam through the doors of the imperial residence like you wanna vaporize them. There's something childishly satisfying about it, like smashing over a block tower or driving your minispeeder off a makeshift ramp. Harmless, but gods does it make a noise.

My parents' rooms are the ideal of imperial elegance, with the kind of luxurious decoration that deserves front page coverage. At first glance, they're perfectly composed and lush, filled with artful sculptures and well-tended plants and balanced with an appropriate amount of negative space.

At second, you start to notice the story. You realize that's Viltian quartz carved into a twining, somewhat human form, a varietal of an orchid now extinct in Hana's razed jungles, a skull of a sea creature native to Chorta. The décor is a gallery of conquest, a trophy hunter masquerading her kills as art. The tall light panels lining the walls are meant to evoke an elegant conservatory in the sky, but once I notice the artifice, I feel like an animal in an enclosure engineered to mimic all the enrichment it needs.

"I take it you got my message," my mother says from her place at the parlor table's side. She's bent over an array of screens that have been splayed out over its stone surface like a patient on an operating table. From here more than anywhere else, she controls the strings that keep the empire's heart beating.

"*Marriage?*" I blurt, because it's the word that's been overriding my thought processes ever since I read my mother's communication.

"I'm surprised," she continues. "You seem upset. From the intelligence I've gathered, it seems like the match would not be . . . unfavorable to you, let's say."

This is a test—a tightrope I've got to walk as carefully as I dare. I rein in the impulse to delve headlong into the rant threatening to boil over inside me. "It's absolutely absurd," I declare, drawing myself up as tall as I'll go. "I thought we were trying *not* to legitimize the Archon upstart."

"We are *trying*," my mother begins, sitting back in her chair with a sigh, "to deescalate this nonsense. They've taken the Osar System in a month. Thousands of people are dead—and none of them are the ones whom I'd like to see dead. We need control of the situation, and a play like this gives us a chance to grasp it before it comes to deploying the Imperial Fleet."

"But offering an alliance is treating them as a separate entity. They're *rebels,* not true governors. The Archon bloodright was forsaken when we crushed them into ash ten years ago."

"These wins are restoring it," my mother says, and my jaw nearly drops. Her thin lips spread into a bemused smile as she takes in my shock. "Dear one, if I block out reality, how can you expect me to shape it? I'll give Archon this much—they are doing exactly what they need to in order to rally those territories. There's a weakness in their culture for nobility and self-sacrifice, and now that their em-

peror has put aside his"—she pauses, looking me up and down—
"obvious bias, they're uniting behind him. Those are people he's
won."

"Are you implying my escape is to blame for Archon's victories?"
I know I could probably make a better move than this, but I can't
possibly maneuver around my mother when my head's still spinning
from what she's put into motion. Better to play petty and keep her
expectations low.

"Just pointing out that it's done wonders for your counterpart's
focus. And for the goodwill of his constituency." Iva waves me over,
then turns the gesture with a practiced imperial hand, pointing to
the chair next to her. I aspire to that level of fluency—to passing
commands like I'm conducting an orchestra.

I wait a daring moment to oblige the empress, partly because she
needs a firm reminder that we share bloodright, but mostly because
I know the temerity of doing so will impress her. When I settle in the
chair at last, she leans in close, carding her nails carefully through
my hair. "I know you didn't want this kind of courtship. We raised
you with a promise for a different inheritance than the one you got.
But we have to live with this reality."

I lean into the touch of the war criminal who birthed me, thinking of the suited knights who died by her command, the systems of
people she threw into turmoil with her War of Expansion, the blood
that soaks her hands. If I can press myself this close to her, if I can
treat her like my mother and hold all that in my head in the same
time, I can center myself in my purpose and play the game without
slipping.

"I want a *story*," I breathe. "Not a travesty. Not a laughingstock.
That's all this farce will be, and don't you dare try to tell me otherwise." My mother's eyes narrow, but if she were going to stop me,
she'd have done it already. "All that careful work that went into restoring my image after the disaster at the academy, after Berr sys-
Tosa threw me to those Archon bastards, after that *usurper* kept me
as a pet and dragged me around in public for months—it would all
be undone."

Her grip goes carefully taut around the curly ends of my hair, fixing me under her unwavering, hooded eyes. "There are larger things in this empire than your image, Gal," my mother murmurs. "Part of ruling is knowing what can be rebuilt and what can't. In a month, you were able to build back the trust of the court—a court that saw every inch of what you went through in Archon captivity, who dared to clamor for it when they thought I wasn't paying attention. You did it naturally, with nothing but a crown on your head and that clever brain we put so much work into cultivating." Her grip softens, along with the look on her face. "*Trust* that you will be able to do it again, and take the freedom that gives you to *act*."

"There's little hope for healing trust twice broken," I reply, and her eyes go flinty.

"Platitudes like that weren't written for imperials," the empress replies.

"So what, we're just going to . . . invite Archon to join our line?" I grind through my teeth.

"You know what an imperial marriage is," my mother says. "Only one bloodright survives it."

Her logic is starting to slot into place. A marriage where bloodright is involved is part ascension, part sacrifice. When she took Yltrast sys-Gordan to be her husband, he forsook his claim to his birth system and instead stepped into sharing the bloodright that governed the entire Umber Empire. If, gods forbid, she decides to dissolve the marriage someday, he can never go back to his old claim.

If we bind Ettian emp-Archon to a similar agreement, he'll be ascended to share the Umber bloodright—at the cost of his Archon title.

"What terms have you offered?" I ask, peppering my tone with enough resignation that a pleased quirk tugs the edge of my mother's mouth. If she thinks I'm taking this seriously, she'll give me the information I need to outmaneuver it.

"If he accepts, we offer a full cease-fire and full forgiveness for the worlds Archon has already overturned," she says, flicking one of the datapads to draw up the precise document she's pulling from.

The way she organizes her thinking astounds me sometimes. Her mind works in maps layered on maps layered on maps. Once something is drawn onto her representations of the galaxy, it's *hers,* and it never gets away from her.

Which is probably why the loss of Tosa and Osar gnaws at her so deeply. Deeply enough that she's willing to recognize Ettian's claim as sufficiently legitimate for a marriage alliance.

"In addition," Iva continues, "we'll allow for the formation of an independent region comprising the former Archon territories, which he'll have the authority to oversee from his position as emperor. He'll make the appointments for all governorships, which will have to pass a review done by the rest of us. If he wants to rule those worlds so badly, I think he'll find it perfectly amenable. And if he doesn't, well. The proposal also included statistics about the forces we're about to mobilize in the region."

My mouth sours. Not because of the cruelty of her proposal or the humiliating way she's moved to sell my hand to broker peace. No, the thing that makes a tinge of nausea trigger a cold sweat on the back of my neck is the fact that I'm not entirely sure what Ettian will do. I'm not even sure what I *want* him to do.

On the one hand, he's Archon, and that comes with a streak of downright ridiculous self-sacrifice that I've never been able to fully wrap my head around. Archon imperials are raised to serve their people in the same way Umber imperials are brought up to wield their power over them. There's no doubt that a promise of a cease-fire would hook him right in that weak point. Forsake his title to save his people from the inevitability of Umber's brutal retaliation?

It sounds like exactly the kind of foolish thing the Ettian I know and love would do.

But on the other, well. Ettian's rise to power has been through the faith of a core council organized under the command of General Maxo Iral. Ettian's always been the unknown factor in this war—and Iral is the one who has Umber nervous. I was intimately familiar with the power struggle going on behind the scenes of the Archon regime, in part because who came out on top determined whether I lived or died. Ettian would never see me harmed.

Iral would have me on a crucifix the moment he was able. The general fought through the worst of the last war and fought harder still when the Archon imperials were executed and the war was supposed to end. He's a man who saw his lover, the suited knight Torrance con-Rafe, assassinated by my mother's agents at Knightfall. A man who saw his twin brother executed at the Imperial Seat in his place. He's spent the past five years plotting bloody vengeance on this empire, and the only thing that's been keeping him from enacting it fully is the fact that he has a green imperial to contend with on the throne.

If Ettian were to abdicate his seat, there's no telling what Iral might unleash.

"The usurper has laid down considerable roots over the course of his campaign," I start carefully. "Archon has never stayed down when they're supposed to. How do we know that binding him into a marriage will quell the unrest? It seems equally likely to set off an even larger rejection of our rule in the region."

My mother reaches around behind her back. There's a soft jingle, a slight clink, and her hand comes back with a dagger clenched in it. She sets it primly on the table between us, leaving me to regard my paling face in its shimmering obsidian reflection. "I've made a study of the Archon people over the years, starting when we first realized we would need to expand into their territories. I like to think I have them figured out. You know, of course, why I chose to open the War of Expansion by killing off their suited knights?"

I think back to the Battle of Dasun, to running Wen Iffan's comms as she tore her way through wave after wave of Umber forces, threw herself down the *Fulcrum*'s engines, and triggered the burn that threw the ship into Dasun's massive, gaseous grip and tore it to shreds. "Because they're terrifyingly effective on the battlefield," I reply.

Iva shakes her head slightly. "They're pests at best—irritating, but small fry compared to the might of a dreadnought. You cannot blockade a planet with a suited knight. Just because one gummed the works of a war machine does not mean they're as invincible as everyone else seems to be treating them."

Wen seems to beg to differ, I think but don't dare say.

"No, it's not that. The Archon people, with all their noble notions of *service* and *honor,* have created an addiction within themselves to people who represent the ideal of those qualities. They hang their hopes so entirely on those people that all it really takes to break their spirits is to remove them. I took the suited knights— I eliminated a whole generation of heroes—and their defenses crumbled within five years."

She slips the blade of the dagger into her palm, tipping it to offer the handle to me. My fingers close around the hilt, my heart hammering so loudly I worry she'll be able to feel the force of it shaking the weapon.

"Now Archon has fielded a new hero. This young man who rose from the ashes, who escaped what should have been a total elimination of his line. The people have fallen back on their old habits. They love him for everything he's given up to serve them—which seems to include you, I might add. They've built this uprising on his back."

I drop my gaze to the glassy edge of the blade. It's far less dangerous than the look in my mother's eyes.

"So we've proposed our arrangement. A marriage, a cease-fire, a regional government. Archon will waver—of course they must. How could we possibly ask them to give up their independence? We'll show them the alternative. Something big, something flashy. Something that'll hurt. Perhaps we'll fire on a continent with an orbital blockade in place. Wipe a city from the map. The Warning Shot we gave them near their precious capital on Rana was a little too lenient, I think."

I think of the massive scar left in the ground to the north of Trost. Of the stories I've heard about the months it took for the smoke to clear, the way farmers in the region lost an entire crop to the abrupt winter that descended, the elderly citizens who died choking on ash. I try to calibrate that as *lenient*.

"Hopefully before it comes to that, Archon will see reason. They'll understand that this is the most peaceable solution possible. One that *serves their people best*," she says with a roll of her eyes. "They'll send us their emperor. We'll stage the ceremony in the Imperial Seat—make it as grand as we possibly can. You two will walk the walkway. You'll meet in the middle."

Her hand slips up the blade to tighten around my grip at the hilt. "And when it's done—when Archon has forsaken its imperial line and laid all this nonsense to rest—you'll pull out the blade."

I feel myself crack. Like a cityscape against the concussive blast of a dreadnought's main battery, my composure shatters. I can't hold back my revulsion any longer, and my mother's eyes light up as she watches my expression swerve from impassivity to terror. She's been waiting for this, I realize.

Her other hand comes up to lock around the back of my neck as her fingers drive mine painfully into the dagger's grip. "You love him still. You've tried to burn it out of you, but it's still there."

I can't enjoy the brief respite her words bring—the relief that she hasn't broken through my secrets completely. Not when she's about to crush the bones in my hand to powder.

"I loved Ximena, too, you know?" she whispers, like it's a tender secret between mother and son. "When she stepped from the shadows and I saw her for the first time, I couldn't help but love her. She was the ideal of our line. I watched her get everything I was raised to inherit, and it broke my heart to know what I would have to do."

I still can't fathom the unspeakable cruelty of my grandparents. How they raised both their daughters to inherit a throne that only allowed for one of them. How they let Iva grow up not knowing that she would only ever be a backup, a fail-safe. My mother has never spoken directly about the way it must have unraveled her before. The only thing she's ever told me is all I need to know: I have no siblings. I am the only Umber heir.

"I loved her even as I cut her throat," my mother says, her deep brown eyes fixed on mine so intensely that I feel pinned in place. "And when I did it, it affirmed the truth I'd always held inside myself. I carry the Umber bloodright. The galaxy is mine by blood. And when you stand before your people and hold the Archon emperor on the end of this blade, you'll know the same rightness."

I don't tell her that I've held Ettian on the end of a blade before. She doesn't need to know about the night before we left for the battlefront, the stolen moment in the Archon palace's service tunnels. I shattered a glass and laid it carefully against his trachea. I'd drawn blood.

And then I let it fall and kissed him. Even with no one watching, even with the opportunity to win the war and break the Archon line with a twitch of my wrist, I chose his lips instead.

But the iron grip locked around my hand tells me that I won't have a choice this time. My mother won't give me a chance to reconsider— a chance to sweep him into my arms and declare him a love-match with a kiss to seal our marriage before the galaxy. That was the wedding I dreamed about as a child.

The reality is a blade in my hand and the expectation that when the time comes, I'll shatter my soul and come into my bloodright the same way my mother did twenty years ago.

The intensity of her hooded gaze gives me no other choice. With my tongue thick in my mouth and nausea roiling in my gut, I pull the dagger closer, close my eyes, and nod.

CHAPTER 5

ETTIAN

I'M LIVING IN A NIGHTMARE. That's the only rational explanation for how this can be happening. I keep on waiting for the logic to break—for the crown to fly from my head or the ground to drop out from under my feet or my arms to turn into Viper engines that launch me away from the chaos that has just descended upon my administration.

Because it's not only that Iva emp-Umber has sent the Archon leadership a marriage proposal to join me and Gal in the most horrific political matrimony the galaxy has ever seen, it's not only that said message also included a vivid threat in the form of the Imperial Fleet's ever-growing masses readying to deploy from the Umber interior—no, that's not enough for this scenario that's so downright cruel it *has* to be a product of my own mind.

On top of all of that, the Corinthian delegation has just arrived.

Wen keeps giving me worried looks. We've been packed in the back of an armored van that's ferrying us at a reckless pace through the streets of Ichano to the governor's mansion. There are a few other guards in here with us, plus my usual entourage of aides, which has created a thorny knot of security clearance issues that have reduced her to making *do you wanna talk* eyes at me across the vehicle's bed.

The look I'm giving her back is somewhere on the spectrum between *wake me up* and *kill me now*.

Iva emp-Umber's play was perfect. I have no doubt she got the intelligence that the Corinthians were sending their ambassadors to rendezvous on Ichano and timed the proposal to arrive precisely when they did. I'm half-tempted to ask my people to backtrace the signal just to confirm the order's been standing by in some communications waystation, waiting for the moment Corinthian ships dropped into the system.

On top of all of that, she made *certain* her transmission wouldn't get filtered through the channels of command so that it reached my ears first. In fact, thanks to my secluded little chat with Wen, I seem to be the last of my inner circle to find out that I've received a marriage proposal. Heavens and hells, *General Iral* knew before I did, which doesn't bode well for the negotiation we're about to enter. He's had a full hour to process the proposal.

All I've got is this chaotic truck ride, and it's nearly over. I hear the sirens cut from the motorcade outside, and a moment later, we come to an ungainly, lurching halt. The guards closest to the doors form a wall with their bodies as they fling them open, and we file out of the van with the frantic pace of a pack of academy cadets who've heard that the cantina's put up a two-for-one special on raw polish shots. An imperial herald cadence starts from the skin drums set up along the drive, making my arrival unmistakable. Luckily the garb I dressed in for the rally—a fine emerald green suit inlaid with curling platinum embroidery—pulls diplomacy double duty just fine. A few aides dart close to adjust my crown and smooth my creases.

Wen falls in step beside me. No one dares try to smooth her down, though she shakes her cape into order with a few self-conscious tugs. She's both the highest-ranking Corinthian in my administration and the farthest thing from the retinue staged to meet us at the far end of the lawn.

Amid their own passel of guards, the three diplomats await. All of them are dressed in trim shirtsleeves that seem a bit simplistic for formal clothing but make up for it in their immaculate whiteness. I recognize the ambassador themself, Biss Xhosi, in the center, marked by the studs of raw granite inlaid along their collar. The two flanking them must be their junior administrators. As we approach, Xhosi dips their head in greeting, and I return the gesture. "Archon," they say, their tone warm but wary.

"Corinth," I reply, and offer a hand. Xhosi hesitates before taking it, a gesture I have to fight not to read as rudeness. I've been briefed on Corinthian diplomatic formalities. A handshake is considered provincial—not offensive, just unbefitting a person who's been elevated to the rank of public servant.

Xhosi seems almost delighted to be doing something so quaint. They crack an easy smile and surprise me by clapping me on the shoulder. "Blessed to meet you, Your Majesty." They withdraw their hand and pull themselves back up to their full, considerable height. "I am Biss Xhosi, speaking on behalf of their excellency Fortis emp-Corinth. I've vowed to act in the emprex's stead and speak on their behalf by proxy. These two are my auxiliaries, Hanna Efir and Alees plan-Cuerto." They gesture to the two women behind them, and I offer both the same short nod Xhosi used to greet me.

"I'm looking forward to our collaboration," I tell them. "Honored ambassadors, I'd like to introduce you to Commander Wen Iffan, Knight of Archon."

If I thought they were being friendly before, it's nothing compared to the way the Corinthians' faces light up when their eyes turn to Wen. She grins pleasantly at them, but I can see the strain of their attention weighing on her. I slip a gentle hand around her back to ground her.

"We've heard of your exploits, of course," Xhosi says. "The footage from the Battle of Dasun was . . . Well, it's been more than a decade since the last time we saw anything like that. I'm blessed, Commander."

"As am I," Wen says, still sounding a little shell-shocked by their reaction to her. She expected to be rejected by the immaculate diplomats. How could they, with their fussy manners and spotless, blinding shirts, welcome a rough-edged, brutally scarred Corinthian who's given herself over so fully to Archon that she's not only ranked, she's become a household name and hero? For a moment a lance of fear needles into my brain, convinced that she's going to forsake me for their obvious adoration. But before that thought has time to settle, Wen adds, "I hope this will be the start of a fruitful collaboration between our two empires. I believe there's a lot we can learn from Corinth, and that our collaboration builds a stronger galaxy."

Diplomatic, yes. Perhaps a tad worrisome in the way she seems to promise deference to Corinth's way of running things. But there's no denying that "we" and the side it places her on in this negotiation, and it makes my heart lift. That's always been my promise to Wen. I met her when she had nothing and no one, and the first thing I could offer her was an "us."

If she really valued "us," she never would have let Gal go, a cruel voice whispers in the back of my head, and it strikes a part of me that twinges like the scar on my stomach. I don't know if my trust in her will ever fully heal, and I don't know that I can survive this war if it doesn't.

Before I can fully process that thought, the Corinthians' attention snaps somewhere above my shoulder with such sudden awe and wariness that for a moment I'm tempted to duck for cover. I glance back and suppress a grimace as I find General Iral striding confidently across the lawn.

He's fresh off his speech and looking as fine as ever, his long, loose braids bound back and his massive frame squared neatly into a handsome dress uniform. My idolatry for the man used to be so straightforward, before I started being measured against him. Presenting himself like this, he's unquestionably the hero who fought like hell to win the first war, and next to him I feel half-baked in almost every respect. I draw myself up a notch taller as he steps up to my side, trying not to let the faint twinge of my scar show on my face.

"Your Majesty," he says, dropping into a perfectly deferential bow. It's not mocking—nothing about it is mocking—but I can't help feeling like he's laying it on too thick for the sake of our guests.

"General," I reply, releasing him with a salute. "Allow me to introduce you to Biss Xhosi, ambassador of the Corinthian emprex."

"Biss," the general says with a wide smile, and I realize the depth of the trouble I've just landed myself in. I watch the two shake hands—no hesitation on the Corinthian's part this time—and exchange a wary glance with Wen.

"The general and I go way back," the ambassador says once they've finished greeting Iral. "I met him when he first landed in Corinth with the scraps of his rebellion. He helped with—well, he *was* my career transition from refugee services to diplomacy. And now look at us. Me, the emprex's outstretched hand, and you with two systems under your belt and many more on the way."

"Let's hope to the gods of all systems that's true," Iral says. "Come, let's continue this indoors."

I can feel myself rapidly losing control of the situation, but I don't want to be the kind of imperial who throws an absolute shitfit over two people I need on my side being friendly with each other. That's not gonna read well no matter how much bloodright I carry. "To the conservatory on the second floor, perhaps," I suggest lightly as I fall into step behind the ambassador and the general.

It's the kind of move I could easily see Gal pulling—both a gentle enough touch not to stand out and a firm reminder of my presence. The thought has me in knots for the entire walk from the estate's lawn to the second-floor study I suggested. My parents didn't live long enough to teach me strategy. Almost everything I know, I've learned from watching the way Gal operated while I had him at my side. He was working at a cross-purpose to everything we were trying to accomplish during most of his time with the Archon rebellion, but he was always so quiet and clever about it that I often didn't realize what he was after until it was far too late. From there, I had to retrace the steps he'd taken to achieve his goal—and often sit back in awe of how seamlessly he did it all.

The Corinthians are already wary enough about the fact that my most recent formal education was at an Umber military academy. If they realize I've absorbed my political playbook by paying a little too much attention to our newly crowned enemy, I'm completely rutted.

Worse, by the time we make it to the conservatory, I realize I've spent what could have been a very productive walk for planning out this meeting thinking about Gal and how brilliant he is. Thank every god of every system the Corinthians haven't figured out mind reading yet—although one Corinthian in particular has all but insider access to my skull and is currently giving me a look that says *You'd better knock 'em dead, buddy*. I clap Wen on the shoulder as I move past her and take my seat at the head of the long, grand study table that stretches beneath the conservatory's majestic duroglass dome.

We've barely had time to settle into Ichano since we claimed this system, and as a result, we're forced to stage our first talks in a room that still bears all the trappings of the enemy. This mansion once belonged to the Umber-appointed system governor we ousted, and she's made sure every room screams Umber imperial might as loudly as it can, from its glassy obsidian tiling to the sharp-edged brass lattices patterning the walls. It's not quite tacky enough to undercut the burgeoning sense of dread I get taking it all in. If we'd had more time, we could have at least thrown up a little emerald drapery to dampen the feeling that Umber looms large over everything we do here.

Iral sits at my right, Ambassador Xhosi at my left, and their juniors take seats farther down the table. Wen stays standing at my back, falling into a wary parade rest. Xhosi quirks an eyebrow at her. "Commander Iffan, you ought to join us properly," they say, gesturing to the seat at Iral's right.

"Honored ambassador, my role on the advisory is purely decorative," Wen says, knocking one knuckle lightheartedly against the fancy armored chestpiece she wears.

The comment strikes an uncomfortable chord inside me. Wen's

elevation to the rank of suited knight wasn't just a boon from Iral. After my assassination attempt, I sent Wen to serve as my representative in the Archon strategy meetings and dig in her heels long enough for me to get back on my feet and back to the table. Iral outmaneuvered me by giving her his dead lover's armor and insinuating that she was better off on the battlefield. Wen couldn't possibly refuse it, and once she demonstrated her value in the Battle of Dasun, there was no going back.

But the fact remains—Wen once tried to hold her own at politics, and because I wasn't there to back her up, she ended up thinking that throwing herself down the maw of a dreadnought engine was the only way to prove herself.

"Sit," I tell her, weighing it with the authority of my bloodright. As she moves to comply, I continue, "Wen was the first Corinthian to welcome me to your empire when I washed up on its shores. It's only natural that she be a part of the conversations that bridge us."

Iral shifts in his chair with a smile that verges on strained as Wen settles primly at his right. "Yes, Commander Iffan has been . . . full of surprises in the time that I've known her, shall we say?"

The ambassador leans in conspiratorially. "Do tell, General."

"Well no one's ever really known what to expect from her," Iral says pleasantly. "The emperor plucked her off the streets of Isla, and from what I understand, she's got a history with the local mob scene there. We had to detain her within a couple of days on the Delos base for tampering with—"

"*Fixing,*" Wen mutters insistently under her breath.

"—one of our ships." He gives her a considered look. "We're all quite lucky that Archon here spoke for her. He kept insisting she could be put to good use. It took me months to come around, but if I hadn't, we'd be trash orbiting Dasun. It's a lesson I've taken to heart."

"Not to underestimate Corinthians?" Xhosi suggests wryly.

"To value aid, no matter the reasoning behind it," Iral replies, leaning forward and folding his hands in contemplation before him.

"You've known me since we fled to Corinth with nothing. Since those Umber bastards hung my brother on a cross. Empires rise and fall with the building and erosion of trust, and mine was ash when we broke ground for that base on Delos. We'd lost too much—I couldn't stand to lose more to the chance someone would worm into our foundations and uproot them."

I realize I'm holding my breath. I've only ever seen Iral's walls come down once before—in the privacy of his study, when I was nothing but a war orphan to him. I'd understood the depth of his suffering then, but I'd been so caught up in the con we were trying to pull, using his rebellion as a vehicle to parade Gal back to the core of the Umber Empire, that I'd never really given much thought to it since.

"I could never bring myself to believe that someone could commit themselves to my cause without the Archon history to drive them. I'd always thought that if you took all that away, I could have been a peaceful man. Perhaps a farmer somewhere in those border-worlds. But Archon pain is not the only pure motive in the galaxy." Iral stares down at his hands. "It's just the thing that was driving me the fiercest. So now I look to you, my friend, and I want to know what drives the Corinthian emprex to our aid."

I need to regain control of this conversation, and fast. I never should have let Iral get that deep into his monologue, but he's managed to twist what should have been stories about Wen's antics into the opening maneuver of our negotiations with the Corinthians. Leaping in now to claim the general doesn't speak for me is only going to make me look greener.

Xhosi sits with the general's words, their eyes closed like they're savoring the depths he's just revealed. They tip their chin up slightly as another smile spreads across their lips. "You're so right, General. There is absolutely no substitute for the suffering of the Archon people. We can claim we have some idea. We witnessed the broadcasts from the War of Expansion. We've felt the pinch of Umber patrols leaning against our border, their greedy eyes peering at the riches of our territory, and we can claim that this is somehow a cousin to the devastation Iva emp-Umber wrought on your people. But the fact remains that these things are happening, and Corinth needs a shield. That's what they used to call you back in the day, isn't it?"

"The Shield of Archon," Iral says pointedly.

I can feel it like a pinch in the side. It's not the moment *I* sense blood in the water. It's the moment Gal would have. The moment I'd realize he'd gone tense beside me. His breathing would slow as he spun the right words into the perfect net, and for a moment I miss him so much that I nearly miss my opening. But before either Iral or Xhosi can get their next words in, I pounce. "General, I believe we all serve a purpose higher than empire. Our duty is not to whichever crown we obey—it's to the people, no matter whose domain they fall under."

All three of the Corinthian emissaries straighten in their chairs with so much uniformity that I have to choke back my impulse to laugh. Wen's got the leeway to smirk, and she's running with it, her lips twisting in obvious delight.

"Our purpose here is not to draw lines and squabble about who defends whom," I continue. "We have a common goal of extracting as many people as we can manage from the grip of Umber tyranny, and as long as we never lose sight of that, I believe our relationship will be long and fruitful."

Xhosi gives me a nod like they're greeting me all over again—like they've finally gotten the measure of me and *now* we can properly meet. "Well said, young Archon. I must admit, there were . . . nerves on our side, when you appeared out of nowhere. When we collaborated with the general, our vision for the territory he reclaimed was closer to our own system of governance. The notion of bloodright has always rankled Corinthian ears, as I'm sure your knight has already informed you. We value choice far too much to leave something so important to the chance that the right ruler will always rise from their predecessor's genes. But we'd also have to be fools to ignore the cases when it's worked—when a young ruler truly is the sum of their parents."

Gods, I wish I could hear that and *not* feel doubt. My parents' legacies loom so large over everything we do that I feel like I'll never be free of their shadow. I've been trying my damnedest to act along the template they were able to pass along, but it doesn't feel like it'll be enough. It wasn't even enough for them—they *lost* the war. And even when they lost the war, they had each other to the bitter end.

"I'm honored," I start, trying to play it like I'm choked with emotion over the mention of my murdered family, not like I'm faltering under the weight of every expectation on my shoulders. "And while I'm obviously invested in reestablishing Archon's imperial line, I believe the empire's second chance is an opportunity for it to evolve, and I welcome Corinthian collaboration in that evolution."

And Iral—oh, he's been fuming the past several minutes. I can feel him rearing back for the strike on his inhale, and though he lets out nothing but a half-audible chuff, it detonates in the room like an atomic bomb.

"Something funny, General?" Xhosi asks pleasantly.

Iral shrugs. "*Reestablishing the Archon line* is certainly one way to phrase it."

Don't, I groan internally.

"Our boy's just received a very interesting proposal to that effect," Iral says. "And I'm wondering if he's seriously entertaining it."

So he wants to go there. A telltale motion of her shoulder tells me Wen's hand is easing onto the hilt of her vibrosword beneath the table, and I feel a similar fury crackling through me. Ever since I came to power, Iral has played this delicate game of implications, holding my image over me like a threat. He knows Gal is the weakest point I have, and he's never afraid to lean hard on what that means about my suitability for my title.

I never *dreamed* he'd try pulling that shit in front of the Corinthians not fifteen minutes after we sat down at a table. I can all but hear the dare. *Either confess to the fact that we've received a marriage proposal from Umber or I'll tell our guests myself.*

But if the general wants to make a fool out of me, I'll do it on my own goddamn terms. "General Iral, you're to leave this table," I announce.

His eyebrows shoot up. "Your Majesty, I'm not—"

"No excuses, General," Wen says mildly from his other side. "Your emperor has given you a direct order."

Xhosi spreads their hands, trying their best to placate the sudden tension. "My fellows, please—surely there's some misunderstanding?"

"There is no misunderstanding," I say, rising to my feet. "Iral has overstepped his bounds, and I would like to speak to you without worrying that he might do it again. The general will leave this table, or I'll have the Flame Knight remove him by force."

Wen shoots me a look that says *Oh don't you dare—he's twice my size easily,* but thankfully it doesn't come to that. Iral knows there are larger things at stake here than his seat on my advisory, and he's not about to make the Archon rebellion look like a squabbling, petty mess in front of our best hope for actually winning this war. He rises, giving Xhosi one last nod before he leaves the table and exits the conservatory by the same way we came.

When the doors swing shut behind him, I fix Xhosi with an imperious look, holding my chin high and trying my damnedest to look settled in my bloodright. "I'm truly sorry for that. I know you expected to open these negotiations with an old friend on the other side of the table."

The look the ambassador is giving me in return is . . . measured, at best. I know I might never get back that moment of admiration I earned from them.

I also know that I'm past giving a shit.

"I would like to know what the general was referring to," Xhosi says after a moment of consideration. "If it was important enough for him to voice it here and now, it sounds like it might be essential to the progression of our talks."

And that's the reality I have to accept. It *is* important. It's not just my personal feelings, not just the way my pulse quickens at even the hint of Gal's shadow. War has obliterated the delicacy I deserve in these matters, and if I believe in the larger picture, like I'm trying to impress on the Corinthians, I believe that my empire's needs come above my heart's.

I catch Wen's eyes, feeling the pinch of the tight-lipped look she gives me. When the choice fell to her, she chose Archon, knowing it would tear me apart. Knowing it could tear *us* apart too.

It was the right call.

I sigh, settling back in my chair. "If you'll forgive the time it's going to take to explain . . ."

"I will, but the war may not, so I suggest you do your best to sum it up."

I allow myself one breath. One moment to inhale deep and close my eyes and wish desperately that I had Gal at my side to talk me through what I'm supposed to do here. Then I open my eyes, lean forward, and start the long, slow, excruciating process of forging the alliance that might save us all.

CHAPTER 6

GAL

When I step into the Wraiths' rumpus room, I have about two seconds to ingest the chaos of it—like someone's taken a squad of academy cadets' belongings and detonated them—before they're on me. Ollins and Rhodes pin my arms to my sides, Rin throws a blanket around my shoulders as a mantle, and they parade me down the gadgetry-strewn floor between their bunks, singing the imperial marriage anthem at the top of their lungs. At the end of the march stands Hanji Iwam, wearing a dour expression she's barely holding in place and a crown made of silvery filings that sits half-cocked on her messy ponytail.

"I see you're all taking this seriously," I mutter under my breath as Rin rounds out around us and lays a hand on both my and Hanji's shoulders.

"This bond is recognized in the sight of the god of Acua," she intones dramatically, with all the usual flair of a chaplain. "As witnessed by this pack of dipshits, it stands in the law of the empire!"

I roll my eyes and grab Hanji by the shoulder and waist, sweeping her around and dipping her like I'm gonna kiss her. Her composure breaks and she squirms away, squawking, "A love match? In *this* economy?"

The Wraiths collapse into uproarious laughter, and I bury my face in my palms. "Ruttin' hell, how am I supposed to pull this off?"

"You need advice about pulling things off?" Ollins asks with a waggle of his eyebrows. I ball up the blanket they've slung around my shoulders and throw it in his face, and he collapses back onto one of the workbenches, giggling to himself.

"You," I fume, rounding on Hanji and pointing my finger accusingly. "You were supposed to wait for me to get down here before you told them about the change of plans."

"What change of plans?" Hanji fires back with a shrug, pulling off her crown and tossing it aside. "You getting hitched doesn't affect the commodore getting her lovely skull lobbed off her shoulders."

"Well no, not necessarily, but—"

"So let's do it one thing at a time," she says. "Come, sit."

Our little war table's set up at the center of the room with six chairs arranged around it. I settle into one, and Hanji drops into another. A third body's already seated—the massive husk of Wen Iffan's missing powersuit hunches daintily next to me like an adult at a child's tea party. The chair beneath it barely seems to be supporting its bulk, and a worrisome pair of inflatable tits are hanging off its helmet. It's an honest-to-gods miracle that the Wraiths have managed to hold on to that thing—or more accurately, that I've been able to block every single effort by Umber military intelligence to requisition it from them. It's their proudest trophy, and even if their security might be lacking, I maintain that everyone's happier with that monstrously overengineered hunk of metal stuck down here in their little bolt-hole.

Suited knights are more trouble than they're worth, after all.

Behind us, the rest of the Wraiths have fallen into their usual *adults are talking* business—here meaning that Rin and Rhodes are bent conspiratorially over some sketches on a workbench and Ollins has started throwing a rubber ball against the wall to amuse himself.

Unlike the imperial quarters overhead, this subbasement room wasn't engineered for its occupants' happiness, much less survival. The lighting comes from dim, mismatched bulbs strung on dodgy wiring, the furniture looks like salvage, and the only comfort is knowing that somewhere in this chaos there's a decent stash of polish.

Despite that—and the Wraiths' tendency to make me want to tear my hair out—this dank little hellhole is the only place in the citadel I feel like I can *breathe*. I spent my childhood in isolation. During my school days, I was up to my neck in secrets, but at least I could forge a few precarious friendships on top of that tower of lies. Now that a crown's been plunked on my head and the need for secrecy has passed, I have the authority to wage war on my loneliness, no matter how much my mother judges the four general nuisances I call friends.

It's her own damn fault for having them kidnap me. When they returned me to the Umber Core, the empress hailed them as heroes, granted them the dubious role of "companions to the crown," and relegated them to these shitty quarters as a reward for their service. They haven't given her a good reason to eject them yet—though boy are we about to.

That is, if I can navigate this marriage proposal without my head exploding first.

Hanji leans back, kicking her long legs up on the table and folding her hands behind her head. "You're a little freaked out, huh, bud?" she asks, tingeing the words with just enough genuine concern to keep me from shoving her feet and toppling her over backward.

"Of all the outrageous power plays I thought my mother would pull with me crowned, I never dreamed she'd lead off with selling off my ruttin' hand to Archon."

"Which is happening first, the wedding or Esperza's execution?"

"The wedding is *not* happening—not if Ettian knows what's good for him."

Hanji gives me a pointed look that clearly says *The dumbass for sure does not.*

"Fine, okay. The execution is still on track. The wedding isn't scheduled, but we can assume that with all the negotiating that needs to happen, *if* it happens, it'll be after . . . well, whatever ends up happening on the execution date." I lean my elbows on the table, running my fingers through the messy strands of my hair. "I just wish . . ."

After a long moment, Hanji slides her boots off the table and says, "C'mon. Finish that thought. What do you wish?"

I stare down at the scratched-up plastic surface, tracing the crude drawings someone's etched in it. "I wish we could move in concert with Archon. We've got five days of distance between us—physics won't bend any further than that. If we could coordinate, if I could just—"

"This is just you wanting to talk to him, isn't it?" she asks slyly.

" 'Talk' is one word for it," Ollins pipes up from the other end of the room, and this time it's Hanji, a wrench, and a hairsbreadth of distance between it and his skull. "I'm just saying, the emperor has needs," he squeaks from the ball he's curled into.

"Not all of us are gods," Hanji says with a patronizing hand over her heart.

I groan, squeezing my eyes shut. "You are *not* a god just because you—"

"Focus, Gal," Hanji says, snapping her fingers in a clear mockery of imperial gesture. "Let's not get off topic."

"I swear on the god of every goddamn system," I mutter under my breath. The Wraiths are best taken in small doses, but with the kind of schemes we're spinning, I don't have that luxury. Hanji in particular is a thorn of a very particular sort in my side. She's the puppetmaster—the strapping tower tech with the golden voice who knows exactly how to aim the rest of the Wraiths and pull their triggers. Nothing gets done without her.

But I can't look at her without remembering the bullet she put in Ettian, and it turns out a working relationship with that at the heart is a little difficult to maintain.

And that's on top of the fact that when she loaded me up in the *Ruttin' Hell* to drag me back to the Imperial Seat, she didn't give a flying rut what I wanted. She and her horrible little crack team were out to prove themselves after Ettian inadvertently tricked them into helping him claim his crown. They saw returning me to get mine planted on my head as their ultimate redemption.

Fortunately, I anticipated the void that would leave in their motivations. During our five-day trip back to the Umber Core, I unraveled every little thing that made these four tick. The Wraiths aren't motivated by loyalty to empire. They don't care about the blood that rules the stars. When they were under the jurisdiction of the man they once called Quartermaster, it worked purely because every suicidal mission he sent them on was a new trick to pull off. The one where they tried to kill Ettian and bring me home was their most ambitious one yet, and I knew it would leave an emptiness behind.

Wen's done me the favor of partially filling it. She sold me to the Wraiths on the promise that they'd return Esperza—and the threat that if they didn't do it in three months, she'd come for them. I couldn't get a drop of the Wraiths' respect if I tried, but apparently they hold Wen in a high enough regard to take her seriously. I've latched myself onto their purpose, pulling all the strings I can to keep my mother from finding out about the plot to steal the most valuable Archon prisoner in five years out from under her nose.

In the process, I've made them an even larger promise—one they can't turn down. If I'm going to hold my crown *and* keep my soul, I'm going to need all the trouble I can get. *Stick with me,* I'm telling them, *and you'll never run out of tricks.* For these four, there's nothing more valuable.

That can't stay true forever. But as long as I keep an eye on what drives them, as long as I never lose sight of what they want, I have the four little monsters who pulled off one of the grandest heists the galaxy has ever seen completely on my side.

Of course, that means if I want anything from them, I have to frame it as a challenge that builds off whatever their current goal is.

Not keeping them focused is how you end up with stuff like fireworks going off in the officer showers or that one time they managed to flood the first-year floor completely.

And the ask I'm coming with today is big. Way bigger than any stunt we've tried so far. "I have a proposal," I start.

Wrong move. "We *know*, dipshit," Rin hollers from over my shoulder.

"Not—I meant I have a new *idea*," I snarl through my teeth. "For the execution extraction extravaganza."

Hanji eyes me with all the caution I deserve. "It's two weeks away, Gal. I know you're used to being just a pretty face, but these things have moving pieces we have to practice. Which reminds me, we need another rehearsal with you and the—"

"I need to see Ettian," I say.

It's bait, pure and simple. Keep them from spiraling into a logistical tailspin by offering up something irresistibly juicy. The Wraiths take it just like I predicted. Suddenly Ollins is sliding into the chair next to me, propping his chin on his knuckles as his eyes beg me for the gory details. Rin and Rhodes abandon their workbench completely—an astounding feat I've rarely been able to pull off—and join us at the table a second later. Hanji's head tilts to the side, her eyes narrowing. "When you say 'see' . . . "

"Look," I say, laying a palm flat and firm on the table. "I have two channels of communication with the Archon Empire open to me. One is through my mother and whatever political machine she's harnessed to lob her marriage proposal bullshit over the battlefront. The other is through your line to Wen Iffan. And neither of those are going to solve this war for us."

"*Win* this war, you mean," Hanji says, eyes going even narrower behind her glasses.

"A war isn't a fight to win, it's a *problem that can be negotiated*. If we could just get everyone to *talk*—"

"I was on the front for months, Your *Majesty*," Hanji replies, a dangerous edge in her voice. "I don't think any of us could have talked our way through the boltfire."

Well, now I've stepped in it. The Wraiths have a sore spot, and usually I'm more careful with it. They've seen the war from an angle I might never experience myself. I don't know if I'll ever get the full scope of the rotating series of hells their Quartermaster threw them in, but if Ettian's taught me anything, it's that you don't *need* people's worst days to understand them. You just have to know the shape of the hole it left in them.

And I know this one in particular isn't to be messed with. "The closer you look, the easier it is to draw the lines—I won't argue that with you," I say, holding up my hands. "But when it's not just 'Take that sector or the enemy will use it as a fulcrum to kill you all,' there's a chance we can use that lack of clarity to leverage it so that—"

"We understand how a war works, Gal," Rhodes says, his voice urgent and soft. "We're just scared we're not going to walk away from this one."

"Speak for yourself, Rhodes—I'm gonna live forever," Hanji says with a shrug, but I can see the false bravado propping it up. The Wraiths may be a rambunctious pack, but when you boil it down, they aren't stupid. They know the odds are stacked against them, and that my mother will rip out their spines if she gets wind of what's going on down here.

"Look, I'm asking this because I know you're the only people in the galaxy with a chance of pulling it off. I need you to get in contact with Wen and set up a rendezvous. With what I have in mind, there's no time for back and forth. We get one window to do this, so we tell them where to be and when, do our part, and pray to every god listening that they can do theirs."

All four Wraiths are looking at me with the same expression, one that teeters on a knife's edge. I've worked so hard to earn their trust, to manipulate their goals to suit my needs, and they've done it all knowing that if it falls apart, the blame will land squarely on their shoulders. I can make all sorts of arguments that I'll take the fall with them, but we all know that when it boils down to it, my mother won't kill me.

"You're asking us to smuggle you out of the capital," Hanji says. "Under the empress's nose, after she just got you back. On top of our original plan to free the commodore before her execution—on the *day* of her execution."

I look her in the eye, tipping my chin with casual grace. "Yes," I tell her, plain and simple. No qualification. No justification. Not even a reassurance that I know how big of an ask it is.

And I see the challenge ignite in her eyes. "Sounds fun," Hanji says, a wicked grin spreading across her face.

CHAPTER 7

ETTIAN

WEN SHAKES ME AWAKE when it happens.

She's the only member of my staff with the necessary clearances to enter my quarters in the middle of the night—though I have no doubt even if I didn't give them to her, she'd figure out how to hack my doors open. After months at war, we're no strangers to this routine, but for the first time I feel a thrill of fear the moment my consciousness solidifies.

Shame follows hot on its heels. I shouldn't have to remind myself I trust her.

"I've gotten a transmission from Iwam," Wen murmurs. "She has a message to hand along."

Years of academy training and an even longer stint surviving on the streets have left me with the ability to shake off sleep like it's nothing, but Wen's words are halfway to convincing me I'm still dreaming. I throw back the coverlet, and the familiar trappings of my stateroom glow into view as the lights ease up to imitate moonlight. We're back aboard the *Torrent* and out in the deep black, far from the welcome of any system's orbit. From here, we can prep for our next offensive and still be ready to mobilize, should Umber decide to make a second try at stealing our systems away from us. I take a breath to ground myself in the moment and all of the machinery in place to protect me, then ease myself to the edge of the bed.

It's nothing fancy—nothing my station requires. When I came aboard, the captain, Deidra con-Silon, made a loud, somewhat performative fuss about getting me set up with a stateroom that befits an imperial, but I shut her down. I've been sleeping on whatever hard surface would take me since I was ten years old, and the academy's crunchy vinyl mattresses were barely an improvement. They tried to house me in the governor's old quarters during the transition period when I took my crown on Rana, and I ended up sleeping on the couch. To placate Silon, I've dressed the bed in a rich, red, satiny coverlet, but beneath it the mattress is achingly firm.

Wen regards me with folded arms. She's dressed in a pajama set and a thick robe, and there's a part of me that wonders whether she was actually sleeping or threw it on to look like she wasn't working through the night before she came to wake me. Her vibrosword's hilt peeks out of one of the robe's pockets. "The message was direct to me, encrypted and unopened," she starts. "I haven't read it yet. I can walk you through all the security if you need the peace of mind."

The words pinch. I wonder if she noticed how I flinched when I woke, if she feels like she needs to reassure me that she's on my side. The care she takes breaks my heart more than the betrayal of letting Gal go. I don't deserve this girl.

"No need," I tell her softly. It's the best peace offering I can give her right now—though I'd be lying if I said it was only that. She's just told me that Gal has sent me a message for the first time in months. I don't give a shit about any of the security protocols wrapping it. I just want to hear from him.

She pulls a datapad out from under the crook of her elbow and hands it to me.

Bent over with my elbows propped on my knees, perched on the edge of my hard-ass bed, I start to read.

Ettian,

I considered saying sorry as an opener, but we both know what you'd say to that. Still, it was never my intention to leave you in the dark for this long. I'm told Wen has explained exactly what happened to you, so I want you to know that once I'd resigned myself to my fate, I knew that there had to be a break in contact.

Well, that's a lie. I tried to steal Hanji's datapad on no fewer than three separate occasions, and all three times I couldn't bust through her security before she'd kicked down the door/dragged me out from under the bed/shot the damn thing out of my hands from across a courtyard and threatened to break my fingers again if I tried it one more time. I hate that I gave up, but I reasoned it was for the best. Both of us had duties—neither of us could afford the distraction.

So I guess that leaves you wondering why now? Or maybe you aren't, because of course you've received my mother's messages (and how I hate that she got a direct line to you before I did). You've been presented with a marriage proposal that I had no part in, which makes me want to raze a ruttin' system—exaggeration, I promise, I know you worry about that sometimes. I wouldn't blame you for taking it seriously, too. I mean, first of all, I'm a total catch,[1] any eligible heir in the empire would be lucky to have me, etc., etc. Galaxy's hottest bachelor coming through. But then there's all it entails, which has to sound pretty enticing. Total cease-fire, annexation of your territories under a governorship tier you appoint . . . I can see you drooling, and honestly I could stand to see it a bit more.

There's just the whole thing where my mother expects me to put a knife in you as soon as everything is settled.[2] Which probably doesn't surprise you either. And that's on top of the fact that marrying me would obliterate your right to rule and nuke the emp-Archon title from orbit in perpetuity.

Why am I telling you things you already know?

The point, because gods know I've gone on for long enough. The galaxy is ruttin' broken. I always knew this—in a grandiose kind of way that comes from reading a lot of history texts and experiencing none of them. I can see all the ways the Umber Empire has fallen into craven violence, but you're the one who actually lived through it. I don't think there are any two people more suited—and in a better position—to figure out how to fix it.

An aside: I imagine a galaxy that wasn't broken, a galaxy that would welcome the idea of the two of us pairing off for the good of two better empires, with no expectation of me murdering you. In that galaxy, I would be so ecstatic about marrying you—I'd burn so brightly they'd have to put a system in orbit around me.[3]

But to the point: we can't fix the galaxy with a five-day time delay between us. That distance works for the fear my mother uses to keep her empire in place, but it's no way to coordinate an effort to save the known universe. We have to meet, and I have a plan. Well, me and the Wraiths (yes, I know, and no, I don't think it's as funny as they do). Attached to this message is an outline of when and where to meet us. I trust you—and more than you, Wen—to figure out the details on how you'll manage that.

Bring your ideas, I'll bring mine, and together, we'll figure this out—like we always do.[4]

Yours, always,
Gal

Beneath that, there's a helpful little section of footnotes so clearly written by Hanji that I roll my eyes.

[1] *Don't believe his lies.*
[2] *I've tried to convince him that trying to kill you is therapeutic, but he claims it didn't do much for him. I don't think he's tried hard enough—I personally got a lot out of the experience.*
[3] *This is disgusting. Imperials should be banned from attempting poetry.*

[4] *There was more to this letter—at least a page of him going on about some very intimate thoughts and feelings. I've deleted it. If he'd been waxing poetic about the shape of your ass, that'd be one thing, but the stuff he was spilling was the kind of shit you tell someone in person. Make the rendezvous, and make him tell you face-to-face.*

I let the datapad drop between my knees, burying my face in one hand. My heart feels like it's about to hammer right out of my chest. I've been so numb for so long. I've buried my feelings for so long. For the sake of the empire, I kept telling myself as I felt everything begin to freeze.

And this isn't a thaw—it's boltfire tearing through me. A dam bursting. I thought finding out Gal never meant to leave me was the flood, but that was barely a trickle against this.

My thoughts are a hurricane, but one stays fixed and solid within their eye. I know it's the worst idea at the worst time. We're two weeks into entertaining the Corinthians, the fleet is resupplying for our next offensive, and the people need their emperor to remain at the center of those operations. But no power in the galaxy could keep me from making that ruttin' rendezvous.

I lift my gaze to find the one power that stands a chance. Wordlessly, I scroll back up to the top of the message and hold the datapad out to Wen. After a moment of hesitation, she takes it and starts to read.

Umber would call it weakness, the way I'm trying to repair our relationship with all these gestures of faith. All I'm doing is handing her the means to destroy my reign entirely. But if there's one thing I take away from her betrayal, it's this: I never want her to feel like she has to go behind my back to do the right thing ever again.

When she finishes, she tucks the datapad into her robe's non-sword pocket and lets out a long sigh. "I'd forgotten," she says with a rueful smile. "When he's not a political prisoner, Gal emp-Umber's an unflappable optimist."

"I used to worry it'd get him killed," I reply, shaking my head. "At the academy, he wouldn't hear consequences—even when they were getting screamed in his face by the officers. Once I found out who he really was, I thought his notions about bending the Umber Empire back from his mother's brutality were impossible. But now . . ."

I don't dare finish the sentence. I'm so used to losing everything that I feel downright repulsed putting what I want out into the universe. It's just daring the gods to snatch it away.

Fortunately, I have Wen. "Now he's crowned—and from that position, he might just manage it," she says with a nod. "But he's going to need all the help he can get, and that starts with this rendezvous."

I fix my eyes on hers, I've half a mind to drop to my knees for the ask. "You'll help me make it?"

Her hand slips down to her vibrosword hilt. For almost anyone else, the gesture is a threat, but here in the half light, she somehow manages to turn it into a vow. "Whatever it takes," she murmurs.

I haven't made this easy on myself. In my efforts to solidify my place at the head of the Archon rebellion, I've gotten myself intricately involved with its operations, and it's no small matter to arrange a leave of absence from the war right at the moment it's starting to gain momentum. We're lining up our next offensive and shoring our defenses for the anticipated retaliation from Umber, which all adds up to every waking hour of my day being spent in strategy meetings that I've designed to be inoperable without me at the head of the table. I have to walk myself back from being the current head of my administration without triggering the panic that might otherwise ensue.

And on top of that, there's the Corinthians.

I'd explained exactly what our political situation was to Biss Xhosi and their auxiliaries. I'm still not sure whether the respect I gained for my honesty was worth the ground I lost for admitting that I was seriously weighing Iva emp-Umber's proposal. But at least Xhosi saw the logic in drawing out my answer. If Umber expects us to entertain the notion that they'd honor the proposal's terms, they can't launch a proper offensive unless we mount a new one. That's a strategic advantage that gives us time to position ourselves for the next attempt to gain ground—and gives Corinth time to muster the forces they're theoretically sending to our aid.

Whether we earn those forces remains to be seen, and my plan to disappear for a week is doing that no favors. For that reason, the Corinthians are the first people I tell about it.

The ambassador and their party have decamped to their own ship, which lingers tucked in the *Torrent*'s shadow. I drop a line to them and take the call in my stateroom's grand antechamber, which has all the security trappings it needs to ensure that any information I disseminate has only one vector out of there. Xhosi greets me with an easy smile when the call connects, their face blown large on my workstation's viewscreen. "Your Majesty, I thought our plan was to save our diplomacy for the meeting in person two days hence?" they ask with a slight furrow in their brow.

"We'll have plenty to discuss at that meeting, but this falls outside its scope and it's something I wished to inform you on before anyone else could."

The furrow in their brow deepens. No doubt they're wondering if my mistrust is directed at Iral specifically.

"I've been put in an uncomfortable position by this Umber proposal, as you're already aware," I continue. "And while you know I have no intention of accepting it, you also must understand that this kind of thing requires negotiation. More than that, it's an opportunity to meet the enemy without running the risk of obliteration by boltfire and get the measure of them. And while it's possible to do these kind of things by proxy, for a negotiation this delicate, I'm afraid the only thing that will do is my presence. I will be leaving to address the matter in three days, and will be away for no more than two weeks."

"As an expert in handling matters by proxy myself, I understand," Xhosi says. "However, I must admit, all this contact with the Umber crown is . . . well, you understand how it looks."

"Absolutely," I reply with a cordial tilt of my head. "Which is why I'm telling you directly, and ahead of anyone else in my administration."

Xhosi's expression goes a tad more guarded. "My trust is not a carnival game, young emperor. You can't keep feeding me tokens and expect that eventually you'll hit upon the reward you seek."

"Fair," I say, with exactly the kind of flippant imperial hand gesture the ambassador expects to see. "I'll just have to hope that in time you'll come to see that my actions are not tokens—they're just how I do things. I want to lead with the truth."

"With respect, Majesty, that doesn't align with what I've heard of the last seven years of your life."

Ah, and there's the meat of it. I'm always going to be doomed to fail at these political games—not because I lack Gal's talent, but because I'm fighting my own history. I buried my identity at the age of ten, in the ruins of the imperial palace on Trost that the Umber Empire bombed to rubble. I entered Umber military service at fifteen to put my life back together—which, to the Corinthians, is all but pulling myself up by Iva emp-Umber's skirts—and all the while, I kept my secret in a little velvet bag buried in one of my drawers.

I want to fume, to ask Xhosi, *What was I supposed to do?* The lie was the only way to survive. There was no *point* in unveiling my identity to anyone in those seven years.

Well, not until I stole a shuttle and flew it into the middle of an Archon military base with the Umber heir in tow undercover. That's the part where my story starts to go sideways. I should have told General Iral who I was the second he walked into a room with us.

Instead, I tried to use the Archon rebellion as a means to deliver Gal emp-Umber to his throne. I set them up to fail, built their plans around our own knowledge of Umber's defenses, and walked them into what should have been the jaws of a trap. The only reason it didn't work was Berr sys-Tosa's cowardice. If the governor hadn't surrendered, our plan would have worked, the Archon rebellion would have been crushed to dust, and Gal—

Well, he got to his crown eventually anyway.

I only revealed my hand the moment it served my interests. The moment it would save Gal. And that tells everyone in the universe enough about my interests, apparently.

I feel myself teetering on the high wire, ready to toss whatever diplomatic competency I've mustered aside and dive headlong into the maw of Xhosi's implications. I'm not the perfect heir they need. I never have been. I'm a liar through and through, and even this conversation, where I'm purportedly being starkly honest with the ambassador, is missing a few key facts that could be absolutely ruinous to our relations with the Corinthians.

But if I've learned anything watching Gal, it's that sometimes one truth can substitute for another. Sometimes people walk away from honesty thinking they've won, never realizing they left the real prize behind on the table. And if we're going to make this work, Xhosi has to understand exactly who they're working with.

"With respect, Ambassador, you have never experienced a war firsthand," I start, trying to keep my voice cool and level. "When you do, I hope you'll grasp the fact that surviving is often antithetical to the moral high ground—and that the former got me where the latter never could."

I end the call before they can point out that I didn't really win the argument. As my viewscreen retracts into my desk, I lock eyes with Wen. She's sprawled on the divan like a cat in a sunbeam, turning her vibrosword hilt lazily over and over in her hands. "Bait is strung?" she asks.

"Now we fish."

The tug at the end of the line comes not from a communication hitting my datapad but from the sudden announcement echoing through the *Torrent*'s halls that General Iral's flagship, the *Aegis*, has dropped from superluminal in our orbit unscheduled and is making ready to dock.

Rather than rushing to the dock along with the officers, I hang back in my quarters, taking extra care in composing my appearance.

Most days aboard the *Torrent,* which has become *my* warship, for all intents and purposes, I dress to blend in with the officers in dull fatigues. I want to remind everyone with my appearance that I'm working right alongside them—that I'm ready to get my hands dirty in the mess.

It's what my father used to do, or so I'm told.

But today I reach for finery. Today I mantle my shoulders with thin platinum chains that fall in elegant twists down a jointed spine that runs parallel to mine. Today I dress in fine white linens lined in rich emerald silks—clearly Archon, but evoking the Corinthian ambassadors' preference for blinding garments. Today, I crown myself not with one of the simpler platinum circlets I often wear about my duty, but with the heavy, twisting, bejeweled wreath Gal placed on my head all those months ago.

Then I make my way to the bridge, where I wait, leaning against the captain's saddle, until General Iral strides through the doors with Captain Deidra con-Silon and Wen in tow.

Wen is the only one who doesn't blink at the sight of me, though she does raise an eyebrow at how thoroughly I've managed to deck myself out. *Laying it on a bit thick, huh?* her eyes seem to say.

But thick is what it's gonna take to get my point across. "General, Captain," I say, accepting their salutes with a casual tip of my fingers.

"Your Majesty, we could have arranged for you to join the welcome party," Silon says, looking mildly flustered that a tidbit of procedure has slipped past her. The captain likes things to be in their proper places. I'm certain that's half of the reason her eyes walk a guilty, well-worn path to Commodore Esperza's old station as if hoping the ex-pirate will somehow magically reappear.

The other half I pretend not to speculate on. Fraternization policies don't work out in its favor, and as long as I pretend not to see it happening, it gets to continue blooming. I'm not certain what stage Esperza and Silon's flirtation was at when Umber took the commodore captive, but I know it was far gone enough that Silon has become a walking ghost in the months since. With Esperza's execution scheduled for mere days from now, the *Torrent*'s bridge command is bracing for the tragedy of it to reach its peak.

"At ease, Captain," I reassure her, snapping her attention back to the fact that I'm still leaning against her saddle. "I knew the general would eventually make his way here."

Iral looks me up and down. "I feel a bit underdressed, I must admit," he remarks. He's garbed in a trim uniform like he's got "parading past some infantry" in the schedule. No doubt he hoped to catch me off guard in my "one of the soldiers" disguise, but I've learned since the incident on Ichano, and Iral's severely mistaken if he thinks he can get the drop on me twice.

Never let me have prep time, jackass. I give the general a sly, almost cocky shrug. My inner child who idolized this man is tearing his hair out.

His lips purse microscopically. "I have an important matter to discuss with you, Majesty."

The tiers of officers around us have gone still, glancing warily between the man they've followed to the Corinthian Empire and back and the man who carries the bloodright of the empire they've kept faith with all these years. I've been working alongside most of them since the Rana campaign, but every day I wonder if I've truly earned my place among them.

General Iral must be having that same thought. "If you prefer, we can do so in a more private setting," he says. *Take the offer,* his tone dares me. *Prove these people don't have your trust.*

"General, if it's a matter of such urgency that you came straight to meet me, I suggest you not waste my time any further," I reply, drawing myself up straight and folding my arms.

He raises an eyebrow at my reversal. "Word has come to me that you plan to negotiate with Umber in person—and that you plan to leave the fleet to do so in a matter of days."

I let the blow hit. Let my gaze dart nervously to the rings of officers tiered around me, let them see both that none of them were supposed to know this and that if my guilty reaction is anything to go by, they probably should have been informed. At Iral's side, Silon's expression has gone particularly sour. Nothing violates the careful order she tries to maintain more than an imperial attempting to go rogue—especially when it's something she has no authority to correct.

This is what Iral was out for. The reason he probably would have tried to summon me to the bridge anyway if I hadn't beaten him to it. He knows my bloodright makes my choices all but untouchable, and the only way he can influence my decisions is by making sure they do the greatest damage to my reputation. By shaming me in front of my flagship's command, he can end this nonsense before it even starts.

So I imagine it can't feel great when he realizes I've started to smile. "That's correct. I intend to leave within the next two cycles, and will be away for a standard week. It will just be me and Iffan in a stealth shuttle to afford us the greatest speed and maneuverability."

"Your Majesty, is it wise to broadcast your plans like this?" Iral asks, his brow furrowing.

"Well, I hardly broadcast my plans. All I did was tell Ambassador Xhosi that I intended to negotiate with Umber in person and give them a timeline for my trip. We were still finalizing the clearances for the shuttle, so I hadn't planned on making the announcement like this, but I'm guessing Xhosi assumed you already knew, and hence—" I spread my arms in a shrug that says *Here we are.*

Iral's lips twitch toward a frown. He's a strategist and a figurehead, but he's not a politician, and I'm not sure he anticipated this sort of move from me. The pilot, the young man crowned, the last-second emperor—I'm not supposed to be playing games like this. Worse, he knows exactly where I learned this. And he knows from the way I'm carrying myself that I still have one more card to play, a blow he's got no way of avoiding.

But damn it, he's gonna try. "I would urge you to consider the security of the mission now that you've announced your intentions so openly," Iral says, his voice laden with the gravity that has pulled so many of these officers to his side. "There's little we can do to protect the two of you once you're out there alone in the black, and the likelihood of an enemy getting wind of your flight plan has just gone up dramatically."

"General," I reply, "if you're suggesting I can't hold the bridge staff of my own flagship in confidence . . ."

"I'm suggesting that word of your trip is going to spread through the fleet one way or another now that such a density of people know about it. I worry that the nature of this . . . *rendezvous* is fodder for gossip among the troops."

My cheeks tighten with a rising heat, but I tamp it down. "Ah yes, the nature of the rendezvous." Am I pulling off nonchalant? My gaze flicks to Wen as if she's going to give me a thumbs-up and tell me *You're doing great, buddy.* "The rendezvous," I continue, "which is going to create an opening for my team to retrieve Commodore Adela Esperza from the Umber capital before her execution."

I was going for gasps, but I settle for the sudden direct attention of every single eye on the bridge. I may not have their loyalty, but they've served with Esperza since the War of Expansion, and until this very moment, I'm sure most of them had written her off as a lost cause. I lock eyes with Captain Silon and give her disbelieving expression a slow, firm nod.

They might betray *me*. Gossip about my fraternization with the enemy. Gal emp-Umber's hold on my heart is a fundamental force of the universe, and I know I can never prove otherwise. But the *Torrent* loves its commodore, and I've staked my crown on the fact that they would never jeopardize her rescue.

I turn to address the rest of the bridge. "I swear to you, I'll return with Commodore Esperza, or I won't return at all." The vow may be a tad dramatic, but I need that imperial flair. They have to understand that my loyalty to my empire can coexist with this so-called *rendezvous*. "Obviously I hadn't planned on distributing the details of the mission like this, but I believe I can trust you all in this matter. Is that so?"

I've made it so easy for them. Dressed up exactly the way they need to see me. I'm sharp as the cuts on the emeralds in my crown, born of the blood that served them for generations. "Yes, Your Majesty," echoes through the bridge in unison, and I bow graciously.

When I rise from it, I find General Iral trying his damnedest to keep from looking like he's been hit over the head. "You . . . The commodore?" he asks, and there's a note in his voice that breaks my heart. Iral was close with my parents. His twin brother sacrificed himself to Umber to enable his escape. He's lost far too many people to Umber's horrible spectacle, and up until a moment ago, he was braced to lose Esperza too.

I step up close and offer the general my hand. "It's a risk, I know," I start, trying to hit the soft tones my father made his music. "But I hope I've proven at this point the lengths to which I'll go to save a single person. And I hope that's enough to earn the crown's place on my head."

General Iral takes my hand firmly. The gesture is one of concord, but his eyes are starting to regain a steel that promises this isn't over. "I still advise caution, Your Majesty," he says. "Keep in mind that risking your neck risks everything that rests above it. Keep in mind what the empire can afford to lose, and what it can't."

"I'll try my best. Now if you'll excuse me, I have a mission to plan," I tell him, then drop his hand and signal Wen, who falls in easily at my side. "Hold the line while I'm gone," I call back over my shoulder as we make our way toward the bridge doors.

Wen locks eyes with the general as she passes him, openly smug where I could never be. "Trust a Corinthian to get the job done, huh?" she murmurs low enough that Iral and I are the only ones who hear, then smirks and spreads her arms.

The closing elevator doors give me only the briefest glimpse of the way the general's expression sours, but I savor every inch of it.

CHAPTER 8

GAL

IN THE DARKNESS of the hypocaust, it's impossible to believe that months have passed since my coronation. It feels like barely yesterday that I rode the mechanism up into the blinding light of day to greet my mother before the people and take my crown. Above us, the crowd's rumble is building toward a fever pitch, but there's a texture to it that was lacking the last time I rose to greet them on the citadel steps.

Last time, they weren't out for blood.

And last time, I wasn't quite this nervous. I'm used to pulling this kind of nonsense with Ettian at the helm, and without him at my side, I can't *trust* in my own plans. My hands are slick with sweat as I try to get my crown to settle over my curls in a way that doesn't look stupid, and having the Wraiths fussing around me is the polar opposite of calming. Ollins keeps bouncing on the tips of his toes like he's warming up for a fight, Rin and Rhodes are pawing at the seams of my clothes to make sure their adjustments are ready for action, and Hanji's uncannily still—which for *Hanji* just screams *Something's wrong.*

She catches my eye and sets a hand on my shoulder. "It's going to work, Gal," she mutters, low enough that the lift operators wouldn't be able to hear. One of them flashes us a hand sign. Thirty seconds until we're on our way up.

I shrug Hanji off, pinching the bridge of my nose and sucking in a deep breath. It *has* to work, but now I'm having so many doubts that I'm tempted to call the whole thing off. It was arrogance—sheer, imperial arrogance—to think I could combine all of our schemes into one ultra-scheme that *has* to work, or else we've lost everything. I guess it really has been months since I was crowned if I've lost touch with reality this fast.

The operator signs again. Three. Two. One.

I bend my knees into the lurch to keep from toppling over as the lift begins to haul us toward the surface. Rin and Rhodes move to flank my sides, Ollins covers my ass—which I'm sure he loves—and Hanji rounds to face me, setting both hands on my shoulders and latching on tight this time. "You do your part. I'll do mine. We've got this, Gal," she says, then reaches into her breast pocket and pulls out a pair of glasses identical to the ones perched on her nose. She slips them into the pocket sewn into the liner of my coat and pats them once—then hesitates. "Should we kiss? Feels like we should—"

"Rut *right* off, Iwam," I groan, shoving her back. She goes with a laugh and a knowing grin, and gods do I hate her for it. Leave it to Hanji to know exactly how to distract me from the anxiety about to reduce me to a fumbling mess.

"See you on the other side," she says with a jocular salute to the Wraiths, then steps up to the edge of the platform. Our ascent is starting to push us through the underbelly of the citadel, and an air duct—whose cover has gone mysteriously missing—yawns into view. Hanji slips her torso effortlessly inside, and Rhodes grabs her boots and shoves her the rest of the way in before the rising platform can take off her legs.

I tamp down a shudder, remembering my own little adventure in the vents of the Archon palace on Rana. I don't envy Hanji's part in this, but I might prefer it to my own.

Above, the portal to the outside begins to winch open, letting in a blazing slash of sunlight. I fold one hand carefully over my chest, feeling the shape of Hanji's spare glasses. "All right, knuckleheads," I breathe. "Showtime."

I break aboveground to the screams of thousands, the Umber Empire greeting its newest ruler with far more enthusiasm than I deserve. I tip a wave that cranks the noise a few decibels louder. Even after months home, I still find myself missing the undercurrent of drumbeats that used to accompany Archon events like this, searching for some pattern in the torrent of sound.

Then again, there were no Archon events quite like this.

The scene is already staged. I've risen into the first pavilion, and across the citadel steps lies the second, where my mother and father are waiting. On the walk between us, a block has been set up with a divot in its middle, and ascending the stairs from the Triumph Way spread below us is the reason the crowd's been roaring and jeering for the past hour.

Adela Esperza is barely on her feet. A brass collar has been locked around her neck, and the six guards that form her escort each have a length of chain attached to it to keep her suspended between them. They've just completed a walk of the Way's full length, and it's clear she's been shown no mercy. She's dressed in linens that must have been white when the walk started. Now they're a patchwork of stains from whatever the crowd has hurled at her, a portrait of the Umber people's displeasure.

The cruelty turns my stomach. These people are citizens of the core, who've probably spent their entire lives in the heart of the empire's abundance. War has never touched them—only the profits of Umber's rapacious expansion—and yet they feel utterly justified in their abuse of a condemned woman shipped in from a conflict at the empire's fringes.

Esperza's locked into the same dead-eyed stare that got her

through most of her trial, but as she takes one last, utterly drained step up the final stair, her gaze finds mine. I see the accusation in her eyes and feel the pinch of it. *You could have prevented this if you had really tried,* the commodore seems to say.

I have no choice when I'm out in the open like this. I lift my chin and let the smuggest smirk I can manage slide easily over my face. Before my people, before the row of governors and representatives that line the lower levels of the citadel stair, I have to be their wicked prince. I have to enjoy this.

My gaze shifts up to the second pavilion, and I have to fight to keep from losing my meager breakfast right then and there. My mother has stepped forward, and in her hands . . .

It was the first death I ever saw with my own eyes. The first my parents deemed me ready for, at the tender age of ten. On the screen, I watched that ax fall on the necks of the Archon imperials—first Marc, then Henrietta—with tears streaming down my face, feeling like my body was far too small to fit the immensity of the terror the sight filled me with. I clutched the front of my father's shirt as he stroked my hair and tried to coach me through it.

To make me understand why the crowd was cheering.

While I nodded along, inside a different conclusion was crystallizing. Before that, the grand destiny I'd been raised to accept was a simple, wondrous thing. But watching blood spill down the steps of the citadel showed me exactly what the cost of that destiny was, and in that moment, I first truly understood that I had to ruin it.

My smirk's gone a little more genuine at the thought, warring with the way the sight of the ax has my palms soaked with sweat. *Don't look up,* I remind myself. *Don't expect anything except what your mother thinks is about to happen.*

But it's hard to resist that impulse when every step my mother takes is another second lost in a plan that only has so much wiggle room. The noise of the crowd crescendos as she gets closer and closer to the block. Esperza tries to root her stance, but her escort hauls on her chain and she's forced to stumble those last few exhausted steps to face the empress.

"Give her a moment on her feet," Iva emp-Umber mutters, scarcely loud enough to be heard. "I want her to hear this."

She pivots to face the crowd, and a sound system around us hums to life as I fall in at her side, hands neatly folded behind my back. My father steps up to flank her, completing the perfect imperial triangle we form—empress, emperor, and heir. The face of the generation that crushed the Archon Empire, and the face of the generation that will crush its last gasps and ensure another prosperous twenty years of Umber reign.

At my back, the Wraiths shift nervously. They've been seen with me often enough to be an incongruous part of my escort, but I wonder how many people pay close enough attention to clock that we're down by one. I can't signal to them to hold steady—all I can do is stand straight-backed and serious and hope that for once in their miserable lives, they follow my lead.

My mother hefts the ax skyward, and the crowd roars its approval. "People of Lucia, people of Acua, people of *Umber*," the empress intones. It's her most favored opener—one that enforces the tiers of power that envelop all under her domain, from the planet all the way to the empire. "Today I stand before you on a historic anniversary. Eight years ago, on this day, I used this very ax to end the Archon imperial line. They resisted the inevitable, refused to concede to the might of Umber, and so they faced the ultimate justice."

The empress is a different woman facing her public. In the imperial court, she's restrained and understated. She knows that posturing in front of the system governors will only end up looking like weakness and that her own stillness is one of the easiest ways to make them second-guess themselves. But before an audience of thousands, she can let loose and project strength from the citadel steps clear down the Triumph Way. Here, it isn't posturing—it's honesty.

Iva emp-Umber is unquestionably the pinnacle of our empire.

And she relishes the hell out of it.

"Before you stands Adela Esperza, an Umber citizen born in the Vargus system, who has betrayed everything we stand for and thrown her lot in with a fringe uprising in the Archon territories. She dared to style herself *commodore* of a fleet of stolen dreadnoughts—dreadnoughts built with the blood and sacrifice of Umber citizens who believe in the greatness of our empire."

Gods, she's laying it on thick, I think, straining to keep my expression neutral. Every second this goes on is shaving years off my life.

"Adela Esperza has elected to die by the same method as her precious imperials. Today I grant her this boon in celebration of all that it represents—a permanent end to Archon rebellion, by my blood and all that it owns." She raises the ax over her head, holding it out like an offering to the masses, and the noise swells with cheers and screams.

Any ruttin' minute now.

And then I hear it. The screams—which should die off as my mother lowers the ax and draws a breath in preparation for another propaganda-fueled tirade—ease louder and louder. I notice some people shaking their heads, others looking to the skies for the approaching flyby.

But it's not starship engines. Not quite.

A shadow flickers over me, backlit by the noonday sun, and it's only then I dare look up. The crack of a sonic boom follows a half second later, sending startled murmurs through the crowd as they squint up against the sky, searching for whatever caused it.

I pick her out instantly. On the far end of the Triumph Way, a speck wheels around and doubles back for a second, lower pass that skims over the heads of the people packing the thoroughfare. Some duck and scatter on instinct. Others freeze in place, their brains taking a second to register that a horror story has just bloomed to life before their very eyes.

Then they run.

"It's the Flame Knight," I murmur.

It doesn't matter how she got here, how she got her powersuit back, how any of this is possible. After what she did to the *Fulcrum,* the Umber people have turned her into a ghost story, and they'll believe any new twist. Of course Ettian's monster would come to save her mentor.

Under different circumstances, I'd laugh myself sick at the way the crowd's illusions have been shattered. Just moments ago, they were raining abuse down on Esperza, feeling like they, too, could claim a little bit of Umber's glory from the comfort of their sheltered lives.

Now they're scattering like rats.

The powersuit hurtles toward the dais, and an arm tucks around my chest, yanking me back into the protective knot the Wraiths have closed around me. In the tumult, I spot my mother and father diving clear as their security team contracts around them and hear the vicious ax clattering to the ground. Esperza's escort tries to close around her, some of them lifting their sidearms as if that's going to do anything against the magnificent Archon engineering.

The Flame Knight kicks up her boots into a brake that tears right through them. As boltfire starts to fly and the Wraiths drag me back toward the lift to the hypocaust, she whirls, grabs one of the guards, and hurls her ass-over-teakettle down the steps of the citadel like she weighs about as much as a stuffed animal.

"Take us *down,*" Rhodes yells into a comm, planting his long-limbed self squarely between me and the knight's rampage as we get into position atop the mechanism. The operators react a half second later, and the platform lurches into a descent that feels far too slow for how quickly the situation outside is escalating into full-blown chaos.

As we slip beneath the surface, I tuck my hand into my pocket and draw out Hanji's glasses. I catch one last glimpse of a guard sent flying into the air before the aperture winches shut above us.

The second it slices the daylight away, the Wraiths get to work. Rin and Rhodes tug hard on my clothes, ripping away the outer layer of finery and transforming what's left into a dress uniform that matches what the rest of them are wearing. Ollins pulls a long brown wig done up in a ponytail out of his sleeve, plucks off my crown, slicks back my hair, and crams the wig over my head. The crown he tosses sideways, sending it clattering down the same vent Hanji disappeared into. A pinch of a trigger inflates the padding wrapped snugly around my hips and chest, and a hidden button activates the lifts tucked in the heels of my shoes.

"I hate this, I hate this, I *ruttin' hate this*," I mutter, settling the glasses over the bridge of my nose. "How's it looking?"

Rin clicks on a penlight, folding her other hand over her chin as she scans me up and down. "Looking good, *boss*," she says with a smirk.

"Great," I grumble, holding out my hand. Rhodes presses an earpiece into my palm, and I slip it in just in time to hear Hanji spitting a truly vibrant string of profanities. "Rut you mother-ruttin' piece of *shit give me two seconds*—" she sputters indignantly against a background of boltfire and the roar of the powersuit's thrusters.

"Wraith Two, sky is yours," I whisper as the platform drops out of the channel and the hypocaust slides into view. We don't give the operators a second to register that the prince is "missing"—or worse, to realize Hanji Iwam doesn't quite look the same. All four of us leap from the platform before it's docked and hit the ground running.

And gods, I'd forgotten how good it feels to run. Not the trudge of an academy drill, not the drudgery of a treadmill workout—to run like every system's hell has opened on your heels, feeling like the breath's about to burst from your lungs. "The Flame Knight's loose in the city! *Move!*" Ollins hollers, and I can't even bite back the smile that cracks over my face. I missed chaos. I missed mischief. I missed *adventure*.

The Wraiths and I rocket through the hypocaust and out to a shuttle deck level, where their darling favorite ride, a quad-rotary beast they've christened *Double Ugly*, is already staged. "If we get in the air fast, we can try to outfly her," Rin yells, flashing hand signals at the technicians. "Asses in seats, all of you. I want cast-off in thirty seconds!"

We spill up the ramp, scramble up the ladders, and tumble into our stations on the flight deck—Rin at the controls, Rhodes on comms, and Ollins and I in the two gunner nests tucked on either side of the helm. Rin spurs *Double Ugly* to life with a vicious twist and a kick, perched primly on a stack of flight manuals that give her just enough clearance to see over the dashboard. "Going hot in ten," she shouts over the rumble of the rotaries warming.

Rhodes relays the information to the deck, and I wrestle my harness over my shoulders, my hands skating over the gun's controls. It's been an age since I ran gunner, but it's what Hanji would do, so here I am. My last second of conscious thought has me checking the edges of my wig and tugging experimentally on the ponytail to make sure everything's secure.

Then Rin lets the engines loose and everything I am is lost to the instinct to hold on to something, *anything*, as *Double Ugly* bucks out of its docking mounts and roars into the sky. The shuttle is a brute—four rotaries is just excessive—and the vertical launch crushes me so deep into my chair that I feel as if my spine's been jammed down like a bicycle pump. On the other side of the flight deck, Ollins is howling like a wild animal.

We catapult into the brilliant afternoon sun, past the razor-edged claws of the downtown skyscrapers, and wheel over the hulking ziggurat of the citadel. The flash and clamor of boltfire gives us our target almost instantaneously, and Rin spurs us onto our vector with vicious aplomb. We dive into a narrow corridor between the buildings, where ahead I can barely pick out the speck of the powersuit fleeing with Adela Esperza tucked neatly under one arm. A squadron of agile watchships are doing their damnedest to keep up with her as they rain boltfire on her rear, but they simply weren't built for this.

"Iwam," I grunt against the brutal press of *Double Ugly*'s acceleration. "We're on your ass."

"Got that, Wraith One," Hanji replies through what sounds like gritted teeth. I miss my station aboard the *Torrent*'s bridge—miss running *actual* comms for a suited knight in combat, where I could see everything from the suit's cameras. The earpiece I'm working with feels like barely a step up from string and tin cans. "Target one thousand meters and closing."

I yank my gun mount up and throw a few perfunctory chugs of boltfire her way. Enough to look like we're trying, without putting her or the *extremely* exposed commodore in any actual danger— with the added bonus of putting a wobble in some of the watch-ships' vectors. Ollins does the same, though the sight of the other gun hot sends a twist of anxiety through me. Ollins has an uncanny aim and a general lack of sense, and the two of those in combination might put this to a premature end.

"City tower, this is *Double Ugly*," Rhodes shouts at the helm comms seat. "Call off the watch. Wraith Squadron has crown auth to handle this."

None of the watchships divert.

"Get them the code," I holler.

"I'm *trying*," Rhodes grunts. "Hard to key it in when Rin is driv-ing like—"

"I'd like to see *you* handle a trench run through a ruttin' popu-lated—" Rin starts.

"*Target in three, two—*" Hanji mutters in my ear.

"Rin, rotaries, about-face, NOW!" I scream.

Ahead, Hanji throws up her boots and sinks hard into her seat, cradling Esperza close to her chest and wrenching her vector sky-ward as the watchships go screaming past beneath her. She shoots up the side of a building and hits the apex of her parabola just as she disappears over its crown.

Rin cranks *Double Ugly*'s rotaries around, throwing us into an ascent to match that has the added bonus of cutting off the Wraiths' snippy chatter. We hurtle up out of the thicket of the Imperial Seat, seconds ahead of the watchships, which weren't built for abrupt al-titude changes like the one we just pulled.

It's given Hanji the time she needs. She's disappeared, but below us, I spot a familiar shuttle outline perched atop one of the sky-scrapers.

My heart can't help but lift at the sight of the *Ruttin' Hell*. She's been staged for immediate departure, and as we pull into a tight turn that circles around, her twin rotaries flare to life. "Wraith One, this is Wraith Two," Hanji's voice announces in my ear. "Ramp's up, and the package has the helm. Get ready to run."

"City tower, this is *Double Ugly*," Rhodes snaps from the helm. "We've got eyes on them. They seem to be attempting to flee in a Beamer." He pauses, chuckling at something the controller's said. "Yeah, you heard me—a Beamer. Leave it to us. This should be fast."

I smirk. *Show 'em what you've got, baby.*

Beamers are a ruttin' joke. A dopey brick of a ship meant for officer transport and little else. But the *Ruttin' Hell* is no ordinary Beamer. She used to be, back when Ettian and I stole her out of the academy and used her to flee to Corinth. Then Adela Esperza got her hands on the ship and worked some sort of chop shop witchcraft on the monstrous lug.

As Rin feints *Double Ugly* like she's going to try to outflank the Beamer and herd her back onto the roof, the *Ruttin' Hell*'s engines blast as hot as they'll go and the ship takes off like boltfire unleashed, leaping from the skyline with an agility no ship of her model should possess. Rin locks on like a cat after a mouse, and my earpiece fills with an almighty clatter that I'm assuming is Hanji being thrown to the back of the *Ruttin' Hell*'s cargo hold. "All right there, Iwam?" I ask.

"The suit took most of it," Hanji groans. "*Most.*"

"You might wanna find something to hold on to," I say as I watch the Beamer claw up and up and up against Lucia's atmosphere. "I've been on the *Ruttin' Hell* with this woman at the helm once. And once was enough for a lifetime."

But this isn't the haphazard, swerving ride Esperza took us on over the skies of Isla's north side. Adela Esperza has been locked in an Umber dungeon for two months, and her only goal at the moment is to put as much distance as humanly possible between it and her. The *Ruttin' Hell* screams for the edge of space, *Double Ugly* doing its damnedest to make up ground against its massive head start. Ollins and I keep up the illusion that we're trying to hit them, Rin keeps us close enough that the rest of the Imperial Seat's ground defenses can't get a shot in, and Rhodes keeps up a steady stream of "No, we've got this, no, no backup, no, we have *crown auth*, what part of that don't you understand?" into his comm lines.

It's not going to work, a little voice in the back of my head insists. My hands are going slippery around the gun mounts, and the vicious ascent has all but crushed the breath out of my lungs. In the raw tumult of noise, I hear Rin announce that a squadron of Vipers is inbound. They're going to shoot the commodore out of the sky. They'll probably take *us* down in the process. I'm a second away from tearing off my wig and demanding that Rhodes patch me through to the towers, even if it blows the whole operation.

But I'm so ruttin' tired of second-guessing myself. From birth, I've been told that my choices are right simply by virtue of being *mine.* All of that bloodright nonsense should have made me as decisive and ruthless as my mother—but it only made me hesitant to offer my decisions to the universe, knowing that the universe would fall over itself to justify them.

This plan is the culmination of months of quiet work. It's an intricate machine I built out of careful observation of Umber's blind spots, from their assumption that the Wraiths are a bunch of loud, useless ex-cadets to the way my mother has suppressed footage of the Flame Knight in action, effectively mythologizing her while making sure no one can really tell that it's not Wen in the suit. And so far, it's *working.*

Maybe I'm just scared—scared like I've always been—that the universe really *does* revolve around my will.

Maybe it's time to accept it.

To *use* it.

But a second thought hits as ahead of us the *Ruttin' Hell* blasts past the atmospheric boundary and immediately winks out of sublight. A half second later, we're clear to do the same. As the black around us snaps to the gray of superluminal, as Rin locks onto the *Ruttin' Hell*'s vector, as the Wraiths collapse into gleeful whoops and howls, I sit back in my gel-seat and admit to myself that the real fear was never about the mission to rescue Esperza. The larger mission—the one that required the indignity of dressing as Hanji, the one that we've just gotten away with—was to smuggle me out of the capital before anyone could realize and lock onto where I was going.

At the end of this journey, Ettian awaits. And now that it's real, now that everything has gone off without a hitch, I have to face the fact that I'll see him at last, and it scares me more than *any* of the nonsense we just pulled.

CHAPTER 9

ETTIAN

THE TOWN OF BREHA feels like it could be the last stop on the edge of the known universe. It's built in the foothills of an expanse of mountains that stretch clean across the planet of Jobal's northern hemisphere, bordered by a massive desert of ruddy sand that's left most of the buildings eroded and tinted red. In the distance, the skeletons of long-abandoned mining equipment loom above the evening haze.

But Breha isn't the edge of everything—in fact, it's the middle. It exists on the tenuous line that once divided the Umber and Archon Empires, an Umber borderworld marked for stripping in the years that led into the War of Expansion. Now there's barely anything left of it. The people of this town eke out a fragile existence on the scraps of those abandoned operations. Few of them ever leave this world.

But one of them did, about fifteen years ago, and she never quite forgot the small, dusty town that birthed her. Adela Esperza left behind a safe-house apartment, a refuge for when times got tough and she needed to lay low—which in her various lines of work was often. Wen and I arrived last night, hoods on and masks drawn over our faces, laying tracks through a thin layer of dust that had settled over the place in the years since it was last used. We've spent a long, quiet day cleaning the apartment out and setting up our security perimeters. I almost loved the work—the way I could lose myself in a task so straightforward and predictable. It was the perfect palate cleanser for the task that's about to arrive.

Now there's no more dusting to do, no more trip wires to set up, no more nasty little Wen-designed traps to rig, and I can feel myself about to boil over from anticipation. I've gone out onto the apartment's little balcony, sat myself down, and fed my legs through the iron trellises, letting them swing out over the street below and daring anyone beneath me to look up and realize that the most wanted man in the Umber Empire is dangling his boots over their heads.

I breathe deep and relish it. It's been months since the last time I had air that wasn't cluttered with the particulate of a city or recycled to death like the air aboard a dreadnought. It only adds to the heady, downright *dangerous* feeling of freedom that's settled over me since we touched down in the town's little spaceport and realized that our anonymity held up.

I haven't been nobody in so long, and I'm shocked to realize how much I've missed it. It feels like flirting with the edge of an abyss, like turning your engines off midflight and gliding for so long that you forget you're still falling. For months, I've felt like the war effort requires my full attention. I fought so hard to stay a part of it when Hanji put a hole in my gut that I think I started to believe the whole thing would topple without the cornerstone of its emperor holding it in place.

But the war is in the Archon Core right now, and I'm here in Umber territory, and the galaxy spins on.

Then again, the only reason I'm able to breathe at all is because Wen's keeping watch. She's set herself up to be the spider in the center of a security web so complicated she's told me not to bother trying to understand all that she's doing here. My safety is borne on the back of her constant vigilance, and the second I forget it is the second I stop deserving the crown I left behind on the *Torrent*.

Like the thought of her is enough to summon her to my side, Wen sidles out of the apartment's sliding door and moseys over to squat next to me. The setting sun lights her up so gorgeously that it nearly takes the breath out of me, rocketing me back to another rooftop, another city on the far side of the galaxy lighting up this chaotic little wisp of a girl who'd just grabbed hold of me and refused to let go.

Up until recently, she was nobody, too, with not much more to her name than a dangerous rainbow umbrella and a mob queen's blood in her veins. I remember the moment I broke open for her— the moment I realized we were bound together by an inherent sameness, that it was *safe* to tell her about the hell I'd lived through because I knew she'd understand. She knew me first, and knows me better than anyone in the galaxy.

And so she knows exactly what I'm thinking right now. "I just got confirmation they've begun their descent," Wen says, laying a careful hand on my shoulder. I reach up and clutch it, and she instantly squeezes back.

The *Ruttin' Hell* and *Double Ugly* popped out of superluminal on the edge of this system a day ago. Iwam transferred from the former to the latter, leaving Adela Esperza free to pick up our broadcast of the coordinates to the Archon fleet and take off for her triumphant return. Meanwhile, the Umber delegation has been on a sublight approach to the planet, trying to fly casual enough not to incur any suspicion from the ground. This isn't the kind of town that gets visitors often, and two cloaked imperials showing up within a day of each other is bound to draw attention.

My eyes shoot skyward, even though I know the plan is for *Double Ugly* to enter atmo on the far side of the planet. The stars are starting to peek through the evening haze, and I don't know if I'm ready for one of them to bring Gal back to me.

"This is the longest we've been apart since the day we met," I murmur. "I don't know what I'm going to say to him. I don't even know where to begin."

"I'm no expert, but I think a kiss on the mouth—"

"Oh come on," I grumble. "You know what I mean. I'm not even sure this is real—it might be an elaborate con you're running on me. Or a dream."

Wen rolls her eyes and pinches my side, making me jolt sideways as I swat her hands away. "There. You're not dreaming. And what would be the point of trying to con you when I know you'd just give me anything I ask for?"

"Fair enough," I chuckle. "I dunno, I just . . . Look, Gal's had these big stupid dreams about changing the galaxy for as long as I've known him. At first I thought he was just a contrarian. Then I found out he was Gal emp-Umber, and I realized he was serious. And I've never been certain if he could pull it off, but I wanted to believe him. To believe *in* him. If not him, then who, right?"

I let out a long sigh, my gaze shifting to the horizon and the hulking, monstrous carcasses of the old mining machinery slumbering against the foothills. The sight is a stark reminder that the Umber Empire's been eating itself just as much as the Archon territories it conquered. At the academy, we were always spoon-fed the image of Umber's unified might—the image you might get from the empire's core looking outward. I'd never left Archon borders before, so I had no grounds from which I could begin imagining anything else. But the dreadnoughts Umber had before they sank their teeth into Archon had to come from somewhere, and now that I've made it to Jobal, I'm starting to see the whole picture with clear eyes.

Here on the fringes, up close, you see the bones sucked dry by empire's cruel mechanics. It makes me wonder how much I know of the places that should be my own borderworlds.

"If not Gal, well, I thought it was going to be me for a time," I continue, squinting against the low light as I try to pick apart how the mining machines once worked. "When we launched the war, I realized that it was my chance to shape the galaxy myself. But it's easy to say things like 'I want the worlds to be kind. I want no one to suffer like I've suffered. I want justice for what was done to us.' I always had this image of imperials as people who could *say* things like that and the galaxy would just . . . snap into place around them."

"Well, I could have told you that's not how it works," Wen scoffs.

"I *know*."

"I know you know. I don't know if Gal knows. I hope he does by now. But you and me—we've both been in the dirt for too long. We know stuff like that takes work, and work doesn't come free."

I close my eyes. "But what if I don't have that work in me? That's the thing that's been ruttin' *haunting* me ever since I took that crown. I know I didn't claim my bloodright for the right reasons. It was for Gal—it was all to save his life. And I've been trying to . . . to build the ship around me as I plummet from the *free fall* of that decision ever since."

"Good thing you know a mechanic," she replies.

I bite down on the urge to snap at her. I know it's just the anxiety of waiting for Gal to arrive making me peevish, and she's only trying to remind me of the absurdly valuable resource that is her existence. "The empire needs a mechanic more than it needs me," I groan.

Wen jabs my side. "Hey. No talk like that. We're gonna stick together, and we're gonna figure out a way through this." She snaps her fingers in front of my face. "Assets, remember? What have we got?"

I give her a weak smile, remembering that low, horrible moment in a parking garage beneath Trost. I thought I had nothing left, but Wen and I put together everything we had and figured out a way through it—a way that led to a crown on my head and a rift between me and Gal that's still in the long, bitter process of healing. "At least one brain between us," I start.

"A real nice sword," she continues, tapping the hilt on her belt.

"An Archon war fleet, though that comes with its own web of issues—"

"Shh," she says, smashing a hand over my mouth. "Assets, Ettian. Focus."

"Fine. My bloodright, but good luck figuring out what use *that*—"

I'm cut off by the hand again. "If you're not going to take this exercise seriously, I guess the galaxy *is* doomed." Wen chuckles. "C'mon. We have a war fleet. We have the belief of the Archon people in your bloodright. They also seem to be pretty big fans of me. We have the Umber heir himself crowned, ready to act from the heart of the citadel, and completely wrapped around your finger."

"Is he, though?" I ask, a panic whiting out the rest of my thoughts. All I've had to gauge Gal's feelings are his words filtered through Hanji and handed to me by Wen. Now that the Umber delegation is on its approach, I'm all of a sudden racked with doubt that any of it has been real. We've twisted ourselves into such complicated knots with the lies we've told and the blank spaces we've left in the three years we've known each other. I feel like it's left me too doubtful of any honesty that comes my way to *live* in that truth.

Wen claps me on the shoulder once more. "Ettian, Gal loves you so much he's been running an elaborate con on the most dangerous woman in the galaxy to align the stars and bring the two of you together. It's *profoundly* foolish—the kind of foolishness you only commit to if you're serious. Believe me, I know. Dreadnought engine, remember?"

I give her a weak smile. She's right—of course, as always. And she's made her other point too. I have everything I need to change the course of the galaxy at my fingertips. The only thing missing is something only I can give myself—the confidence to see it through.

"Speaking of," I say, tipping a finger at Wen. "Greatest asset in my arsenal."

"Stop," she groans flatly.

"No, I'm a man of the truth now—the Corinthians have put me on the straight and narrow, don't you remember? I only say true things."

Wen shoves me hard, and I grab her by the wrist, cackling as she rears back trying to wrench herself away. When that doesn't work, she switches tactics, looping her free arm around my neck instead.

"I'm trying to say I appreciate you," I whine against the pressure on my throat. "At least let me look you in the eyes while I do it."

"*Never*," she replies with a laugh. Then, right as I'm about to warn her she's squeezing a bit too tight, Wen abruptly shifts her grip, lunging to catch my torso in a firm hug.

Against the backdrop of a ravaged world, under the shadow of a war that nearly tore us apart, it feels like a little miracle.

"They're going to be here soon," she murmurs in my ear. "I'll bring 'em in from the edge of town. You . . . should probably shower."

I move to swat her, but fast as boltfire she springs to her feet and dances out of my reach, laughing merrily. As Wen slips back into the apartment, I give my pits a sniff just to confirm that yeah, she's right about that too.

The shower doesn't do much good. By the time I get the ping from the security perimeter showing Wen entering with five unidentified individuals in tow, I've stained another T-shirt with anxious sweat that a vigorous pacing session hasn't helped.

Deep breaths. In two three. Out two three. But over the sound of that, there's the creak of footsteps on the stairs. Only one pair. I freeze, my heart feeling like a hand's just closed around it. Every step seems to come at a slower pace than the last. I swear you could fit an entire imperial line in the gap between the final stair and the landing.

And then there's a slight judder of a hand shaking the door handle. A breathy laugh that cracks me in half—a laugh I can't help but mirror. "You didn't give me the ruttin' *key*," Gal's voice hollers back down the stairs.

Of course she didn't. Of course she's gonna make me choose this. I cross the room and set one hand on the handle, my other coming up to fidget with the lock mechanism. On the other side of the door, I think I hear his breath catch.

I open the door, and there he is. The person I took a crown for.

The person I'd take another bullet for, knowing exactly how agonizing it feels to have your guts shredded. Gal emp-Umber has locked up like an academy cadet in an officer's flashlight, his eyes wide, his hands unsure what to do at his sides. His hair's grown longer since I last saw him, but his curls are artfully tousled as ever. His hooded eyes have darker shadows around them. I'm sure mine mirror them. The burden of empire has fallen heavy on both our backs.

But the weight feels like nothing as I step to collapse the distance between us. I pull him hard and fast against me, burying my nose against his neck as he locks his arms around my back and squeezes so hard that my scars nearly scream in protest. I bite down against the ache, tears swelling in my eyes. "Gal," I breathe, not caring that it comes out halfway to a whimper.

"Ettian," he murmurs against my collarbone.

The world has dropped away so thoroughly that confusion pings through me when he draws back slightly and glances down the darkened maw of the stair.

"The Wraiths—" I start.

"The Wraiths will wait where I've told them," he says firmly, and a thrill traces up my spine.

"Wen—"

"—says we have an hour," he finishes, reaching back with one hand and swinging the apartment door shut behind us. "And an hour is barely enough time for everything I need to do to you."

His lips find mine as the latch clicks into place, and it's a Viper at full burn, it's a skyscraper coming down, it's dreadnought boltfire plowing into a planetary surface. It's worth every sacrifice, every crumbled empire, every drop of blood I've shed to bring me to this moment. I clutch him like he's going to disappear—like if I don't, a girl in a powersuit is going to drag him away from me again.

There's no room for doubt in the way he kisses me back. I can feel myself reflected so perfectly that the tears in my eyes are threatening to spill over. I used to fear that Gal would never—*could* never love me the way I love him. But here he is, crowned like he was raised to be, in possession of everything he could possibly want.

And he wants me.

The relief takes my legs out from underneath me. I pull Gal down with me, laughing at the surprised noise he makes as we hit the floorboards in an ungainly mess. It was worth it to sow the seeds of discord I'll no doubt reap when I go back to my administration. Worth it to wage this war, worth it to save his sorry ass from the academy when this whole mess started. I've said it before. I've wanted to believe it so badly, and now I can.

No empire is worth it if I don't have him too.

CHAPTER 10

GAL

THE FIRST DAY of plotting to save the galaxy is hell.

It starts at the asscrack of dawn with Hanji Iwam kicking open the door of the back bedroom, beating a pot with a spoon and singing some horrible drinking song she must have picked up in the academy cantina. I hurl a pillow at her with vicious accuracy while Ettian stuffs his hands over his eyes and groans. She cackles and slams the door before I can find something harder to throw.

The situation doesn't improve by the time we make it out into the common area. The Wraiths have wreaked their usual havoc on it, somehow managing to coat a place that was *pristine* when we arrived last night with their detritus. Ollins is puttering around in the kitchen, overseen by Rhodes's nervous hovering. Rin is flat on her face, fast asleep on one of the bedrolls haphazardly strewn across the floor. In the center of the room, Wen is bent over the powersuit, whose innards look like they've detonated out from its torso, with Hanji peering curiously over her shoulder.

But of course, all of that freezes when I step into the room. "Gods of all systems," I mutter, pinching the bridge of my nose.

"Sleep well, Your Majesty?" Hanji asks, her eyebrows waggling so hard they're threatening to detach.

"None of your ruttin' business, Iwam. Ollins, your breakfast is burning."

As he yelps and scrambles to save it, I take a moment to savor the strangeness of this moment. This combination of people shouldn't be able to coexist under one roof, but the fact that we've all come together gives me hope that maybe—just maybe—we'll be able to figure something out.

I was a little too distracted last night to get the measure of Esperza's apartment, but in the morning light I can't help but feel like an anthropologist in the face of something so strange to me. My whole life I've bounced between dorm rooms and imperial grandeur, and the normalcy of an average living space feels like a forbidden thrill. It's as spare as you'd expect a safe house to be—not many valuables, plenty of nonperishables lined up in the cupboards Ollins has left open—but personal in a way that tells me more about the ex-pirate-turned-commodore than she's ever likely to tell me about herself.

A scattering of photos is tacked along one wall, depicting Esperza with a host of friends I don't recognize. It's not until I notice one wearing the armor of a suited knight that I realize it's likely many of them are dead by my mother's hand. Like my mother, Esperza seems to be a bit of a collector, but her gallery is less trophies of conquest, more weird little doodles and obvious jokes. My attention snags on a gold tooth, lovingly framed and accompanied by a placard that proclaims, "Punched out of Boss Caprica's mouth."

Ettian comes up behind me, setting a hand on my waist with so much tenderness I want to whirl around and warn him that people are watching. Sometime last night, it finally clicked why he's always been so ruttin' careful with me. Ettian emp-Archon has had a good thing ripped out of his grip one too many times. He's learned not to hold tight.

"What's the plan?" he asks, muffling a yawn. His eyes find Hanji's, and for a moment I worry I'm going to have to step between the two of them. Before I'm needed, Wen snaps her fingers, and Hanji's attention immediately drops back to the powersuit mechanism the two of them were fiddling with.

Maybe "coexist" isn't the right word yet. I press one hand over his, curling his fingers tighter into my hip, reminding him that it's okay to do so. "First things first, we eat whatever Ollins dares to serve us. After that . . ."

Well, after that, we take the mess we inherited and figure out how to escape it.

By the second day of plotting to save the galaxy, it's become clear that before we can form a plan of action, we need to get our philosophies ironed out.

Placing everyone under one roof was just the start. Now that we've had a day to acclimate and pool our data, the factions are starting to rise to the surface. Surprisingly, the lines aren't clearly drawn between Umber and Archon. On some issues, Ettian and I stand apart from the other five by virtue of our imperial blood and upbringing. On others, Wen, Rhodes, and Rin branch off from the group due to some technical aspect of the challenge that the rest of us lack the brains to see. Occasionally Wen and Ettian will form an island of their own, the only people here who've lived through ruin. Sometimes a talking point will split us into people who have seen the rawness of war versus the people who were shielded from it—which in this case is just me.

Those moments are the worst. Not because I'm all by myself trying to argue that their foot soldiers' perspectives are obfuscating the larger picture, but because Ettian, who by all rights *should* understand the larger context of ruling an empire, has an annoying tendency to discard that and fall in with the rest of them. He's been crowned for longer than I have, but he was crowned at the launch of a war that he's been fighting ever since. I want him to know better, but a part of me fears *I'm* the one who doesn't know enough.

After all, I've been coddled my entire life. Listening to the others tell their stories has made it starkly clear that the shadowing process that was supposed to instill me with a broader perspective on the empire has been a grand failure. I got to live among the people, but living with them isn't the same as living *as* them. Even when I was sleeping on a rooftop next to Ettian and Wen, I had the security of my bloodright humming through my veins. I had a history that had never betrayed me, a childhood of means, and utter certainty that neither of them shared that somehow we'd find a way out of our predicament.

Now I feel the pinch of it more keenly than ever. "As the only person here who's had any sort of political training," I start to a chorus of groans. "No, shut up, you little monsters—I mean it. I'm just saying that if we try to delay the Imperial Fleet any more than it already has been, the system governors are going to smell blood in the water."

"That's *good*," Ettian says from the kitchen table, where he, Rhodes, and Wen have an array of datapads splayed out. "Destabilizing Umber creates distraction. That gives us more openings to get away with more—"

"Just because *your* default plan is to throw something into chaos, duck in while everyone's busy putting out fires, and waltz out with exactly what you want doesn't mean that kind of thing works on a *galactic scale*," I retort, running an exasperated hand through my hair. "I thought you Archon folk were supposed to be all about serving your people. I've got people, too, and I don't know how to explain to a farmer on Naberrie that the reason their local economy crashed is because their system governor called a percentage of adults to crew their portion of the offensive."

"Gal's right," Hanji says, earning her a glare from Ettian. She shrugs, sprawling back on the futon. "Look, Umber system governors are a different breed. Trust me, I've got four little sisters who will ruttin' *eat* each other if it means they get to stake the family bloodright that my older sister's claimed. Your mother poisoned what it means to hold power in an Umber context."

"We only make it worse if we aggravate it," I conclude, but Hanji shakes her head.

"Nah, we need to . . . I don't know, we need *Archon* to look like the big dog here," she says.

Ettian's glare sharpens on her. "I will not sink my empire to Umber standards just to put a bunch of system governors outside my domain in their place. We're trying to *avoid* violent conflict, not exacerbate it."

"If all you want is a peaceable solution, one's already been proposed," Rhodes reminds him. "The two of you get hitched, the war freezes, the territories get annexed under your governing directive, and no more blood has to be shed. Well, apart from yours, if the empress gets her way."

I meet Ettian's stricken gaze. We've talked about this—in murmured side conversations, in bed with our foreheads pressed together, flat on our backs on the apartment's roof, watching the spidery pinpricks of abandoned dreadnought build struts cross in the night. I've told him about the knife my mother forced into my hands and watched his face crumple as he realized that even if he takes the easy way out, it won't be the easy way out for him. I think both of us have held on to a quiet hope that we *could* make this work through a marriage.

Which is why it broke my heart so keenly to hear him say out loud, "I won't marry you."

"That's out of the question," he says now. "That's not true peace—it's peace on the terms of Umber tyranny, and it's not a peace I'll lay down my life for."

Rhodes shrugs, as if Ettian's free to dig his own grave if he's gonna ignore the logic of it all. Next to him, Wen squeezes her skull between splayed fingers and says, "So then we accept that the fleet will mobilize, which means Archon has to be ready to hold it off. We need a cavalry, and the only one we have is the Corinthians. Which means we need to secure their aid as fast as humanly possible."

As in all things, she's infuriatingly right. But that opens up a whole new can of worms. The Wraiths and I don't know the Corinthian ambassador. Ettian and Wen have barely gotten to know them, and it's clear we don't have a finger on the pulse of what makes them tick. The most we know is that they like Wen, they're on upsettingly good terms with General Iral, and their ultimate goal is to reestablish Archon's territory as a buffer zone keeping Umber's hungry jaws from expanding down the galactic arm.

It's not enough to fix a war. It's barely enough to start a conversation.

Ettian shoves himself up abruptly from the table. Wen sets a hand on his arm, but he shrugs her off. "You all can keep going. I just . . . I need a breath." He eases around the chairs and clutter, making not for the balcony but for the door of the apartment. There's some perfunctory murmuring about how it isn't the greatest idea for him to be outside at the moment, but it doesn't do much and it all stops when the door closes behind him.

Then everyone's gazes swing back around to me.

I close my eyes and haul in a deep breath. "I'll talk to him."

I know exactly where to go. He needed to cool off, and for Ettian that always means open sky. It never made sense when he first explained it to me at the academy, the way he went on about the freedom and the possibility of it all wrapped up together. To me, the possibilities that came to mind first were flying, which I hated, and assassination, which I also wasn't a big fan of. But later I learned that Ettian was buried in rubble during the final days of the War of Expansion, trapped in the subbasement of the imperial residence when Trost was bombed. I think I'd love the sky, too, if the sight of it once meant salvation.

When I step out onto the rooftop, I find him standing a reasonable distance from the edge, his arms folded as he stares out over Breha's uneven silhouette. The sun's easing into the golden hour, the afternoon heat starting to break, and it makes him luminous.

It catches up to me all at once how far I've fallen. For most of my life, I accepted that nothing *real* could happen between me and anyone else until I turned eighteen and stepped from the shadows. I flirted and flitted, nursed quiet hopes, tamped down incandescent jealousy when Ettian would stumble in late at night, rumpled and wild-eyed from some tryst with a girl in the next year, and bit back *deeply* unexamined smugness when all it would lead to was him sourly nursing his polish in the cantina a few weeks later. I reveled in my anonymity sometimes—in the way nothing really mattered because I wasn't really Gal Veres—and I think that was part of the reason that by the time I realized I was fully in love with my roommate, I was already too far gone.

Now I've fled the Imperial Seat to meet him in a dusty borderworld town, and whatever we decide here will determine the galaxy's fate. And despite all that hanging over our heads, it isn't enough to outweigh the blazing joy of just being with him. There's no such thing as normal for imperials. There never will be. But here in Breha, it feels like we've stolen a slice of it, and I can't help but savor it.

So for a moment, I just take in the view.

"Sorry," Ettian mutters without turning around. "It's . . . I feel like the more we talk about this, the more it's clear that the best possible thing I can do for my people is die."

I slip a hand onto his shoulder and squeeze. When he doesn't respond, I snare my arms around his waist and pull his back against me, tucking my chin over his shoulder on tiptoes. "That can't be the only way to fix this," I murmur in his ear. "We'll think of something."

"We're running out of time," he seethes, but I can feel the tension in his body starting to slacken. "I can only be away for so long. And I'm sorry—" He unravels my grip just enough to twist in it and snare one arm around my neck, planting a quick kiss against the side of my head. "I don't want you to feel like you're not living up to my expectations because . . . holy shit. But we're trying to solve the hardest problem in the galaxy with four dipshits, one genius, two emperors, and five days. And if we don't, there goes the universe."

"I get it," I tell him, squeezing him harder. I've come to understand that Archon imperial upbringing has corrupted Ettian almost as much as my Umber childhood did me. Where I learned that my power was so inherent that I was above questioning, he learned that his was a burden he was nobly born to bear. Worse, he never claimed his bloodright with the intention of bearing it—he stepped out of the shadows because it was the only way he could save my life. He's never felt ready for his crown, and when you combine that with the fact that he's missing *years* of experience meant to prepare him for it, you get the moment we're frozen in and the terror that's wrapped him around me.

"I've been trying to understand power," he says, the words coming thick up his throat. "Trying to understand what it is and how to use it for the best. But power is *smoke*. I can't grasp it. I can only point at it and hope that my enemy sees something monstrous in its form."

I reach one hand up to cup the back of his neck, brushing my thumb carefully along the stubble at his hairline. "Power can be smoke. I've seen my mother make threats, watched people believe her wholeheartedly, and never been quite sure whether she'd follow through if they hadn't. But I see power as balance. Everyone is weighted. Everyone holds a place. Everyone leans. And I have my hand on the rug beneath it all."

He lets out a little huff that's halfway to a laugh—a victory I'll take, because this day needs *some* sort of win. "Gods of all systems— *neither* of us should be running empires. Maybe the Corinthians are on to something."

I roll my eyes, clapping him on the back as we both step back from the embrace. "An appointed emprex is still an emprex. They just delude themselves into thinking that any decision their leader makes would have been their choice too."

"But fools like us wouldn't even be in the running in the first place."

"Oh come on—have you *seen* me?" I strike a gallant pose that he knocks over with a shove to my shoulder within a second.

"No one with an ass like yours has any business hiding it on a throne," he says with a smirk.

"Should have told Iwam that before she dragged me off to be crowned," I fire back, but he's already reeling me in for a kiss. I let him bend me into a dip, laughing against his lips as I clutch the collar of his shirt, even though I know he'd never let me fall.

When he pulls me upright and draws back, he keeps his eyes closed an extra second, giving me a moment to relish his uncomplicated happiness. "Gods of all systems," he murmurs. "I just want . . ."

He's not allowed to not end that sentence. "What do you want?"

Ettian's eyes slip open. His expression is light-years away from the weight of his empire as he breathes, "You. You and a life with you."

My thoughts hit a fork as I stare into his eyes, feeling like I could break the universe in half over my knee for this man. On one branch, there's the urge to pinch his side and call him corny. But the other, darker path I find myself stumbling down has the glimmer of an idea at the end of it.

Ettian squeezes my arm. "Gal?"

"Mm."

His eyes sharpen. "What's wrong? You never use filler words unless—"

I press a finger against his lips. "Thinking."

"That sounds dangerous," he mutters against me.

"I have an idea."

"Gonna need a qualifier on that one."

"I have a *good* idea."

He gives me a look.

"Okay, it's a horrible idea, but if it works . . . If we pull this off . . ." My hands have started shaking. My heart is racing—and it was *already* at a good clip thanks to him. I'm pretty sure Ettian thinks I'm on the verge of a panic attack. I'm not sure if that thought is wrong. "Look, I know how it sounds. I'm not promising you the magic solution to every problem in the galaxy. But . . . I think I know where we start."

On the morning of the third day, I step out onto the balcony with a datapad and fire off a message.

By the sixth day of plotting to save the galaxy, we're almost to the point of monotony. The plan we've concocted has so many moving parts that we have no choice but to put our heads down and study for it like a tactics exam. The apartment's gotten so quiet I can barely believe the Wraiths are here at all. Rin, Rhodes, and Ettian are deep in some research-and-development task on the living room floor that Ollins is "supervising," while Wen tests out the fit of her retooled powersuit, assisted by Hanji, over by the balcony.

Sandwiched between them, I'm bent over the kitchen table, staring at my datapad like at any second it's going to divulge the secrets of the universe.

I've done the math—even had Rhodes double-check it. We're now within range of when everything goes to hell, and I have to convince myself that I'm ready for it. But so far, all I've managed to do is hyperfixate on my datapad's message queue and its blistering emptiness.

"It's too tight," Wen chokes, and my gaze snaps up to find Hanji prying awkwardly at a piece of paneling on her back. "Rocks and rust, longshot—are you trying to collapse my rib cage?"

"Says the woman who insists on keeping a pulse of charge in that nasty thing she's got strapped to her hip," Hanji fires back, twisting the implement in her hands in what's clearly the wrong direction, based on the snarl Wen lets out. "Try using it on me, I dare you."

I've yet to decipher the bond that's locked into place between the two of them over these long months of scheming. They're clearly capable of working together—and seem to, whenever no one's watching. But there's always a boiling point, one I understand all too well. Hanji's still working on penance for the bullet she put in Ettian, and Wen's constantly on guard for the next moment Hanji's gonna surprise her. And since Wen never relaxes around her, Hanji's nerves get worn thin fast. Flare-ups are inevitable, but usually short.

When they're not snapping at each other, they actually manage to get a terrifying amount of work done. In the time since we arrived in Breha, they've finished a complete tune-up of the powersuit, reencrypted all of our communication networks, and only had something blow up in their faces once.

As they fall into another round of bickering, I sigh, clamping my head between my hands and squeezing. The pressure's not doing anything for my focus. *Be rational*, I try to argue with myself. *There's going to be some overhead time. Even if she sprang into action the second she got the message, putting together a response takes time. It's not like she's going to—*

But the universe just *loves* to throw my plans into tailspins, so of course that's the precise moment the message pings into my notifications.

I slam one fist down on the table, and Wen and Hanji's sniping goes immediately silent. Every eye in the room is fixed on me as I rise from the table, clutching my datapad in one shaking hand. "Six dreadnoughts have just dropped from superluminal into a planetary blockade, commanded by Iva emp-Umber. Not by proxy. By presence."

I hold up the datapad and hit *ACCEPT*.

My mother's face fills the screen, a slow smile spreading over her lips as she takes in the room. From his place on the living room floor, Ettian rises to face her, looking wan. He's never looked into the eyes of the woman who killed his parents before, and a raw fury has taken over his posture as his gaze slips up to me and he murmurs through his teeth, "This wasn't the *plan*, Gal."

"Best to leave the planning to the true imperials, Archon," my mother replies. "Let me tell you exactly how this is going to go. I have six cityships in orbit around this planet, all of them in position for full offensive coverage. This world is deserted enough that I'm not terribly concerned about what a stray shot would do to the local ecosystem. So when I say that either you'll follow my instructions or I will not hesitate to reduce you to ash, trust that I'll make good on that."

I wonder if she notices how badly the camera is juddering in my grip. I can scarcely believe that she rode out—that my message was enough to bring her screaming in with a dreadnought fleet to make sure the Archon usurper stood no chance of escaping her clutches. She hasn't left the Umber Core since the War of Expansion. The whole thing reeks of a desperation that makes me wonder what I'm about to return to in the core. Has my disappearance thrown the political situation into a tailspin?

"Now," the empress continues. "You're to come quietly with my heir and his cohort up to my flagship. We'll depart for the capital and have you and my son wedded on the citadel steps within the week. And then we will finally, *finally* put this nonsense to bed."

I keep the datapad's camera fixed on Ettian's look of crumpled betrayal. If I didn't know better, I'd swear it was genuine. A twinge of guilt hits me alongside the realization that his performance is rooted in truth. Ettian sells betrayal well because he's been betrayed so often. By me in particular.

But not this time. This time, there's a larger game at play.

With the datapad's camera pinned on Ettian, my mother doesn't see the Wraiths sneaking around behind me, throwing together their go-bags. She doesn't see Hanji fumbling through the process of seal-ing the Flame Knight into her powersuit. She doesn't see the mecha-nized thumbs-up Wen throws my way.

Go time.

Ettian opens his mouth as if he's finally come up with a rejoin-der, but another voice interrupts him before he can get the words out. "Over my dead body," Wen announces, and I swing my cam-era's spotlight to her.

Several things happen in rapid succession. Wen makes like she's going to lunge for Ettian, but before she can move, Hanji's arms have locked around her powersuit's shoulders. With a mighty heave, the two of them stagger back through the plate glass window, shattering it, and topple over the edge of the balcony. Ettian lunges in turn like he means to throw himself after them, but Ollins and Rhodes grab his arms and wrench him back. Both of them look to me.

"Cuff him," I snap. "Rin, get *Double Ugly* and bring her around for immediate evac." I spin the datapad around and look my mother in the eyes. "We're on our way."

CHAPTER 11

ETTIAN

WHEN THE CUFF LOCKS around my wrist, *that's* when the reality of the situation locks into place. But before my brain can get past the obviousness of *gods of all systems, it's actually happening,* I hear another click that isn't paired to a sensation on my other wrist, look down, and find that rather than cuffing my hands together—

"Ollins, you dolt," Gal groans, practically vaulting over the kitchen table as Rin crashes out the door. "I meant cuff his hands *to each other,* not cuff him to *you.* No, don't bother—there's no time," he says as Ollins starts slapping every single one of his pockets, feeling for the key. "We'll make do. Rhodes, grab his legs."

"Wait—" I blurt, but before I can get my full objection out, Rhodes has jammed my knees together and hoisted them up. Ollins grabs the wrist he was supposed to cuff, and Gal jumps in to support my midsection as the three of them barrel toward the apartment door that Rin's left swinging wide open in her wake.

There's no way this is faster, I want to complain, but it's all I can do to keep my breakfast from creeping up my throat as we stagger drunkenly down the stairs. I squirm against their grips, trying to wrench my head upright, but that only makes them clutch tighter. Over the clatter of three pairs of feet, I can hear the muffled chaos outside that tells me Hanji survived the plummet out the window and is currently going full tilt against the Flame Knight in the middle of the street.

"Watch his head!" Gal yelps as Ollins yanks us around the landing and shoulders out the fire door. I wince against the harsh afternoon sunlight, biting back the urge to search the sky for the empress's dreadnoughts in orbit.

Breha is a sleepy little town on a normal day, but the commotion has brought everyone out all at once. Heads pop up in windows, folks peer from doorways, and the few pedestrians on the street go diving for cover as a blast from Wen's boot thrusters sends the tangle she and Hanji have created rocketing down the town's main drag. My eyes catch on two people who've just flattened themselves against the storefront next door. "*Help,*" I choke before Ollins slaps a hand over my mouth.

It's not part of the plan we discussed—right now is all about *spectacle*—but I'm hoping for some spark of rebellion in these people who've eked out an existence in this town long after the Umber Empire used it up and abandoned them. All I get is blank stares that elide slowly into confusion as they start to grasp exactly who's being bodily dragged past them—and who's doing the dragging.

But before they can decide to do anything about it, thrusters scream from the far end of town as the Flame Knight arcs up over the marketplace, resplendent in her powersuit, her vibrosword drawn. As we start scrambling toward the spaceport where the Wraiths put up *Double Ugly*, Hanji barrels past, a steady stream of profanity pouring out of her lips as she glances back over her shoulder at the knight-shaped bullet that's set its sights on her.

Gal, Ollins, and Rhodes have all gone a little slack-jawed at the sight of a true Archon knight, and I feel their grips start to loosen, reminding me that if I really want to sell this, I need to be fighting back a bit more. As the sweet, sweet pop-kick of Wen's thrusters snaps through the air, I take the opening. My elbow makes contact with Ollins's stomach at about the same time my knee drives into Gal's crotch. Gal drops my midsection immediately, giving me all the torsion I need to kick free from Rhodes's grasp as the young emperor keels over with a whine.

The scream of Wen's approach fills my ears, and I pray to every god listening that her aim strikes true. I yank my wrist away from Ollins, stretching the cuffs taut between us with enough force that the metal bites viciously into my wrist.

The whine of Wen's vibrosword keens through the air, that single remaining charge pulsing so close I feel it in my teeth.

A half second later, the chain falls limp against my arm, smoking slightly at the point where it was cleaved. Ollins and Rhodes scramble back, their eyes flicking on a disbelieving, predictable path.

First, to the chain dangling from Ollins's wrist.

Then to me, freed and on my feet.

Then to their emperor, shriveled on the ground.

And finally to Wen, who's just thrown her heels up, spun around, and set her vector on us.

Rhodes is the smart one—before Wen can close the gap, he lunges for me, tackling me just out of her grasp. She lands in a skid, plowing a rut down the dirt of the main road with one knee as she slams up a palm thruster to slow herself. I wrench my elbow back into Rhodes's side, giving me the space I need to break out of his grip, but before I can stagger toward Wen, a hand locks around my ankle.

"That was a cheap shot," Gal seethes, and yanks hard.

I hit the dirt with a wheeze, and barely have a second to recover my breath before Ollins throws himself on top of me and starts trying to wrestle my arms behind my back. I choke under his weight, my mind reeling through a thousand scrapes on the streets of Trost, where I was fighting for far less dire stakes than the fate of the galaxy. But before I can sink too far into the seething ex–street kid rage, there's the thud of mechanized boots slamming into the dirt next to me, followed by a sudden release in pressure as Ollins is lifted bodily from my back and flung clear across the thoroughfare.

Wen's powersuited hand dips into my field of view. I slam my palm into hers, wincing at the heat of the thrusters as she drags me to my feet. "Well, this is going splendidly," she mutters, and turns, pressing her back to mine as we take stock of the situation around us.

We had no opportunity to rehearse this part, and the only guidance we have for choreography is making sure there's no obvious window for me and Wen to flee. At the moment, the Wraiths are a little too far on the back foot. Ollins is groaning to his feet ten meters away, while Rhodes is trying to get Gal both upright and as far away from the suited knight as possible. Which just leaves—

"Hey, firecracker!" a voice calls from the far end of the street, and both Wen and I whirl. Hanji stands with her feet a cocky span apart, her sniper rifle nestled snugly against her shoulder as she levels it at us. "Time to give it up. No, I *really* wouldn't try it," she says as Wen squares up like she's about to lunge. "I know that suit as well as you, and my aim's only gotten better since I had my crack at the emperor."

My mouth has gone dry, and suddenly the slight twinge in my gut might as well be the hellfire of the bullet that caused it. Spending a week with the woman who shot me was uncomfortable enough. To see her pointing a gun at us now has me shrinking against Wen's bulk, praying Hanji's finger doesn't slip. Trying to make a scrabbly little street fight look real was one thing, but this is a hair too close to reality for my taste. Slowly I hold up my hands. After a moment of hesitation, Wen retracts her vibrosword, clips it to her belt, and does the same.

"That's right," Hanji says. She lifts a hand to her earpiece. "Rin, bring her around."

The murmur of shuttle engines in the distance sharpens into a roar. To any passerby, they'd be indistinguishable from any other ship. But even with a crown on my head, I'm still a pilot, and I can still tell the difference between a dual-rotary craft and a quad.

"*Move!*" I bellow.

The *Ruttin' Hell* blasts down the thoroughfare, throwing up an unholy whirlwind of dust and dirt as it pivots into a skidding landing. I throw myself to the ground, with my hands over my head, landing on the softness of another person who convulses under my weight. With the debris whipping across my cheeks, I don't dare open my eyes, but I know the shape of the body beneath me better than anyone—and I'm fairly certain he knows it's me.

With the *Ruttin' Hell*'s rotaries screaming mere meters away, there's no space for words. So while no one else can see us, I find the back of Gal's neck, yank him up into a furious kiss, and hope that says enough—about everything I dreamed of, everything we may never have, everything we're fighting for together. He clutches me back so hard I grunt, his teeth catching against my lips. He murmurs something, but it's lost in the chaos.

It was probably *"goodbye,"* though I desperately wish that it wasn't.

There's no time to linger—I shove Gal back into the dirt and scramble off him, holding one hand up against the furious dust storm as I try to triangulate the *Ruttin' Hell*'s position. The roar of the engines is so all-encompassing that I can't be sure if my steps are carrying me in the right direction.

But then her silhouette looms out of the dirt—this horrible souped-up shuttle I love with my whole ruttin' heart. Glee sparks through me as I break into a sprint for the ramp slowly lowering to the ground.

That lasts all of two steps. A shadow lunges out of the dust, grabbing me by the collar. I plant my feet and let out a snarl of frustration as I twist to lock my hands around Hanji's wrist. "Not so fast, Your Majesty," she coughs.

Then her eyes go wide, and I have only a second to relax before I'm lifted bodily out of her grasp and spun back toward the *Ruttin' Hell*. "Go!" Wen shouts, one hand dropping to the hilt on her waist. The dust billows around us as her sword unfurls, the soft *shick* of it stolen by the shuttle's screaming engines.

A shadow lurches in the murk behind her. Wen sees the way I'm about to shout and whirls, already slashing.

Hanji Iwam surges out of the dust to meet her with the barrel of her rifle. I scramble back as the Wraith leader shunts Wen's blow aside, the scar on my stomach twinging again. But the feeling scarcely has a chance to settle before Wen is ducking into Hanji's guard, her sword whirling into a second strike that whiffs past Hanji's shoulder.

"I said *go!*" Wen hollers.

And then they're whirlwinds. Twin dervishes, the dust eddying around them with wild abandon as Wen's sword flashes and Hanji's rifle spins to counter it. The Wraith doesn't seem to care that she's going up against a blade with a gun that wasn't made to be wielded like this. She throws herself into the fight with gleeful enthusiasm, and the Flame Knight meets her with quiet, brutal efficiency, her swordplay a stone wall that leaves no opening for Hanji to get a shot off.

They're putting on such a hell of a show that it kills me I can't watch, but the blockade in orbit overhead is only getting tighter. I duck up the *Ruttin' Hell*'s ramp, scramble across the hold and up the ladder, and worm through the narrow corridor to find Commodore Esperza leaning back over the pilot's seat. Her hair's swept back in a messy ponytail rather than the neat military bun I've grown used to, and in civilian clothes, she's less the fearsome commodore, more the former pirate to whom I once sold this very ship. Captivity's taken an obvious toll on her, but she's got a familiar diabolic spark in her eyes and she keeps a steady hand on the controls with a gleaming prosthetic. "Welcome aboard, Your Majesty," she calls.

"Thought you would have booked it to the core by now," I say, slinging myself into the copilot's chair.

"Iffan told me there might be some fireworks. Said to stick around in case you needed an extraction."

Wen left out the part where this whole "betrayal" is an elaborate ruse, which means the next order of business here is keeping Esperza distracted enough that she won't notice where the punches are getting pulled. "What about . . ." I feel a heat building in my cheeks, a line I know I shouldn't toe. "What about Captain Silon?"

Esperza lets out a bark of laughter. "You kidding me? My wife's probably *relished* two months without me meddling in her command."

I gape.

"Oh don't give me that look—you clearly don't have a leg to court-martial me on, *Your Majesty*." She gives me an eyebrow waggle so loaded with implication it could give Hanji a run for her money.

Speaking of—

"What's taking Iffan so long?" Esperza mutters, eyes dropping to the comms. "Wen, we leaving this rock any time soon?"

"Just. Give. Me. A. Second," Wen's voice grinds out, punctuated by the sounds of her grappling with what sounds like a pack of wild animals.

"Ruttin' hell," Esperza mutters. "Here, take the con. I'll go."

I dive sideways to claim the controls as she ducks out of her seat. "Wait—" I choke, but she's already launched herself down the corridor, throwing herself into a slide that drops her clean into the cargo hold with the kind of piratical flair I thought they made up for the broadcasts. I bite down on a frustrated snarl. We don't have *time* for these shenanigans, and Esperza stands a good chance of taking out one of the Wraiths for real.

But for the first time in months, the *Ruttin' Hell*'s under my hands and gods—it hits like a drug how long it's been since the last time I flew. I sink into the familiar embrace of the pilot's seat, wondering how badly Gal would try to kick my ass if I told him it's the best thing I've felt all week. With a few twists, I tease the rotaries left and right. Everything's just like I remember.

The comms board I remember a little less well—it takes me an extra second to recall how to bring up the feed from the rear cameras. When I see the tangle outside, I almost wish I hadn't.

Not just because Wen and Esperza are in an all-out brawl with three of the Wraiths. Not just because Gal is prowling the edge of the fight like he's not sure whether to get involved.

No, the thing that chills my blood is the shadow that flickers over it all as a set of quad rotaries blasts my dust storm away. *Double Ugly* has arrived on the scene.

If a Beamer is the minivan of starships, a Bucker is a monster truck. *Double Ugly* is big, nasty, and excessive on all fronts. Rin Atsana pilots it with flair, splaying her rotaries wide as she stabilizes into a hover and wheels the gun mounts to point at the five figures scrabbling in the dust. "Wen," I shout into the comm over the scream of its engines. "Get the commodore onboard. We gotta move *now*."

"They're after you," she grunts. "You go. We'll hold them off and catch up."

On the one hand, the logistics of that don't make total sense.

On the other, she doesn't have to tell me to fly twice.

I spur the *Ruttin' Hell,* maxing out its burn and blasting the ship skyward. The acceleration chokes every last drop of fear out of me, and I throw my head back and howl with the screaming rotaries, knowing full well that Wen's rolling her eyes. The thought borders on sacrilege, but it's inescapable—*this* is what I was born to do. To burn like I'm trying to outscorch this system's hell, to flirt with my circulatory system's limits as the g force crushes me into my seat, to grin so wide my face aches.

I haven't felt this alive since Gal put a crown on my head.

Breha shrinks to a small, dusty smudge in my periphery as I wheel the nose toward the stars, lock the rotaries into ascent, and sink into the euphoria of the controls in my grip. With the line still open to Wen's helmet mic, I can hear the faint sounds of the Wraiths' panic as they realize their prize has made a break for it earlier than anticipated.

I pull up her helmet cameras just in time to catch Wen seizing the moment of distraction. She turns and sweeps the legs out from under Commodore Esperza, throwing her mentor over her shoulder like a sack of potatoes. Before the commodore can get in a word of objection or warning—or possibly delight—Wen kicks her boot thrusters on and launches after the *Ruttin' Hell*'s rear.

To their credit, the Wraiths are on to us far faster than I'd like. Within a minute, *Double Ugly* springs into the sky, locking onto our vector and putting all four of its monstrous thrusters to good use. In a contest of vertical acceleration, the Bucker has my baby beat. I draw up the distance I've got left to clear between here and the edge of the atmosphere, run some quick numbers, and let out a long-suffering sigh between my teeth.

"I know that sound," Wen's voice chides over the comm.

"*Double Ugly*'s coming up too fast."

"Rocks and rust," she mutters, and I see her helmet camera feed swivel as she dodges a glance back to confirm it. A streak of boltfire snaps past her nose, and she lets out a fuming snarl. "Oh, those ass-holes think they're free to fire on *me*?"

I bite back the urge to remind her that if they don't, it's going to look suspicious as hell. "We gotta get the commodore in the ship before we break atmo," I tell her instead. A little thrill rushes down my spine. "I'm gonna put down the ramp."

Now *this* is gonna take some flying.

Wen's coming up fast behind me, the brilliance of powersuit engineering closing the gap like it's nothing. "Not gonna have time to do this daintily," she says. "How fast do you reckon that door closes?"

I catch her meaning and grin. "Fast enough." The *Ruttin' Hell* fills with howling wind and the scream of the engines triples in intensity as I drop the rear open. I unlock the rotaries and use the attitude thrusters to cant over the body of the ship until it's level with the ground, my stomach swooping at the sudden adjustment. Aerodynamics work viciously against me with the Beamer's flat top suddenly square to our direction of travel, but I need the deceleration anyway. "How's that throwing arm?" I call over the ceaseless noise.

"Think it's gonna do the trick." On the camera feed, I watch as Wen carefully slips the commodore down from over her shoulder and takes her by the forearms. I catch a flash of Esperza's panic, followed by a brief glimpse of the *Ruttin' Hell*'s open rear. "On my mark, close that door as fast as it'll possibly go," she says, nosing up beneath the ship.

"Copy that."

"Three," Wen starts, shifting Esperza so the commodore hangs from her wrists in front of her.

"Two," she says as she fires her boot thrusters with an extra burst, angling them outward.

"One," she grunts, flipping over the commodore's head in a graceful arc that leverages the powersuit's considerable weight into momentum that snaps Esperza up like a whip.

"Mark," she says, and lets go.

I jam the door button down and lock my focus on the feed from the hold. The blurry form of Adela Esperza rockets up into sight, reaches apogee, and then slams down on the half-closed ramp. My stomach clenches as she tumbles over, but then the commodore's prosthetic darts out and latches its iron grip around a binding on the floor, and I breathe a sigh of relief as the door locks into its seal and the vicious winds go quiet.

"Your Majesty," Esperza's indignant, half-breathless voice thunders from the rear of the ship. "I think you owe me a new pair of pants."

CHAPTER 12

GAL

I CRANE MY NECK, peering up out of *Double Ugly*'s windshield as I try to wrap my brain around what just happened. From the right gunner nest, Hanji puts it to words. "Did she just . . . *throw her?*"

"So unnecessary," I mutter, which does nothing to cow the look of disbelieving admiration Hanji is beaming at the pinprick above us. This whole exercise is unnecessary, but I know the second I try to raise that point to this crowd, they're going to claim I'm just mad I got hit in the balls.

Which isn't *not* true, but right now there are bigger fish to fry.

And even bigger fish hanging in orbit overhead. The *Ruttin' Hell*'s flight path has led us straight into the shadow of the *Precipice*, my mother's flagship, which already seems to be targeting from the telemetry on Rhodes's screen. "Rin, get us *up*," I warn, my hands clawing fruitlessly into the arms of my chair. My mother's made it clear that if Ettian fails to comply, she'll take him out.

He's failed to comply, of course. So it's up to me to do what I always do—jam myself squarely in the crossfire and pray my value outweighs his in the empress's eyes.

As if on cue, my datapad chimes. I wrestle it out of my pocket and answer the call. "Dear one," my mother says evenly. "What the *hell* do you think you're doing?"

"I have it in hand," I lie through gritted teeth.

"Footage of the scrape on the ground is already hitting the feeds. If the usurper gets away, your reputation may never recover."

Which was the whole idea in the first place, but I fire back with an astounding degree of unearned confidence, "Then let me handle the matter and earn the people's trust in my ability to wrangle Archon."

The second the words leave my mouth is the precise second the Flame Knight's boots slam down on *Double Ugly*'s hood. "Oh, don't you *dare*," I holler, clutching my datapad to my chest as Rin wrenches the ship in a valiant attempt to throw her off. This wasn't part of any plan we discussed—Wen was supposed to catch up with the *Ruttin' Hell* and make a clean getaway.

Rin's roughhousing does nothing. Wen's magnetized her boots, locking her into a predatory crouch against the hull in front of the windshield. As her hand drops to the hilt on her waist, every whispered horror story I've ever heard about the suited knights flashes through my imagination. Fighters carved clean in half by a vibrosword's stroke. Knights riding a sputtering ship like a falling star through an atmospheric burn. The *Fulcrum,* wrenched into Dasun's unforgiving grip.

I can almost picture the smirk behind Wen's faceplate as the vibrosword extends. The Wraiths catch her intention, and all four of them start hollering as she carves a long, deliberate scratch across *Double Ugly*'s hull. Now she's not only off-script—she's being an asshole. Uncharged, the sword's not enough to pierce the plating, but Hanji takes it like a mortal wound, bucking in her restraints, howling obscenities, and flashing rude gestures that I'm not even sure Wen can see.

In return, she tips a salute that almost certainly pairs with a cheeky smile and vaults backward, her boots leaving behind two blistering scorch marks on the shuttle's nose.

"Now hang on—" I mutter, but I'm cut off by an unholy muffled screech.

"We just lost a rotary," Rin says, her voice so flatly accepting of it that it takes an extra second for me to register what that *means*.

"Oh, rut me sideways," I groan as *Double Ugly* cants viciously into its newfound lack. I glance up at the *Ruttin' Hell*'s rapidly re-treating form, and for the briefest moment I allow myself to imagine Ettian at the helm, his hands firm on the controls and a grim edge to the smile he can't help but wear when he flies. The ghost of his part-ing kiss is still tingling on my lips.

Then I plunge back into the reality of our situation as *Double Ugly* starts to spiral. No time to worry about how Ettian is flying full tilt at a dreadnought with what seems like absolutely no forethought—now my primary concern is the fact that we've lost all chance of staying on the same vector. "Rin, what's our status?" I croak as the ship lurches in a desperate attempt to stabilize.

"I'm trying, I just—" *Double Ugly* jolts like it's hit a rock, and she gives her readouts a puzzled look. "We're stable, but going down. It's almost like . . ."

"You gotta be ruttin' kidding me," Hanji says, her seat swiveled so she can peer out toward the rear of the ship. "Looks like Iffan's lending us a generous hand."

This I have to see—I unclip and grab the straps overhead, using them to swing an unsteady path over to Hanji's gunner nest. Most of her view is occluded by the smoking wreckage of the rotary, which looks like someone's torn it apart with their bare hands.

Someone *has* torn it apart with their bare hands, and that some-one is currently wedged beneath the fallout of her bad decisions, her boot thrusters firing at full force to keep *Double Ugly* from spiraling into an uncontrolled descent. Her helmet jerks up toward us, and I know for sure we're sighted. I jab one finger at the sky—at Ettian, getting farther and farther away. At the person she's sworn to protect, the person I'm *trying* to protect, the person I need her to save.

The Flame Knight gives an almost imperceptible shake of her head, shifts her grip to free one of her hands, and jabs a finger down toward Jobal's surface beneath us.

"We can make the landing unassisted!" I shout fruitlessly, throwing up my hands, but Hanji claps me on the shoulder.

"Trust me, you're not gonna talk her out of it. Now get out of my lap and strap in. This is gonna be rough."

I grit my teeth, feeling any sense of control I had over the situation slip like sand through my fingers as I wobble back to the command chair, throw myself down in it, and pull my restraints back on. This, *this* is why I used to hate flying so much. Too much can go wrong, and when push comes to shove, the yoke in your hands is a ruttin' illusion meant to convince you there's some way you can save yourself. "Rin, we're gonna have to drop."

She gives me a wide-eyed look. "But Ettian—"

"I know."

"But the rotary—"

"I *know*. Flame Knight's gone rogue for some reason, but at least she's being heroic about it. I'd rather take her up on that offer than trash the shuttle any more than she already has."

My pint-sized pilot exchanges a wary look with Rhodes. "Your funeral, Your Majesty," she says at last, and cuts the thrusters back.

As we start our gut-tangling plunge back toward the planet surface, I pull up the line with my mother again. I feel a wave of childish shame rising like a tide in me—or maybe that's just the way the ship is plummeting. My failure today has been loud, public, and extremely witnessed, and even if it wasn't part of the plan, getting my ass saved by the Flame Knight's goodwill is admittedly the perfect final touch to my total humiliation.

And despite it all, I'm remarkably clearheaded. This is exactly what I called my mother out here to see, baiting her with the claim that I had the Archon usurper in hand. I sold her on the idea of bringing him in together, planning for it all to collapse in a hideously embarrassing fashion the second she arrived. I still have one last card to play, and it's nowhere near my reputation.

I make the call, and a communications officer on the *Precipice* picks it up in an instant. "Put me through to the empress," I demand before they're halfway through the breath they'll use to greet me. I'm transferred with all the ease of slipping through the void, and when my eyes meet my mother's across the connection, the sight of myself reflected back in her features grounds me so thoroughly in my purpose that the last dregs of my fear slip away.

"Gal—"

"You listen to me," I interrupt, thrilling at the sight of her taken-aback blink. "The man in that ship is the love of my life. I will forge a life with him if it's the last ruttin' thing I do, and if you dare fire on that Beamer, I vow I'll make myself absolutely useless to you. You can cull me and start your line anew for all I care—but good luck explaining that to the governors."

"The man in that ship is the bloodright the Archon rebellion is staked on," she counters through a snarl. "We have our opportunity here and now—right in front of us—to eliminate the dregs of that line and restore the empire before it's torn irreparably."

"Rut the empire," I declare, which earns me worried looks from three of the Wraiths and a gleeful thumbs-up from Hanji. "The empire has been diseased and corrupt for generations, but with you it festered into rot. *I* am the empire. *I* am the culmination of your great works. *I* am the future of the galaxy, not you. Kill Ettian emp-Archon and you destroy your own line once and for all."

Iva emp-Umber gives me a long, considered look, one so withering she might as well have turned the *Precipice*'s main battery on me. I've been keeping my defiance of her so indirect for the past two months that declaring it openly now is like staring into the heart of a star. I expected her disappointment to taste like ash on my tongue, but instead I find I'm savoring it.

"I have broken systems over my knee and built them back brick by brick into Umber glory," my mother says at last. "You will be no different."

The call cuts. The plummeting sensation intensifies a thousand-fold. I raise a shaking hand to my lips, my eyes turning up to the sky above, my thoughts whiting out to nothing but a prayer to any god listening that the pinprick of the *Ruttin' Hell* isn't the last glimpse of Ettian I'll ever get.

CHAPTER 13

ETTIAN

MY SKILL AS A PILOT has always come from gut instinct. Maybe it's something my time on the streets of Trost uniquely shaped me for—the sense that keeps me from wasting time checking a readout that's only going to tell me something I already know. The feeling that guides me more than any vector marker.

But right now, after a knock-down, drag-out fight and a furious vertical burn into Jobal's atmosphere, my gut is just aching, and I'm starting to fear I might not have the sense I need to fly us out of this mess. Or maybe that's just my gut telling me there *is* no way to fly out of this mess.

The *Precipice* looms over us in all its inevitable monstrosity. I'm still struggling to wrap my head around the fact that I'm spitting distance from Iva emp-Umber, galactically speaking, which isn't doing my sense any good. The woman who ruined my life, ruined my empire, and took an ax to my parents' necks is just scant miles away from me, wrapped in the impenetrable cocoon of a dreadnought's hull. There's a furious, animal part of my brain that doesn't give a shit how foolish it would be to take on a beast like the *Preci-*

pice in the *Ruttin' Hell*. For a moment, I sustain a fantasy of finding some secret exploit—some exhaust port engineering flaw that will down the 'nottie in a single hit.

It would be impossible. A single person taking out a dreadnought only happens when you're Wen Iffan, and she nearly killed herself in the process. The only hope we have right now is escaping to superluminal while the dreadnoughts are still oriented in an inward blockade.

Which was so much easier the last time I did it. When Gal and I first fled the academy, we found ourselves facing a similar dreadnought blockade set up by Berr sys-Tosa. But Tosa's aim was to capture Gal and use him as leverage to bolster his position in the Umber hierarchy. He couldn't fire on the Umber heir without igniting the fury of his mother, which gave us the opening we needed to act like we were surrendering and then leap to superluminal before anyone could stop us.

Iva emp-Umber wouldn't fire on her heir—of that I'm fairly certain. But her heir is miles beneath us, about to be grounded on Jobal. Aboard this ship is only me and the commodore, and I'm fairly certain the empress views that as a *two birds, one stone* sort of situation—a situation that will only turn to *three* if Wen manages to catch up with us.

"*Double Ugly*'s down," she announces through the comm. "Heading back up your way."

"You didn't have to peel him completely off us," I mutter as I check her telemetry. The powersuit's thrusters catapult her toward our retreating tail with such furious speed I worry about the heat shedding off her helmeted head, but it's not enough to close the gap before we reach the atmospheric boundary that will allow us to leap to superluminal.

A boundary that barely matters when you consider our chances of making it there before the *Precipice* shreds us. I switch the instruments over to our scans of the dreadnought, searching for the inevitable guns targeting.

But none of them are preparing to discharge. My brow furrows.

"Yeah, I kinda did," Wen says thickly against the sweltering heat her suit's coolant must be trying valiantly to combat. "Empress talks big, but she still values her heir. She was willing to fire, damn the consequences for the planet. Didn't sit right with me, so now it's a planet her son is stuck on with no means to escape in time to duck the fallout of a shot like that. As long as you keep a line between the 'nottie's big guns and his position on the ground . . ."

I blink. "Ruttin' hell. You really do think of everything."

"That's my girl," Esperza grunts, and I turn to find her crawling up out of the hallway, gritting her teeth against the ascent that's doing its damnedest to drag her all the way back down into the hold. Her ponytail's barely holding on, her skin's slick with sweat, and she's decorated with a brand-new scattering of scrapes and bumps that will no doubt darken into bruises, but the set of her jaw is all business. "What's her ETA?" the commodore asks as she rolls over onto the bulkhead behind me.

I check Wen's speed against ours, against the distance between us. "We're gonna have to hold out for at least ten minutes. And we've got fifteen minutes minimum before we hit the boundary for super-luminal."

On my readouts of the *Precipice,* an alert starts to flash. Launch tubes on the dreadnought's surface are peeling open. If the empress can't take me down with the main batteries, she'll make it a free-for-all target practice for her pilots. I can picture them as they rocket down those tubes, eager for the glory that awaits the person who wipes out the Archon bloodright.

It's been so long since I flew combat. I'm an entire galaxy away from the boy I was when I strapped my Viper to Gal's and dragged him through twenty of our classmates trying to kill him. The same goes for the moment I flew this very ship through an active field, using the human shield I had aboard to sow chaos through the battle as Archon overran its first dreadnought. I'm rusty—and that's on top of how exhausted I am. I let my head droop as above, the *Precipice* begins to spew a horde of gleaming fighters into the afternoon sun.

A cybernetic hand comes down on my shoulder. "Your Majesty," Esperza says. "Leave this to me."

Part of me wants to protest—to fight like hell for the pilot's seat I've missed for so long. But the other part of me wants to live.

I've only been in a ship with Adela Esperza at the controls once before. This ship, in fact, before all the outrageous modifications she socked into it in her chop shop program on Delos. She was trying to take it off our hands for cheap, and so she flew it deliberately into every weakness it had—but she did it with the confidence of a pilot who's been flying ships dangerously for longer than I've been alive.

So I abdicate my throne. I unclip, heave with all my might, and drag myself sideways into the copilot's seat as Esperza hauls herself up to replace me. She's barely had a week to recover from her time in Umber captivity, and Wen tossing her into the *Ruttin' Hell*'s hold did her no favors, but there's a glint in her eye that tells me if I try to make a case about it, I'm going to get a fistful of metal for my trouble.

I clip in, pull my comms setup over to the copilot dashboard, and brace myself for what she's about to unleash.

Ahead, an entire Umber cavalry has set sights on us. Hundreds of Vipers stream from the *Precipice*'s skin, flocking into formations I know by heart from my time at the academy. I can all but feel what it would be like to fly at the point of one of them—to hunt in a pack of the fastest, most agile ships ever to roll off an Umber line.

At my right, Esperza sighs. "Well, this won't be very interesting."

I'm halfway to asking her what she means by that when she throws us into a sharp turn, cranking the rotaries around so hard that it nearly sprains my neck. I sink back hard into my seat, biting down on the urge to close my eyes. I don't want to miss a second of this.

And within seconds, I've decided that Adela Esperza is utterly wasted in her role as commodore. She wheels the *Ruttin' Hell* wide around our pursuers, twisting the body of the ship with the attitude thrusters to let loose a barrage of boltfire that strafes a line of pure destruction across their perfect formation. Rather than fleeing their revenge, she plunges gleefully toward the wreckage as the Vipers scatter like a school of fish someone's just hurled a rock through.

The light fighters' weaponry is nose-mounted, only capable of firing at something they're running directly at, a weakness Esperza is all too happy to exploit. As she fords the debris field of her initial carnage, the attacking squadrons quickly discover their possible angles of approach drastically cut. Esperza's created a cocoon of dead Viper guts that she shoulders the *Ruttin' Hell* into, using the rotaries to turn us into a whirling cannon mount. In the broad scope of things, it only buys us a few minutes while the squad leaders reformat their ships. A few minutes might be all we need.

According to my telemetry, the *Precipice* is intent on not giving us that time. Putting Gal on the ground took the main batteries out of the picture. Iva emp-Umber can't annihilate us with the full might of her flagship. But the smaller batteries are starting to go hot, starting to target. They aren't maneuverable enough to hit us when we're tearing unpredictably across the battlefield, but now that we've hunkered down into a fixed position, it's open season.

"Commodore, the *Precipice,*" I grunt against the monstrous G's she's pulling.

"Hard to miss, kid," she replies. "Sit back, loosen that jaw."

She doesn't have to tell me twice. I jam myself back in my seat an instant before the *Ruttin' Hell*'s acceleration does it for me. We bolt from the thicket of our cover, setting a vector on the fastest possible line to the edge of the atmospheric boundary keeping us from going superluminal. The Viper squadrons are forced to swap tactics once again, giving us the scant extra seconds we need to create distance between us and them before we have to start putting some loops in our flight path.

This time I squeeze my eyes shut. There's nothing else I can do here—it's all down to Esperza's flying, the *Ruttin' Hell,* and whatever gods are watching.

So I miss it when the first fighter falls abruptly off our rear. Esperza's whoop jolts me from my resignation, and I open my eyes just in time to watch another speck get wrenched off-course on our read-outs.

"Wen?" I ask the comm, scarcely believing what I'm seeing.

"You really shouldn't be surprised," she replies as a third Viper gets snapped back from the flock like it's reached the end of a rope. "Come on, my acceleration was nowhere near linear. With the atmospheric falloff?" She punctuates her question with a crunch that radiates through her suit like the toll of a bell—a sound I'm fairly certain is her *elbowing* a ruttin' light fighter out of her way.

"You don't even have a charged sword—what do you think you're doing?"

"The most," she says through what's almost certainly a wicked grin.

The formation has no idea how to adjust. Umber hasn't flown combat against suited knights in a decade. Never once in my years at the academy did we run that scenario. The knights were gone and dead, obliterated by Iva emp-Umber's Knightfall, and no one dared to imagine the possibility that they might one day rise from the ashes.

And even if that were the case, I don't think anyone imagined a knight quite like Wen Iffan. The Archon knights came in all shapes and sizes, but they were united by a common thread of noble purpose that characterized their work, from the way they addressed the public to the way they fought. Wen has come a long way from the streets of Isla, but there's a part of her that's always going to be the kid who survived that with nothing but the tricks up her sleeves and a rainbow umbrella. It's not a noble knight bearing down on these fighters—it's a half-feral street girl who grew up in a chop shop with the blood of a mob queen in her veins.

And yet. She *is* noble—she knows the weight she's throwing around is downright unfair, and despite the fact that these fighters are shooting to kill, Wen's defanging and disabling them where she would be well within her rights to shoulder clean through them. Her scrap with the Wraiths was playtime—a warm-up to the methodical, relentless way she tears into the Vipers pursuing us. They scramble to reformat around her, but she weaves through them handily, all but skipping off their wings as she claws through the scrum closer and closer to the *Ruttin' Hell*.

In all our months at war, I've rarely gotten the chance to watch her work live, and I always forget that the joy and fear in equal measure feel like they might rip my heart in half. Like all Archon kids, I idolized the suited knights—and with Iva emp-Umber herself on the field, I'm achingly aware of how easily they can be snatched away.

"Next part's on you, Majesty," Esperza says, jolting me back to my own precarious position. "Need that hold door sealed. Not gonna be an easy walk back. You up for it?"

In response, I unstrap my harness, sucking my lips between my teeth as the Beamer ducks into another gut-tangling maneuver. *You're not getting out of this without bruises,* a little voice in the back of my head warns me—but rut it, I'm bruised already. If Adela Esperza can fly this defense run after months in Iva emp-Umber's cells, if Wen Iffan can fight her way through all of this and still think of a way to save the planet beneath our feet from the empress's wrath, I can crawl down the hall and push a button.

I slither out of my seat and flatten myself against the floor, trying not to laugh at the absurdity of it. There's no safe way to do this on my feet—not with the way the commodore's flying. Even with the precaution of grounding myself, there's the complication of moving. Handhold by handhold, scrabbling foot by scrabbling foot, I shove myself across the cockpit floor and grapple my way down the hall. It's a battle just to keep my head from hitting anything as we tilt and tumble through the crossfire the remaining Vipers are laying down, and in a strange way, it's utterly freeing.

I'm not an emperor. Not overseeing a system that encompasses billions of lives and hopes to reclaim billions more. I'm just a dumbass trying to close a goddamn door.

"Uh-oh," I hear from over my shoulder, which is the only warning I get before Esperza wheels the rotaries around and plunges the ship into a dive that sends all of my mass hurtling toward the ceiling.

I manage to latch onto the crew bunk's doorframe in time to keep me from cracking my head open on the bulkhead above. We're far enough out that gravity's become an afterthought, but Esperza hasn't spun up the ship's generators yet. The only thing keeping me pinned to a surface is acceleration, and it isn't kind.

"Commodore, call your directions—" I grunt through my teeth, but it's too late. She's spun the rotaries again, this time pointing them aft and gunning them as hard as they'll go. My grip gives out, my mass takes over, and I hurtle down the hall, clawing at the walls to no avail. I roll clean past the door and out into the hold, and this time there's nothing to save me from the vicious impact that drives the breath from my lungs and sends a searing stab of pain through the scar in my gut.

This is bad.

This is very rutting bad.

I roll on my side, taking stock of where I've landed. I'm pinned against the hold's ramp, the ladder up to the living quarters and cockpit a solid fifteen feet above my head. There are struts and straps lining the wall, but with the way the *Ruttin' Hell* is flying, there's no way I can trust I won't end up dangling haplessly from one of them or outright losing my grip, flying across the hold, and cracking my skull open.

"You okay back there?" Esperza asks. She clearly doesn't have the capacity to look away from the fight at the moment, but I can't help wishing I could scream, *What do you think?*

"I'm stuck in the hold," I croak against the rumble of the Beamer's machinery. "I need you to fly straight and cut the engines for two seconds on my mark."

"I can't just *cut the engines*—we're gonna be boltfire magnets."

"Two seconds," I repeat with all the force I can put behind the words in my current state.

It's not much, but it must register as imperial enough. "Standing by," Esperza shouts.

"Three. Two. One. *Mark.*"

I shove myself as hard away from the ramp as I can as the *Ruttin'*

Hell's acceleration melts to nothing. The sudden loss of gravity threatens to pull my brain into utter disorientation, but I keep my gaze fixed on my target, arms outstretched as I sail across the hold.

"That's two!" Esperza shouts from the fore, and I swing frantically, my fingers barely catching on one of the rungs of the ladder before she guns the engines. The acceleration tries to yank me back again, but I lock my grip tight and pray to every god listening that it holds as my legs stretch out behind me.

A sinking feeling settles in. I'm dangling on the wrong side of the door. Maybe at my peak physical fitness—when I was running academy drills every morning—I could pull myself up and wedge myself into the corridor, but that was before I got crowned and shot in the gut. There's only one way we pull this off, and it's a gamble I'm not sure if I'm ready to take.

But the alternative is unthinkable, so I heave with all my might, swinging one hand off the rungs to catch the door mechanism, and tug it shut before I have a chance to second-guess myself.

"Your Majesty?" Esperza hollers from the front of the ship, her voice muffled by the door's seal. A light clicks on to confirm it's airtight, and equal parts relief and dread flush through my system.

"You're gonna have to do it with me in here," I yell back.

"Absolutely not," the commodore snaps without hesitation. "You can't order me around this one, Your Majesty. Your safety supersedes all other imperatives."

I grit my teeth, using another vicious twist of the ship to swing my legs up and hook my toes into the rungs. "I have a firm hold. If we time it right—if you only open the door for as long as she needs—"

"*Ettian,*" Esperza says. "You are our *emperor.*"

"And if that weren't true, you'd save Wen in a heartbeat," I reply. "And so would I. And it's what we're ruttin' gonna do, because nothing in this universe matters more than her."

I promised her no more dreadnought engines. No more lighting herself on fire to keep the Archon flame alive. There's no circumstance where I'd ever leave her behind on a battlefield to save my own ass—damn the consequences, damn whatever it means for the future of my empire. *She's* the future of my empire.

Esperza's gone quiet. My muscles are starting to shake from the holding on. "Just . . . Just tell me when it's time," I yell.

"You got it," Esperza replies, her voice resigned but firm.

I try to ready myself. Try to remember every last bit of the mandatory safety lessons we always zoned out through at the academy. The total loss of pressure is about to do absolutely horrific things to every pocket of gas in my body. *Don't hold your breath*, I remind myself—but I'm terrified that I won't be able to curb the impulse when the moment comes. I use a sudden pitch of the ship to haul myself up close enough to weave my arms into the rungs I'm gripping, doing my best to lock myself into my current position. If I lose consciousness, I'll drift—and I'm almost certainly going to lose consciousness.

"She's coming up fast," Esperza hollers. "Opening the hold . . . *NOW.*"

I close my eyes and let go of my breath. The machinery of the ramp rumbles, there's a soft *whumph* and a whistle of wind, and then everything around me goes quiet, quiet, quiet.

The sweat on my skin evaporates in a searing prickle, and I can feel myself swelling, stiffening, my body suddenly pushing larger than its usual bounds. I fight the urge to choke as the moisture in my mouth and nose blisters into vapor, but my willpower starts to go soft around the edges.

My grip loosens. The dark behind my eyes melts toward a larger darkness, but the last thing I feel before I go completely is a set of metal arms catching me in their cradle, and the last thought I can hold is that no matter what, in Wen's hands, everything will be okay.

CHAPTER 14

GAL

MY MOTHER ISN'T speaking to me.

Normally, this would be cause for celebration. Ever since I took my crown, I've been desperate for any moment away from her constant attention. In the weeks after Breha, I've been braced for consequences.

But by the third week back in the Imperial Seat with absolutely no communication from my parents' quarters, I've decided we're well beyond "too much of a good thing."

I've spent most of that time in my rooms, watering my sad little plant and watching the news of my gloriously public rut-up explode through the empire's newsfeeds. I've even gone through the pains of making a spreadsheet of each video source that managed to capture the event and which major feeds have distributed it—a somewhat masochistic way of visualizing the way it's spread. At this point I think I've memorized every moment in every angle.

The Wraiths, predictably enough, have turned watching reruns of it into a drinking game. I've taken to lurking in the back of their rumpus room with a glass of warming polish dangling from one hand, watching them tip back joyful shots every time the moment of me getting kneed in the balls replays. The memory of the pain should invoke some sort of sympathy, but every time I watch it, the only thing I can focus on is Ettian.

I miss him. Miss him like a planet flung from orbit, miss him like a dying star gasping for hydrogen. Hanji tells me I'm being dramatic, but Hanji doesn't take anything seriously enough to know how horrible it feels to have nothing but the cold comfort of the fact that the *Ruttin' Hell* slipped past the blockade unscathed. Ettian has yet to make a public appearance since his return to the liberated Archon worlds.

Like us, he's regrouping. The first stage of our plan has succeeded with my humiliation and Ettian's escape. The next part hinges on the empress's response. The Breha incident has sent shock waves through Umber politics, and I have no doubt that part of my mother's silence is because she's a little preoccupied wrangling the fallout.

So when it breaks, I know I'm in for it.

The summons comes directly to the rumpus room—a knock on the door announces an imperial aide, who in turn announces they're meant to escort me to my mother's side. The Wraiths make a bunch of *ooh Gal's in trouble* noises, hiding snickers behind their hands. I decide I might as well play the part of temperamental prince I know will amuse them the most and heave my polish glass at Hanji's head. She snatches it out of the air like it's nothing and blows me a sardonic kiss as I turn and storm out on the aide's heel.

I've had weeks to prepare myself for this moment, but I've given up on trying to predict what I can expect. Despite all her attempts to educate me, I lack the imagination to replicate my mother's cruelty. Normally it's a blessing.

Today, it's putting a cold sweat on my palms.

We trek an arrow's path through the citadel, carving through the most direct corridors that take us from the Wraiths' basement haunt to the elevators that rocket us into the spires above. Up here are mostly administrative offices for the governors and representatives who've leeched onto the heart of imperial affairs like desperate remoras. The penthouse level is reserved for a suite of conference rooms for less formal meetings and an audience chamber for more formal ones.

It's the audience chamber I'm directed toward. The aide hangs back, which never bodes well, forcing me to shoulder my way through the massive doors myself. I don't dare do it with anything even remotely *resembling* an attitude. Now is not the moment to pull that kind of shit in front of my mother. At least, not until I have a better sense of how she's taking current affairs.

But when I step into the room, I realize that no entrance could have made this any less of a mistake. I'm greeted by the sight of my mother lounging on the throne in the center of the room. An elegant rendering of the Umber Empire radiates from her feet, done in brass ingots set against obsidian tiling. A dagger—the same one she pressed my bones into—dangles from her fingertips, wet with blood.

Before her stands my father, and before *him* lies a man flat on his back, dressed in simple prison linens that were probably white at the start of all this. His limbs have been chained to the floor, though at this point that doesn't seem necessary. The chamber is utterly silent, but for the ragged sound of his exhausted breathing.

My mother gives me a moment to soak it all in, then rises from her throne with a broad, welcoming gesture. "Dear one, come closer. As you can see, we've gotten started already, but let me bring you up to speed."

I let the door fall shut behind me, circling the carnage at the center of the room with a wide berth. As I approach my mother, she lifts a hand to my jaw, her eyes narrowing as she tips my head back and forth. When I was younger, her careful inspection used to be a comfort. I'd soak in the full focus of a woman with an entire galaxy under her control, feeling like the center of the universe had shifted to me.

Now all I can think about is the dagger in her hand and the man bleeding out on the floor. All I can see is the cruelty that brought the galaxy to heel under her in the first place. I could never be the center of this universe—right now, all I can wonder is if I'll survive it.

"Do you recognize this man?" she asks, pressing my face to turn my gaze inexorably to the bloody wretch.

I've listened and learned well at court, and though his face has seen its fair share of the knife's attention, I place his features without hesitation. "Lorne sys-Acua," I blurt, my voice a tic higher than usual. He governs this very system, making him a frequent fixture in the Imperial Seat. Without his court garb's fine brass detailing and the obsidian charms that make him sound like breaking glass every time he moves, it's difficult to see him as a man with an entire star and everything in its orbit under his domain.

My mother nods. "I've been aware of Acua's ambitions for years. He has never been wholly content with the bloodright the gods have bestowed upon him. He's always been hungry for more, waiting for an opening—though he never dared voice that fervent wish. I could see it in the way he moved. The way he withheld his fleets from the War of Expansion, claiming that it would be more pertinent for him to focus on our core defenses. He drove a wedge between his dreadnought captains and the rest of our forces, readying them for the moment they would have to wall up Acua System and let him play out his coup."

"It's not true," Acua hisses against a burbling wad of spittle and blood. "I am loyal . . . to the Umber crown. I protect the Imperial Seat . . . with all that my lineage commands."

"I earnestly wish that was the case," my mother says, closing her eyes and shaking her head. "I didn't want to believe it when we received the transmission from your second daughter. You covered your tracks well, but when word got out that my heir was caught trysting with the Archon usurper, you decided it was time to act on your plan."

"My daughter orchestrated this," Acua begs. "She fabricated the evidence to implicate me so she can claim my bloodright over her siblings."

My mother lets out a long sigh, holding up her free hand and counting something out on her fingers. "That's five lies, all in a neat little row. I thought we'd established the ground rules here."

"No, no, *nonononono*—" the man begins to plead as my father crouches at his side, raising a gleaming obsidian dagger. With a lover's tenderness, he draws it methodically over Acua's upper arm five times. The blade's edge must be lethally sharp—it takes several seconds before blood starts to bead from the cuts. Acua seethes through his teeth. "Please. Listen. I'll do anything you want. Just let me live. I'll go into exile. I'll strip myself of title."

"What you have is not something that can be stripped away by banishment," the empress says. She steps away from my side to crouch at Lorne sys-Acua's head. "You were born into bloodright. You've spent your whole life holding it—you know nothing but the fated power running through your veins. And yet you had the audacity to reach for more. So I'll take it from you drop"—she uses her own dagger to trace another cut along his cheek—"by drop."

I am not drunk enough for this. The polish in my stomach is at absolute war with the terror of this moment. I tuck my sweating hands behind my back, pressing down a swell of nausea. *This man made his own choices,* I try to tell himself.

Choices driven by the fallout of the disaster I toppled into the public consciousness. Choices that might as well be me whispering in his ear, telling him the empire is destined for a weak heir.

My mother's gaze tilts slowly up to me like a predator sensing weakness. "You seem uncomfortable, Gal."

"I'll confess," I start, my voice thick against my gorge, "I don't understand why this is a private affair. If sedition is to be punished, should it not be punished openly, for the edification of his peers?"

She rises, settling into a prowl around Acua's splayed form. Her hard, flat heels ring against the stone like gunshots in the quiet of the empty chamber. "Public displays are for enemies of the empire. Acua here, for all his faults and failings, sought not to destroy Umber but to redefine it under his rule. For that, the punishment must be handled with a more . . . delicate hand."

The system governor lets out a soft moan as the empress traces an elegant line through the air with the knife edged in his blood.

"We will release pictures of the body, of course, when the time is right. But never forget that the governors with the most active imaginations are the ones who will give you the most trouble. You can work wonders simply by giving them a hole and letting them fill it with their worst thoughts." As my mother steps up to my side once more, her eyes search mine for understanding.

I can't give her anything in return. "Why cut him slow? Why drain him drop by drop? Why is any of this necessary?" I ask, the presence of the blade in her hands humming in my awareness like a charged vibrosword.

My mother reaches up to cup my cheek again. "Dear one, there *is* an audience for this affair. The system governors aren't the only ones who need to be educated. You will one day stand where I do, and I do not intend to leave behind an heir who can't keep these slavering dogs in line." She ruffles my hair lightly, with so much tenderness that it almost cracks my brain in half to exist in a moment with both my mother's playful affection and a man bleeding out on the floor.

I haven't forgotten her solemn vow to break me over her knee, and I know this moment is her opening salvo. She means to make this normal—to let the realities of empire mold me the way she was molded. Her parents must have done the same to her, to raise a woman who'd cut her sister's throat for the throne.

She expects me to sink to her depravity as a way of groveling for forgiveness. I can never give her the satisfaction.

"This man has you to thank for his predicament," she continues, slipping her hand down to my shoulder and turning me so I can't look anywhere but at the carnage splayed out on the ground before me. "He saw your weakness and thought that meant the time was ripe for his play. Lorne sys-Acua, do you believe my heir is weak?"

"No, Your Majesty," he croaks.

My mother lets out a disappointed huff. My father bends down with the knife. I close my eyes. If the point is for me to see this, I won't. But there's nothing I can do to block out Acua's keening groan as yet another line carves down his skin.

"Come now," my mother croons. "You know you won't leave this room alive—why bother with the act? Will you really die a simpering sycophant? If you're the kind of person who dared to make a play for the throne, surely you'll meet your end with more pride than this."

I sneak a glance at Acua, at the complicated expression playing over his face. Pain has left him with so little capacity for anything but feeling it—and yet, there's something starting to harden into resolve in the way he clenches his jaw. "You want me to have pride?" he snarls. "I didn't act in pride. I acted in *shame*. Shame that the blood that rules us has grown so thin. Umber deserves better than that boy, and it clearly isn't coming out of your line any time soon. I tried to save my system—the system my blood rules by a right passed down for generations—from the ruin he'll bring on it."

My father sits back on his haunches. Yltrast emp-Umber's expression is implacable. Between his tacit silence and the way he's melted into the background of my mother's rule, I genuinely have no idea what makes him tick. Why does he go along with this cruelty? Why are his hands the ones soaked with blood right now?

His deep brown eyes tip up to lock on mine, and I realize the whole room is holding its breath, waiting for my response. *I'm* the one who's just been insulted. Who's being blamed for the impending collapse of a diseased empire that the accident of my birth has forced upon me. This is the part where my parents want me to grab a knife of my own and make the governor's words another lie I carve into his skin.

Instead, I turn to my mother and say, "I have nothing to prove to this man. You're just going to kill him anyway. If you want me to prove my worth to the empire and clear my name in the eyes of the public, I have a better proposition."

Her lips twist into a sour smirk. "You may have nothing to prove to this man, but he's not your only audience. So tell me—what's your bright idea?"

"Send me to the front."

I can feel a past version of myself clawing at the walls for even *breathing* this suggestion. When I was imprisoned in Ettian's court, the mere idea that I would accompany him to the war's ragged edge terrified me so much that I made a half-assed attempt at squirming to freedom through the vents.

Now, it's the next stage of the plot we cooked up in that dusty little apartment. If I'm to follow through on my part, I need to secure a command. It's bold and reckless to show my hand so early, but I can't let the empress think that Breha has smothered my ambitions.

"I'll take the Wraiths," I continue in the measured silence my mother allows. "Gods know you'd rather have them out of the capital. They've fought on the lines before, and they'll watch my back. You give me a wing of the Imperial Fleet, and I'll make Archon wish he'd let me drag him back here. These pissants can keep squalling about how unfit I am to rule. I'll make them eat every word."

My mother's eyes have lit up, and for a brief, foolish moment, I think I've impressed her. Then the snort escapes. She collapses into a giggle that works at terrifying odds with the knife in her hand. "Gods of all systems," the empress scoffs. "After the nonsense you pulled with the Archon commodore? With the Archon emperor? How could you possibly expect anyone to fall in line under your command?"

"With the bloodright in my veins—" I start, but she cuts me off with a snap of her fingers.

"You are not a tactical commander. You are an emperor—and that means that your first duty is to governance, not warfare. And governance, my dear, is *this,*" she says, emphasizing her point with a vicious jab of the knife toward Acua. "You must establish respect in the core, not at the warfront, and let it bloom outward. What's more, you can't be trusted anywhere remotely *near* Archon territory after the last stunt you pulled."

My hands ball to useless fists. "The last stunt I pulled had the usurper in hand—the only reason it fell apart was because the knight outmaneuvered us."

"The knight is a foot soldier," Iva emp-Umber declares with a dismissive flip of her hand. "A desperate artifact Archon insists on propping up as their beacon of hope. You weren't outmaneuvered by a pawn—you were outmaneuvered by the person who put her on the board. And until you can properly identify who your true enemy is and crush him with all the power inherent in your blood, there is no place for you on the warfront."

There's a quiet rage building in me, urging me to protest. Why not make an utter fool of myself, begging my mother to send me off to the front lines? My play was utterly transparent. She knows right now all I want is to be closer to Ettian—even if there's a field of clashing dreadnoughts between us.

"You want command?" she asks, her eyes narrowing. "Then you'll prove to me—and to all of Umber—that you can put your empire before your personal feelings. I have something in mind. Your penance for that complete travesty at the border and the prisoner you cost us in your bid to get yourself out there."

A chill washes over me. I knew my actions would have consequences. Knew I'd have to be ready to do whatever it took to weather them. But in my mother's cold stare, I see the way it'll test my soul and wonder if I'm prepared to win my command on her terms.

As if she can read my mind, a slight smirk tugs the corner of her lips. "If you'd like to practice beforehand . . ." The empress holds up the knife, slipping her fingers tenderly around its bloody blade as she tips its hilt toward me.

The last time she pushed a knife at me, I took it without question. It was just me and her in the room, and I had no illusions about using it on either one of us. Now I know that laying my hand on the blade is a choice I can't take back.

Well, if my mother wants to see mettle, this is all she gets—the quiet, unblinking look I give her as I fold my hands carefully behind my back.

Iva emp-Umber clicks her tongue in disappointment, spinning the blade in her palm so quickly that I almost miss the moment her fingers tuck seamlessly back around the hilt. "I should have involved you in the work sooner," she says, stalking toward Acua. "But you'll get your taste for it soon enough. Watch carefully. See what it takes to govern. And once I'm certain you can apply it—only then will I unleash you on Archon."

She crouches at the governor's side and lifts him by his sweat-slicked hair.

I close my eyes.

CHAPTER 15

ETTIAN

FROM THE OBSERVATION DECK of the Tyrol repair yards' main station, there isn't much to observe. I stand with my hands folded behind my back, staring out through the duroglass at the hulking, shadowy forms of warships in the clutches of the station's spidery struts and the lines staging behind them, some still trailing debris in their wake. Most would say that the hits these ships took were worth it, for it seems that General Iral has struck a decisive blow in the battle to liberate Duvar System from Umber tyranny. But the losses were heavy, and Duvar still isn't completely ours, and all I can think about is how many people can't say the sacrifices were worth it because they *were* the sacrifices laid down for the sake of a half-baked victory.

I returned to my empire in a daze, barely grasping that something momentous had happened in the time that I was away. The medical wards were overflowing with soldiers recovering from hull breaches, and I slid seamlessly among them, just another in an assembly line of decompression sickness for our doctors to treat. I was still reeling from the events of our rendezvous, still disoriented from my brush with the void, and in absolutely no condition to dive back into the chaos of war.

Unfortunately, I didn't get a choice in the matter. Wen did her best to barricade the ward against my administration for long enough to let a doctor take a look at me. The physician said I should make a full recovery with adequate bed rest.

Naturally that's been in short supply.

"Your Majesty," a low, sonorous voice announces, tearing me from the sight of the scarred members of my fleet. I turn to find General Iral crossing the deck, dressed—as I've rarely seen him these days—in simple fatigues, no markers of rank anywhere in sight. "I was hoping to speak with you."

We spoke just this morning, in the daily briefing where he laid out the extent of the damages to the fleet, once again trying to frame them in the context of what it bought for us. But that was before the rest of the administration. Now, Iral approaches me without so much as an aide in tow. It's no doubt some kind of play, which means I need to stay alert. "I have a moment," I reply, inviting him to my side with one hand as with my other I signal for the two guards watching over me to take their distance.

"First of all," the general says, joining me at the window with a respectful incline of his head, "I never properly thanked you for restoring the commodore. While it's clear your meeting with the Umber delegation did not go . . . entirely as planned, it's impossible to dismiss that you brought Esperza home, and for that you have my eternal gratitude."

"It was Wen's operation," I offer with a humble shrug. "Really the most I did was act as bait and fly the ship for part of it."

The general's brow furrows. "Yes, I've just come from a meeting with the Flame Knight where she told me all about how she staged it. It almost sounded like she had the plan in motion *before* she brought you in on what she was planning. I worry, sometimes, about the amount of rein you give her. Her reach has a tendency of exceeding her rank."

It's a favorite thread of his whenever he has a moment alone with me, but I'm not new to my crown anymore, and I fix General Iral with an imperious look. "Like how you ran an offensive against Duvar the moment I wasn't around to oversee it? My order, if I remember correctly, was to hold the line."

"The line remains held," Iral replies tersely. "And now we've punched a hole in Duvar's defenses that will take months to fill, leaving us an opening to liberate those worlds before Umber has a chance to tighten their grasp again."

I stare out at the nearest dreadnought, my eyes drawn to the horrific hole torn clean through its outer hull. The sheer scale of it sends my mind reeling, and I wonder how many people were on the outer deck when the strike obliterated it. At this distance, the build struts the repair yard workers have laid over it are gossamer thin, and a line of prefabbed plates stretches up beneath them, vying to do their part to fill the hole.

I've been trying to win this war with trickery and misdirection. General Iral has been trying to win with force, the way wars are *meant* to be fought. The sight of the damage a single victory has wrought makes me wonder if I'm fooling myself, thinking there's any way out of this disaster that doesn't involve punching straight through it.

"Your Majesty," Iral starts, his voice shockingly gentle. For a moment, I'm rocketed back to the only private conversation I had with the man before he knew who I was—when I was just an Archon kid begging for a place in his rebellion and he was my childhood idol brought back from the dead. He had pictures of my parents hung on his wall, the empty shell of a powersuit standing in the corner of his office, and a dream to revive Archon I could scarcely believe. "With respect, you are the emperor—I fight for the sake of all that your bloodright claims. But I've also been a soldier as long as you've been alive. Decades of experience went into the decision to mobilize at Duvar. I don't make these decisions to challenge your rule—I make them to enforce it. And I don't make them lightly. I have decades of costs weighed upon my shoulders. I feel the weight of these losses, and it's part of my job to keep them from corrupting your ability to rule, as it was when I served your parents."

What ability to rule? I stop myself from blurting. So far the most I've done for the Archon Empire is provide a rallying point. People have united under the notion of restoring my bloodright, but I don't know what to do with the millions of eyes that have turned upon me, convinced my rule is the answer to their suffering under Umber tyranny. I want to give the people something better than myself. I don't want to have to give my whole self to do it.

"I appreciate your service and your experience," I start. "I wish I had the experience Archon needs from me."

"In my experience," Iral says, a half smile on his weathered face, "often some good sense is enough to fill in the gaps."

I sigh. "You're referring to Breha again, I assume."

Iral closes his eyes. "Do you want my counsel?"

My heart's already been given so many reasons to ache, but Iral's words press into it anew. I know I need guidance. I know there's no one better to give it than him. Protecting Gal from him while we had him captive tore an irrevocable gap between us, one that forced me to work in opposition to the general during one of the most fraught parts of the campaign.

Now, well. Maybe it's time to see if we can mend it. "What would your next course of action be after an . . . incident like the one on Breha?"

Iral's eyes fix on the work being done out in the yards, tracking the progression of a tugcraft as it begins to maneuver one of the patches toward the wounded dreadnought's hull. "The first thing you must do is absolutely everything in your power to distance yourself from the notion that you're sympathetic to Umber. After the footage from Breha, the people are beginning to gossip about the implications of your meeting with the Umber heir. The marriage proposal is still a tightly held secret, but I've seen speculation that it's on the table. That has the greatest chance of creating problems."

"You'd think clawing free from him in an all-out brawl would read clearly as a rejection," I mutter, which earns a chuckle from Iral.

"I'm just the messenger. That's how things are developing. And unfortunately Biss let me know that the Corinthian delegation has developed some serious reservations about moving forward with an alliance."

"I suppose that's within their rights," I sigh. "No chance you'll put in a good word for me?"

"Depends on what your plan of action is, Your Majesty," Iral says with a wry smile.

"So I have to figure out some brilliant move that shuts down all suspicion of a pact with Umber, wins back the Corinthians, and proves once and for all that Archon will be restored?"

"And bolsters recruitment," the general adds casually. "If we're to sustain this war, we need to grow our forces, and our rates have taken a hit. We may need to start discussions about a draft if current trends continue."

I grimace. For a moment there, I almost felt like the two of us were united in purpose. I wanted to cling to that feeling, to feel like I have proper guidance for once. But I don't know if I can ever condone forcing my people to fight my war. It goes against everything my crown stands for, against the very notion of existing to serve the people. I can see the monstrous necessity of it from the general's perspective, but it's something I know my parents never would have allowed.

Then again, my parents lost.

I let out a long sigh. Out in the yards, the pinprick sparks of laser welders start the work of stitching the patch plate against the dreadnought's hull, work that looks unfathomably delicate from a distance. "I imagine the Duvar offensive didn't do much to help with that either."

"No," Iral admits. "The reality of war is rarely inspiring. So this brilliant move of yours is probably not something played out on a battlefield."

"Corinth wants me to shut down all possibility of our movement capitulating to Umber," I muse. "So I have to commit to Corinth—or at least the idea of forging an alliance with Corinth. Something big. Something public."

Iral hums in agreement. "I . . . hesitate to even mention it, but Iffan raised an interesting point. Honestly, I believe it was more of a joke, but once she said it, I couldn't help but think there was some truth behind her remark. Granted, my expertise is in war, not politics," the general says with a deferential hand gesture. "So I'm not entirely sure if such a thing is feasible. Or . . . desirable for you. I wouldn't move on it until we're certain the Corinthian delegation thinks it's a good idea. But I believe there's an option."

Well, if it's coming from Wen, it's probably both a horrible idea and the thing that's going to save us all. "Enlighten me," I tell him.

I'd missed Rana's gravity. Nothing pulls you down quite like your homeworld, and I haven't been back since I departed for the warfront all those months ago. Now I find myself in yet another shuttle, circling a crowd as we wait for the security sweeps to clear, and even though there are a thousand reasons to worry, the steady feeling of the planet I was born on beneath me is a balm that soothes them all.

The skies are clear, the winds are gentle, and the pilot flies with a steady hand. Even though my nerves are strung taut, it feels like the day's been bolstered by good omens.

Wen catches my eye from the other side of the hold. Unlike the last time we did this, she isn't dressed to drop. Her lower half is free of the exoskeleton cage that kept her makeshift boot thrusters stable, and even though the galaxy knows the powersuit is back in her hands, today isn't the day for it. Instead, she wears a fine set of armor trimmed in curling platinum threads. Her hair has been woven into a complicated braid stitched with more silvery metal, and the total effect is downright stunning. She's rough and fine all at once, and impossible to look away from.

Until she pulls a face at me, and my composure breaks. "That's better," she chuckles as I bury my smirk in one hand. "You looked like we're about to go to war."

In a way, we are. Sure, we've been at war for months now, but what we're about to pull is going to be a defining moment. Umber's response to our slow crawl through the Archon systems has been lackluster at best, always held back by the vague promise of diplomacy.

This is a tactical nuke to their reservations.

The shuttle touches down, the rumble of the engine replaced by the murmurs of the gathered crowd. They know something big is happening, but we need the first news that Umber receives to be the most effective punch we can manage, which means that so far, the details of the event have been kept on a strict need-to-know basis. I'm sure many of them have guessed that their emperor and their knight are aboard—and probably they're disappointed that Wen didn't take to the skies for the pre-rally antics they've come to expect.

The cheers start the second the ramp cracks. Both of us unstrap and rise from our seats as our guard moves in to do the same. Side by side, we face the spill of brilliant winter sunlight that blasts into the hold.

Side by side, we process out into the public eye.

The whispers start the moment we emerge and chase us along the long walk up the lawn of the palace, audible even under the triumphant thunder of the imperial skin drums that flank our path. Mixed with the hum of the deflector armor I wear under a decorative shell, it's driving my stress to a fever pitch. I try to keep my eyes steady on the dais ahead, but the temptation to sweep my surroundings for gun barrels is overwhelming. My gut twinges. I can't tell how much of the noise is from the way my image has been tarnished by the Breha incident and how much of it is people realizing what's going on here. I'm not sure what's worse.

"Keep flying," Wen murmurs between her teeth, a sunny smile locked onto her face.

My nerves calm slightly as we reach the rows of officers stationed on either side of the walk. All of them are dressed out, their uniforms pressed to perfection and their platinum polished to shine. I slow our progress, making eye contact with each of my soldiers as we pass. Most maintain their implacable composure, their gazes locked to the middle distance, but there are three exceptions, all of them standing nearest to the stage.

Adela Esperza can't help smirking.

Deidra con-Silon can't help rolling her eyes at her wife's lack of decorum.

And Maxo Iral gives me a slight nod. I don't know if I've ever seen him look more proud of me.

As we mount the stairs up to the raised dais, I offer my arm, and Wen takes it, tucking one calloused hand into the crook of my elbow with a coy smile as the sight of it sends a little shock wave through the crowd's noise. I've been careful with my conduct in the public eye—up until Breha annihilated any dignity I had left. I knew there were rumors floating around about my relationship with Gal, and I always maintained a careful distance between myself and my subordinates to quash any extrapolations people might make about my character.

If they're this scandalized by me guiding Wen up the stairs, they're going to lose their minds when the chaplain appears.

There's no going back now. The time to call this off was back in the shuttle, and the person whose call it was is the one matching me step for step up the stairs. As in all things, Wen walks fearlessly forward, her head held high and her lips turned to a half smile that promises she's already thinking twenty steps ahead.

At the top of the stairs, I turn toward her, glancing back over our shoulders at the sprawling crowd. The drums fade to a quiet, simmering roll. My heart feels like it's about to break the deflector armor casing my chest with the way it's hammering. I don't know what I'm hoping to find in the sea of upturned faces. Approval? Forgiveness? A divine sign that I'm altering the course of history the *right* way?

I suppose Gal would say that my bloodright is the only assurance I need.

But really, the only assurance I need is the wicked smile Wen gives me when she catches my eye. It's a look I know all too well—a look I've seen her pass my way a hundred times, from the day we first met to the parking garage where I lost all hope to the first time I saw her resplendent in a powersuit. It's the look that says *Stick with me, buddy. You're about to see some serious shit.*

I grin back, knowing a thousand lenses are capturing the moment, hoping desperately that none of them are attached to sniper barrels. Together, we turn to face the chaplain who has just mounted the dais from the opposite side.

The crowd's hum ramps up into a dull roar, but I don't hear any objections in the wave of noise that crashes over me. The chaplain stretches out his arms, setting his hands on our shoulders. "Under the sight of the god of this system and witnessed by the assembled," he intones, "I invite you to take your oaths."

One of the aides in my escort steps forward, bearing a cushion with two platinum rings.

Wen picks up the larger one, turning it over in her hands so that the intricate, spiraling grooves carved into it catch the light. She takes my hand and lifts it to her chest, placing it over her heart. Through the layers of decorative armor and the rattle of the deflector shielding, I can tell it's hammering just as hard as mine. She's made a career of leaping without looking, trusting herself to stick the landing—whether it's getting into trouble with the Isla mob, throwing herself into the *Fulcrum*'s engines, or turning Gal over to Hanji Iwam.

But this is a leap on a whole new scale. A leap that requires absolute faith not only in herself but also in me. We've been in this together since the moment we met, but now, in the sight of the galaxy, we're formalizing it.

She slips the ring over my trigger finger and in the clearest, most honest voice, announces, "On my blood and all that it owns, I swear loyalty to you and no other."

They're the same words my mother once spoke, brought from the distant edge of the Archon Empire to ascend to its rule side by side with my father. But even though her origins were humble, Henrietta emp-Archon was still forsaking a bloodright with that vow. Framed from an imperial perspective, Wen has nothing to forsake.

I picture Iva emp-Umber's lip curling at the sight of this farce. Umber's method of imperial courtship is founded on the belief that the best partner will come from the upper echelons of their gentry. She thought she could defuse the war by framing me as an adequate match for her heir and shoving us together.

I pick up the second ring, take Wen's hand, and pull it to my chest, wondering how many people can guess that the soft smile I wear is at the thought of how ferociously I'm slamming that door shut in the Umber empress's face. I move with care as I slip the ring down over her scars and calluses, the signs of a life of humble labor not even the greatest Archon imperials could brag. "On my blood and all that it owns," I tell her steadily, "I swear loyalty to you and no other."

I'm not sure what I expected to feel, but it certainly wasn't the relief that floods through me as the door to peaceful alliance with Umber latches and locks. With this vow, I'm not just declaring allegiance to my empire but to the principles it stands for, the principles without which we might as well be an annexation of Umber. We're a people who believe our rulers are at the service of our people, that their highest duty is to uplift the best among us to the roles that best suit them, no matter where they come from.

Now I choose Wen to share my bloodright, and while it aligns with Archon values, it's also something utterly new. Wen is Corinthian, and my gesture extends to the Corinthian allies we hope to court in this fight. Their political system hinges on elected bodies and appointments, the concept of bloodright somewhat barbaric in their minds. By marrying someone who once lived on the streets of their fringes, I declare my friendship and my commitment to a brand-new way forward for the governance of the reforged Archon Empire. It may be difficult for my people to wrap their heads around, but my wager is that they prefer it far more than the alternative.

I hazard a glance at the Corinthian ambassadors, whose blinding white garb makes them impossible to miss in the crowd. Biss Xhosi seems to be biting back a wry smile. I'm hoping that's a good sign.

The chaplain tightens his grip on our shoulders. "With oaths sworn and rings exchanged, this bond is recognized in the sight of the god of Tosa. As witnessed by the Archon people, it stands in the law of the empire." His hands slip away as he takes a respectful step back.

There's one more stage to this plan—one we haven't consulted any of the rest of the administration about. I meet my new wife's eyes and find them shimmering with a merry challenge. The crowd rumbles around us, murmurs growing as they wait for the first action we take as a wedded pair. In past imperial weddings—in my parents', where there was no love match to declare—the newly joined couple typically bows in deference to the people they serve. There will be some among the people watching who call this whole thing a sham, convinced I still carry a torch for the enemy's heir.

I move to silence them with my left hand, reaching up to cradle the scarred side of Wen's face as I draw her forward. She slings her arm around my shoulders as I fit one hand to her waist, sweeping her around and dipping her.

This I feared even more than marrying her, even more than doing so in front of a crowd. *Sell it or else,* a dire voice warns in the back of my head. *But not too well, or Gal's going to kick your ass.*

With the way Wen's looking at me—with that sly smile that says everything's going to be okay as long as we're together—I can't help but grin back, honest as I've ever been, the second before my lips take hers.

CHAPTER 16

GAL

THERE ISN'T A BOTTLE of polish strong enough for how drunk I need to be right now.

If I had my way, I'd be locked in the Wraiths' rumpus room, smothered by the suffocating noise of Hanji's abrasive oldies playlist and drowning in their stash. Instead, I'm crowned, primped, and quietly suffering before the entire Umber court.

The dinner service has just begun, dulling the noise of the gossip that's been flying nonstop since the first guests arrived. I pick at my food, but I haven't been able to muster an appetite in three days.

The sight of Ettian emp-Archon marrying someone else will do that, apparently.

My mother made damn certain I watched the full footage of the wedding the second the news arrived. She hovered over me like I was a newborn, waiting for the moment my rage broke me down so she could sweep in and start sticking the pieces together. I tried to show her I was in control, keeping myself at a careful simmer.

Tonight, she hopes I'll sputter into a full boil.

I catch her making a careful study of me from the high table, where she sits resplendent in her finest glass-black gown, side by side with my father. I should be seated with them, elevated as an equal by my crown. The fact that I'm not—that I've been relegated to an adjacent table with my Wraiths—is fueling a good portion of the rumors our guests are circulating tonight, with the rest amply charged by the Breha incident and its fallout.

The empress holds my gaze and jerks her knife up ever so slightly, the signal so clear she might as well have snapped, *Sit up straight, you little shit,* for the court to hear. I oblige her, but only barely. Tonight's performance has an arc, and that arc requires a bit of buildup.

I've already made the rounds through the system governors and their attachés, doling out time to each table like I was dividing toys among a pack of toddlers. Some needed to be rewarded for good behavior with a long, pointless conversation about supply lines. Others needed to be rebuked with stiff, brusque words for their insufficient support for the war effort—sorry, the *quelling of the rebellion,* because half of being at war is never admitting it to the general populace.

Most chilling of all, I shook hands with the newest governor among our ranks, the beautiful young Vera sys-Acua. If she had any qualms about the way she deposed her father and took his blood-right out from under him, they didn't show in her delicate smile and the bright laugh she gave at something I said that was nowhere near funny. I nearly rolled my eyes at her transparency. *Oh, I just happen to be the governor of the Umber Core's most critical system, of an age with you, and I love your jokes?* Give me a ruttin' break.

Then again, given the strength of her play against her father, I suppose I should be watching less for a proposal and more for a knife in the back.

I've been treating the evening's security like a dare, mostly to spite my mother. I imagine her knuckles going white beneath the table as I lean just a little too close to everyone I greet. Am I tempting fate? Possibly.

Am I trying to find a way out of this dinner by any means necessary? Absolutely.

Eager anticipation suffuses the room, floating on the whispers of gossip and sparking through the clinking of silverware. Our guests know a state dinner like this means a spectacle, and they're waiting for it to arrive, wondering what it might be, and praying to every god listening that it doesn't involve them. Historically, these have been popular venues for surprise assassinations, spur-of-the-moment executions, and occasionally grand announcements of bequeathment as newly acquired territories were handed out to the eager and the loyal. The Umber elite are so addicted to the thrill of it that it cancels out any dread they might feel.

I, on the other hand, feel like I'm made entirely of dread.

"Loosen up," Hanji mutters from my right. "Acua is making eyes at you again."

"Stop saying that like it's a good thing," I mutter, scowling at my plate.

"Look, if Ettian gets a hot wife, you should at *least* be able to—"

I silence her with a kick under the table. I know she's just trying to get me out of my head, and on any other day I'd appreciate it. Hanji's constant antagonism has spared me from more panic attacks than I can count in the days since we returned to the heart of the citadel, but if I fail tonight, all of our schemes will be for nothing. The fate of the galaxy is at stake—I'm well within my rights to stay tense.

And with the main course wrapping up, it's almost time for tonight's entertainment.

The room's anxious atmosphere has hardly touched the Wraiths. Ollins is shoveling a second helping of food down with gusto while Rin and Rhodes argue loudly over some inscrutable bit of engineering. They look so at ease that I can't help smiling—though of course it drops the second I realize Hanji's grinning back at me.

"You sentimental little—"

I cut her off again, this time with a twitch of a gesture. I can feel my mother's eyes on us. The weight of what I have to do next grinds down heavy on my shoulders.

But the moment has come—I can feel it in the chatter of our

guests growing louder as they wait for a new course to appear, some of them craning their necks as they scan the court for their next amusement. It's now or never.

Now or no wing of the fleet under my command.

I rise to my feet and feel the way it *pulls* this room. A hundred hungry eyes snap to me, conversations sputtering to a halt. I've dressed to command their attention, my suit a slick liquid black woven through with brass threads so fine that they're only visible when they catch the light. My hair's smoothed back, tamed under the weight of the angular crown set upon my brow. Tonight is one of the rare occasions where I need to unquestionably outshine my court's splendor. I try to remind myself I'm not prey in a predator's sights—I'm a star with the gravitational force to capture an entire system. Doesn't make it any less disconcerting, because I know exactly what all these governors are after.

In the wake of Breha, there have been plenty of rumors that I've fallen out of favor with my mother, bolstered by my carefree court appearances and my well-known history with Archon. Vera sys-Acua was able to use those rumors to wrest a system from her father's grip and feed the old man to the empress's cruelty. Those who wish to follow in her footsteps—or stave off any members of their family who might be plotting something similar—know they have to watch carefully for openings. Chances to apply pressure.

And this certainly looks like it has potential.

"I'd like to propose a toast," I announce, casting my voice loud enough to echo off the looming brass panels that hang overhead. With a crook of my fingers, I pull one of the roving stewards to my side and pluck a bottle and five empty glasses from her tray. "A toast," I continue, laying out the glasses and filling them one by one with a generous pour, "to my finest companions."

Now I feel like the court's proper blazing center. A few murmurs filter from the back, but nothing can hold a candle to the way I've commanded the room's attention. Out of the corner of my eye, I spot a few of the governors I passed curt words to earlier go noticeably looser as they realize they've been spared the court's merciless focus.

"Some of you may not know my Wraiths," I start with a magnanimous sweep of my hand. "You may not know Hanji Iwam, the only person in the empire who's managed to put a scratch on the Archon usurper. It was her bullet that downed him on Ellit, just as he thought he was celebrating a moment of triumph. Give her a hand."

Hanji takes the applause with a cocky smile and a flip of the wrist that reads as *oh, stop.*

"You may not know Rin Atsana, who flew the harrowing run to rescue me from Archon's clutches—and did it all in a Beamer, if you'll believe it."

Rin looks like she's about to interrupt with the necessary corrections—that we were in a Beamer that had been cleared to leave the Archon fleet by Ettian himself and that the *Ruttin' Hell* barely qualifies as a Beamer after all the enhancements Adela Esperza socked into it—but then she thinks better of it and gives the court's noises of admiration a dainty, almost bashful wave.

"You may not know Rhodes Tsampa, who engineered an infiltration of a rebel dreadnought that allowed this team to live in the vents for *weeks* with security none the wiser."

Rhodes flashes me a warning look as the court seems to waver between continuing their sycophantic applause and wondering whether it's really a good thing that dreadnoughts can be hacked like that.

Before they can start to dwell on it, I continue, "And you may not know Ollins Cordello, who . . . has *many* fine accomplishments, though the one I find most impressive personally is that he's the only person in the history of the Umber Imperial Academy on Rana to successfully streak the officer quarters all the way to the head's door."

Ollins tips a bow to the applause and laughter, cracking a blinding smile at a daring whoop from a young staffer near the back.

"It's no understatement to say that these four have saved my life. They pulled me from Archon's grasp, right out from under the nose of the Flame Knight herself. When the Flame Knight dared to show her face in this very capital, my Wraiths leapt into pursuit without hesitation."

I bite down on the urge to check whether my mother buys any of these outright lies. Whether or not she believes them hardly matters—it's all about the narrative I'm selling our guests.

"My Wraiths. My companions. The bravest, most loyal friends a young emperor could ask for."

Breaths start to catch around the court. The more seasoned governors present recognize this oration style. They know this part is the buildup.

The next is the reversal.

"I could stand here all night singing their praises," I say, letting my voice drop from a sonorous projection to a low, level, lethal tone. "But none of them would outweigh how they've failed me."

The conspiratorial grins drop from the Wraiths' faces. I notice some of my audience sneaking looks at my mother, no doubt wondering if this is sanctioned or a surprise. I keep my back square to the high table. Any backward glance will only cement their notion that I'm doing this because the empress forced me.

Even if I *am* doing this because she gave me no choice.

Her voice echoes in my head, cruel and inescapable. *Public displays are for enemies of the empire.*

"Oh, don't give me that look," I mutter, meeting Hanji's blazing eyes with an expression I'm certain I learned from my mother's court sessions. "Surely the four of you realized there would be consequences for Breha. Breha, where we had the Archon usurper *in hand*," I seethe, clenching my fist, "only for the four of you to let him escape."

The performance is killing me inside, but I give it my all. Breha went exactly as planned, even with the slight hiccup of Wen going off-script. The Wraiths followed orders to perfection. I wish *that's* what I could shout to the court—that my friends did the ruttin' impossible and staged an escape for Ettian and Wen from right under Iva emp-Umber's nose. I channel that frustration into the fury I'm trying to sell.

"We were up against the Flame Knight," Hanji spits.

"Flame *Empress*," Rin corrects, which gets a few nervous laughs from the court's fringes.

"There are four of you, and you *still* can't keep up with a Corinthian street rat," I reply. "What use are you to me?"

"We're your friends?" Ollins offers, and I have to fight to keep from letting it show how deep that one strikes.

"You four," I say against a rising tide of bile, "are a childish distraction. I understand that you earned yourselves a modicum of respect for rescuing me. Then you squandered it on cheap debauchery in the capital as the rebellion boiled over into not one but *two* of our justly won systems. And when it mattered most, you rutted up our one shot at galactic peace so badly that the only reason we're still alive is because of the Flame Knight's mercy."

Thus far we've been able to obscure the fact that my sudden disappearance from the Imperial Seat was planned under the empress's nose. To the public, I took the Wraiths on a covert mission in pursuit of "the Flame Knight" and Esperza after the failed execution, tracked them to their rendezvous with Ettian on Breha, and called in the fleet to block Archon's escape and bring him in loudly, publicly, and decisively. Only my mother knows that we were cozied up together for nearly a week in the intervening time, but for the sake of the crown's reputation, we're keeping that bit under wraps.

That leaves us to reckon with the humiliation of letting that plan fall apart and the way it's tanked any faith that I'll be a worthy successor. I have to show the Umber people—or at least the people who govern them—that I can be ruthless.

"I'm not so arrogant that I expect the people who serve me to be flawless," I say, picking up the drinks I've poured and circling the table as I distribute them one by one. "I understand that some mis-

takes are lessons. Some mistakes are calls to do better. And so tonight, I would like to toast to my Wraith Squadron, and to their
failure. My friends, drink with me."

I lift my glass, and the Wraiths join the toast. Their hands are
steady as they raise their drinks, but their expressions have gone
grim. Hanji's eyes catch mine through the warped prism of her glass,
and my breath goes still in my throat at the rage etched into her
gaze. Her whole life's been shaped by the vicissitudes of bloodright
and she, more than any of the others, understands exactly what I'm
saying—and exactly why I've been backed into this corner.

I realize after a second that I'm waiting for some clever words,
some jab to undercut the tension—something so quintessentially
Hanji that it feels wrong to proceed without it. But for once in her
life, my Wraith waits in silence for my next order.

I tip my glass to her, then knock it back with a single swallow.
The polish strips my throat raw, but I stone-face through it, watching as the Wraiths follow suit. To their credit, none of them so much
as wince, though Ollins lets out a little burble of a cough into his
fist.

The court's dropped into a cold silence, a chorus of held breaths
waiting for my next move. I set my glass back on the table, and I
swear the sound of it ricochets like a gunshot off the brass paneling
that swoops down from the ceiling.

I will not look back at my mother.

I will not—

Rin, tiny Rin, is the first to crack, her hand clawing up to her
throat as she releases a hacking cough. Noises of alarm bubble up
from the crowd as Rhodes joins in, clutching his stomach as he bends
over a protracted wheeze. Ollins's face floods red, and he fights back
a grunt.

Only Hanji manages to keep completely quiet. Her furious gaze
burns into me as she fights, fights, then slumps slowly forward into
her half-finished dinner.

I fold my hands behind my back and watch with a downright
heroic impassivity as my Wraiths go still and silent. I can feel the

anxious gazes of the courtiers who were paying attention—who saw me drink from the same pour—but the only surprise I have to offer them is my continued existence. I'm the Umber heir, and before the eyes of my governors, I'll show them I'm not so easily toppled.

Beneath it all, my gut roils. I once dreamed I'd defy my mother's cruel spectacle, that I'd forge a kinder empire. All I've done—all I *could* do, in the end—is let her mold me into exactly the monster she wanted all along.

"This I swear to you," I say, fighting back the nausea as I turn to my audience and spread my arms wide. "I have learned from my failure. I loved my Wraiths, but I must put the good of the Umber Empire ahead of my heart and let them reap the rewards of their mistakes. And no doubt you already know—I once held the Archon usurper dear to me."

At this, I turn at last and meet my mother's cold, dark eyes. She's tilted ever-so-slightly forward in her seat, eager and hungry and the proudest I've ever seen her. I lift a hand to her, gesturing over my friends' bodies, over the consequences, over the price I've paid.

"I am ready to redeem myself from my failure with him too," I announce, and feel the horrible power of my bloodright rattle through the court with the weight of the words. "Give me a wing of the Imperial Fleet, and let me burn him to the ground."

"You won't just have a wing," Iva emp-Umber replies, her eyes blazing with sickening satisfaction. "It's time the fleet deployed in full, with your bloodright at the helm."

CHAPTER 17

ETTIAN

"I THINK MARRIED LIFE SUITS ME," Wen emp-Archon says, hands square on her hips as she stares out at the sun dawning gloriously through the thicket of Trost's skyscrapers. She's dressed in a robe with her hair a disheveled mess, all but daring the one-way duroglass that surrounds our balcony to fail.

I'm flat on my face in bed, one arm halfheartedly slung to spare my eyes from the worst of the brutal lighting. Wen's always been improbably energetic, but that was never a *problem* until I started sharing quarters with her. I let out a long, slow groan as I heave up onto my side. "What time?" I manage.

"Such imperial dramatics," she tuts.

"You're imperial too," I mutter—partly to make the point, but mostly to see the way it makes a grin even more brilliant than the rising sun break over her face.

Her coronation was a much quieter affair than the wedding. We staged it in the court, before all the ranking officials we could muster and an array of cameras to capture the moment for posterity. On that dais, before the assembled, I set the crown upon her head and felt the same relief I knew when I met her. We hold the same burden between us, and I can scarcely believe how freeing it is to share the load.

Then came the work. With any possibility of a peaceful alliance with Umber sufficiently crushed, Wen and I have been fielding non-stop meetings with the Corinthian delegation to formalize the terms of our alliance. At the same time, I've been wrangling the system, planetary, and continental lineages I've appointed to manage the fallout of my sudden decision to marry so egregiously outside of the system of bloodright. Another one of those is the first thing on the schedule for today, and it's got me less than willing to leave the comfort of my bed.

"Come on, *sweetheart*," Wen chides as she pads across the room and drops a knee on the mattress. "Empire's not going to run itself."

"Can we take 'sweetheart' off the table completely?" I grumble into my pillow. On top of the exhausting work of overhauling Archon politics, we're also mired in the charade of presenting our union as a love match. At times, it's a delightful grift and the only spot of levity in otherwise overwhelming days. Other times it's just another chore on top of all the others.

Too often it's a chance for Wen to be her delightfully annoying self. She smirks, trying to tug the pillow out of my grip. "Fine, how about . . ."

"Don't."

"Sugar lips?"

"I'll ruttin' kill you."

"Baby cakes?"

"Gods of all systems."

"Lovey—"

A rap on the door cuts mercifully through her noise. We exchange a glance, then move all at once, rearranging ourselves so that she's sitting cross-legged on the mattress and my head is lying peacefully in her lap.

"Enter," she calls with the authoritative ring of an imperial, trailing one gentle hand along my stubble.

An aide peers through the door, then quickly averts their eyes when they realize the quiet intimacy they've intruded on. "Majesties," they start, their voice professionally stiff. "Your first audience of the day is in one hour."

"Thank you, Torvin," Wen says. "We'll be dressed in fifteen minutes."

As the door slips closed, Wen reaches for her datapad. I'm halfway to the wardrobe when a sudden surprised hum from her stops me in my tracks. "What is it?" I ask.

"News from Umber," she murmurs. "It's done. Gal got the fleet—not just a wing, the *whole rustin' fleet*—and they're readying for full deployment. But he had to . . . Look, you should just read it."

When I finish taking in the report she shoves my way, I glance up to find Wen uncharacteristically curled in on herself. "Hey," I breathe, sliding back into bed at her side. "Talk to me."

"It's fine," she says, turning to give me more of her scar. I don't round out and force her to face me this time. I'm just as shell-shocked as she is. The report includes some choice excerpts from Umber news media—excerpts that show the bodies. Of course Iva emp-Umber would make damn certain her son's ruthlessness would be on full display to friend and foe alike, but I don't think anything could have prepared us for the sight of the four Wraiths slumped against a banquet table, their eyes half open and their skin graying.

It seems like just yesterday we were all under one roof, drinking and laughing like those nights we'd sneak into the academy control tower as we plotted to save the galaxy. That plan was going to have unknowns—places where we'd have to work around whatever the empress gave us.

This, though—this is a bigger hiccup than we anticipated. Gal was supposed to secure a command, and now he's got the whole Imperial Fleet at his fingers. But to convince his mother to give it to him, he had to pay the highest price she could ask.

I didn't think it would hit Wen this hard, but in this moment, I realize exactly what she's thinking. I let my hand slide from her shoulder to her back, rubbing a careful circle there. "I couldn't . . . I *wouldn't*. No matter what. Not even if the fate of the galaxy was on the line."

"As if I'd ever let you get the drop on me," Wen mutters thickly.

"That too," I huff around a laugh that feels outright wrong at a time like this. But there's an edge of a smile curling into Wen's cheek, and I know I've said what she needs to hear.

"C'mon, honey," she says, bumping her shoulder into mine. "Time to do our part."

Fortunately, our first meeting is over coffee. Unfortunately, it's with Bette sys-Tosa, matriarch of the lineage of system governors who fled the fall of the Archon Empire eight years ago, and she isn't exactly thrilled with me.

"We were under the impression," the governor begins, swirling a truly absurd amount of sugar into her drink with a tiny spoon, "that your intent when you took your crown was to reestablish bloodright rule throughout the reclaimed territories."

I force myself to keep from pulling a face. "Are you not restored to the lands that your lineage has held for generations?"

Tosa gives a humble nod, her eyes darting to the sweeping view of Trost's skyline that the observation deck where we've staged our little meeting offers. Something in her goes a little softer at the sight. "Your Majesty, you have my eternal thanks, and I don't wish to downplay all that you have done for my family. We never *dreamed* we might have a chance to serve our people again after Umber ripped us from our homeworlds. It's just . . . ."

There's no need to prompt her. I watch the governor levelly, knowing that at my side, Wen is doing the same. Under the combined weight of our gazes, Tosa has no choice but to continue her line of thought.

"Well, it's just that your choice to marry came as a bit of a shock. It is not, as I'm sure you're aware, how that sort of thing is traditionally done."

I set my own mug down, folding my hands together in front of me as the older woman fidgets in her chair. "My rule has been untra-ditional from the start," I point out, my tone soft and coddling. "We are not in the most typical of successions, and I don't have time to follow in my parents' footsteps."

"If I may," Wen adds after a moment of silence. I nearly grin at the deftness of it. Her question is directed at Tosa, all but forcing the governor to acknowledge the way power lies in the room.

"You need no permission from me, Your Majesty," Tosa says dip-lomatically.

Wen smirks. "You've been comfortable in the core since your in-stallation, correct?"

The governor nods, taking another sip of her coffee.

"I have been . . . less than comfortable. I'm sure word of it has made its way all the way back to Trost. I've been on that front. I've fought and bled for this empire and seen the scope of what we're fighting for."

"Majesty, I don't mean to downplay any of your accomplish-ments," the governor interjects hastily. "Gods, the Battle of Dasun—I fully recognize that I would not have my title and lands if it weren't for your heroism."

Wen holds up a hand, the gesture so perfectly imperial that I know she must have learned it from Gal, not me. That thought blooms sour as it settles, but I can't allow myself to get sidetracked. "Governor, what this all boils down to is a difference of opinion. You think I'm unfit to rule."

"I would never suggest—"

"That is patently untrue," Wen says, cutting off the governor's stammering. "You've done nothing *but* suggest it since we first sat down with you, even though by your own admission you would not have your position if it were not for my actions. Furthermore, you've been comfortably seated in the core ever since Rana was reclaimed at the start of this offensive, have you not?"

The older woman's mouth catches, halfway open for her next retort. She seals her lips and sets her mug carefully down on the table. "It is my duty and my inheritance to serve Archon from this position, and I've been privileged in my placement outside the immediate battlefront."

Wen spreads her hands beatifically. "There we go. Was that so hard? And there's one more piece to the puzzle, which I'm sure you'd be willing to elaborate on."

Tosa lets out a long sigh through her nostrils. "I have a son of an eligible age, and I had hoped that when the time was appropriate, he would be among those considered for the emperor's hand."

"Ambitious, I'll grant you," Wen says with a smile that veers on simpering. "I'm still somewhat new to Archon philosophy myself, but I must say your brand of it seems a little misaligned with the empire's core values. Little self-serving, no?"

"It's in the empire's best interest to be supported by a strong union," Tosa offers levelly.

"Define 'strong,'" Wen fires back. Her voice has a teasing edge to it, but her words are unambiguously a command, and Tosa has no way of ducking it.

The governor leans forward. "The revolution will only succeed with the right framing. It's been eight years since the conquest and six since Iral's last stand. The territories are *raw,* and we had accounted for that when we planned this movement. Having your bloodright to rally around became the focal point of our efforts," she says, nodding to me.

"I believe I understand where the governor's going with this," I say, tilting my chin. "We have to be careful to frame this as a restoration of the former order, not another conquest that will uproot what peace the people have managed to find since Umber took our worlds and wrung them out."

"Exactly so."

"And so your concern is that the notion of marrying a Corinthian with no bloodright to her name promises a new regime, not the one we've so carefully established as the foundation of our rebellion?"

"Your Majesty, what's done is done," the governor says helplessly. "Yes, as the empress points out, I would have preferred for you to choose a partner through the traditional tour of your holdings—and yes, I would have liked for you to consider my heir, but that ship's on its vector. All I'm urging now is that you let it be the boldest choice you make."

I drop my gaze to the black depths of my coffee. I knew my decision would ruffle feathers—especially among members of my administration who never knew that Umber was attempting to pressure me into a far worse marriage. But those feathers deserve to be ruffled. The mutters, the sideways glances, the way Tosa's trying to talk circles around her discomfort—they're all symptoms of a necessary fever that has to run its course.

"Governor," I start, placing my palms flat on the table. "I respect your experience and the wisdom it has granted you. You were governing these territories before I was even *born,* and I would be nothing without your faithful service. But as my wife has so rightly pointed out, your point of view is rather narrow. Your experience is in politics at the system level. We're fighting a war that impacts entire empires, and I hope your years have given you the wisdom to realize that falls outside your scope."

I turn one palm upward, and Wen slips her hand into it with no hesitation. I let a slight smirk curl over my lips, knowing she must be doing the same as we pin the governor under our haughty imperial gazes. We're light-years from two kids scheming in a garbage bin on the edge of the Corinthian Empire, and yet I know that's exactly what the governor sees when she looks at us—two street rats who've plotted their way to the pinnacle of the galaxy.

"The aim of my rule is not to restore the Archon Empire to its former glory," I continue, squeezing Wen's hand tight. "I believe we can be better. The restoration is an opportunity to reexamine the way we've distributed power and ask ourselves if it's truly what's best for our people. If anything, I think the past decade of Umber rule—the past *several* decades of Umber rule, if we factor in all the internal strife caused in the wake of Iva emp-Umber's succession—has proven that bloodright succession can so easily be led astray."

The governor looks like someone's spit in her coffee. "You want to dismantle a system that's worked for generations, that you yourself have profited from to the *extreme*, in the midst of a war?"

"I want to give the people of Archon an ideal to strive toward," I reply, fixing my eyes on my wife with all the shameless love in my heart. Wen lifts her chin, still staring at the governor, daring Tosa to counter that statement. *Go ahead,* her smirk says. *Say I'm not the ideal. Say every last horrible thing you think about me. I've proven everyone wrong so far—step right up to be next.*

"A noble intention," Tosa says at last, her fingers fidgeting around her mug. "Spoken with the confidence of youth—and perhaps we need that if we're to win this war."

"I have a proposition," Wen offers, her eyes narrowing cannily. "While we're putting our faith in the confidence of the young. Tell me about this son of yours."

Once again, Tosa can't duck a direct order—though I see the calculation splay over her face as she tries to figure out her response's angle of approach. "He's an honorable young man. Nineteen years of age. Spent his formative years at my knee in the refugee camps on Delos, learning the art of service and the ins and outs of governing our people. I claimed him openly as my heir ever since the fall of Archon—no point in shadowing him when Umber held our bloodright."

"Damn, maybe you're right," Wen chuckles, tapping the back of my hand. "Babe, this guy sounds like the total package. Maybe we *did* rush into things—"

"*Wen,*" I warn through gritted teeth, biting back the heat building in my cheeks.

"Kidding, kidding—the crown looks too good on me. *Anyway,*" Wen says, releasing my hand so she can clap hers together. "I've been working on an initiative with the Corinthian stakeholders. They've entered this war hoping to put distance between themselves and a bunch of bloodright-worshipping, power-hungry monsters, and that extends not just to beating back Umber but to making sure Archon doesn't become the enemy they're trying to defeat in the process."

"At the risk of sounding like a glitchy transmission," Tosa says, "I worry that the Corinthians are introducing too much complication. Is it not enough to let Archon govern itself as it always has for the span of this conflict? Must we turn our already overtaxed territories into a volatile testbed?"

Wen raises her fingers, her eyes lighting up. "See, that's the thing. I know my perspective is broad, but it doesn't include these matters. Yours does, but of course you're far too busy governing Tosa System to be involved in such a complicated effort. This son of yours, however . . ."

The governor's brow furrows. Wen's just told her that the new order is inevitable—and in the same move offered her a part in its legacy. Something tells me my empress has struck upon precisely what it is Tosa desires here. The governor's original hope was that she could broker a place for her son at my side, thus securing her family's position in the emperor's confidence.

I have a suspicion there's even more to it than that. Bette sys-Tosa was ripped from her bloodright eight years ago, and now has an heir of age at the moment she's restored to it. She seems to be passionate about governing, if not a little too ambitious, and that leads me to think that offering up her son as a potential partner wasn't just about the benefits she might reap by having an emperor in the family—it was also about getting her heir out from under her feet so she could enjoy her restored position a little longer. Her next oldest child still has five years until they can begin the succession process, giving her plenty of time to arrange things to her liking before she has to hand over the reins.

Of course, that's if the position of system governor hasn't been made obsolete by then.

"I know," Wen says, sensing the sticking point the governor's hit. "The Corinthians' ideal is a representative democracy that makes appointments, much like their own. The express goal of this initiative I'm talking about is to establish an elected council of planetary representatives who'll collaborate on issues within their systems. It's the kind of thing that could get overwhelmed by Corinthian thinking, which is why we need Archon guidance coming specifically from the system level. From my research, your son sounds like the perfect candidate."

Tosa sits back in her chair, letting out a long, weary sigh. A smile seems to be tugging on the edge of her lips despite herself. Her gaze slips to me. "Where did you say you found her again? Are you *sure* she's not from some long-lost line?"

I let out a short laugh, shaking my head. "Governor, I found her in a Corinthian junkyard. I know it violates your core principles to imagine that great leadership can come from outside an established bloodline, but we'll work on broadening that perspective."

The governor smirks. "Perhaps. I'll broach the topic with my son. Have your people send over a spec of what he's in for."

Wen beams. The crown has never looked lighter on her head, and once again, I'm astounded by how far she's come. It really shouldn't surprise me. She has a mind for systems, something that serves her equally well whether it's a dreadnought she's figuring out how to take apart or an empire she's trying to drag together. In a matter of weeks, she's learned the ropes of being an empress and applied that knowledge to prodigious effect.

Sure, winning Bette sys-Tosa over coffee is a small battle, but I can't help but believe it bodes well for the war to come.

The imperial court has come a long way since the day I first stormed into it, waving a platinum ring on my finger and demanding my blood-right. Under Berr sys-Tosa, the room was garishly Umber, boasting towering angular brass-plated statues and a ceiling that glimmered with inlaid obsidian. It's taken months to strip and redecorate, and the dusty scent of construction and fresh paint still lingers, but the results are terrifically worth it.

The walls have been painted a lush emerald green, textured by the holes left from the obsidian that's been pried away. Curling spirals of platinum threading creep toward the arched ceiling like vines. At last I feel like I can breathe in this space.

But the greatest improvement of all is the second throne that's been added to the dais. Wen sits primly upon it, dressed in a fine black suit with a flowing green cape hung from its shoulders that pools around her feet. The crown upon her head is twin to mine, the finest in our rotation, meant for occasions that merit a show.

Commodore Esperza has tried to convince us she doesn't warrant this fuss, but we easily overruled her. "You rejected the release from service I offered," I told her. "You live with the consequences."

Truthfully, I'm amazed she's returning to duty after barely two and a half months in recovery from her time as an Umber prisoner. She's shrugged off all attempts to grant her a longer period of rest, even when I essentially begged for it. It's the closest my marriage has come to an argument—Wen's a little more ruthlessly practical than me, and maintains that the whole goddamn *point* of extracting the commodore from Iva emp-Umber's clutches was because we need her on the field. *She's the only one who can make the call when to return,* my empress insists, *and she's made it.*

I tried to argue that the game has changed significantly since she made that call. With the Imperial Fleet about to enter the warfront under Gal's command, there's a significant chance Esperza's leadership could actually hinder more than help us if she does her job a little too well.

Leave that part to me, Wen declared with all of her usual confidence, and there's no countering that.

So this is my petty revenge—an extravagant ceremony to commemorate her departure for her renewed post that no one really *wants* but everyone is willing to suffer for the sake of appearances. Everyone is dressed in their finest, and the applause when Esperza appears at the grand door of the chamber swells to fill the ceiling's vault.

Wen and I rise to greet her as she processes down the aisle in the center of the court. The commodore is light-years from the woman I met in the *Ruttin' Hell*'s cockpit on the day we escaped Breha, her wild inky hair sleeked back into a practical bun and her fatigues swapped for a dress uniform laden with platinum honors. Even her prosthetic looks like it's been polished to perfection.

She looks well, too, which relieves me. At Breha, she was scarcely a week out of captivity, and I knew she was putting on a brave face to get the job done. Tossing her bodily into the *Ruttin' Hell*'s hold did her no favors either. Proper recovery time has lightened the dark hollows beneath her eyes and rounded out her sunken cheeks, but there's a slight stiffness to her gait I can't help noticing.

Or maybe her uniform's just riding up her ass. No one's comfortable today.

"Your Majesties," Esperza announces, setting her heels together as she draws herself up tall before the dais. "I am at the service of the Archon Empire. I come to accept my posting, wherever you'll have me."

"Commodore Adela Esperza," I announce, throwing my voice loud enough to fill the massive space. "You have served our empire faithfully for many years, and we are eternally grateful. After your ordeal at the hands of Iva emp-Umber, I offer you a full release from service."

"I decline," Esperza says firmly.

With the formality out of the way, I plunge ahead. "Very well. I call upon Captain Deidra con-Silon of the dreadnought *Torrent*."

Silon steps out of the ranks of assembled officers and makes her way to the front of the room. I can't tell if the pleased little smirk on her lips is at the thought of going back to war with her partner at her side or the clean formality of this ceremony, which I *know* gets her rocks off. She places herself at Esperza's left and offers a crisp salute.

I release her from it with a loose flip of my hand, earning me what looks like the most restrained of exasperated sighs. "Captain

Silon, the *Torrent* will regroup under General Iral's wing with Commodore Esperza aboard. Upon arrival at the fleet, she will resume her command."

"As you wish, Your Majesty," Silon says. Her gaze darts sideways to Esperza, who gives her a shameless lopsided grin.

"And one more thing," Wen says. The room goes collectively still. They haven't adjusted to the two of us working as a unit, and everything she does still feels like a rude interruption, a line she's overstepping. "The emperor and I have come to a critical decision."

With the Umber Imperial Fleet now under Gal's command, it's time for our plan to advance. For the next stage to work, we'll have to meet him in the field—not just with our forces, but with the full force of our bloodright present. The thought of it sends a shudder through my scar, and I draw myself up tall with a thick swallow.

"We will be accompanying you back to the front."

CHAPTER 18

GAL

I OVERSEE THE IMPERIAL FLEET'S departure from the bridge of the *Precipice,* and the only thing I can think is that it's far too quiet.

Not the sudden snap to superluminal that catapults us from the fringes of the Acua system—that's always been far gentler than it should be, especially shielded in the command core with the hum of the dreadnought's drives miles away. Not the noise of the *Precipice*'s officers as they dig up long-haul procedures these ships last ran nearly a decade ago. No, the thing missing, the thing I used to rely on to drown out my anxious thoughts, is the Wraiths' chatter at my side.

"Course is set, Your Majesty," Captain Yser sys-Gordan grumbles from his position in the bridge's saddle.

I spare my uncle a withering glance. He's an old-timer, a veteran of the War of Expansion who's run the *Precipice* with a firm hand for over a decade. He was comfortable—*far too comfortable*—tracing lazy circles around Acua before my little excursion forced my mother to drag him out to Breha and back. Now I'm knocking the dust off his long-established routine, and the way he resents it is one of the few joys I can take in my command. "Come now, Captain," I drawl. "Aren't you thrilled to *finally* have something to do?"

He looks like he's considering inventing time travel just so he can go back and kick his brother in the balls hard enough to keep me from being born. "It is my honor to serve the empire," Gordan grits out.

I should be a little more careful about how I play this next part, but without the Wraiths, I find myself making trouble just for the sake of it, as if I'm hoping it'll fill the void they've left. Sure, it'd spice things up a bit if one of my officers tries to smother me in my sleep, but I need to make it to the front.

"The honor of having you serve me is all mine," I reply, then sidle out of the bridge before the captain can throw something at me.

One might accuse me of having a little too much fun with this.

Or simply not giving a shit.

I spent most of the voyage back from Breha shut up in my quarters, but preparing to deploy has given me more than enough time to familiarize myself with the *Precipice*'s command core. Much like the *Torrent*'s, which I got to know intimately during my time in Archon captivity, it's a maze of honeycombing corridors and elevator throughlines that connect the beating heart of the cityship, making it possible for all the ranking officers to live in comfort and execute their roles without once leaving the safety of the dreadnought's interior. I move through it with cold confidence, biting back a smirk as I blow past officers tripping over themselves to duck out of my path.

Now that we're under way—and free from any potential interference by my mother—I have a bit of housekeeping to attend. Or a bit of theatrics to commit, depending on one's point of view. I shoulder through a conference room door to discover that my counterpart's arrived well ahead of schedule.

"Fleet Admiral Norsat," I drawl as he rises to salute. I let him hold it while I cross the room and throw myself down in the executive chair at the head of the table, then wave his formality away with a flap of my hand. "Please, sit."

Norsat looks like he was cast from the same mold as General

Iral, but a few decades earlier than his Archon counterpart. I have a suspicion he's been skating by on that imposing appearance, though there's a glint in his eye that warns me I might get myself in serious trouble testing that theory.

Here goes nothing. "Remind me of your service record," I command, kicking one leg casually up on the edge of the conference table.

Norsat's lip wrinkles in obvious distaste. It's exactly the reaction I'm trying to provoke, but the fact that he dares to scowl so openly tells me enough about the hold my bloodright has over him. He wouldn't dare show that kind of insubordination before his empress.

I'll let it slide. For now.

"I've been in the service for forty years, Your Majesty," the admiral starts. "I was educated at the Umber Imperial Academy on Lucia and departed for my first tour upon graduation. For five years—I'm sorry, am I *boring you*?"

I break off midway through an exaggerated yawn, raising my eyebrows. "No, do go on. Don't mind my exhaustion. It's just a bit taxing, you know, preparing for such a large-scale deployment. Perhaps you have some wisdom to share from your . . . somewhat excessive term of service."

Norsat scrubs the disbelief from his expression. "Your Majesty, why am I really here?"

"I am to command this fleet, am I not?" I reply, giving him the most amicable smile I can muster.

"As the empress has decreed, yes. You are to command this fleet."

"A chain of command is only as strong as its weakest link. Before I send this glorious flock of ships careening into battle, it's my duty to run my fingers over every link and test its mettle. So what can you prove to me, Fleet Admiral?"

The admiral leans back, sinking into his seat. "I'm sure you've already perused my record, Your Majesty. Does it not speak for itself?"

I make a show of digging my datapad out of my pocket, drawing up the admiral's information with my fingers held in a crude gesture. "Your résumé is impressive. But no more impressive than, say, Vice Admiral San, who has also served this empire faithfully for forty years. Tell me what you have that she does not."

The admiral has to bite back what looks like a visceral reaction to how offensive that demand is. He reaches up and taps the brass sigils that denote his rank on his shoulders as if it should be obvious. *He's* fleet admiral.

"Yes, I see," I coo as if talking to a toddler. "Very good. You've been granted the title. Look, I can do it too." I knock my knuckles against the crown resting at a jaunty angle on my brow. "What does that prove?"

"That the empress, infallible in her bloodright, has seen fit to bestow the honor on me, not Vice Admiral San," Norsat replies through his teeth. "And that the empress, infallible in her bloodright, has also seen fit to crown you as her heir."

"But that's not quite how we do things, is it?" I muse, tapping my fingers on the armrest of my chair. "Bloodright means nothing if it cannot be expressed. And I intend to express my bloodright clean through this Archon rebellion, which means I need people who're going to work swiftly and decisively to enact my orders. Your service record is extensive, but"—I give the datapad a long, slow, lazy scroll—"I would say woefully inadequate for my purposes. After the War of Expansion, it seems you swooped in on the first posting available for the interior. *You,* my friend, are the central reason this fleet's gotten choked with rust. What happened to that glorious ambition that won you your rank in the first place?"

"Your Majesty," Norsat says, his tone edged in venom. "I urge you not to confuse maintaining the peace of the core—at the behest of the empress, I might add—with inaction. If there's anything my years of service have taught me, it's that a military is so much more than the battles it fights. Young people like you only see the bloodshed. You think that's all there is."

"If my mother's taught me anything, it's that bloodshed *is* all there is," I reply, my lips twitching into one of her sharp-edged smiles. "Everything else is the veneer of politics. Like, for example, this conversation."

With one smooth motion, I pull out the dagger. In the reflection of the obsidian blade, Fleet Admiral Norsat goes strikingly pale. It's the same knife my mother pressed into my hands all those months ago, the one I clutched as I swore fealty when she officially awarded me command of the fleet. It's everything I swore I'd never become.

But I can't deny the effect. The fleet admiral has never seen the way I struggled to accept violence when my mother forced it on me. He's only ever seen me poison my four closest friends in the middle of the Umber court.

I give him my wickedest grin.

To his credit, he sits forward in his seat, laying his hands carefully on the table. "Your Majesty, I can't see how it'll be inspiring—or indeed useful for your purposes—to kill your way through the ranks until you find someone malleable enough to take your orders," Norsat says, with only a touch of nerves quavering in his voice.

"You're right, Fleet Admiral." I let my foot slip from the edge of the conference table and catch myself on my elbows, turning the dagger carefully end over end. "Which is why I've brought you here today. I have an offer for you. You'll serve me through this campaign. You'll follow orders without questioning them. And if you serve me well enough, you'll have proven yourself a worthy ally to the throne—one who must be rewarded. According to your service record, you were born on Naberrie. Is that correct?"

Norsat nods, a slight furrow digging into his brow.

"How would you like to govern it?"

He's utterly transparent. A military man, whose emotions matter so little to his day-to-day operations that he's never fully learned the art of hiding them. His confusion lasts a half second, and then he registers the scope of what I'm offering. An entire planet under his command. A core world where he can reap the fruits of his long, worthy career. A bloodright earned in the crucible of battle, supplanting whatever poor sod currently calls themself plan-Naberrie.

Supplanting is a somewhat gentle term for what it'll take, but I've read Norsat's record, and if the way he tore through Archon is anything to go by, I think he'll be up to the task. This man's stoked wildfires that committed entire worlds to starvation, leaving them raw for strip mining. Surely he can stomach a little murder.

"I'm a generous man," I continue, spreading my arms wide. "This campaign is not just for my own bloodright's sake. Think of it as a proving ground for new blood. The last time this fleet rode through the Archon worlds, it was to claim new territory that necessitated fresh leadership. My mother used that as an opportunity to audition hungry officers for the governorships of the systems and territories she was stringing one by one on her belt. But those worlds are scarcely a reward for dedicated service—especially now that we've had our fill of them."

The admiral's brow wrinkles. "Naberrie already has a governor—one whose family has held the planet for at least three generations. Have they fallen out of the empress's favor?"

"Admiral Norsat, I suggest you moderate your concerns. The empress's favor has very little bearing on your future. The empress does not oversee this campaign—I do. And I am the future of the empire. I have a grand vision for the shape of things to come, and I need the right people to enact it. Are you one of them?"

The admiral's spine stiffens as he grasps the fragility of this moment. I need my ruthlessness matched, or else he has no value to me. Every brick I've laid has built up to this question, and only one answer will spare him the dagger I'm toying with.

"I am at your service, Your Majesty," Norsat says, bowing his head.

"Excellent!" I tap the hilt of the dagger against the conference table for emphasis, then spin it once in my palm and slide it back in its sheath. All show, no substance, but I think the man's just relieved to see it go. "I'm glad I have you by my side, Fleet Admiral. May our campaign be bloody and prosperous. You're dismissed."

I beckon him up with a flick of my fingers, accept the neat bow he gives me, then slump back in my chair with a sigh when the door slips shut behind him.

The relief won't quite take. It's still too quiet.

I pull up a comm line to the aide standing outside the conference room. "Right then. Bring in Admiral San."

By the time I make it back to my quarters, I feel like I've been put through a few rounds on the academy's meanest centrifuge. Shaking down the Umber admiralty has its fun parts, but my whole body's been tense for hours. When the door latches firmly behind me, I let it all go, a wave of dizziness forcing me to catch the frame.

I may have been born for this, but I wasn't built for it.

The *Precipice*'s imperial suite feels like a slice of the void, all rich black wall panels, refined brass edges, and plush silken padding. Like most dreadnought officer quarters, it's a security black hole, with surveillance on the outside only. Here, I'm afforded complete privacy—including the freedom to pull my mother's knife from its sheath and hurl it across the common area. It bounces off the wall and lands on the couch with a completely unsatisfying thump.

I throw myself down next to it, letting my head fall back as I stare up at the vent in the ceiling. "Everyone comfortable?" I mutter.

"Cozy as can be, boss," Hanji replies.

I let loose my first real smile of the day.

Killing the Wraiths was easy. Reviving them from the drug they injected at the moment they downed their drinks—that took some doing. They had to stay convincingly dead for long enough to fool my mother and mysteriously disappear somewhere between the morgue and the incinerator. It took wits, guts, and intimate knowledge of the citadel's layout, and if I hadn't pulled it off, this next stage of the plan would have been nearly impossible.

Fortunately, once revived, they took care of the rest. The Wraiths had smuggled themselves aboard the *Torrent* and lived in the vents for weeks while planning my kidnapping with Wen, so they already knew exactly what to do. They hitched a ride on the pleasure cruiser I flew in an ostentatious circuit around the capital before making my way to the *Precipice,* then slipped into the air ducts with the dreadnought's security team none the wiser.

Now I have four roommates hiding in my ceiling, taking advantage of the surveillance dead zone around my quarters as they bide their time.

"I've met with each of the admirals," I tell them, handing up my datapad. Hanji unlatches the vent and squirms down to pluck it out of my hands. Either she's been working her core like hell or Ollins is sitting on her legs—rather than withdrawing, she just hangs there, paging through the transcripts of each conversation. "All of them took the bait."

"Of course they did," Rhodes interjects from somewhere deeper in the dark. "It's bloodright. You don't turn that down."

Hanji snorts, her glasses slipping precariously down her nose. "So what are you thinking now?"

"You with Norsat, for sure. Hardisson will be sharing a bridge with him—I trust you can handle both of them at once. Rin's the best fit for San, but as for Venta . . . I'll need a little more time to think."

"You've got three days," Rin chirps helpfully.

Three days of superluminal to reach the edge of the Archon territories. On that third day, the fleet will come to a full stop to supply the ships and figure out our angle of approach. From the latest intelligence, it seems like Archon forces are currently chewing their way through the Duvar System under the command of General Iral. As we prepare the fleet to enter the war, we'll have to decide whether to plunge in at the hottest point and start carving our way through Archon's beefiest forces or attempt to anticipate their next offensive and shore up an unbreakable defense there.

All that strategizing will be the perfect cover to smuggle the Wraiths out onto the admirals' flagships.

Which means the next three days could be all the time I have left with them. The conditions aren't ideal—if I could have somehow gotten hold of the fleet's command without staging their deaths, we could have spent this whole ride blasting Hanji's horrible music and drinking ourselves into oblivion. Now we have to stay sharp and keep the Wraiths off the radar of the *Precipice*'s internal security, leaving us little room to savor what could be our final days.

The notion tears me in half a little bit. Even though I knew the plan to revive the Wraiths, it didn't make it any less horrible to see them "die," and the weeks since have left me wondering how I could possibly feel so damn *lonely* in the midst of arranging a massive military deployment that scarcely gave me a moment alone. I want to soak in their reckless nonsense for as long as I can.

"Three days, no showers," Ollins muses. "It's gonna get *fun* in here."

Well, maybe not for *too* long.

CHAPTER 19

ETTIAN

By the time we arrive at the Duvar front, General Iral is already mopping up.

Wen insists that we use it as an opportunity to take our newly christened flagship, a sleek cruiser named the *Dawn*, for a spin. It's far more maneuverable than a dreadnought—a fact we use to stick to the skirts of the massive cityships and keep out of danger as we skim the edges of the battlefield.

The *Dawn*'s bridge is a cut above a dreadnought core, fitted with a looming viewscreen wall that provides a real-time look at the battle flickering outside. Wen and I sit side by side on the command dais, our heads bent close together as we shift our gazes between the view of the field and the data scrolling across the monitors of our personal stations.

"We should get closer," she murmurs, fingers sketching out a proposed vector.

I shake my head. "It's still too bloody out there." Duvar may have fallen decisively, but Umber never gives quarter, and they can be their most dangerous when they have nothing to lose. My memory flickers back to the Battle of Dasun—the active field I flung myself recklessly into to save her ass—and the vicious way Umber smashed itself to pieces against our ships after Wen took out the *Fulcrum*.

"I could take my suit for a walk," she muses, then glances sidelong with a smirk that tells me she's kidding. She wrenched an entire battle off-course the first time she took the field as a suited knight. There's no telling what Umber might muster if she steps out as empress. "I'm just saying now's the time to establish our presence."

"Is it?" I muse, my gaze tracing an Umber cruiser's suicidal vector toward one of Iral's dreadnoughts. The sight of it puts an ache in my heart. "We said no more dreadnought engines."

"This isn't a dreadnought engine—this is a chance to show the people how their imperials fight for them." Her voice has risen from a murmur to a stern, firm tone that has a few heads in the command center swiveling our way. There's been a burgeoning curiosity about the particulars of our marriage that's chased us through our arrival at the front, and nothing draws their ears faster than the scent of discord between their emperor and empress. We'd meant the love match as a distraction, but now it seems almost *too* effective.

"We fight for our people in ways that go beyond careening recklessly into battle," I remind her, lowering my voice and bending my head so I may as well be whispering sweet nothings into her ear.

"But careening recklessly into battle is my *specialty*," she whines. "And besides, this wouldn't be reckless. It'd be calculated. This was what we were supposed to do at Imre, remember? General Iral wins the day. We pick up the pieces. It just went sideways at Imre on account of the army fleeing to Dasun—and then we had to get creative. This is so straightforward."

I let out a long, hissing sigh. This is exactly what I signed up for when I married her, but that reminder does little for the growing ache in my chest. I don't think I fully accounted for the way returning to the front would affect me on a purely physical level. Ever since Breha, I've been wrapped in so many layers of safety that I feel like I've lost the wary edge I used to rely on to keep me alive. There's a part of me that tries to argue I deserve to feel safe, but it's crushed by the overwhelming guilt of knowing that so many in my ranks have forsaken that luxury. The least I can do is join them.

But it should be enough just to be here, on the front lines of this war, staking my life on this campaign. I am not Iva emp-Umber, who purportedly never so much as left the citadel during the War of Expansion. I'm throwing myself right down in the dirt with the rest of my soldiers.

Just . . . not right now. Not yet.

Wen must sense the frustration building in me. She lays one careful hand on my arm, her fingertips pressing gently against my pulse points. "I'm sorry," she murmurs. "I'm just trying to be what the people need us to be. I have so much more to prove than you."

I catch her fingers and squeeze. "You have *nothing* to prove," I mutter back fiercely. "The crown on your head is proof enough. Never forget that."

She sighs, slumping back in her chair and using her free hand to prod at her circlet—a simple daywear band—until it rests comfortably. Then she remembers herself, and her spine straightens back into a prim, proper posture. I've watched this dance play out a thousand times, watched her skip haphazardly down the line between what an imperial should be and what an imperial *could* be.

And that thought sticks and festers. Because who are we to dictate what an imperial should be? Who are we to limit what an imperial could be? The whole point of elevating Wen to empress is to expand the Archon imagination beyond the structures we used to accept as a given. The right ruler can come from anywhere. The right ruler can be anyone.

I believe Wen emp-Archon is the ruler the empire needs. But if she's going to rise to that, she needs the people behind her. The ache in my heart gets keener as I remember the Battle of Dasun. Not the moment she tore through the field, not the moment she flew into the *Fulcrum*'s engines and burned, but the moment that preceded all of those moments—the moment she begged to be loosed upon the full might of Berr sys-Tosa's forces and I told her no.

Maybe this time, I can do better. Maybe this time, I can listen to her from the start.

"You know," I muse, squeezing her hand gently. "Taking the suit for a walk isn't a half-bad idea."

A spark kindles in her eyes. "Thought it was too bloody out there?"

"For a decorated cruiser with both imperials aboard, sure. But I've yet to see an Umber warbird land a hit on you in that suit. Careening recklessly into battle is your specialty, isn't it?"

She grins. "You're sure?"

"I don't have to be sure—that's on you. If you think it's the move . . ."

Wen darts in and pecks me on the cheek, then slips her hand from mine as she pushes up from her seat. "Attention on deck," she announces, and heads whip up across the bridge, lit by the soft, flickering glow of their screens. "I'm stepping out for a little bit of air. I'll need an escort—four Cygnets should do it."

I settle deeper into my seat as the bridge spins into action around Wen, watching as she lifts her head high and strides for the door. That confidence—to give an order, trust that it gets followed, and keep moving forward—is something she's slid into as natural as breathing. Wen's never second-guessed herself, and it's exactly what I need at my side if we're going to make it through this fight.

Thirty minutes later, the Flame Empress takes the field, resplendent in her powersuit. After its stint in Umber captivity, she's finally had the time to tailor it, polishing out the scuffs and—after a heavy heart-to-heart with General Iral, whose dead lover once wore the armor—setting her own brand-new sigil, a curling twist of fire wrought in Archon platinum, over the sternum.

She wheels up into the bridge's viewscreen and fixes herself in front of the cameras with careful pulses of her thrusters as the four Cygnets she requested for her escort squadron form up around her. Slowly, deliberately, she pulls her vibrosword from her belt, unfurls it, and lofts it over her head. The bridge erupts into cheers and hollers, the war drums roll into the knight herald cadence, and I can't help the proud grin that creeps over my face.

I may never be able to join her on the field—and maybe it's better that I don't. Wen deserves a spotlight all to herself, a chance to show the empire that she means business, and every inch of the applause for doing so.

She lets the sword drop, brings up her free hand, and pantomimes blowing a kiss, prompting more than a few whistles across the bridge.

"Go get 'em, sweetheart," I murmur as she kicks up her heels, throws her boot thrusters as hot as they'll burn, and hurtles off into the flickering remnants of Iral's victory.

The effect is instantaneous—almost frighteningly so.

Archon has always held Wen at a careful distance, ready to cut ties the moment her trouble tipped over into something more destructive. Back when I had her running loose in Trost to scourge Umber out of the city, she nearly crossed that line, so much so that I pulled her back and reassigned her to guarding Gal. When we moved to the front, I did my best to get her ranked and trained, hoping it would bolster the public's image of her, but all of those months of hard work was a drop in the bucket compared to the Battle of Dasun.

There, she showed the lengths to which she was willing to go to fight for Archon and nearly lost her life for it—and it was there Archon started the slow process of embracing her. They cheered for her as she wheeled over crowded arenas, celebrating that the suited knights had returned at last. But even then, it seemed like they were celebrating the notion of our old heroes more than *her*.

And then I married her, and once again they had to recontextualize this scrappy little Corinthian in the eyes of the empire—this time as their empress, sworn to serve them. No one knew what that meant. No one's ever seen an empress like her. Ever since I set a crown on her head, I've watched everyone we meet second-guess how they're supposed to treat her, like they can't wrap their heads around it.

Turns out all I had to do was toss her on a battlefield again. I can understand how the logic lines up, even if I never thought this way myself. True Archon imperials work at the service of their people. Before the Duvar victory, she was a fluke that took out a dreadnought and a mascot for our revolution. Then she had the audacity to seat herself on a throne with no bloodright sacrificed for her title.

But now she's the woman who had the crown on her head and still suited up and threw herself into the mess.

And they ruttin' love her for it.

"Gods of all systems," I mutter, low enough that only she can hear. We're seated around a conference table for a strategy session, surrounded by the fleet's leadership, and I'm moving slowly but steadily through the dreadnought status reports logged in my datapad's inbox. Most are damage logs listing off the various scars the second Duvar campaign incurred. The leadership is meant to comb through those and decide which ships get packed off for Tyrol for repairs and which can stand to take a little more. Some of the reports are bold requests for more personnel, more support ships, more important positioning in the fleet's formation.

But nearly every single one of them has a note at the end of it. It's written differently every time, clearly voiced by each captain or whatever aide drafted the actual message, but they all express the same sentiment.

As Wen shoots me a curious look, I tip my datapad her way and she reads the latest. *An additional note: Captain Reed Symon of the dreadnought* Vanguard *would like to express his admiration for the empress's efforts on the battlefield and let her know that he is at her service.*

Wen raises an eyebrow. "What was he asking before?"

"He wants the *Vanguard* at the spearhead of the next push. They've spent most of the campaign in an ancillary position, and he's arguing that with so many of our dreadnoughts bound for Tyrol, now's the time for his 'nottie to serve."

"It's really about that?" she asks, darting a nervous glance aside to make sure none of the other officers clock what she's questioning. "Service? Not glory?"

"It's always difficult to tell," I reply just as softly. "But I want to believe the best of my officers. The second I start suspecting they're out for power is the second the ones who *are* genuinely out for power sense the blood in the water and move in. Even if the nobility is a façade to cover a genuine lust for glory in battle, it's my job to prioritize nobility—to cultivate it until it's the firm foundation of my empire."

"And that's why they're all being so nice to me now," Wen grumbles. "It wasn't *noble* enough when I took out the *Fulcrum* single-handedly?"

"Not when you gave up nothing but your life to do it," I remind her.

"I happen to like my life very much. It felt like a pretty large sacrifice at the time. Y'know, when I was roasting alive inside a dreadnought engine as I flung it at a rustin' planet? But now I go out, punch through a few warbirds, gut a barge, and do absolutely nothing for a battle that's already won, and *that's* when I start getting every dreadnought captain in the fleet singing my praises?"

I twitch a finger toward a shushing motion, catching General Iral's eyes narrowing in our direction. "A life is not much to give up to them," I murmur. "A crown is."

Wen scoffs. "Guess it's down to a difference of opinion, then."

"Important thing is they've come around—and we can use that."

She gives me a sly look and a subtle wag of her finger in lieu of outright shushing me.

"Your Majesties," Iral interrupts. "If I may draw your attention back to the matter at hand."

"Draw away, General," Wen says with a sweeping gesture. The boldness of her confidence should rankle Iral, but I've noticed that the two of them have been on *strikingly* better terms since the wedding. Is it Iral's innate deference to bloodright? The fact that now that she's crowned, she's been meeting with him one-on-one to go over strategy rather than doing things her own way and pulling him along for the ride? Whatever the case, it's a relief to have two of the most potent figures in my military in sync at last.

Iral gives Wen a nod and pulls up the room's central projection screens. Splayed across them is the shape of the galactic arm. Umber's lands have been drawn in brutal, engulfing red, with Archon's three reclaimed systems an emerald green nestled within their fold. The Corinthian border gives way to a swath of gray that marks their territory.

"Today," Iral begins, "we must decide the shape of the war to come. With victory secure at Duvar, a portion of the fleet will remain to support and defend the system. The rest, we will commit to a new offensive. We have three viable targets, which you've already been briefed on." He taps his datapad, and three systems glow a blinding white on the map.

Utar. Sohla. Lusan. I can't help the way my gaze zeroes in on the first—the site of General Iral's most humiliating campaign. I still remember sitting in an academy classroom, silently fuming over the gloating way my instructors would describe his failure. The campaign was staked on incomplete information that led to Iral botching the supply lines, which in turn led to a fundamental lack of resources. The general fought well, but the academy teachers loved to hang the defeat on his neck alone, and it was brought up time and time again as a textbook example of the weak Archon leadership that *deserved* to fall to Umber.

I want to give Iral a second chance for victory in the system, but on top of that, it also has immense strategic value. Utar connects the systems we hold already to the Corinthian border, creating a valuable channel between us and our allies where they can safely stage the distribution of resources and reinforcements to our fronts without worrying about Umber interference. If we liberate Utar, the war gains a whole new dimension—one we sorely need.

Then there's Sohla. Its key benefit is its adjacency to Duvar. If this were a linear campaign, Sohla would be the logical next stepping-stone. It's easy to mobilize to that system, but it doesn't have much strategic value beyond widening Archon's stake and liberating the people pinned under Umber rule there.

Finally, there's Lusan. When Umber first began clawing their way through the Archon Empire ten years ago, Lusan fell before any other system. As Utar shares a border with Corinth, Lusan shares one with Umber, making it the go-to access point for any Umber forces mobilizing from their interior. If we take it, we can effectively cut off any reinforcements they try to send and shore up a defense that will allow us to scourge the remaining Umber forces from our systems.

But taking it isn't my primary concern—*holding* it is. I worry that Lusan will become a drain on our already fragile forces, that Umber will be able to gradually siphon away our strength simply by forcing us to commit ship after ship to the system's defense. It's a bold move to push directly toward Umber and attempt to create a choke point, but we have to be sure it's one we can maintain against what's sure to be vicious retaliation.

"I'm of the opinion that we should focus our efforts on Utar," I announce to the room. "Our talks with Corinth have progressed considerably, and they're ready to begin a concrete contribution to our effort. After Wen's latest negotiation with them, Ambassador Xhosi has been coordinating shipments of supplies to the Tyrol Yards to assist in rebuilding the 'notties we lost taking Duvar, and troops will be following not long after." I tap my datapad and the territory we'd gain from driving Umber out of Utar lights up in green, illustrating the border we'd gain with Corinth and the protected channel it would create between their lands and our newly established interior. "With a unified corridor established, our alliance can flourish, putting us in the best possible position to root out the remaining Umber occupation."

Iral folds his arms, his dark gaze locked on the map in contemplation. "Utar has been historically difficult to sustain a campaign in. While I agree that we'd benefit immensely from a channel to the Corinthian border, I worry about the viability of an offensive in a system that's been stripped even further than the last time I waged war there."

"Surely your familiarity with the system will give you an edge you may not have had last time," I suggest.

Iral's expression shutters—a microflinch that speaks volumes. He's a professional. A man who's been serving as a soldier for longer than I've been alive. But Utar's a wound in his psyche that's yet to heal. "That may be true," he starts with clear reluctance. "If it's truly your wish to make Utar the focus of our next campaign, we can begin—"

"What about Lusan?" Wen asks from my right.

Startled, I glance sideways to find her hunched over the data, her fingers combing through it as she nets the stats she's interested in. "Well, Lusan is an *option*," I say cagily. "But it's in our better interests to strengthen our defenses before we attempt to take that system—which we can do best by establishing a corridor to the Corinthian border."

Wen frowns. "I'm not so sure about that. Yes, we'd be better positioned for Corinthian support, but I've been over the numbers with Xhosi and I don't think any amount of aid they can offer will be enough to counter the full force of the Imperial Fleet if it gets a foothold in Archon space. Based on our scouting, the fleet's vector would carry them to Lusan first. It's the most logical place for them to establish operations, and from there they'll pivot right into razing every system we've managed to claim. But if we can head them off before they even enter Archon space—"

"That's a pretty significant *if*," I counter. "We have no idea what we'll be up against. This fleet hasn't deployed in a decade. The closest they've come is the contingent Iva emp-Umber trucked out at Breha, but that was just a show of force—they turned back for the interior once . . . Well, once they realized they couldn't collect what they came for," I finish, tamping down the heat that tries to climb my cheeks at the mere thought of Breha.

There's a subtler argument at play, a tightrope Wen and I are walking above the heads of the rest of our staff. The incoming Umber fleet is under Gal's command, just as we planned, but he's impressed his mother a little *too* much after his stunt with the Wraiths. We were betting he could wrest a fraction of the fleet out of the core, but he's managed to get the whole damn thing deployed. Worse, we were operating on the assumption that the Wraiths would be able to act in the open. We're still not sure they can do their part while playing dead.

I think we need to regroup, to figure out what we're really up against before we move to the next stages. Wen thinks we can dive in headfirst—because of course she does.

She throws her information up on the screens at the center of the room, and a sobering quiet drops over the officers as they take it in. Wen's drawn up the shape of the Umber Imperial Fleet and the data on all the ships at the empress's command, from the dreadnoughts down to the Vipers. The numbers themselves are staggering, but when I try to visualize what those numbers look like physically, I can feel my brain shutting down at the sheer scale of it. "If a force like that establishes a presence in Lusan and uses it as a gateway to our systems, it's all over."

"We have no hope of countering a force like that without Corinthian aid," I argue, pulling my datapad up to put together some numbers of my own: the forces we have available to us and the rate at which we can expect to lose them if we acquire Lusan before the Corinthian support comes through.

But it's too late. I can feel the tide of the room ebbing toward her. The numbers she's presented, coupled with Iral's reluctance to revisit the site of his great failure, have my people nodding and consulting their own datapads, no doubt already running projections for how quickly they can mobilize their portion of our forces for Lusan.

I could rage that *I* am their emperor, that I carry the bloodright of my line, that my will should eclipse all here, but Wen has positioned herself perfectly. By taking the field for the Duvar victory, she's won the goodwill of every officer in the fleet. By aligning herself with General Iral's opinion on our next advance, she's placed herself on the side of our people's most respected war hero. And on top of all of that, she shares my bloodright as an equal. That was the entire ruttin' *point* of marrying her. With so little support from the room, any further attempts to argue for Utar as our next campaign will be seen as self-serving, and as Archon's emperor, I'm supposed to be anything but that.

Wen catches my eye and shakes her head softly. "We have to claim and fortify Lusan before it's too late. Corinth can still send aid through occupied territory to shore up our strength, and we can make the Utar push once we've established an Umber border that will hold off any attempts to reinforce that territory."

I take a quick estimate of the room, my gaze darting up and down the table of assembled officers. I'm met with eyes all but begging me to concede to my wife.

So I draw myself up tall and say, with perfect imperial grace, "Very well. We'll pursue a strategy at Lusan."

It takes less than a week to mobilize the full force of the Archon fleet. Those who've been approved for repairs disappear on a vector for the Tyrol Yards to lick their wounds, and the rest of us wrench onto a superluminal journey that deposits us in the shadow of Turrot, the stabilizing gas giant that orbits in the far reaches of the Lusan System. The giant's captured a tenuous ring of icy bodies that cloak our fleet's arrival and make our numbers difficult for any Umber monitors to estimate, giving us the time we need to get oriented in the system.

Once again, Wen and I sit in the relative comfort of the *Dawn*'s bridge, taking in the sprawling expanse of the ring through the viewscreen wall. The parts in sunlight are blindingly brilliant, while the parts covered by Turrot's shadow drop to a deceptive dark that blends with the blackness of the void.

"You look tense," she observes.

"You look overprepared," I counter. We're still in the process of mustering our forces with no engagement anticipated today, but she's kitted out in her powersuit all the same, as if she expects to take the field at any moment. It's an effective reminder to the bridge command that the empress isn't just here to lord over them as they go about their work—she's ready to jump into the mess the second it's needed.

Which, to me, is just showing off.

"You know me," Wen says, prodding one massive mechanized finger into my ribs with such absurd gentleness that I can't help but gape at how deftly she controls her suit. "Contingency on contingency on contingency."

"Let me know how that works out for you when your ass has been wrapped up in that suit for a full day," I scoff.

She opens her mouth for some witty rejoinder, and it's at that precise moment the bridge sirens scream to life.

My academy training kicks in before any other instinct. My spine goes ramrod straight as I drop my focus immediately to my monitors, drawing up the real-time map of the fleet and everything the sensor array has logged. And there, painted in brilliant enemy red, I see the scale of the reckoning that's finally descended on us, just like I feared it would.

At my side, Wen's done just the same, her HUD cycling the data in front of her eyes. "Rocks and rust," she mutters. "Maybe you were right."

The Imperial Fleet has come to call in full force. The sight of a single Umber dreadnought—a miles-long war machine wrought from metal they stripped from our empire, built for nothing but annihilation—still freezes me in my tracks with dread, even after months at war. A single dreadnought's firing power is enough to scar a planet permanently.

We face forty of them.

With their numbers, they've dropped from superluminal directly into an impenetrable blockade of Turrot, and my mind can barely grasp the sheer scale of what they've enacted in one fell swoop. They knew we were in the gas giant's orbit, and even with the debris in the rings obscuring our true position and numbers, all they had to do was lock us in.

But we still have one card left to play. "Navigation," I call across the control room. "Prepare for immediate egress from the ring followed by a superluminal vector set for Rana."

Wen's head snaps up, her suit tensing with predatory grace. "Hold that order!" she shouts.

I whirl on her. "Do you not see the ruttin' *armada* that just dropped on top of us? We don't have the numbers to fight that thing. Our only hope is to break for the interior."

Wen surges up from her seat, striding to the center of the bridge. "We can do this. We have cover in the rings. They think they have us pinned, that *they* have the element of surprise, and it'll make them sloppy. We'll never have another opportunity to strike like this."

The plan's going to work, she's begging me with her eyes. *Let us see it through.*

I pinch my brow, letting out a seething hiss. The scarring on my stomach twinges as I push myself up to join her, trying to strike as confident a pose as I can manage to counter the inherent power of her armored figure. "Even if the fleet could hold out and do some damage, *we* have to go. The Archon imperial line—the future of the empire—is aboard this cruiser."

Wen opens her mouth like she's going to counter, but then her eyes snag on some piece of data in her HUD. "Communications," she calls instead. "What's their flagship and its command?"

The officer gulps, her eyes darting to me as if unsure whether it'd be helping or hurting to take the empress's order. "They're heralding their arrival under the dreadnought *Precipice,* under the command of . . . Gal emp-Umber. Not by proxy. By presence."

I can't let his name affect me, but it hits like another shot to the gut. We've been a galaxy apart since Breha, and the mere notion that he's orbiting the very same planet sends electric chills coursing through my fingers. The stricken expression on my face must be transparent as the void. Communications is looking at me like I might as well have blurted my love for Gal to the entire ruttin' room.

And worse, his mere presence on the field has just effectively destroyed any argument I could make for running. It's been generations since an Umber ruler rode into battle alongside their troops. His own mother was content to conduct the War of Expansion from safe within her interior. But now Gal has gone and made this not just a battle between Umber and Archon forces—it's a battle he's staked his own bloodright on, and if I flee the field, I'll as good as admit that his right to rule is superior.

Wen's play was outstanding, executed with tactical precision. Either I listen to her, or I look like a complete, imperial ass.

I grit my teeth. I'll be damned if I let a galactic pissing contest be the reason my empire falls, headless, back into the dust Umber ground us into. "I don't give a shit who's commanding their forces," I snarl. "Navigation, get us out of here."

"*Hold,*" Wen repeats with equal furor. "If that fleet gets its foothold in this system, there'll be no stopping it. We are *not* turning our backs on these people to save our own necks."

"It's not turning our backs on them, it's acting to preserve the whole empire! This empire is nothing without the bloodright I carry—the bloodright every single one of you fights for," I seethe with a sweeping gesture around the bridge.

"The bloodright *you* carry, huh?" Wen mutters. "What was the point of marrying me and elevating me to share it if it all comes down to you and what *you* think is best?"

I swallow back a bark of laughter. "If I wanted a partner who'd throw my empire into a ruttin' black hole, I guess I should have taken the Umber proposal."

It cues more than a few sharp inhales across the bridge, but what do I care? That's ancient history at this point, and if they want to read anything damning into it, I'd encourage them to look outside where the man in question is riding the full force of the Imperial Fleet into a blockade around us.

"If you were only ever planning to betray your people to save your own hide, I guess you should have," Wen replies.

The storm starts to whip into a fury at the fringes of my vision.

The *Dawn*'s bridge is scrambling to react in the absence of imperial guidance, the outer ring of officers desperately trying to glean orders from the inner ring—all of whom can't look away from the spectacle of me and Wen facing off against each other. I can feel the tension of the moment drawn taut as a bowstring, waiting for the inevitable snap.

Her searing gaze is locked on mine.

Her hand drops to her waist.

There's only one way to clear the deadlock. Only one way she can save us all. It's a choice she made before—my heart or the future of the galaxy.

Her answer hasn't changed.

Wen moves like lightning in the storm clouds of Turrot, the vibrosword hilt swinging up as she lunges. With the perfect, intimate aim of a lover, it strikes me right in the same place as Hanji's bullet, bending me over the scar.

The snarl of a blade tearing through the back of my uniform. The spatter of wet heat on my shoulder blades. I feel none of it—only shock as with her free hand my wife, my empress, carefully tips my chin up to look me in the eyes. I expect a smile, that same smile I saw peeking out from underneath a rainbow umbrella on a sweltering summer day in Corinth. The grin of a girl about to sink her teeth into a con she's been preparing for so, so long. The beginnings of a life turned upside down in nothing but the flash of her slightly crooked teeth.

Instead, there's a horror in her eyes I've never seen before. The awful necessity of what she's just done is hitting like a hammer, leaving her wretched in its wake, her hand straining against the weight of my jaw like she's trying to keep me upright—like doing so might undo the finality of the choice she's made.

It's on me to smile, then. It's the last thing I do before the darkness closes in.

CHAPTER 20

WEN

It's come to this. To me, alone.

I thumb a trigger, and the blade sprouting from Ettian's back collapses from whence it came, leaving only a dribbling gash in the back of his jacket. Pulling back my hilt, I find my hand's come away painted as red as his was the day we stormed the Archon court together. He cut it open before Iral in a bullheaded attempt to prove his bloodright.

Now that bloodright settles on my shoulders with the weight of a thousand worlds. The emperor slumps, but I catch him by the collar before he hits the ground. With a quick pulse of my boot thrusters, I propel myself up onto the bridge's central command table and cradle him carefully against my chest.

It's at around this time that the rest of the room catches up on exactly what's just happened. I give them two extra seconds to chew on the shock and horror, then lift my bloodied fist, clutched around my vibrosword's hilt, over my head. Tears sting my eyes, but I blink them back furiously. There's a war fleet bearing down on us and no time for the breakdown my heart's demanding. I'm the mechanic, and the engine room is on fire. Time to get fixing. "Ettian emp-Archon would have you run. Would have chosen his own life over defending his empire. Would you have chosen that with him?"

This is the moment that decides everything. With Ettian's blood pooling at my feet, these people have to choose me as their empress all over again. Does my marriage legitimize me enough to give me the right to make this move? Or was I only ever a Corinthian street rat scamming my way to the top? I have plans for every possible way this could go, but no idea which will be set in motion until this moment passes.

"Your Majesty," our captain, the honorable Addisit Pura, says. Great start. "Our oaths are to Archon above all else. If I may be so bold as to point out," she continues with a voice that barely shakes, "you seem to be borrowing not from Archon or Corinth, but from Umber in your . . . current state."

Fair point. Regicide features in only one imperial playbook—though I'm sure if you go back far enough in any empire's history, you're bound to find that no one's completely innocent. I sincerely doubt Iva emp-Umber wanted to fall to her knees and scream after she carved her sister's throat open, but that's not the argument I should be making at the moment. "Sometimes one goes a good way toward resembling the enemy on a journey to defeat them," I reply, meeting her gaze as steadily as I can manage. "Captain Pura, I know you're a discerning soldier—and I hope you can discern that I'm not your enemy."

"The enemy out there may kill me," she fires back. "But you're a lot closer to pulling it off at the moment."

Also a fair point. I lower my vibrosword hilt until I feel the tug of the magnets on my hips, then let it snap into place at my side. "I know it's not much when I'm wearing a powersuit, but I hope you get the point of that gesture," I say, spreading my empty hand. The motion jars Ettian, his head rolling to tuck against my chest. "I think we want the same things. I saw the way all of you hesitated when the emperor tried to get you to turn tail. You want to stay. You want to fight. You want to tear clean through anyone who'd stop you from protecting your homeland, but you didn't have the bloodright to strike him down. Only I could, and so . . ." Something dangerously close to nausea swells in my throat—*don't look down don't look down don't look down*—but I bite it back. "So I did."

This is the thing I bet on above all else. That Archon would understand the ugly necessity of what I did. That they would see this war was as good as lost if they followed Ettian's command. That they would breathe a sigh of relief that I acted where no one else could. That doing so would validate me *just* enough to allow my haphazard step from co-rulership to a single-person throne.

But I think what saves me is that I'm treating with Addisit Pura first. I see it in her eyes—the moment she realizes that I haven't made any demands beyond her perspective. I haven't ordered her to patch me through to Iral or even to the system emissaries who represent the governors' interests in the fleet leadership. I'm not going straight for the powers that would validate the . . . let's be honest here, *coup* I've just initiated. My priority is the people who just watched me strike my husband down—the people who've just found themselves wrenched into terror and uncertainty. If they're not on my side, I know I have nothing, and Captain Pura must realize that makes me a different sort of imperial. One worth listening to, I hope.

I've read her file—her homeworld, Atran, resides within this very system. It was one of the first Archon worlds captured and stripped in the War of Expansion. Captain Pura fled with her family and both she and her partner dedicated themselves to the service not long after. Now she clings to the glimmer of hope that we could restore her to the world that birthed her.

Which is precisely why I chose this cruiser to christen as our flagship.

"You really think we can win, Your Majesty?" the captain says, her gaze flicking uncertainly down to her screens and then back to me.

I nod once firmly. "I have a plan. Well, I have about eighteen major forks of a plan, depending on how this engagement goes, but trust me, you'll be briefed." I crouch on the console, forcing my eyes to look past the body in my arms, the blood, the *consequence,* and tab through the ship's systems until I reach my encrypted set of files. A quick retinal scan and a passcode later, my strategy unlocks. With a twist of my wrist, I distribute it to every station on the bridge.

A few murmurs of surprise rise from the junior officers as they realize the scope of what they've been given. Battle strategy's a matter of utmost security, and under most circumstances, they'd get their marching orders from a superior and never know the full scale of what they're participating in until after the fact.

I'm aiming to be a different sort of commanding officer. I can't buy trust, but I *can* inspire confidence in the fact that I have these contingencies at my fingertips. If they doubt my stability—and rocks, they really ought to, given the amount of blood still leaking over the console—let them see my competency.

Let them see that not only did I push for an offensive at Lusan, I planned for an engagement with a fleet of this size. I've evaluated all the forces at our disposal and run the scenarios in my head over and over and over again.

Let them remember that before I struck Ettian down, before the Umber Imperial Fleet dropped on top of us, I was the one who suggested using Turrot's rings as our mustering point. I wasn't just recklessly tearing through the field at Dasun—I was paying attention. I saw the way Berr sys-Tosa's forces got the drop on us by using the cloak of the gas giant's clouds as cover. Turrot is an even more ideal candidate for a maneuver like that. The rings of this world are uneven, perturbed by massive bodies that trawl through the particulate and create gaps and disturbances in their wake. The disk of the ring is thick, its composition metallic enough to scramble sensors. The cover is just what we need to counter the size of Umber's forces.

But more than that, it's enough to inspire Archon's confidence that we can take them. The contingencies I've just dropped on their stations may look extensive, but it's only a fraction of the plans that branch through my head—all of which depend on having the Archon fleet comfortably and competently under my command.

I give them the time they need to read, scanning the bridge carefully as most of the eyes on it peel off me. No hands itching for blasters. No fury burning in anyone's gaze. Archon has accepted that what I did was just—a pruning to save the empire from Ettian's tactical failings.

He did a masterful job, even without my help. Everything that led up to the blade jutting from his back felt natural to the point of inevitability. Of course he would try to steer us toward a less risky campaign. If we had followed through on his naïve notion of taking the fight to Utar, the Imperial Fleet would have torn through the three restored systems while we had our attention turned toward the Corinthian border. He came to Lusan with such reluctance, and when the Umber fleet dropped on top of us, his first, loudest instinct was to run. Then, when I pushed back, he had the audacity to try throwing the Umber marriage proposal in my face—in the process, revealing that he entertained that bargain in the first place to the officers on deck.

It kills me, how seamlessly it all came together, but I can't let it show.

Captain Pura's a fast reader—or at least she knows how to skim. It's her head that snaps up first, her gaze zeroing in back to where I'm still crouched on the console. "It could work," she says. An appropriate amount of caution, but it's not what I'm looking for here.

"If you believe that," I reply, "put me through to the general."

Her mouth settles into a grim line as she realizes exactly what I'm asking of her. I'm not using the weight of my station to bully her into action. She has an out—or at least an avenue to raise any further questions or concerns. But she also has to know that with the Umber fleet locked into a blockade around us, every second counts. If we're to act, there's no room for her to stall.

"Communications, hail General Iral on his direct line," Captain Pura declares.

I draw myself up tall and step off the console, hitting the bridge's deck with a thud that tolls like a bell. With as much care as I can manage in the powersuit's might, I lay Ettian carefully back in his seat. I still can't bring myself to look at him directly.

A communications officer hauls up a camera arm and swings the lens toward me. Appearances are critical right now, and it would send the wrong message entirely to take this call sitting on what is for all intents and purposes a throne. "The general has accepted the call," another one announces. "Live in three. Two. One."

A screen unfurls from the camera I'm facing, just in time for me to see the microsquint of confusion Iral makes when he realizes which imperial is addressing him. "Your Majesty," he says with exactly the calm I'd expect from an officer as seasoned as he is.

"General," I reply. "There's been . . . a bit of a restructuring over here." I lift my right hand in a demonstrative wave, flashing the darkened blood that slicks the powersuit. "The emperor attempted to use his bloodright as a cudgel to force our fleet into retreat. I disagreed rather pointedly. I'm transmitting my plans for the engagement to you now. Please distribute them to the rest of your officers."

The transmission gives him time to process my blatant confession—perhaps even time to notice the crumpled figure on the chair behind me. His face has settled into a grim mask. Maybe he's reflecting on the fact that once again he's failed to defend the Archon line—that the Archon line he vowed to serve is *over*. Or maybe he's reframing what the Archon line really means, coming to understand that it can exist solely in me. Or maybe he's thinking about the amount of time it would take to get a dreadnought gun targeted on the *Dawn* to remove the complication of the problem entirely.

Every option is possible, but I'd wager most aren't probable—a wager I've staked my life on. In the weeks since my marriage, I've taken time to get to know the general one-on-one, and I think I have him pinned. Iral is noble, but more than that, he's a man who understands priorities. And right now, Archon infighting only weakens us to the fleet bearing down on us. If we're to engage, we have to unite.

He can decide whether to kill me or not after the battle.

"The cover of the rings only gives us so much," Iral says, clearly skimming through the plans I've just dropped on his station. "It will take hours for a courier ship to reach Tyrol and marshal the Corinthians, and everything you've outlined here hinges on being able to hold out until then. You seem to be making some key assumptions about how the dreadnoughts will move with their targets obscured."

The powersuit holds me straight-backed enough to keep from showing the slump of relief that hits my shoulders. I was fully prepared to have to fight tooth and nail for the general's collaboration, but if he's already moved on to tactics, we're doing this the easy way. "That's founded on our experience at Dasun," I reply, drawing up my sketch of Turrot and its orbit on my suit's HUD. "Perhaps it's optimistic of me to assume Umber will keep from pointing their dreadnoughts directly at a gas giant's pull after the way I took down the *Fulcrum*, but—at least if *I* were them—I'd keep my ships broadside to the planet."

Iral gives a satisfied nod. "We'll be ready to reassess if that changes, but as it stands, are these your orders, Majesty?"

"No, General." I take a moment to savor the flicker of confusion, hoping all the while that I'm going to have a long, fruitful career during which I'll manage to get *bored* of surprising this man. "I defer to your experience. I can claim to be a tactician, but the somewhat barbaric practice of handing command off to whoever can claim the most substantial bloodright is something I don't intend to perpetuate in my term as sole empress. You are the man most suited to lead this fight, and the Archon fleet is best managed under your steady command. Can I entrust this to you?"

Once again, it's a question that can't fully be considered—not when we have to start withdrawing our ships into cover as fast as we can manage. But Iral takes as much time as he can spare with it, his brows furrowing as he realizes the depth of the paradigm shift that's just happened. "This is the fight I've been preparing for since the day the empire fell," he says at last, his voice just as steady as I need it. "I will give it everything I have."

"Thank you, General. *Dawn* command out."

The communications team cuts the transmission, and I shift my focus from the camera lens back to Captain Pura. "The general has assumed command of the field. I'll be operating primarily as a strategist from here on out, and I would prefer if you defer to his instruction over mine. If you're still on board, I'd suggest setting this ship on a course for the perturbation in the shadow of moonlet T-2394. It's in this sector of the rings and its primarily metallic composition, combined with the disturbance it causes in the particulate, should serve as adequate cover."

Captain Pura's eyes narrow cannily. She's picked up on the shift in my language—a shift that's persisted, even when speaking with Iral. I'm no longer hurling my bloodright around the way I was just moments before I ran Ettian through. In fact, ever since, I haven't given a single order with the force of command. She's wise enough to know it could all be a scam designed to lull her into a false sense of security, but I hope she's open-minded enough to accept that it's a promise—one I intend to hold for as long as the throne is mine.

Bloodright is broken. It's torn the Umber Empire apart and turned it monstrous, and if I love Archon for all the ways it's saved me, I owe it to the empire to curb its relationship to inherent and inherited power until I've saved it in return.

But it does have its applications. As Captain Pura gives me a stiff nod and turns to Navigation, I shift my attention back to Communications. "I do have a personal missive I'd like you to send, if you wouldn't mind."

"As you wish, Your Majesty," the chief officer replies.

"Excellent." I turn back to the seats we once shared and let my gaze drop at last to Ettian—sprawled, ashen, and so, so still. I stoop, using the powersuit's strength and weight to scoop up my husband's body as easily as a child, slinging him carefully over my shoulder. "Make a broadcast to the area hailing the Umber heir," I say as I head for the bridge doors. With Ettian's weight bearing into me, it takes everything I have to make my next words come out steady and sure. "Let him know who's in charge."

CHAPTER 21

GAL

WHEN THE BROADCAST HITS, I wish I was alone.

The timing is impeccable. Here I am, seated before a meeting of my fleet leadership, with all of their faces arrayed on screens before me, watching them watch me learn that the man I once called the love of my life, the object of my most ardent affection and most furious hatred, has been murdered by the woman he betrayed me to wed. No amount of practice with my mother could prepare me for the challenge of hearing the news, ingesting it, and controlling my outward reaction all at once.

Ettian is dead. The words won't fit in my brain.

Wen has killed Ettian. Equally untenable.

You claim you were ready to burn him to the ground. That one sounds like my mother's voice, the one I used to hear crooning for me to lean into my worst instincts. Like she's daring me to admit— here before all of my admirals—that I never meant it.

I clench my left hand, feeling the ache of the bone I broke on my ring finger the last time my bluff got called. Hanji shot Ettian through the gut, and I beat her face in. The same boiling rage should be rising in me now, looking for an outlet. A target. Another place to smash my fists.

But all I feel is numb, and I know that's just as damning. Under the scrutiny of the fleet leadership, numbness is a confession of its own. My head reels as I try to piece together the *right* reaction—the one that salvages this moment before I lose my leadership's confidence. All of them received the broadcast at the same time. All of them have taken the news in stride, naturally. I see sick smiles, leering grins, and above all, eager eyes fixed on what must be my own feed, looking for the first sign of weakness they can fall upon. Never before have I been more aware of how right my mother is about these people. They're monsters, all of them, and the only way to survive their hunger is to turn it outward.

"The usurper is dead," I say, my voice perfectly, impregnably flat. Eighteen years of imperial training culminate in the way I'm clawing tooth and nail away from slipping into a panic attack in the sight of my fleet. "Archon's rebellion now falls under the command of his murderer, Wen emp-Archon."

I notice several people drop their attention to their readouts—no doubt to comb their files for what we know of her. Wen's been a thorn in Umber's side ever since Ettian took the crown, but our data on her betrays the unified opinion that's formed behind our lines. Our briefings have the basics logged—that she's a nobody uprooted from Corinth and tasked with much of the emperor's dirty work during the rebellion's early days, that she's a pilot skilled enough to handle a powersuit, and that she struck the decisive blow at Dasun. But there has never been an effort to *know* her deeper than her actions, even after Ettian married her. After all, she had no bloodright. Even when Ettian gave her one, it was easy to dismiss as the politicking of a green young emperor. It didn't *mean* anything.

But if there's anything that validates a bloodright claim, it's cold-blooded murder. It's the same maneuver that elevated my mother from her sister's backup to the Umber throne. The same maneuver she hoped would restore my people's faith in me once we'd bent Ettian into forsaking his empire for a love match. Wen just got there first.

And I may be imagining things, but I think it's putting sweat on some of my officers' brows. They knew Ettian. After months of battling him, they've come to anticipate how the Archon forces operate under his command. There was a sense of relief when we dropped into the Lusan system and discovered that the fleet here was commanded by the emperor's presence, not by proxy. Not only did it give us the confidence to strategize, knowing the playbook Archon would likely employ, but it dangled a shimmering bit of bait before my leadership's eyes. Glory to the officer who takes out the Archon usurper once and for all.

Now that glory's been snatched by someone we *can't* anticipate. Someone I've never been able to predict in all the time I've known her. My fleet leadership is looking over their plans for this engagement and wondering how many of them we'll be able to retain in the face of this paradigm shift.

It falls to me to embolden them. "Wen emp-Archon is even less suited for the throne than the usurper," I proclaim. "She's uneducated. Unfinished. She's had less than a year of training for command, and if she expects to hold out against the finest the Umber interior has to offer, she's in for a surprise."

As I speak, my attention drifts to the four screens I've positioned in the center of my display. On them are Admirals Norsat, San, Venta, and Hardisson. Norsat oversees fleet command, and the other three are his direct reports, tasked with maintaining the fore, rear, and body of the fleet respectively. They're distributed across three nimble flagships, with Norsat splitting Hardisson's bridge in the core of the fleet.

None of them are wise to the fact that those flagships have been infiltrated by my pack of should-be-dead knuckleheads. The Wraiths have taken up their postings, each assigned a member of the high command and tucked safely in the vents off their bridges. They're waiting for my signal.

But all I can think of is how far away they are. No one's been left behind to watch my back, and with regicide in the air, I know more than a few people on this call are getting ideas. My fingers twitch toward the encrypted comm line set up on my clip, the one that goes right to Hanji's ear. Every system's hell has truly iced through— I can't believe I'm thinking this, but gods, I wish she was here. I need her chattering vulgarities in my ear, trying to get a rise out of me with inane nonsense. The fact that she's not means that this is really happening. We're really about to put the endgame in motion.

I can picture her giving me the slightest of smirks, the slightest of nods—one that's part reassurance and part dare.

So I plunge ahead. "The Archon fleet is more vulnerable than we ever could have dreamed in this moment. If we act decisively and without hesitation, we can end this once and for all. Let these bastards join the dust of the ring they hide in like cowards. There's no life on any of the satellites within Turrot's orbit. You are free to fire as you wish. Blow the whole ruttin' thing to ash for all I care."

A sickening sense of relief begins to loosen the tension in my chest as I see the shift in my leadership's attention play out in real time. They've stopped scrutinizing me, looking for a weakness to exploit in the wake of Ettian's murder. By giving them permission to tear through this planet's ring system with impunity, I've dangled a piece of bait in front of them that's enticing enough to divert their focus. I've had plenty of practice at this with the Wraiths, and I know exactly how this game is played. It will only hold until the battle's through—then I'll have to find something else to catch their eyes, some other seed of discord to sow. I can see the long, catastrophic process chaining on and on and on, until I've built a reign as tyrannical as my mother's on the backs of a thousand vicious distractions for no higher purpose than to keep these animals from tearing the throne out from underneath me.

This is the pinnacle of my bloodright. This is everything I was raised for.

I let my voice drop down to a snarl. "This world is mine. These scraps of territory they cling to and call their empire is *mine*. And by the end of this engagement, I expect they won't forget it. Show no mercy. Give no quarter."

The trembling wrath in my voice will inevitably prompt extra scrutiny. My officers have come to expect the cold, casual cruelty my mother drilled into me, but now I'm starting to veer from the Umber ideal of rational, inevitable violence. I have no doubt they're wondering whether my fury is motivated more by a genuine desire to reclaim my empire or—as perhaps they're right to assume—a need to crush the woman who dared to steal the man I loved. Those who decide it's the latter must weigh whether that's motivation worth following into battle.

So it's up to me to remind them what's at stake here. "There is glory to be won on the field today, for every last one of you. Some say that the Imperial Fleet has grown soft in the time since the War of Expansion. That you've drifted aimlessly around the interior, 'defending' the empire from an absolute drought in serious threats. When I was trapped behind enemy lines, I heard the whispers that the fleet was coming—and the laughter that followed."

The barb lands visibly on some of my screens. Norsat and Hardisson in particular both look like they've taken a hearty swig of engine polish.

But hurt pride alone isn't enough to get these rusty-ass officers' blood pumping. "Make them eat that laughter, but never forget why we fight. Remember what's on the line. Remember the glorious shape the galaxy can take under unified Umber rule. These Archon bastards have besmirched the perfect order my mother built. I will build it back on a higher tier of perfection, and *you*—" I let my gaze sear into the camera, praying every officer to whom I promised territory feels the heat of it. "*You* will be that perfection's instrument."

The admirals sit up a little straighter—all of them, in near-comical unison. Loosening their leashes was just the beginning. This is the real bait. The promises I made them, the territory I dangled in front of their eyes. A chance to establish brand-new bloodright legacies, earned in the blaze of Archon's destruction.

It should disgust me that this—*this,* this hollow promise of power—is the thing that locks my leadership in, but a different feeling is rising in me faster than my gorge. The numbness that set in when the broadcast hit announcing the Archon handover is melting to a rising, righteous fury. "Captain Gordan," I announce, and the *Precipice*'s bridge snaps to attention around me, alarmed that my attention has abruptly shifted outside the world of the call I'm hosting. "The *Precipice* will lead the charge. Get this ship to the head of Admiral San's formation."

"Your Majesty," the captain objects with an absolutely *bold* degree of firmness, given that he's speaking back against a direct order. "It would be prudent to consider your safety before executing such a maneuver."

I go still, straightening predator-smooth as I fix him with the full weight of my gaze. I've always been told I have my mother's eyes, and now I turn them to their oldest purpose—bending the men of the Gordan bloodline to their every capricious whim. "Do I look," I start, my voice low and molten, "like a man who gives one single *rut* about my safety? I am the blood of Umber. My right to these systems is etched in my very veins. If I am not safe, it's because the gods themselves have decided to strike me down. Put us at the head of the forward group."

The captain's made it this far by staying in my mother's good graces, and clearly he still has the instincts locked in. He moves without hesitation to the central saddle, mounting up and shouting for Telemetry to plot the course.

I sink back in my seat, my wrath quelled but not fully satisfied. My gaze drops back to my screens—to the waiting faces of my leadership. It may be my imagination, but I think a few of them look *nervous* where before they were only eager. *Is the emperor letting his personal feelings pull us into this battle?* I can hear them asking. *Will he drag us into a reckless engagement to avenge the death of an enemy?*

I let my lips curl into a sneer. *So what if I am?*

"That's all. Happy hunting," I declare, and cut the call.

CHAPTER 22

WEN

I WAS BORN WAR-READY. I've been at war my entire life, from the moment I was pressed against my mother's heaving breast, screaming like I already had a bone to pick with the world. She raised me at her knee as she made her bid to rule the north side of Isla, and through her I got my earliest lessons in how to run an empire.

Then when I was eight, that empire crumbled beneath me. My mother died in battle, and I was left to the whims of the man who killed her and devoured every last bit of the world she'd built for me. I saw how easy it was to gut a hierarchy for parts, to convince everyone involved that this was just the natural order of things and it would be easiest to use this as an opportunity to advance rather than stake themselves to someone who'd already fallen and failed. I spent eight years biding my time, convinced I wasn't one of those people. I was going to be careful. I was going to watch and listen and learn, and on the day I knew I had it in the bag, I was going to take my revenge.

So I climbed the ranks from runner to chop shop girl, all the while keeping my eyes on the throne. But the throne had its eyes on me in turn. I hadn't yet learned how to be *watched*—how to move beneath notice—and so Dago Korsa saw me coming from a mile away. He knew he had to keep me down, and found all the little ways he could make sure I never reached him.

It was never quite enough. I think he wanted me broken, and I never so much as bent—not even on the day he had me thrown from the chop shop for what he claimed was an attempt on his life. He handed me over to a lieutenant with a known temper, and wouldn't you know it? A few weeks later, the bastard melted half my face.

If I concentrate—really concentrate—I can almost believe in the person I was before the fire of that Solstice-VI scorched away the illusions I clung to. The kid who thought she could play Korsa's game. Who thought she was clever enough to win it. In the aftermath, there was nothing left but fear, pain, and the certainty that everything I believed to be special about myself could be charred away in the blink of an eye.

I ran. I hid. I felt Isla closing around me like a trap. Felt myself get reckless, because at least that was more fun than getting desperate.

Of course, it was barely a month before another revelation cut the engines out from underneath me. I tried to sell a stolen skipship to a hapless-looking boy who turned out to be far more trouble than he was worth—and yet.

And yet.

There was something in his eyes. Isn't that what they say in the stories? *One look and I was gone.* Except it wasn't the first look that had me. I marked him for a sucker with money in his pockets, and when I found out he and his boyfriend were Umber deserters, I saw my long-awaited ticket onto the base outside the city where an Archon rebellion was amassing and Dago Korsa would have to get past an army to get to me.

But then we spent a night on a rooftop in Isla, caught in that hazy half sleep you get to when you know you can barely afford to let your guard down. Gal slumbered on his other side, dead to the world—a boy who'd never known the kind of fear that keeps you wary through the dark.

In the deepest part of the night, a skipship lifted off on the next block over, and Ettian's eyes snapped open at exactly the same time as mine. He looked to Gal first, because of course he did, but when his gaze made its way around to me, I met him. Really met him.

That was the look. The one that told me everything I needed to know about the guy who called himself Ettian Nassun back then. I caught him reacting to an instinct that had been ground deep into his bones by years of survival on the streets, but there was more to it than that. In that look, I saw the pinch of it. The unfairness—not because no one should have to live in that kind of terror, but because he had been meant for something else, and this wasn't it. *That* was the sameness I saw in his eyes, and that was what told me I'd be with him 'til the end.

And now it's the end.

I take a moment for myself before I reenter the bridge, listening to the smooth hum of the *Dawn*'s engines and the muffled rudiments the war drums are pounding through the corridors. I know the instant I step through those doors, I'll need to be the empress they expect, forged in fire, but here on the other side, in the darkened hallway, I can let my body sag into the powersuit's cradle, setting the limbs to lock and support me as I try to release the tension I've been carrying ever since I set this madness into motion.

There's no room for hesitation when I retake the bridge, so I let it all out of my system now, savoring the pause like a child with a stolen sweet. I let the war fall completely from my mind and switch my focus over to the thousands of subsystems wrapped around my body, from the temperature regulators to the extra comms tech not even my mechanics know about, checking each one to ensure it's fully operational.

Then I slip the suit's governance back over to my muscles' guidance, draw myself up tall, and step forward, triggering the doors to sweep open and admit me to the *Dawn*'s bridge.

"Empress on deck," Communications hollers, and every operation that can afford it ceases as the soldiers rise and salute.

I dismiss them, praying I've gotten the gesture down. It takes such careful balance to be efficient without flippancy, but I hope I've managed to pull it off. The situation is far too tender right now, and I can't afford to incur any doubt about my commitment to the role I've just promoted myself into.

The soldiers take the dismissal and drop back down to their seats and their tasks—with the exception of Captain Pura, who releases her hand but remains standing as I approach her station. "Your Majesty," she reports. "We've just locked into position at T-2394. The Umber blockade is beginning to cinch. Our telemetry seems to indicate their flagship, the *Precipice,* has lunged to the fore of it."

"Is that the one Gal emp-Umber is aboard?" I ask, setting my hands against the central console as I lean in to examine her charts. In the time since I left the bridge, General Iral has done an admirable job of tucking our fleet into defensive positions throughout Turrot's rings, but several vulnerabilities catch my eye like stars gone supernova. I purse my lips.

In principle, the idea of supplanting the Archon tradition of bloodright by refusing to exercise one I've clearly earned is solid, but it crumbles so easily in the face of what we're up against. The battlefield laid out before me is a puzzle, and I want to solve it so badly that it pains me to keep my mouth shut. I know I'm fighting a second war with stakes that go far beyond the outcome of a single battle— stakes that will determine the course of history, if we make it through this—but I can't help thinking of all the souls whose lives are on the line. Whose lives I could be saving if I just take the power the philosophy of bloodright decrees I've earned.

"It would seem so," Pura replies, oblivious to the minor crisis detonating inside my skull. "Though it doesn't make much sense why the Umber heir would be flinging himself to the forefront."

"Maybe he expects an easy victory?" I offer, my pursed lips sliding into a lopsided smirk.

It's a temperature check, and Pura's tightening jaw tells me all I need to know. The Archon fleet has accepted committing to this offensive as a last stand, but my flagship captain has a good head on her shoulders, and in her estimation, this could very well turn into an Umber landslide.

It won't, but my belief hardly matters. If Archon is going to do this without me aping centuries of imperial bullshit, they need a strategy that will convince them not only can they hold the line—they can win, and win decisively.

Fortunately I've got a few in the tank.

I drop into one of the seats at the main console's side, grimacing at the squeal of protest it lets out under the powersuit's bulk. My eyes ease toward a red smudge still lingering on one of the screens, but I can't let it steal my focus beyond a mental note to run a cleaning crew through here sometime before the engagement goes hot. Now that I think about it, the air's still tinged with the raw iron scent of blood.

Pura notices the way I've frozen. Probably has her suspicions about what did it. Her eyes narrow, and she drops her voice to a murmur as she asks, "The body?"

"Burned it," I reply steadily.

She tilts her head, a move that reads like *I don't know what I expected,* then settles into her own seat at the console and starts cycling through the *Dawn*'s operations.

Knew I picked her for a reason.

To the task, then. I was born war-ready, and now it's time to prove it. I pull up our rosters on one screen and the reporting of the Umber forces on another. We're sorely outnumbered, both in dreadnoughts and support craft, but Umber has always been a little *too* dependent on overwhelming force, and it makes them sloppy. Makes them rush into situations that are a little thornier than their first appearances. The Imperial Fleet dropped into their blockade assuming they'd be trapping us for easy pickings, but the "terrain," for lack of a better term, is far more complicated than that.

As I predicted, the Umber dreadnoughts have turned broadside to the planet to avoid any gravity-assisted maneuvers like the one I used to take down the *Fulcrum.* This far out from Turrot's grasp, the gesture is fairly senseless—not only does it present their largest sides as a target, but it removes half of their main batteries' firing capacity with all of their targets on the planet-facing side. On top of that, it forces them to make all course adjustments on a single plane or else risk reducing that capacity to barely anything at all.

I feel the possibilities branching inside me, solidifying with the field. In the time since I left the bridge, Archon forces have moved to consolidate into two wings: one made up of dreadnoughts and their ancillaries under the command of Commodore Esperza in the *Torrent,* and the rest composed of ships classed at corvette and below, which General Iral himself heads in his flagship, the *Aegis.*

Umber has tracked the movement and responded in kind, shifting their blockade to solidify their coverage of the two bodies. I trace back our readouts of the way the dreadnoughts move, sorting and circling as the formation shifts across my screen. Their command is broken down in thirds, it would seem—a fore of lighter, faster ships ready to move into the ring itself, a body of dreadnoughts cruising sideways, and a rear of lighter ships with heavier artillery meant to provide coverage.

My gaze narrows on the *Precipice,* which has just shoved itself to the fore, heedless of any branch of command. Gal is aboard, all right, riding that bloodright wherever his whims carry him. Some of the dreadnoughts local to his position have shifted to provide cover. On the one hand, it's broadcasting to every enemy in the vicinity that the *Precipice* bears the Umber heir himself.

But on the other, it draws their resources to defense. The *Precipice* has just made itself a huge, obvious distraction, and *that* is something I intend to work with.

The possibilities branch. I prune the tree. "The *Precipice* has placed itself like a prize, and they've shifted valuable coverage to defend it," I murmur. Pura's head jerks up from her own operations. "They intend to lead with their lighter craft—craft that can weather the planet's pull and root us out of the rings. Esperza's dreadnoughts should lay down the coverage necessary to beat back that advance so we can preserve the cover we've managed to stake. Iral's wing will run offense against the dreadnoughts—not the ones at the core of their formation defending the *Precipice,* but the ones on the outside that have their firing power free to use offensively. With their maneuverability cut, we can use our own lighter craft to focus fire on their less-defended rears and the engineering cores there."

"Are these your orders, Your Majesty?" the captain asks, her fingers shifting to hover over the Communications section of her station.

"Suggestions," I say, consolidating my findings into a data packet and dropping it into the fleet strategy channel. "Though I do hope they're welcome. Umber's aboard the *Precipice.* Jammed himself forward like bait. We'd be fools to take it."

I keep my thoughts to myself, but a vein of worry has begun to pulse inside me. I've committed my fleet into General Iral's hands, an act I can't revoke without using my bloodright to override him. I want so badly to believe in the general's experience. I want to believe he'll see the value of the strategies I'm laying out. Ever since my coronation—ever since Breha, really—I've been working hard both building up his trust and making sure I know exactly how he thinks. But the general lost his twin brother to Iva emp-Umber's cruelty, and with her heir dangling so tantalizingly before him, my predictions are tenuous, more wagers than equations.

I know what it's like when the impulse for revenge scorches you from the inside, and even so, I've staked my carefully tended tree of strategies on my assessment of the general's behavior. He'd better not prove me wrong.

Both because the survival of the Archon fleet depends on it, *and* because if my larger strategy is going to work—the one I need the fiddly bit of comms tech in my suit to enact—Archon needs to behave exactly as I've ordained.

A slight ringing in my earpiece tells me the channel's still open. "So we'll whittle away at the dreadnoughts Umber would be using for offense," I continue. "Meanwhile . . ."

CHAPTER 23

GAL

THE *PRECIPICE'S* BRIDGE feels far too silent for the situation coming to a boil outside the dreadnought's hull. This is the first time I've ridden into battle without the constant hammering of Archon drums pulsing through my skull, and I think I'm starting to understand their purpose more and more with every passing second. It's not that they're a distraction—they're a refinement. A meditation, a focusing of thought that doesn't allow for fear or anxiety or anything else beyond the simple order of their call.

In their absence, I've crafted a rhythm of my own, an internal mantra that cycles through my skull over and over and over again.

I am my mother's perfect heir.

I am my mother's perfect heir.

I am my mother's perfect heir.

No amount of repetition will make it true, but I let it focus me all the same as my flagship shoulders into its place on the front.

"Rin, status report," I mutter into my comms. I've commandeered a workstation in the central ring of the *Precipice*'s bridge and spread my nonsense over it, dialing myself into a five-way line that connects me to the Wraiths' postings spying on my admirals' bridges.

"Whatever the opposite of ruttin' right off is, they're doing that," she says, her audio nearly obscured by the frantic tap of her fingers against her datapad. She must be plugged into the bridge's intelligence directly, trying to process a battle spanning millions of miles on a screen barely bigger than her palm. "We're still working on a numbers estimate—gonna be impossible to pinpoint exactly with the cover this thick."

I bring up the latest models from our scopes, which render the fog of Turrot's ring tenuous enough to see right through. It does us no favors when the fog itself keeps their ships off our instrumentation, and all I'm left with is a map of several known objects larger than a mile in diameter floating in the planet's orbit and a scattering of anomalies that *could* be Archon ships. For the larger ones, it's a safe bet—even with the ring for cover, a dreadnought sticks out like a sore thumb. But the cruisers, corvettes, and other support craft are much harder to pick out. They could be flocking to the dreadnoughts' skirts, ready to defend their larger cousins.

Or they could be settling into attack formations and ready to launch on a vector pointed straight at us.

The eerie silence of the bridge is starting to sound like a held breath. This isn't like any battle I've been in before, where ships drop onto the field from superluminal with their batteries hot and ready for action. There's a boundary drawn here. Someone has to be the first to cross it.

And I think everyone knows it's going to be me. In this murky field, I have to pick our first victim and pray I get it right. If the *Precipice* breaks the stillness with a total whiff of a shot, well, there goes any respectability my command hoped to establish.

That's assuming you had any shot at respectability in the first place, the voice in the back of my head reminds me.

The best-case scenario for my imperial reputation is to get it in one—figure out which ship Wen's aboard and vaporize it—but I'm never going to be that lucky, even if we had sightlines on the entire

Archon fleet. The message, the . . . *taunt* she threw out was simulcast from multiple origin points and impossible to backtrace to a single ship. But she's out there somewhere in the ring. No Archon ships have fled the field on a superluminal vector.

I sigh, leaning back in my seat and pushing up my crown to knead my forehead. Every second we wait is a torturous moment in a galaxy without Ettian, and I just want it to be *over* already.

"Steady, boss," Hanji's voice urges. "We have a plan, remember?"

Rut this. Rut this to every system's hell and back. I surge abruptly from my seat, feeling every eye on my bridge snap up to me with sudden terror. "Archon thinks they can hide themselves in the rings," I snarl. "Let's chum the waters. Captain Gordan, have the main batteries fire. No targeting. Fast as they can cycle."

My uncle rears back in his saddle, his brow furrowing. "If I may advise, while the representation may look condensed on your screen, the chances of hitting anything are—"

"Did I say I want you to hit something, or did I say I want a *ruttin' light show*?" I snap, slamming one fist down on my console as my other hand drops to the hilt of my mother's knife on my belt. "I do not need your advice, Captain. I need your compliance without hesitation."

"As you wish, Your Majesty," the captain mutters, then sinks meekly back down into his operations. "All batteries, lay down untargeted scattershot through the rings."

I settle back down into my seat as the screens around me plunge into the chaos of unstructured fire, each gun warming at its own pace as the order shuffles through the *Precipice*'s outer decks. "Admiral San," I call out over the channel that links me to the fleet's high command. "I want every dreadnought on the front lines following the *Precipice*'s lead."

"Your will be done," she replies, then drops her mic levels low enough that I don't get blasted with the full volume of her shouting my orders across her own ship's bridge. San took to my offer like a natural pilot to a ship fresh from the machine shop. In another life, I might have admired her for her ruthless hunger for power, but right now all I care about is its utility. I pull up my readouts from the fore of the fleet just to watch her command ripple over them, guns warming across every dreadnought.

A faint thrum pulses through the *Precipice,* and I know the first salvo has been made.

Then another. Another. Arrhythmic, pounding, shuddering through the floor beneath my feet. They're no Archon drums, but the first beats of my chaos make lovely music in my ears all the same. My readouts light up with the trajectories, then burst into fireworks as the rest of the forward group begins to add their own shots to the fray.

"Admiral Norsat's trying to get his communications team to hail you," Hanji chuckles into my ear. I can all but hear her shit-eating grin. "Think they're about to discover our little jam."

I let a smirk curl over my lips. As part of my bid to keep the admirals in line, I've let Hanji wreak havoc on their comms lines, rendering my flagship absolutely inaccessible to any of them on a direct line. She, Rin, and Rhodes have worked up some disgusting black magic code that I won't even pretend to understand and used my imperial security overrides to bury it hopelessly deep in the dreadnoughts' systems.

"Ah, they just caught on," Hanji says. "Expect a scolding over the shared line in three . . . two . . ."

"Your Majesty, I believe our communications have been sabotaged," Norsat says. "The hack seems to be internal—we're running analysis now—but I can't pull up your direct line."

"Your communications are working exactly as they should, Fleet Admiral," I reply through an incorrigible smile. "This is a bit of my personal design. You'll also find it a little difficult to hail San or Venta without keeping me in the loop, but feel free to chat with Hardisson all you like."

He takes a moment to process that, to form his theories about what, precisely, I think I'm doing. "I was under the impression," he begins through what sounds like gritted teeth, "that this offensive was *my* operation. The agitation your sudden tactical swerve has caused disrupts all the effort we've been putting into scouting the battlefield before we engage."

I lean my cheek into my knuckles, my jaw pulsing tight at this man's outright temerity. "Fleet Admiral Norsat, I'm disappointed you're so inflexible. Especially after Admiral San took my instruction with no resistance whatsoever. It's giving me doubts about those potential . . . future prospects we discussed."

"Forgive me if it's a little difficult to imagine myself governing Naberrie after being atomized by a bit of Archon boltfire we weren't prepared for," Norsat snarls.

A beat of silence crackles through the channel.

"Now hold on one moment," Admiral Venta says, his voice sharpened to a lethal edge. "I thought *I* was getting Naberrie after the campaign."

In my private line, the Wraiths start to giggle.

In the admirals' channel, the shouting starts.

I let out a light sigh, my gaze roving up and down the scans projected on my screens, watching as bolt after bolt tears haphazardly through the rings, watching as objects skirt the blasts with enough prescience that they can easily be pinpointed as Archon ships, watching the dirt I've kicked up with the detached disinterest of a lonely god. Umber rides into battle in its full glory, all guns blazing, and here at the end of all things, I only feel empty.

Without Ettian, I'm just so . . . *tired* of it all.

At least the Wraiths are enjoying themselves. The admirals blustering at one another over who's been promised what has reduced them to wheezing laughter they're struggling to pin down before it gives away their locations.

"Shut up," Hanji hisses a full octave higher than her usual pitch. "Quiet, all of you little monsters, you're gonna—"

A crackle of static overtakes the line, whiting out the Wraiths for a solid thirty seconds. Has Norsat's comms team managed to pinpoint the source of their problems?

"Sorry about that," Hanji says, her voice cutting through the noise as the channel stabilizes again. "Got another call." Before I can ask for clarification, she announces, with cold precision and absolutely no hint of her usual smile, "Wraith Squadron, detach."

The dread that floods me is so instinctive it's a wonder I have any capacity for rational thought in its wake. I last heard those words—those *exact* words—in the cockpit of a Viper the day my life should have ended. *Would* have ended, if it weren't for Ettian swooping in to save my ass. They were the words that announced the original Wraith Squadron, a coordinated attack group of twenty academy students hell-bent on ending my life. My Wraiths took their name in jest.

Only it doesn't sound like a joke anymore.

"What the hell is going on? This wasn't the plan—" Before I can get another word out, the line goes suddenly dead in my ear, leaving behind a piercing ringing tone that only seems to get worse when I tear out my earpiece. Whatever's happening on the other end of it, it isn't good. My gaze slips up to find Captain Gordan watching me warily, the command of his ship fallen to the wayside as he tries to discern why his emperor has gone from vicious to clammy in the space of a heartbeat.

I ignore him, leaning forward to thumb through the independent lines I should have with each of the Wraiths. All dead. Rin, Rhodes, and Ollins all individually pulled contact.

It's happening. It's really happening. I try to twist the words into a new mantra that'll ground me in the reality of my situation, but my brain is racing a light-year a minute. It should be crushing me into my seat, but instead I feel as if the grav generators have cut, as if I'm about to float right out of my chair. The cold sweat is giving way to heat, the numbness to a fire crackling through my bones.

A sudden bang rocks the bridge, and a vent cover bursts from the ceiling with explosive force, pummeling into the floor so hard it leaves a warped impression in the metal. Bridge security leaps into action, but by the time they have their blasters out of their holsters, a blacked-out figure has plummeted from the opening, firing as he goes. His stunner bolts catch the officers square in their chests, sending them to their knees one after the other as he lands in a crouch and immediately rolls to the shelter of the nearest station.

By the time I draw my next breath, he's dropped half the crew and sent the other half ducking for cover like the cowards they are.

I rise from my chair to face him, fighting to keep my eyebrows from creeping into my hairline. Ollins Cordello's been a haphazard mess the entire time I've known him—a truth that obfuscates his jaw-dropping competency when you put a gun in his hands and point him at a target.

I'd burst out laughing if it weren't for the blaster he's just leveled at my forehead. In my periphery, I see jaws falling open and faces going pale as my officers struggle to rationalize the dead man who's just single-handedly taken the bridge.

"No one move a muscle, or the emperor gets it!" Ollins shouts, ducking close as he loops an arm around my neck and presses his armored body against my side. The surreality of the moment has me by the throat so badly that I'm tempted to swoon for dramatic effect.

Instead I dig deep for a voice that won't shake and call out, "Do as he says!"

The bridge stills under the force of an imperial command. The vibrations of the distant firing of the *Precipice*'s batteries shudder up my legs, clashing dissonantly with the hum of the deflector armor Ollins wears and even worse with the hammering of my heart as he pulls me roughly toward the bridge doors.

"C'mon, Umber," Ollins says. "Let's go for a little ride."

CHAPTER 24

WEN

"GOT A REQUEST from the *Torrent* for Your Majesty, direct,"
Communications calls across the *Dawn*'s bridge.

I lift a hand and beckon, and the line opens on my screens a half
second later. "Commodore, I figured I'd be hearing from you
sooner," I say, trying my damnedest to partition my attention between the predictive modeling keeping our ships clear of Umber's
haphazard firing through the rings and stringing a sentence together.

"Been a little preoccupied," Esperza replies tersely. Through her
line, I can hear the faint pattering of her fingers working furiously
against her station. "And I had a feeling I wasn't going to get much
out of this conversation."

"Meaning?"

"Meaning you have a plan, and I've got the sense we've only seen
part of it."

"You know me," I concede, the corner of my lips pulling taut.
"Then to what do I owe the pleasure?"

She lets out a short wheeze that might be a laugh. "So you're
going to tell me that there's a plan, but you're not going to share?"

I feel the pinch of it. Ever since my marriage elevated me far beyond her station, I've felt downright awkward speaking to the woman who's been my mentor and fiercest advocate since the moment I arrived at the front for the first time. With Iral, I was forging a new relationship where only scaffolding existed before. But with Esperza, I felt as though I'd just knocked down a building and found myself faced with the task of putting it back together brick by brick. She didn't teach me everything I know, but everything I am is thanks to the framework she gave me to rise above my oh-so-humble beginnings. There's guilt in surpassing her, and worse in the power differential between us suddenly inverting to an exponential degree. A part of me still wants to prove myself to her, and I'm trying to see it as a good thing.

"Maybe part of the plan is you not knowing the breadth of it," I offer. "Maybe all I need from you is for you to continue serving admirably. And I must say, the dreadnoughts under your command are holding the line beautifully."

"Don't pull that trick on me, Iffan—I *taught you* that trick," she grumbles. "Look, I've been getting my marching orders from General Iral, but as I understand it, he's moving based on a plan *you* concocted. Iral's a good soldier, a great leader, but a bit of a shit strategist if we're being honest here. So I'm sure you explained what you were doing just enough to get him thinking it was good enough to give us a shot. But from where I sit, this plan has some pretty fundamental holes."

"Such as?" I ask, shifting in my chair as I draw up the readouts from the general's attack groups. They're heartbeats away from breaching the ring's cover and starting their first runs against the front line of Umber dreadnoughts.

"Your foundations are sound. You're using the cover elegantly, baiting their fire in the right direction, and running purposefully at their weak points. That's enough for the first wave. But the way I see it, Umber's first line of dreadnoughts is only your first set of problems. The strategy you built isn't sustainable. And as you said, I know you. So I want to know what's up your sleeve."

I turn my head slightly, the reaction so baked-in that I do it despite the fact that she can't see me through the audio-only line. Even if we'd been face-to-face, I'm not sure anyone but Ettian has ever picked up on that tic—the way I give people a little more burn than usual when I'm trying to keep a secret.

Because yeah, I've got a few things I'm sitting on. Things ranging from little surprises that'll hopefully cement the Archon Empire's goodwill toward me to world-shattering secrets I'll take to my grave. The trick is to have enough of the former to shield the latter.

The other trick is knowing exactly when to pull back the curtain. "If I tell you you're right, will you promise to still act surprised when it happens?" I ask, tucking my head down into my powersuit's collar to shield my words from Captain Pura, who's still sitting right across from me.

"Gods of all systems," Esperza mutters, but there's a smile behind it. "Fine. I swear—three claps, at least. But I'm saving the standing ovation for when you genuinely surprise me."

"It didn't surprise you when I killed my husband and took sole control of the Archon throne?" I ask mildly. An ugly twinge of guilt hits me at how easily the words come.

Esperza hesitates. I can picture the thin line her lips have tautened into. "You've never quite made sense to me, Iffan." I'm not sure whether I should be reassured by the fact that she's still not addressing me by my proper title. I can't tell if it's familiarity or an act of resistance. "I could always tell you were thinking about more than you were saying, and that you had desires that went deeper than anything you expressed. So when I found out about the . . . *change-over*, it clarified some things—and thus it didn't exactly knock me over."

I sit with that. Turn it over as I watch the guns on Iral's attack groups go hot. So much of what I've put in motion is an act for an Umber audience, designed to strike fear in their hearts. Ideally it should also galvanize Archon, showing them that I'm willing to choose the empire's well-being over my own bleeding heart, but playing to both sides simultaneously is a delicate balancing act.

I remind myself that Esperza's still here, still talking to me. I wouldn't doubt that if she really thought I was about to drag the Archon Empire down the wrong path, she'd have ordered one of her dreadnoughts to obliterate my flagship the second she found out what I did to Ettian. She sees the larger picture—and knows there's cards up my sleeve I'm not playing yet.

But she still felt the need to call. To make sure.

I can feel her trust starting to go brittle in my hands. I need to salvage it before it's too late, or else everything I've done to get here is for nothing. "Over the past months, I've been working with embedded operatives in the Umber fleet," I tell her. Pura's head snaps up—I've just spoken frankly, no longer concealing my words in my powersuit's neck. "About ten minutes ago, they threw over all four of the admirals governing this offensive. We should start to see the effects of that at any moment."

Esperza lets out a low whistle. "Dasun wasn't good enough for you, was it?"

"Dasun was proof of concept. Umber gets distracted by fireworks too easily to properly learn from their mistakes. All of their tactics have adjusted to protect their dreadnoughts from another nuisance in a powersuit, but they didn't take a long hard look at why they actually lost the battle. Umber fleets are vulnerable to decapitation. Take out their leadership, and all the firing power of a hundred dreadnoughts won't save you from the internal chaos. I got my people in the right place at the right time, and I pulled the trigger."

"You say you took out the admirals," Esperza ponders. "But according to the arrival herald, this fleet's leadership goes a little higher than that."

"Which is precisely why I'm telling you this," I reply with a grin. "My operatives have secured a high-value asset and need safe passage through the scrum. They'll be aboard a small pleasure cruiser, designation *Spearhead,* departing from the *Precipice.* I need you to make sure that ship has a clear path from there to the *Dawn.*"

"Need" is perhaps a bit too strong of a word for it. All the *Spearhead* has to do is make it into the rings and then it's all but free and clear, and given the much more pressing concerns Umber has to deal with, it's unlikely they'd fire on any defecting craft, much less the empress's personal cruiser. My need is less tactical, more . . . well, in some sense it *is* tactical, but more about internal politics. I need Esperza to be needed.

The commodore lets out a hum, one I know for sure is accompanied by a shake of her head.

"Something wrong?" I ask, trying—and I'm sure failing—not to sound anxious.

"I've pulled my fair share of nonsense," she says, her voice dropping from the polished "officer tone" she tends to use before her subordinates to the provincial, piratical borderworld drawl that has always been Esperza at her realest. "You've heard the stories of my younger days, before I had a suited knight to sort me out. I was teetering toward the edge of something then, something Omoe saved me from. I could feel the trouble getting too big for me. If I didn't pay the favor forward, I'd be downright disrespecting her memory, so tell me honest—you're not feeling anything like that right now, are you?"

It's a better reassurance than anything she could have said direct, and it pulls a softer smile out of me. "Don't go soft on me, Commodore," I mutter. "Gonna need you sharp as hell for this next part."

"That's not an answer, Iffan."

I huff. "No trouble in my life has ever felt like too much for me, but you'll be the first to know if that changes." My suit's HUD lights up with an incoming communication, and adrenaline spikes through my system. "The *Spearhead*'s just launched."

Esperza pauses for so long I want to leap through the comm line and shake her. "Got it on our scopes. Sending a message across the dreadnought line that its vector is not to be interrupted. You're sure your people are aboard, right? Would hate to have nothing but 'the empress told me to do it' as an excuse for Iral when he asks why exactly an Umber ship was able to run straight at the *Dawn*."

"Tell the general it was my request," I say, drawing the *Spear-*

head's flight path up on my HUD. "And don't worry—the *Dawn*'s got its own guns if they try anything funny."

Which I'm not putting entirely past them. There's what Esperza would call a general tendency toward nonsense with this bunch. At times, it's well-suited for my own brand of chaos. At others—for example, the mess at Breha, which I'm *still* in awe we pulled off—the nonsense has a tendency to take over.

Rocks and rust, I think as I watch the Wraiths' approach. *Please, let this work.*

CHAPTER 25

GAL

YOU'D THINK I'D be used to this by now.

I try to convince myself this isn't anything I haven't done before, reeling through every experience that's led me to here. The betrayal above Rana, when my classmates turned on my Viper in a coordinated instant. My capture during the first wave of the Archon rebellion, when General Iral dragged me into the Archon court and started preparing for my execution. The moment Hanji Iwam kicked my door in, stuffed me in a breach suit, and hauled me back to my mother's knee as I scrabbled and fought to stay by Ettian's side.

I've done this so many times. But I'm never any more prepared for it, and no matter how much I steel myself, I can't reckon with my own reckoning, for what's sure to be the last time.

Not even when the airlock unseals and admits us to the *Dawn*'s stark, imposing halls. I walk through them, feeling as if I'm in a dream. The Wraiths are packed tight around me, moving with the same coordination we practiced a thousand times when we prepared to free Esperza moments before her execution. We breeze past Archon security officers, who watch us go with hands on the hilts of their blasters, ready for the second the situation turns ugly.

I want to tell them not to bother. The turn's already happened. Everything from here forward is inevitable.

Maybe I should have fought when Ollins dragged me off the bridge of the *Precipice.* I clawed tooth and nail trying to free myself from Hanji when she dragged me off the *Torrent,* after all. But that was when my only audience was my nightmare second-in-command and the even worse nightmare who had conspired to tear me away from Ettian's side in exchange for her precious commodore. Sure, Ollins downed most everyone between us and the *Spearhead* on the path we cut through the *Precipice*'s core—and sure, the Wraiths probably jammed the camera feeds—but I should have given more careful thought to what my people's last memory of me will be, and what purpose it'll serve.

That worry drains from my bloodstream the second the bridge doors peel open. Wen, it seems, has thought of everything. She probably remembers the day I was dragged into the Archon court, when Iral's people wasted so much time they could have spent killing me setting up the cameras that were supposed to capture the moment.

I step onto the *Dawn*'s bridge to find the lenses already prepared and Wen emp-Archon, Flame Empress triumphant, standing between them in the splendor of her powersuit.

Her eyes go to Hanji. "Longshot," she says with a smirk and a nod.

"Firecracker," Hanji replies. "Brought a little gift to commemorate your ascension. Express delivery. No dings whatsoever in transit."

At that, Wen's gaze finally settles on me. I've seen her in a hundred broadcasts since her coronation, watched her image dissected by a thousand Umber pundits, but seeing the platinum crown on her head in person is something else entirely. It glimmers faintly in the bridge's scattered lights as she lifts her chin higher, lording the monstrous height the powersuit grants her. I search her expression for cracks that hint at remorse or regret, hoping for a peek behind the mask she wears for the cameras, but she's better than that. My image was an afterthought—hers is a carefully constructed battleship, weapons hot at every angle.

I shake my head, rolling my eyes. What does it matter if it looks frivolous? These are my last moments. Might as well do whatever I damn well please with them. I've never been able to live on my own terms in the public eye. From the moment I was first unveiled to the galaxy, I've calculated every move, second-guessed every impulse, lived in perpetual fear of myself. I'm so close to being free of it all, but just this once, I want to feel like I'm allowed to both exist in my body and be seen in it.

"Gal emp-Umber," Wen begins.

"Wen emp-Archon," I reply. Her marriage legitimized her in the sight of Archon law, striking Ettian down legitimized her in the sight of Umber's fears, but me calling her by her proper title, doubly won, is perhaps the final blow needed to obliterate any doubt of her legitimacy. Even in the face of the inevitable, I address her as an equal.

"Your fleet is teetering on the edge of chaos. Your admirals and their bridges have been struck down, your communications severed, and you, the masthead of this army, have yourself been removed from your command and brought before me." She turns on a heel, setting her sights on the primary camera in the array that's been set up. "The Umber emperor has ridden out to subjugate the worlds his mother unjustly seized and reinforce a decade of tyranny that has turned Archon from a glorious, wealthy empire to a husk scraped clean for the profit of the Umber interior." Her gaze slips back over her shoulder to me, eyes narrowing. "Have you done this under your mother's command, Umber?"

The weight of the galaxy's eye rests on me. "No," I snarl, leaning perhaps a bit too hard into the theater of it. "*I* command the Imperial Fleet. *I* set them on this vector. I had the empress's blessing, but the empress has crowned me as an equal, and as her sole heir, the future of the galaxy is *my* bloodright."

Wen's lips tease toward a smirk the second the words "sole heir" leave my mouth. The cards are on the table. My mother's legacy rests on my shoulders, and this is what I've managed to do with it—bring utter ruin on the most glorious fleet the empire has ever mustered at the hands of a lesser force. *This* is my bloodright and everything it's earned me.

There's still a part of me reeling for an alternate scenario, even as the reality of this one firms up around me. I had a childish dream once—a dream to dismantle my mother's violence and supplant it with an empire run on *my* terms. That dream's been dashed on the rocks so many times I can scarcely keep count, from the moment Ettian stepped into his bloodright and reframed the reality of everything my rule was destined to uphold to the moment I stepped into my own and my mother began to educate me on exactly what it took to keep the Umber Empire from tearing itself to shreds.

It was only ever a fantasy—it never could have worked. At first I believed it because I saw an Archon uprising that wouldn't stop until the carefully cultivated peace Umber had established was pulled up from the roots. Then because I thought I could defect from my responsibility entirely and join Ettian's righteous fight. *Then* because I convinced myself I was finally in a position to achieve my childhood dreams—that it was possible to dismantle my mother's empire, serve true justice to Archon, and build my own vision for Umber's future from the throne I'd been reluctantly restored to.

This is that vision made real. The only way it ever could have ended. I was never destined to be a peacemaker. Peace made by Umber could never be called a just peace in the first place. All we were ever good for was outsourcing our internal strife into the trappings of unity by dumping it on others. And in the end, I did what I was born for—emulating my mother's lust for blood right into my own ruin.

"And what do you have to say for yourself now?" Wen asks. Her tone's dropped soft, almost gentle. It's so hard to reconcile her with the chaotic little tempest I first met in a rented room on the other side of the galaxy.

I take a deep breath, then ease carefully down onto one knee. "I offer unconditional surrender and immediate cease-fire. On top of that, I offer an exchange. I am willing to trade my life for the lives of my people. Take it, and allow them to retreat to the border of the Umber Empire in peace. If any of them should fire on your ships in defiance of my command, count them disavowed from the bonds of this pact and do with them what you will, but my express order to my remaining troops is this: quiet your guns, surrender, and leave Archon to its justly won spoils."

I can imagine how that's going to go over with my fleet command, but all the same, I feel part of me loosen in relief. No imperial directive that can possibly supersede my own will be able to reach them for days. Either they follow my orders and withdraw, or they operate in direct defiance of the man they've sworn to serve and invite the wrath of the woman who's handed them their asses before the worst of the fighting even starts.

They'll choose the latter—I'm all but sure of it. I don't have the time or the skill it would take to deprogram them from the ruthless Umber mindset, and I *certainly* haven't built the fleet's respect in the brief time I've helmed it. The Wraiths have taken out the admiralty, leaving a power vacuum far too tempting to pass up, and I know for certain the remaining officers were handpicked to be exactly the sort who would jump to fill it.

But the surrender is the most I can do for the peace with the time I have left. If I have to go now, I go honest, on my own terms.

Wen nods. "I accept your terms and offer my own promise," she says, keeping her eyes fixed on mine. "Mark the time of the emperor's order. This broadcast is going out wide, unencrypted. I'm giving one hour, galactic standard, for full compliance. Should be enough time to rein everyone in and withdraw those dreadnoughts. But anyone who's not burning to escape Turrot's orbit by the time that countdown is over has accepted the consequences. And anyone who dares fire on my fleet in the interim will be met with equivalent force."

The question hangs in the air. How much do my officers value the sacrifice I'm making? How much is an imperial life and a final imperial command worth to them?

I probably won't be around for the moment they decide on their answer.

Wen's hand slips down to the hilt of her vibrosword, and I feel as if a hand has clamped around my heart. A shadow's dropped over her face, and she finally ducks her gaze, staring down at her power-suit's bulk as she murmurs, "If you have any goodbyes . . ."

I rise, willing my legs not to give out underneath me. I don't know if my palms can get any sweatier. It takes every last bit of courage in me to turn my back on Wen and face the Wraiths, who've arrayed themselves in their usual line behind us.

Before, I hadn't really felt the weight of the cameras looking on. They were part of the usual theater of my life. But now I look at the lineup of my four closest friends, the four operatives who will forever go down in history as the traitors who dragged me to my death, and I realize that this moment can only ever be performance. What parting words can I possibly give them that will sum up the breadth of what I feel looking each of them in the eye right now? Nothing truthful. Nothing fully real.

"For your sakes," I mutter, "I hope it's worth it. Every last inch of everything you've done."

Hanji's eyes meet mine. I trust she knows me well enough to know everything I'm not saying. I couldn't even pretend to know what goes on inside her skull enough to say the reverse. She tips her head to the side. "We'll miss you, Gal."

"Kiss my ass, Iwam."

The surprised smirk that flickers across her face is the sweetest comfort she could possibly offer me. With that, I turn back to Wen.

The Flame Empress arches her eyebrow at me. "Any other last words?"

I spread my arms in a shrug, barely biting down on the urge to tell her to *just get it over with already*. There's nothing left to say, and nothing more I can do. The galaxy's drawn its lot. All that remains is for Wen to seal her victory.

And for me to face it. On my feet, arms outstretched, eyes open.

Strike me down, I dare her with every inch of my body. *Like you did with Ettian. This is the easy one.*

Wen pulls the vibrosword hilt from her hip and steps in close. Her free hand settles on my shoulder so casually that for a moment she looks less like an empress in power armor, more like a teammate taking the baton for the next leg of the race. "You'll be with him," she breathes, soft enough I'm certain no one else in the vicinity heard.

The last of my tension loosens at her words. She brings the hilt up against my chest and thumbs the trigger.

There's no pain—only a *thud,* a weight, and the distant wet flush that begins to soak into my jacket as my vision goes dark, dark, dark.

CHAPTER 26

WEN

FOR THE SECOND TIME TODAY, I wipe an imperial bloodright from my vibrosword's hilt.

The peaceful look on Gal's face is at odds with the blood pooling around him. He was ready—I have to believe that. But I can't let myself get bogged down in contemplating whether I gave him the right ending. That end's not set in stone yet.

"*Dawn* bridge," I call out, turning to my officers once more. "Umber made his last breath a call for surrender. I'm not sure that order's going to take. These four are my operatives." I gesture to the Wraiths. "Ever since they faked their deaths and stowed away on the Imperial Fleet alongside Gal emp-Umber, they've been embedded in the bridge commands of the admirals who constituted the fleet's leadership. They brought more than just the prince over enemy lines—they've come armed with an arsenal of information on this fleet's leadership, tactics, and fighting capacity. Wraiths, if you would."

This is the test I feared the most, but the four of them pass with flying colors, moving with absolutely no hesitation—not even a nervous glance at Hanji or at the body on the floor between us. Most of the coordination we've done over the past months has gone between me and Iwam, and while I know the other three Wraiths are on board with the plan, I also know that she's the de facto wrangler of these little monsters. That idea can't make it to the minds of my officers. I need universal confidence that I have a handle on the Wraiths— that I *haven't* just introduced a team of elite Umber operatives who answer to no one in my hierarchy, even if that's exactly what I've done.

Ollins, Rin, and Rhodes pull out their datapads and move to Communications, but Hanji stops short. I brace myself for the snag, casting a nervous glance toward Captain Pura, but it seems the information the Wraiths are offering is a juicy enough distraction that none of my bridge staff notice that one of my new additions is taking an extra second to stare down at Gal's crumpled form.

"You good, longshot?" I murmur. More than anyone in the galaxy, I know what's going through her head. She didn't see the first execution, and I'm barely numb to this one.

"Tell me it's gonna work," she mutters back, eyes still fixed on Gal. "You've never been wrong."

I restrain myself from telling her I *have* been wrong—a million times over thousands of branches of possibilities, just only ever in my head. And I'm trying like hell to keep it that way. "It's already in motion," I reply. "See it through."

The command lands nebulously between us, an order passed from the empress of one empire to a citizen of another to any outside observer. But no outside observers have been in the encrypted lines Hanji and I have been exchanging messages over ever since I gave her both Gal and an opening to haul ass back to the Umber interior. They'd call Hanji my equivalent among Gal's inner circle. They'd argue she served the same purpose for him as I did for Ettian.

But then again, I'm sure any outside observer would be rethinking some things in light of recent events. Hanji Iwam, they might be thinking, was less Gal emp-Umber's operative and confidant and more Wen emp-Archon's.

Which is closer to the truth, but can never capture the whole of it. No one will ever see the long months of work, the thousands and thousands of messages we exchanged as we built a scheme that would pull the rug out from under not one but two empires. No one will ever understand that even though bloodright decrees my post above her, I never could have pulled this plan together without her guidance. I can feel the ghosts of the sleepless nights I should have had—the sleepless nights that never touched me because Hanji knew exactly what to say to put me at ease.

Now I have the space of my bridge's distraction to return the favor. I set one hand carefully on her shoulder—the one that isn't visibly stained with an emperor's blood. "Steady," I remind her, firm this time, loud enough for anyone to hear me. "I'm going to take out the trash. Be back before you know it."

Hanji's eyes brighten, like they always do when a new stage of the plot takes root. "All right, comms jockeys," she calls, hauling her datapad in the air overhead as she turns to Communications. "I've got the hot stuff. Who's hungry?"

Perfectly loud. Perfectly eye-catching. Just like I need her. As my bridge's focus solidifies on the Wraiths, I duck to one knee and scoop Gal into my arms. I have to strike a balance here—can't look like I'm being *too* gentle with the remains of the enemy's heir. I flop him gracelessly up over my shoulder, wincing as the still-thickening blood squelches against my armor. I *just* got Ettian's off me.

I don't rush off the bridge. I don't add any flair or act like I'm trying to make a spectacle out of my exit. All I do is stride with purpose toward the bridge doors and let that speak well enough for me. My officers may note the boldness of leaving the Wraiths unattended after so recently welcoming this quartet who decapitated the Umber admiralty to my bridge. They may wonder at the wisdom of that.

Which is fine, because it keeps them from wondering too much about where I'm taking Gal.

The nearest airlock is no good. Too close to the bridge, and thus too integrated with the *Dawn*'s systems. I don't need one meant for egress of the leadership if the ship fails catastrophically—I need maintenance. Routine. Easiest ones to trick, with the fewest eyes watching. Undoubtedly the ship's internal security is tailing my progress for my own sake, but I have a contingency for that, too.

Not the most elegant of contingencies, I muse as I bring up my internal HUD with a twitch of my fingers and inject a loop into the right camera feed the second I turn a corner. But it's worked once already today, and by the time a team comes to investigate, my business at the airlock will be finished.

I step through the inner door and seal it behind me for good measure. There's a narrow window, but the camera outside wouldn't be able to see much through it even if it were operational. Confident I'm moving unseen, I crouch and lay Gal down with far more care than I let show picking him up.

Then I pull up the nearest bench and draw out one of the emergency breach suits.

Dressing a body's the kind of work I'm not skilled for. By the time I'm stuffing his arms into the sleeves, I start to wonder how much of my caution was wasted on trying not to knock him around too much. Not like I can afford to go any slower, though—and not like he's complaining.

I lock the helmet over his head and double-check the seal. The suit's indicators let out a confused whine as they try to latch onto any signs of life, but they confirm that apart from the shockingly still body they've found within their embrace, all systems are operational.

I shift him upright and let him drape like a towel over one arm, using my free hand to snap up my powersuit's helmet, run a lightning-fast diagnostic, and then jam down the button releasing the outer airlock door. The void creeps in with a breath that fades into nothing as the vacuum's silence takes over. I ease Gal up to the edge, feel-ing him start to lighten in my grasp as his mass flirts with the edge of the *Dawn*'s gravity field.

Then I push him forward, planting my boot squarely in his ass and shoving with all my might to send his limp body flailing out into the void.

"Go get 'em, babe," I murmur to nothing but the quiet.

CHAPTER 27

HANJI

IF YOU ASK either of them, they'll tell you Wen's the cornerstone to this whole thing.

They're not wrong. Someone's ass had to end up on that throne, and that someone had to be *really ruttin' sure about it*. And really ruttin' ready for it, as only Wen Iffan could be. When they came down from that rooftop with the embers of a wicked idea sparking in their eyes, they went to Wen first. Ettian pulled her into the back bedroom as Gal manned the door and weathered the barrage of innuendo we hurled at him to cover the fact that we knew *something* had just changed but had absolutely no notion of what it might be.

But just to set the record straight, it never would have worked without me. Which Wen soon-to-be-emp-Archon realized the second she worked out that the hasty explanation Ettian was fumbling through was taking the shape of a proposal. Her answer wasn't "Yes," "Definitely," or "Absolutely"—it was "Let me talk to Iwam."

"What are you actually asking me here?" was the first thing I blurted when she finished said talking.

"What do you think I'm asking?" she replied—always with that tone of mischief. Pissed me the hell off when we first met. I wanted to shake her by the shoulders and go *We can't both be the fun one.*

"You're asking me what I think would be best for the galaxy like I haven't been saying for *days*—"

"You've been the pessimist we needed, but I don't know what you actually *want*," she clarified, spreading her hands in a gesture I didn't realize until much later was her testing out an imperial method. "You strike me as someone who loves playing the game, but wishes it didn't exist in the first place. Is that accurate?"

I rolled my eyes, spreading my hands right back. "I'm not in the business of solutions. I'm a voice in a tower. A finger on a trigger. Someone else does the pointing."

"You're selling yourself short. *And* dodging the question. I'm not asking for the right answer. I'm just asking what your answer would be right now, and if you don't start shooting straight, I'm gonna push you off this roof."

I bit down on a retort about how I'd like to see her try—she's of a height with Gal, and while I respect her knight training, I was pretty sure it wasn't enough to move me from the center of the universe. Instead, I stared out over the rooftops of Breha and tried to find the words for all of my impossible desires.

"I always fancied myself the galaxy's focal point—no, I swear I'm going somewhere with this," I warned as she seemed to brace for the shove that would end it all for me. "I wanted to be in the middle of this huge-ass web, pulling on strings, but that kind of thing only works when you're born into the right bloodline. I missed the mark by two degrees, and instead I got stuck with a bloodright claim that's absolutely no good when there's one older sister with her hand firmly on the family's inheritance and four younger sisters sharpening their knives. And even if I *were* in the center of that web, I meant what I said before—I think bloodright's too broken to fix after Iva emp-Umber's reign."

I paused, just in case that was enough for her. I really should have known, even by then, that it wasn't. She twirled one finger lazily in the air, daring me to make her ask.

"That doesn't bode well for your boy, though," I went on. "He's as reliant on the concept as Gal. Even more so, I'd say. Gal's got powers that be who have things riding on his rule. Ettian seems to just be in the way."

I glanced sidelong at her, waiting for her to jump to the defense of the Archon throne—or if not of the throne, of the man sitting on it. I knew her well enough by then to know that the latter meant more to her than the former. But she surprised me again. She didn't make a snappy retort. She didn't brace to topple me over the edge of the roof. Wen Iffan just nodded. After a moment, she said, "We have to end it. And we have to save them from it in the process."

I blinked. Took my glasses off and rubbed them on my shirt—a senseless habit, but when I didn't think I heard something correct, it felt right to make sure I was seeing clearly. "Ah, yes," I muttered when the silence stretched long. "Let's just . . . end bloodright. Why didn't I think of that?"

"Because you're not in the business of solutions," Wen countered.

"I hate you so ruttin' much."

"Not ideal for what I have in mind. Or, well, credit where credit's due—what *they* have in mind."

"Which is?" I glanced sideways in time to catch the glint in her eyes, the grin that caught the corners of her lips, and the terrible thought that struck me at the sight of it: *Oh no. This is going to be good.*

"In short, a wedding and two murders."

When she'd finished explaining the emperors' proposal, there was a part of me a little bit ready to tip over the edge of the roof before anyone could go through the trouble of shoving me. "So your bright idea—"

"*Gal and Ettian's* bright idea—"

"No, rut off with that—it's yours now. *Everything* is yours now if we go through with this. *Your* bright idea to fix the whole problem where bloodright sucks and we need to get rid of it is to . . . establish more bloodright?"

She held up a finger in objection—another testing of imperial gesture I only caught in hindsight. "Establish a bloodright that *breaks* bloodright once and for all. I'm Corinthian gutter trash. My origins couldn't possibly be more humble—which the Archon people will eat right up because it meshes with their mythology of the ideal imperial pairing being an elevation of a worthy party from an unknown corner. And that notion of bloodright will neatly—or not so neatly, depending on how we stage the deaths—transition into a bloodright *Umber* is forced to accept because it fits *their* mode of power transitioning with blood running down a blade, claimed by those bold enough to take and hold it."

I could scarcely argue with that part, having let the bitter point of that metaphorical blade guide my life choices from the time I was old enough to understand exactly how my position in my family's birth order shook out. If an Archon-crowned Wen killed Gal under the right circumstances, all of Umber would be forced to reckon with the fact that either she deserved to do so or the willful acceptance of violence as merit might *not* be the best foundations for a galactic empire.

Wen's gaze burned a fierce line out to the twisted husks of abandoned mining equipment slumped against the foothills. "I could place myself so unshakably that the weight of it will shatter them," she murmured.

I threw my head back and laughed. "Heavens and hells, you're already talking like Gal when he gets in his moods." I was absolutely trying to goad her into kicking my ass at that point, but rather than taking the bait, she only grinned.

"That—that exactly. That's why I need you, longshot." She faced me, the full intensity of her half-scarred face like looking into the heart of a star. "If we're going to try to pull off something so unreasonable, I need a voice of reason in my corner. But not just an adviser, not just a confidant—I need someone to be with me at the center of the web, someone who can pull on all the strings I can't and think in all the corners I've never been trained for. I'm the right warm body to put on the Archon throne while we guide it into an ethical transition of power with assistance from our Corinthian buddies, but I need eyes on my back and operatives who can work where I won't be able to."

I could see the moving parts of everything in that moment, clear as day. Saw the way I'd been lined up like a shot, the way she pulled the trigger with barely a look and knocked down my ambitions great and small. I could have started to dig in my heels, could have made noise about how ludicrous this whole notion was, but I think at that point, I wouldn't have been able to hide that I was absolutely starting to buy into her bullshit.

There was a quiet thought I'd been nursing ever since the long ride back to the Umber Core with a recently radicalized prince in tow. I listened to his arguments. I let him sway me into committing myself body and soul to his plans to tear down his mother's empire from within. All the while I could never quite work up the energy to say to his face, *But it's all bullshit when it comes from you, right?*

I'm sure if I had, I'd get a perfectly adequate answer—something along the lines of *Look, if I have the power in my hands, what good does it do me not to use it?* And it's not like I didn't want him to use that power. From the throne, he could do far more than any of us, and with his mother's vicious reputation, he certainly wasn't doing it from a place of safety.

But at the end of the day, he would still be just another in a long line of Umber imperials deciding the shape of the galaxy. I saw the same thing happen when Ettian stepped out of the shadows to take his crown. A radical uprising spearheaded by Maxo Iral and backed by Corinthian sponsorship transformed in an instant to a push to restore not just Archon's governance of their territories but the entire system of Archon bloodright that Iva emp-Umber thought she buried. It was righteous to the Archon people and welcome after seven years of Umber rule stripping their territories, but underneath it all was the notion that some people were born with inherent power and it was their right to use it however they wished.

Archon had always tried to point to its most generous leaders to justify that system. Umber always pointed to the most ruthless. All I saw in those broken mirrors was the fragments of my family and the promise of what my sisters and I could have been if the blood we were born into hadn't doomed us from the start. As long as blood-right existed, there was no fixing it.

I met that star-bright stare with a crooked smile. "So you need the best right hand in the galaxy to pull this off?"

"Position's yours for the taking," she replied.

The months were long, the particulars nasty.

The Wraiths took up the technical aspects of the grand finale. Rin and Rhodes poured their all into the design of a rig that would mimic all the pageantry of being stabbed through the gut without any of the actual stabbing. Ollins played willing test subject, ruining so many shirts that we had to start incinerating them and disguising our backchannel bulk orders to avoid suspicion. Once we had all the kinks ironed out, I sent the design along our secure line to Wen so she could replicate it and familiarize herself with it.

Then there was the drug—a concoction Rin and Rhodes whipped together after a long, sleepless research bender. Both Gal and Ettian needed to drop convincingly dead and remain that way long enough to put aside any doubts that this was all an act. It took a few iterations to get right, including one close call where we had to perform a full-on resuscitation to get Ollins back from the waking death we'd dropped him into.

Thank every god of every system we finally nailed it, because not a week later we had to put it through the field test of a lifetime. And I mean that quite literally, because there's no way in hell I'm ever doing that again. Dying sucked ass, waking from the dead was worse, and both the last and first thing I saw was Gal's face. Disgusting.

Even though they weren't putting their lives on the line, the Archon side's task was far more daunting. I watched from afar, both through the newsfeed coverage that leaked our way of the confusing internal shuffling that seemed to be happening in the Archon administration and through Wen's bleary messages, which she only ever seemed to compose in the dead of night after a long day of peeling apart Archon's imperial structure.

Don't get me wrong—I know the ins and outs of manipulating people. I've just never done it at *scale* before, and that was the thing that had me breaking into a flop sweat every time a new message came down the tunnel. I signed on for this, but I don't know if I ever fully believed a wide scale dismantling of Archon bloodright was possible. I expected we'd all be regrouping in a few months to rethink the strategy—if Iva emp-Umber hadn't nailed us to the wall before then. Their moves were so blatant that even though I knew it would be outrageous for anyone to draw the connection, I couldn't help that paranoid little voice in the back of my head whispering that somehow they were going to get *us* caught.

But here's the thing—you never win betting against Wen. So I could only watch from the other end of the galaxy as she not only proved wrong every fear I ever harbored, but did so with so much grace and elegance that I was forced to admit those fears might have been ridiculous in the first place. She and Ettian slowly but surely established the council of planetary representatives, involving the Corinthians in every step of the process without making it seem like they were the ones running the show. They made it look effortless.

I feel like only I knew the truth. The connection between our two teams was a weak point that had only ever been entrusted to me and Wen, and I realized even before we set this shenanigan into motion that part of my job was to be the filter that kept the Umber side working with confidence. So, despite multiple attempts by Gal to sweet-talk me into handing over the line, command me with the force of his soon-to-be-worthless bloodright to just let him send a quick message to Ettian, or straight up have Ollins distract me so he could steal my datapad, I held firm.

And I watched as Wen doubted. She wondered. She barely slept. She stayed sharp through all of it, but sometimes it was too sharp for her own good, so sharp that she was thinking herself in knots. That was another part of my job—to drag her back down to solid ground, reining in the scope of her problems before they got unmanageable. *Is that a problem for you to solve right now,* I'd often ask her, *or a problem for me to solve once I'm installed at your right hand?*

It could *be a problem I solve right now,* I'd often get in response, but I learned long ago that sometimes even if an answer isn't sufficient, the asking of a question does enough.

The last time I talked to her one-on-one was through the encrypted channel we'd set up, while she was doing her damnedest to get Ettian's blood off her powersuit. She was using an interpreter to whisper her comments into the suit's comms array and translate them into text that appeared on my datapad. Even without the tone of her voice, I could tell she was rattled.

The blood, after all, was very real—both emperors had been drawing a collection over the past several weeks. It was a careful balance to strike, gathering enough that we could make the deaths look realistic without rendering either Gal or Ettian too woozy to keep up the complex lies they were spinning, but we knew anything else wouldn't hold up under scrutiny.

We hadn't anticipated the psychological effect of being doused in the stuff.

My part's done, her text read. No more than that—no details in case this line was intercepted. With our signals spanning a battlefield, we had to be far more cautious than our usual communication, and with us Wraiths wedged in vents, waiting for the next stage of the plan to play out, audio was a no-go. *Cleaning up now, then back to the bridge. I need whatever flight plans you can get.*

I pulled up the necessary data, then added a message of my own: *The juice went down smooth?*

I regretted it the instant I hit send. It was my job to absorb her worries, not the other way around—and what I'd just asked was fairly transparent. I knew the vibrosword trick looked good. The blood was unimpeachable. But the drug was horrible, and even after my turn in its clutches, I still didn't trust it. Before we put Gal through it, I had to *know.*

It wasn't pretty, but it got the job done.

Did not like the sound of that one bit.

It was at that point I knew I had to let go of the outcomes I hoped for and focus on the ones that *needed* to happen. My confidence could only carry so much—and the fate of the galaxy rested on its shoulders. Even if that meant Gal might—

A new message blipped into my datapad. *Steady, longshot.*

Damn her intuition. Damn her empathy. Not only did she know I was starting to let the doubt creep in, she knew the slightest nudge from her would prop up my tilting architecture just enough to get us through the rest of this. I started this whole endeavor wanting to believe Wen could be the right person to place on the Archon throne more than I actually believed it.

Damn me for not locking in fully until she said the exact right thing at the most critical moment.

I fixed my eyes on the back of Admiral Norsat's head, just visible through the vent covering I was lodged behind. From somewhere on the other side of the bridge, I could hear Hardisson barking orders to the fleet body in a voice that annoyed me so much I was counting the seconds until I could silence it. *Squadron's in position here,* I typed without looking. *Ready to act on your signal.*

Couldn't do it without you, Wen emp-Archon wrote back, and she's never been wrong. All that remained was for the two of us to see it through.

CHAPTER 28

ETTIAN

SHE COULD NOT HAVE *possibly* made this more difficult.

"I could undo it all, you know?" I mutter to myself as I fire up the skipship's engines and set it into a lazy drift away from my camping spot nestled in one of the moonlet's crevasses. *"Hey everyone! Guess who's not dead! It was all a trick to beat Umber at their own game. Yes, I said some things I regret, but look at the results before you hold it against me, huh?"*

I'm kidding, but would it be any less believable than the truth?

The fact remains: she was supposed to *push* the body. Let it drift gently into the void on an inescapable course that gives me *plenty* of time to match speed, line up the hold doors, and catch him before he pancakes on this ruttin' moonlet.

Instead . . . well, it's going to be one hell of a catch.

Fortunately I'm one hell of a pilot.

The skipship is eager under my hands, moving like a god-sent dream. Its hull is blacked out and shielded, nudging any attempts at detection from the *Dawn* gently to the side. I know Wen's already taken significant pains to keep me invisible ever since I cast off, and I'm not about to blow that on some showoff maneuver.

But gods, I want to, and I can't help throwing a little flair into my movements as I spin the ship around its rotaries—540 degrees, just because—and line myself up along the predicted vector of that tiny, frail, defenseless figure in a breach suit drifting limply through the void.

See? Easy, I can almost hear Wen chiding me. *Nowhere near as tricky as when you had to catch Esperza over Breha.*

But Esperza was conscious, and Wen was *aiming.* Now it's no one's fault but mine if Gal drifts into one of my rotaries instead of the hold I'm slowly cranking open.

I pulse the ancillaries until I'm matching his speed, pointedly ignoring my windshield's view of the looming rocky surface of the moonlet that's just daring me to get closer. Another goose of the thrusters slows the skipship enough that Gal gains on it. My eyes are fixed on the instrumentation, my hands starting to go damp around the controls. I watch him approach on the rear cameras, my breath caught in my throat.

The second he clears the ramp, I jam down the trigger to close it, not trusting that he won't bounce out of the hold by the time it winches shut and begins to repressurize. I nudge the thrusters softly, injecting the gentlest deceleration I can manage into our vector as I line up the ship's nose with the crevasse that's been cloaking me for the past several hours. It's agony to keep my focus on flying when all I want to do is stare at the limp body drifting around the hold, but I manage to keep my vector steady until we're wedged back in the safety of the moonlet's crags.

When I've scaled the ship back down to stillness, I tear out of my harness like it's burst into flames. I don't dare reenable the gravity generators—there's no telling what position he'd land in. Instead I navigate with my hands, shoving off the console and twisting in midair to glide down the narrow hall that leads from the cockpit to the hold door. With shaking fingers, I check the hold's air levels to be sure it's equalized completely, then rip open the door.

And there he is, floating still as the void as his rag doll form bounces slowly off the ceiling.

I kick off the floor to catch him, twisting up and over him to let my body take the blow from the next wall we bounce off. I barely feel it, too caught up in the equal parts thrill and terror of feeling him in my arms again—and feeling just how lifeless he is. As another wall approaches, this time I reach out with my free hand and grab the webbing that coats the hold, anchoring us before we can careen into another ricochet.

Fumbling, nauseated, I crack the seal on his breach suit's helmet and pull it slowly off.

I expected him to look peaceful, like he could be sleeping, but whatever's in the cocktail his injector dosed him with is far worse than that. Gal's gone completely ashen, his hooded eyes looking even more deeply sunken against the graying cast his skin's taken on. I smooth back his weightless, wild curls, then drop my hand down to his neck.

No pulse. *No pulse, but that's fine, that's to be expected, if he had a detectable pulse, this wouldn't have worked in the first place, gods of all systems how did Wen see me like this and not lose her goddamn mind—*

Deep breaths. In two three four, out two three four.

I pull the counteragent injector out of my pocket. It's already worked once today, but I find my hand hesitating as I position it over his clavicle. I can't pretend to know what I'm about to hit him with—I only know that I'm not sure anything else in the galaxy felt quite as strange as the sensation of being wrenched back from the dead. There's a beading ache from the matching pinprick on my own collar, a phantom echo of the shock of adrenaline that brought me gasping back to life.

"Come back to me," I breathe, seal the injector against his skin, and jam down the depressor.

For a terrible, far too still moment, nothing happens.

Then I feel a twitch. A spasm. An entire limb locked rigid. I do my best to hold Gal in place as the drug flushes through his system—

sluggishly, at first, as it kicks his heart back into some semblance of order, and then with such violence that he nearly cracks his head on the hold wall. The first audible breath he draws sounds like it's dislodging half the wall of his throat in the process. It might be the sweetest sound I've heard all day.

I resist the urge to hold him tight, to never let go. My own resurrection was disorienting bordering on downright panic-inducing, and Gal has always been even more anxious than me. Wen held tight to one of my wrists through the whole process, from when I was bucking and fighting to get her off me to when I finally had my senses and needed her touch to ground me in the groggy reality of being *alive*. I try to strike a happy medium between keeping him from bouncing off the walls and keeping him from feeling like he's being held down.

I'd say the results are mixed, to the point that I start to feel seriously guilty for not having the patience to get him laid down somewhere soft so I could spin up the gravity generators. His eyes are open, but they're rolling haphazardly and I can tell he isn't really *seeing* anything. I give up on holding on to the rigging, instead bringing my hand up to cradle his jaw. "C'mon, c'mon, c'mon," I breathe. My nerves can't handle another minute of uncertain twitching.

He blinks once, twice, his eyes coming home to mine as his focus sharpens. I feel some of the tension in his muscles go loose. "Ruttin' . . . hell," he rasps.

"There he is," I murmur, barely caring how my voice breaks.

A shaking hand drifts up to lock around the back of my neck, and I feel like I'm about to crack in half from the joy of it. Months of planning, months of distance, months of tiptoeing carefully around secrets that would ruin us, and this is the final result—the very notion of empire knocked loose from its bearings, and the two of us drifting weightless in the hold of a hidden skipship, dead to the galaxy and so, so alive in each other's arms.

"Never doing that again," he croaks.

The notion of it is so absurd that it breaks me immediately. I duck my head, clutching him like it'll help me brace against the laughter that's seized me. And of course once I'm laughing, Gal's laughing too, even though I can tell his throat's not quite up to the task. Tears were already welled up in my eyes—from fear, from stress, but now they burn with furious joy as they cling to my vision and render it warped enough to make me question my whole reality.

But then he tugs hard on the back of my neck, seals his lips over mine, and banishes any notion that this could ever be a dream. I pull him closer, hooking one leg around his to keep us locked together as I sink hard and sure and desperate into the reality I've chosen, fought, and for all intents and purposes *died* for.

I choose him again. And again, and again, and again.

By the time we've pulled ourselves together, the battle is in full swing. I feel the peculiar ache of it as we glide into the skipship's cockpit to find the instrumentation a scrambled mess of telemetry that barely touches the surface of the chaos going on outside our little hideaway. I've had months to make my peace with the fact that going forward, the empire no longer needs me, but it's another thing entirely to see the war churn onward, completely outside my realm of control.

Gal seems similarly transfixed, his fingers floating hesitantly over the comms station as if he's dying to start diving into the thicket and untangling strategies. His face asks the same question I feel rattling around the chambers of my heart. *How can we possibly sit back and watch?*

I clap one hand on his shoulder, then lever off him to swing around and plant my ass in the pilot's chair. "Bringing the gravity up in three, two, one."

With a tug that feels like a hook yanking at my bones, the generators pull me down into the cushion of my seat and swing Gal's boots to the deck. I'd hoped it would ground me in the sight of the galaxy still spinning without me at its center, but the comfort of the pilot's chair beneath me only does so much.

"Imagine how pissed she'd be if we blew it here," Gal says on a sigh, rounding his chair and dropping into it.

Instead, I imagine her. Wen emp-Archon, Flame Empress triumphant, sitting carefully atop the throne we carved for her, flanked by
the Wraiths, *her* Wraiths, as she fights for the soul of the galaxy with
bloodstained hands. I've never made peace with leaving it all to her.
I know part of it is selfish—an indignant voice that demands I get to
live out my bloodright for the rest of my days. Part of it comes from
fear, a fear I've tried to justify as unfounded. I've learned not to
doubt her when she says she can do something, and more than that,
I've learned that I can rarely stop her. But when she said *this* is something she can do, with total confidence that hasn't wavered over the
long months, I couldn't help but worry. I watched carefully as we
maneuvered her into full control of a reborn empire at war, watched
as she proved over and over again that I have nothing to fear.

But the real reason I can't quite let the notion settle is the one
that aches the most. It's not that I don't believe Wen will wrench the
galaxy back on track with the unwavering hand of a mechanic. It's
that I've left a part of my heart with her, and I'm not sure when—or
even *if*—I'll see it again.

Gal snaps his fingers in front of my face, breaking my unfocused
stare through the skipship's windshield. "Hey. This was the point of
it," he says, clapping me on the thigh. "We were in the way. Now
look."

He dives into the telemetry, sorting it until the tangle of signals
resolves into the artful constructs that guide the engagement outside. Archon's claws have come out, attack groups surging from the
cover of Turrot's rings as they hurl boltfire against the Umber dreadnoughts, rounding from the rear to avoid the main batteries' full
power. The Umber fleet has taken Gal's order to surrender predictably, in that they've completely disregarded it. Their dreadnoughts
fire with impunity, searing brilliant holes through the ring's particulate as they try to draw out the larger Archon ships.

On a whim, I start recording our telemetry from the Umber
dreadnoughts, making sure my visual includes timestamps. It's the
kind of footage that could do significant damage if it got enough
airplay to reach the Umber elite. After all, Gal was crowned, his

position in the Imperial Fleet's leadership given Iva emp-Umber's explicit blessing. His commands were spoken with the weight of his bloodright, and now they're being openly defied without any retribution.

With no admirals left to guide it, the fleet is governing itself, throwing off any notion that Umber's power all trickles down through the throne. An optimistic thought strikes: perhaps this will do just as much damage to the notion of bloodright rule in Umber as Wen's active dismantling of it in Archon. If that's the case, I'm happy to help it along with an eyewitness report.

Gal raises an eyebrow at me. "Little gift for your mother," I tell him with a smirk. "By way of her system governors."

"We haven't talked much about what comes next," he says. Fair point. With no room for error in our plotting, our focus has always been on getting us to this moment, not what we do once we're in it.

"I'm guessing you have a list," I reply.

"Some ideas," he says, pulling a datapad out of his inner jacket pocket. "Just because we're not at the heads of our respective empires doesn't mean that we can't participate in the fun of tearing them down. But I think that's gonna have to be a remote position at first. And given we're best served laying low in *your* former domain . . ."

I've given it plenty of thought in the long, lonely hours waiting for Wen to toss him to me. "How do you feel about beaches?" I ask.

Gal's expression goes soft and contemplative. "Don't know if I've ever been to one. Why, you got a recommendation?"

"Secondhand, but I hear it'll ruin you for all others. And I've got a bit of business there. A little bit of good we can do."

"I like the sound of that," he murmurs.

"There is one thing we have to take care of before we set our vector, though."

Gal's brows drop into a confused furrow.

I lean forward and slap the dashboard. "This is a top-of-the-line skipship. Fast as all hell, handles like a dream, and the hottest piece of tail its yards have ever produced—don't look at me like that." I chuckle as Gal throws me an exasperated smirk. "It's a ship fit for two former emperors. And it needs a name."

"I'm assuming the *Ruttin' Hell II* is off the table?"

"Gods of all systems," I mutter.

"You should name it," Gal says, spreading his hands in a mockery of imperial deference. "Consider it my belated wedding present."

"Oh, rut right off with that," I chuckle. "Fine. It'll need to be something that's not vulgar."

"Something that's not going to get us flagged on a dock's ledger."

"Nothing overtly tied to any empire—or anyone we know personally."

"I wasn't going to name it after my mother anyway."

I smirk. "But it should mean something. To both of us."

"But something unassuming, from the outside."

I bow my head, feeling like the criteria are bouncing off the walls of my skull as I try to synthesize an answer. Something small, something no one would think twice about—but something with the potential to tip two empires into utter chaos and walk away without a scratch. A soft smile slips over my lips as I lean forward and pull up the ship's registration.

Gal peers over my shoulder, then lets out a short laugh when he sees what I've keyed in. "You romantic," he chides. Then, softer, "That's perfect."

We watch for a while, just to make sure—though with far less decorum than any imperial could ever get away with. With no need to hide our emotions from our bridge officers, we perch on the edge of our seats as the battle begins to work toward a fever pitch, fists clenched, murmuring every time a dreadnought's main battery scores a direct hit. Gal was brought up to revere the might of the Imperial Fleet, and his terror at all that firepower being leveraged at our friends is palpable.

I know Archon victory is a sure thing. I know never to doubt Wen. But even so, I need to see it, to prove to my stubborn pilot heart that I can take my hands off the controls and the galaxy will stay on its axis.

By the end, our feet are kicked up on the skipship's dash. Gal's found a few bags of snacks stowed away in the kitchenette, which we demolish without a second thought for who's going to clean up the crumbs or what we'll do with the wrappers. The embers of our bloodrights flicker out as Wen and the Wraiths rout Umber so thoroughly that by the time a comportment of Corinthian supply cruisers fresh from Tyrol drop onto the field, there's hardly any need for them.

And once the relief—that we're no longer needed, that we're beholden only to each other—settles in with devastating finality, I spur the *Firecracker*'s engines, wheel us out of the rings, and set us on our vector.

EPILOGUE

U S

WE COME DOWN over Chorta on the night side, breaking into the troposphere over an ocean that seems, from a distance, to be a starfield unto itself. Bioluminescent jellyfish spread as far as the eye can see, painting the moonlit waters in vibrant blues and purples. We put the *Firecracker* down on an atoll that, as far as our scans can tell, is miles from any of the planet's scattered settlements. With the ship's running lights turned as low as they go, we steal down the ramp barefoot and plunge our toes into sand still warm from this system's sun, whooping and howling like wild animals at how impossibly alone we are in the vastness of Chorta's night and its biological reflection.

One of us has his shirt over his head in a second, plunging into the surf without a second thought for the chill. The other hesitates— but can't for long when the company is so inviting.

We give ourselves a week of nothing. A week of shedding the burdens and bruises of empire from our bodies until we're both walking taller than we have in months. It won't ever be enough to undo the stressors that have doubtless shaved years off our lives nor any of the scars we've earned, but it helps us settle into the notion that our lives are our own.

And it gives us time to think about what we do next.

At the end of the week, we start trawling what signals our ship can pick up. Life on Chorta is rarely anchored to land—there are a few stationary stilt-cities, made to adapt to the rising and falling of the tides, but most of the world roves on flotillas that move with the flow of the planet's currents. It's not ideal for tracking people down, but one of us has picked up enough clever comms tricks at the knee of Hanji Iwam to get the job done by the fifth day of searching.

In another life, under other names, we heard a kindhearted soldier with an audiobook habit tell us about his moms, their skiff, and the jellyfish we've been swimming with every night. He'd sworn to us that he'd make it back to this world someday to see if they'd made it through the war okay. He's still off fighting another war with his moms none the wiser that he survived the first one.

That's the first little bit of good we can do. The smallest drop compared to the galaxy-breaking power we once wielded, but we have to get used to small steps, to being mere mortals walking among the common people. When we were shadowed as children, we were meant to go out into the galaxy and learn how others lived, to better serve us when we returned to take our thrones. But that little taste of humanity was never meant to be permanent. We were always going to be dragged back to our higher destiny. It's another thing entirely to be a man with nothing but a ship and the love of your life, standing on the shore of just one of the galaxy's many oceans, wondering what the *point* of you is.

We've been making lists. Some are crackling with ambition and might as well be titled "Everything Two Faceless Men Can Do against an Empire." Others are full of people who've helped us along the way, people we can help in turn. There's an apartment in a borderworld town that needs to be cleaned up. Four sets of next of kin who deserve some sort of explanation for why their shithead kids have defected to the enemy empress's side. Even a bit of business from that empress herself, who's left with us the devious little challenge of making sure the man who killed her mother knows she still has his number. It's more than enough to keep us driven, and there's plenty of room for those lists to expand.

Now there's a new goal fixed in our hearts, one we're going to spend a lifetime chasing. We once lamented that we might be more good to the galaxy dead than alive. That's the blazing star we're hurtling toward, the reason we stay up long into the night, sitting cross-legged on the beach with datapads scattered on a blanket around us, scheming about everything we can possibly do. We *will* be more good. We believe that we can be.

And without crowns on our heads, there's a life we can live parallel to that life of ambition. A life where we wake one curled around the other and don't leave bed for a solid hour. A life where one of us flies, one of us navigates, and both of us criticize the other with merciless glee over inconsequential rut-ups that leave us laughing until we're sick. A life where one of us can get overwhelmed by all that he's left behind, all that he never lived up to, and everyone he misses with every beat of his heart and know that the other will be there to hold him through it. A life of a thousand stolen kisses, some quick, some grease-spattered, some languorously pressed against the *Firecracker*'s sun-warmed hull.

We chase our hearts' desire across the stars. Not crowns or thrones or a galaxy at our feet. Just the words one of us once shaped it into, the words we sometimes breathe to each other in the deepest part of the night, scarcely believing we finally have it.

You and a life with you.

ACKNOWLEDGMENTS

When I first started noodling around with the idea of a book that married my love of tricksy con men with my love of bombastic space opera, it was the beginning of 2016. I write this as we round the bend on 2021, and I'm not sure how I can properly sum up the intervening years that produced this trilogy—or the past two years in particular, when I wrote this book.

I started my first draft of *Vows of Empire* in March of 2020, just days before shelter-in-place orders in response to the COVID-19 pandemic went into effect across the United States. *Bonds of Brass* came out a month later. In all of my grand imagining for this trilogy, I never could have imagined that it would release over the course of a global pandemic. That there would be no bookstore events, no conventions, no coming together to celebrate and commiserate and share the joy I hoped these books would bring. But despite that, so many people put their hearts into making this series special, and I don't know how I can possibly convey the depth of my gratitude to everyone who's carried me through the grief and horror of these years.

Thank you to my wonderful editor, Sarah Peed, who's been the boys' biggest fan from the start, and to the entire team at Del Rey for putting so much loving care into the Bloodright trilogy. To Scott Shannon and Keith Clayton in publishing, to Tricia Narwani and Bree Gary in editorial, to Julie Leung and Ashleigh Heaton in marketing, to David Moench and Jordan Pace in publicity, and to Cindy Berman and Sarah Feightner in production—thank you so much for your outstanding work bringing this story to its triumphant conclusion.

Thank you to Charles Chaisson for turning my blobby sketch of an idea into this book's gorgeous cover, and to Ella Laytham for the eye-popping design that ties it all together.

Thank you to all the authenticity readers who have lent their insights to the series and helped me do justice to these characters. Any mistakes and missteps that may remain are my own.

Thank you to Thao Le, my agent, my champion. I couldn't do any of this without you in my corner. Thank you to the entire Sandra Dijkstra Literary Agency team, especially Andrea Cavallaro and Jennifer Kim, for supporting my career with their continued hard work.

Thank you to my critique partners, Tara Sim and Traci Chee, for every late night "whine and cheese," for every virtual escape room, for every emergency phone call. Tara, you magnificent goth bitch, I set out to entertain you with a fun Boy Story all those years ago, and I can't believe we made it to the final chapter without you pulling my hair out. Traci, I'm chasing the shining light of your brilliance, and I'm so lucky to count you as my friend and fellow creative.

Thank you to the Cobbler Club crew for all the support over the years—Alexa Donne for writing sprints and hot goss, Gretchen Schreiber for neighbor shenanigans and baked goods, and Alyssa Colman for the wine glasses. Even though our friendship now spans the country, I hope one day we can all come together again.

I've said it before, and I'll say it again—publishing isn't survivable without a complete life outside it, and I'm deeply indebted to all the people in my life who barely know a thing about my weird side job. Thank you to my day-job cohort, who make it a joy to have health insurance and a 401(k). To my D&D buds, board game dickheads, and climbing partners, thank you for lighting up my life with hobbies I'll never dream of monetizing. Thanks to Wop House for the regular virtual hangs that make it feel like we never left the Hill. This book is due in print just days before we finally get to see each other again, provided that the third time really is the charm for this Vancouver shindig. To Mom and Dad, whom I haven't seen in person in two years—though I booked my flights this morning to finally come home. To my sister, Sarah, my first creative partner, whose spectacular artwork has brought some of my most profound nonsense to life. And to Mariano, who carried me through the worst of these years and was undoubtedly the brightest part of them, a resounding third *no u*.

Thank you to the librarians who brought this trilogy into their collections, to the booksellers who handsold it to their customers, to the book bloggers, booktubers, bookstagrammers, and booktokers who featured it for their audiences, and every single one of you who told your friends to read it. The more I do this weird little gig, the more I understand that authors cannot really do anything significant to move their stories, but the love of a single vocal reader can send a book to the stars. If you're one of those folks, I cannot thank you enough. I'd be nowhere without your support.

And last, for the third and final time—to you, the reader, whoever you are. Thank you for sticking with this roller coaster through thick and thin. It's been a joy to share this galaxy and these disastrous boys with you, and I hope you'll join me on another adventure soon.

ABOUT THE AUTHOR

EMILY SKRUTSKIE was born in Massachusetts, raised in Virginia, and forged in the mountains above Boulder, Colorado. She attended Cornell University and now lives and works in Los Angeles. Skrutskie is the author of *Oaths of Legacy, Bonds of Brass, Hullmetal Girls, The Abyss Surrounds Us,* and *The Edge of the Abyss.*

skrutskie.com

Twitter: @skrutskie

Instagram: @skrutskie

ABOUT THE TYPE

This book was set in Sabon, a typeface designed by the well-known German typographer Jan Tschichold (1902–74). Sabon's design is based upon the original letter forms of sixteenth-century French type designer Claude Garamond and was created specifically to be used for three sources: foundry type for hand composition, Linotype, and Monotype. Tschichold named his typeface for the famous Frankfurt typefounder Jacques Sabon (c. 1520–80).